INSIDE THE INSTITUTE

Someone had executed a sculpture of two snakes. Or maybe they were dragons. This looked like the sort of place where people would be terribly interested in dragons. The figures were luridly detailed, arm-thick, molded of bright synthetic stuff that had dried to a porous simulacrum of skin. (Though why not scales?) One was fuchsia red, the other essentially white, or smoker's-tooth yellow—not pure hues but tacky swirled amalgams that averaged out in the observer's eye. The two creatures squared off in petrified, unconvincing combat across something Turner could only think of as a laminated birdbath. The white one looked like it was winning.

Our observer was getting increasingly involved here, picking apart the pretentious symbology. But really: color-coded dragons wrestling on a sundial. It just so painfully *meant* something. And the fact of its meaning something meant something too.

It's some kind of emblem, I bet: of this place, this preposterous Institute. Perhaps I should ask this woman here, absurd stick-legged creature signaling me to follow her.

"*Do* come now, young man"—five-ten, school-marmishly smiling—"or you will miss one of the most interesting experiences of your life."

Other books by Richard Grant

Rumors of Spring
Saraband of Lost Time

VIEWS FROM THE OLDEST HOUSE

A NOVEL
BY
RICHARD GRANT

BANTAM BOOKS
NEW YORK · TORONTO · LONDON · SYDNEY · AUCKLAND

VIEWS FROM THE OLDEST HOUSE

A Bantam Spectra Book / published by arrangement with Doubleday

PRINTING HISTORY

Doubleday edition published December 1989

*I'LL COME RUNNING, ST. ELMO'S FIRE and GOLDEN
HOURS
Copyright © 1975 EG Music, Ltd.
Used by permission.
ALL RIGHTS RESERVED*

*BACKWATER
Copyright © 1977 EG Music, Ltd.
Used by permission.
ALL RIGHTS RESERVED*

Bantam edition / December 1990

*Bantam Books are published by Bantam Books, a division of Bantam Doubleday Dell
Publishing Group, Inc. Its trademark, consisting of the words "Bantam Books" and the
portrayal of a rooster, is Registered in U.S. Patent and Trademark Office and in
other countries. Marca Registrada. Bantam Books, 666 Fifth Avenue, New York,
New York 10103.*

For Matthew

With a tip of the hat to Ned Rorem
and to Brian Eno

There was the heating up and then the cooling off. There are bright, confusing, terrifying moments when things are done, and calm years when they are talked about.

Prophets speak of entropy as though it were the same thing as chaos, or disorder. It is not. A cup of hot wine, laid on the snow, will cease its Brownian frenzy. Its impetuous vapors will disperse; its droplets will fall into crystalline alignment; its larger molecules, sugars and tannins and other remnants of the old grape, will be frozen apart like insects trapped in a perfect web. That is Order, ladies and gentlemen. That is the direction of history.

In the old days, the hot days, when prophets sang of entropy and physicists dreamed of infinite fire, the future seemed an impatient monster: a dragon, to be eluded or appeased. But in April it is difficult *not* to believe the sun will grow ever warmer. September is already cold, on this mountaintop.

I am not a prophet. But I knew a prophet who believed he was a physician. I knew a general who loved music. I knew an enchantress. I knew a king. They are gone now. Only I am left alive—if this silence, this lingering, is still life. Alone in the cool rooms of my house.

—Tristin Maleish
[From an incomplete early MS. Given here for contrast with his final, more exuberant style. R.G.]

HANGING ON

1

All unhappy students are alike

Turner Ashenden left the road unsafely fast where a sign had once mentioned the population of some town. The old spirit-burner gave a pained glub as the contents of its tanks sloshed about and resettled, forcing an interesting pause in the sideward acceleration of the vehicle, an abeyance, into which Turner's attention moved without alarm, only confusion and moderate annoyance. The physical world had gotten beyond him. His only hope now was to gain enlightenment and come to understand such things as inertia and momentum through direct intuitive means. First, of course, he would have to quit drinking beer. The sun seemed lower today than the last time he had driven up the mountain, but that was another problem.

It was not yet fall. An air of relief had settled over the trees and grasses: relief to have gotten August done with. Complacence at having the countryside to themselves. World-weary languor of midafternoon. None of the weeds growing brazenly through the cracks of the exit ramp cared one way or the other about the young man's fitful passage. They merely waggled in what scant breeze his aging craft could generate as it puttered and sloshed its way around a stand of *Pinus virginiana* thrusting sunward from the mouth of a culvert. These trees, in their collectivity, managed to look ennobled, despite the fact that regarded individually they were among the ugliest living things in creation. It is an imperfect world, Turner reflected. When I come to set down my philosophy of life I must take this strongly into account.

The road past the exit ramp was suspiciously clear. Its paving was broken but still discernible among patches of bare clay and windblown loosestrife—the product of local cement, not imported asphalt, which to an archaeologist might mean any of several things. But the era was a bit young for archaeology.

The thing about drives in the country, thought Turner, is that you find all these places, these perfect little worlds, tucked around every corner of the road. One minute you're in cool moody woods and the next you're staring out from a bluff over derelict pastures, part of a farm someone had lost, maybe, or given up on. You could imagine yourself living here and living there—erecting a dome or an A-frame at the crux of the latest small valley, there beside the stream, with a prospect of flood-prone meadows and scrubland. He surveyed each possible homesite in turn for defensibility, for protected flanks or narrow causeways. You never knew how things would turn—if the Easterners, for instance, would give up at last on their crumbling cities, or the Southerners on trying to live in what one gathered was essentially a great kudzu-covered parking lot. Or, worse luck, the oldest dream of the latest government might come to pass, and someone would try to enforce the Settling Out Laws.

At heart Turner did not believe in such dire eventualities, but you had to keep them in mind.

You had to consider everything. Trust in nothing. Guard the future like a child against all dangers imaginary or real.

The spirit-burner hesitated, gasped, lunged ahead—air pockets in the tubes probably—and Turner from stern habit paid it no attention. Nothing he could do until the next stream-crossing, anyway, unless he came upon a farmhouse whose pump still worked. On top of which, the afternoon out here was unbelievably magnificent, and this was no time to worry about breakdowns, bubbles in the tanks, or other forms of worldly corruption.

Meantime the unfamiliar road continued upward, blindly turning, fastidiously clear. Soon it had lifted Turner out of the hills altogether and onto an indisputable mountainside, stunted trees and wind-eroded gorges all around him, and where for God's sake were the guard-rails?

But God is horribly absent, Turner reflected, from the mountains. As from the seven sacred volumes of Proust. Stone tablets and Saint-Loup notwithstanding. And the Black Angel spreads his wings above the earth. Orbiting low. A great dark all-seeing satellite. Irresistible. And much more colorful, anyway, than the Absent Father, his white-hatted bland *bête noire*. As Ashley to Rhett: the Fallen One always treated more sympathetically. Sporting soul you see in MacLeish. Lost his seat but kept his manners. And fiendishly handsome, if Milton is to be believed. Only down on his luck. By sorrows beset. As aren't we all. His countrymen.

Turner took the serpentine curves of the road energetically, mimicking powerful-engine sounds in his mind to drown the suck and glub of the spirit-burner. *Vrrwwwwurrmmm*, he thought. Like fading thunder. The devil's tympanum. Invisible orchestra crescendoing while the dancers leap antigravitationally into each other's arms. *Le sàcre du* late summer. Prelude to the afternoon of a fall.

Vrrrowwwwwrrrrr!

So that was Turner Ashenden:

Hair the color of chestnut veneer blown back from a narrow brow by air curling around the spidered windshield. Eyes an indefinite color, but tending toward lavender, like the Michaelmas daisies they spied blooming in a roadside ditch. Nose and mouth a good way down the delicate slope of the bell-curve, causing one to imagine a mother somewhere—intense, solitary, rereading *Middlemarch*. Well, ma'am, your boy is handsome enough. Though his shoulders are, yes, a bit hunched. As his long fingers clutch the steering-lever. And his stomach tautens, empty and tense. Yes—

And this, *this*, was a warm afternoon in the country, forty-five minutes by spirit-burner west of the University at which Turner Ashenden was unhappy. Splendid views of a verdant mountainscape just yellowing. Benign clouds brushing the sky. Not yet autumn, not yet late afternoon.

Nothing is over yet. No possibilities have been excluded. That is probably all we need to know.

Fin de siècle

Not without some startlement—but calm, remaining calm, which was always important—Turner registered a spot of brightness and color blinking at him through the fringe of ailanthus flanking the road, judged it by its size to be some eighty feet ahead, and refused on general principle to translate this into meters. You had to take a stand somewhere. Remaining so very steadfastly calm that his hands began to quake, he reached under the steering console and fingered like a touchstone his shockgun, reassuringly still present. The spot of brightness drew nearer, an illusion, as in fact the spirit-burner bore ignorantly upon it. Turner dearly loved this quarrelsome old beast of a vehicle because it was his and it did not often fail him and neither of the two of them gave a hint of knowing any better.

Around another turn, the brightness resolved itself into a well-made almost-level sign that could not possibly have been more than a generation old, whose sunstruck background was the very color Turner's friend Malachi described as swami yellow. ("The yellow that struggles against the frailties of human paint to glow like the halo on a cheap icon"—but that was Malachi.) Unable to work up sufficient cynicism not to be amazed by it, Turner read the sign from bottom to top without achieving the faintest comprehension.

Open Noon to 5 Weekdays, the last row of fine black lettering said.

Madame Gwendola, Co-Founder and Self-Realized Adept, said the next line up.

And above that, seeming to hover before its swami yellow backdrop —in kingly purple, for God's sake—was:

BAD WINTERS INSTITUTE
OF
SCIENCE AND PHILOSOPHY

Immutable: it remained there, word for word, as Turner read it again from top to bottom. Nor had there been any change in the narrow weedless drive behind it, quickly sloping upward out of sight between native great-leaved rhododendrons.

Well, he thought.

Bad Winters Institute.

His fingers had left the shockgun and showed no inclination to go back. The spirit-burner shuddered impatiently. In Turner's brain a voice among the thousands whined: *I wanna ask, I wanna know. . . .*

My God, thought the unhappy student, I am nothing but a palimpsest. Overwritten in a thousand hands not my own.

Beneath his loins the engine growled, as though sensing an alien approach. Turner tightened his grip on the steering-lever.

"Be quiet," he said seriously. "I am making up my mind."

The fact was (as he realized, shifting gears), Turner could no more easily have passed a purple-on-swami-yellow sign stuck beside a mountain road than his friend Malachi could have failed to scoff at it. That was perhaps the meaning of *personality*, the elusive hard center of one's otherwise squishy selfhood. Turner was pleased at the momentary feeling of having bitten into it. Until an instant later the spirit-burner bumped up the sloping drive and his eyes slid unexpectedly across a wide croquet-worthy stretch of emerald lawn, where they were brought up short and stupid by a building—a mansion? a schoolhouse?—unlike any that one might ever have expected to see here. On top of this godless mountain. Where one's expectations were after all constrained to scrub pines, dysfunctional ski-lifts, shaky cottages, and—if one were imprudently tardy—an impressive sunset or two. But not this. This.

Fin de siècle, prompted Turner's chattery mind.

Fin de *what* siècle? he demanded. Fin de siècle *what*?

(I wanna ask, I wanna know. . . .)

But yes, there was certainly that feeling. About this thing, this aesthetic monstrosity, across the unearthly perfect lawn. Too large to be a house; too small to fulfill the purple promise of *Institute*. Too grand to be an inbred mountainman's folly; yet too chaotic, its elements too unbalanced, to have sprung from the pen of any competent architect. It was a hodge-podge of misremembered styles, whimsically assembled, as though at intervals, with whatever materials lay at hand. Its façade was a bad miss at alabaster white. Its lines were out of plumb. Windows were undersized and overpopulous for their walls. A columned portico did not quite meet one's gaze head-on.

Turner throttled down the spirit-burner and coasted to a stop before a more intimate sign—meant for familiars, he guessed—that stood pedestrian-high at the edge of the lawn. Trained against the sign, then arching away, a yellow rambler rose framed the entrance of a path. Which led, one was intrigued to note, not to the building but catwise around it, out toward a dramatic drop-off the mountain made just beyond. The little sign said:

QUIET, Please!
Weary SPIRITS are
at rest.

Oh my God, thought Turner mirthlessly. What would Malachi say now?

The path it was, then: moustached aromatically with creeping thyme, *T. serpyllum*, which crunched under the heels of Turner's borrowed boots. How green, how wonderfully level the ground was!—an elevated plain, or was that plane, among the clouds. Rougher mountainsides ran down on alternate sides of it, and the weird building we must try to have a better look at reared up like an affronted promontory just there, cold-shouldering us, its stare eternally turned. Yet seeing us all the same. Watching as we creep crunchingly by. Giving us goosebumps.

How old do you suppose the place is? wondered Turner. Not nearly as old as it would like. But how old really? No smartmouth answers now.

From somewhere—or everywhere, as all directions are one from a mountaintop—came a sound of tinny music: bad speakers, or the richer sonorities had been spirited by the wind. Though come to think of it, there was really little wind aloft here. *Der Tod und das Mädchen*. The strings through cool air calling. Second slow movement of the quartet. Broad face of the building as still as a marbeloid deathmask. Turner, *andante*, hummed encouragement to the cellist, whose part was most conspicuously underdone, reinforcing the broad and solemn chords. Dark resonances Schubert had understood, if anyone. *Der Tod*, ever present among us: an angel they call him, shrouded in black. Hum him a hymn. The harvester. Who grinningly waves his scythe on trite tarot cards. Who took Franz only eleven years older than Turner, a singer of melodies, merry haunter of bars—and now called him forth again fleetingly to this godless, architectless terrain. From the vasty deep plugged him into Turner's unoriginal mind. There to sing once more. To vainly, stubbornly hang on.

The path changed: sank a bit, the lawn near its edge acquiring a bevel. The music's soft theme repeated in upper octaves. As Schubert's maiden lightly sighed. Turner paced a row of badly placed and hollow boxwoods, dying before their centennial, and rounded a two-story wing of the mansion that now loomed; then the great, dying plain leapt to fill his vision, its last stands of Indian grass burning in the sun like a glaze of raw sienna, and tears from nowhere, begotten not made, trembled within the corners of his eyes. And as quickly dried, unshed and tiny, already—in being noticed—made too much of. At the edge of the gray-boned cliff sweet autumn clematis hugged a handrail, vanilla-scented, in bloom.

Death and the Maiden. Life and the unhappy student.

And then from an undersized window at scalp-level, through leggy geraniums, a woman's voice called down:

"Come on now, hurry! Madame has been awake seventy-two hours. She is speaking in the library. Hurry now. For today, there will be no charge."

Übermensch, mentioned in passing

Someone had executed a sculpture of two snakes. Or maybe they were dragons. This looked like the sort of place where people would be terribly interested in dragons. The figures were luridly detailed, arm-thick, molded of bright synthetic stuff that had dried to a porous simulacrum of skin. (Though why not scales?) One was fuschia red, the other essentially white, or smoker's-tooth yellow—not pure hues but tacky swirled amalgams that averaged out in the observer's eye. The two creatures squared off in petrified, unconvincing combat across something Turner could only think of as a laminated birdbath. The white one looked like it was winning.

Barely, though. The red one—older, Turner guessed, than its rival —hung on. Its reptilian features were set in weary stubbornness, and its foreclaws enclosed a fin jutting up from the pedestal. Which maybe, then, was supposed to be a sundial. So much the worse: fake pagan astronomy. The glaring plastic face of Time.

Our observer was getting increasingly involved here, picking apart the pretentious symbology. But really: color-coded dragons wrestling on a sundial. It just so painfully *meant* something. And the fact of its meaning something must mean something too. Some unintended summing-up.

Obiter dictum. Trivial, probably, but something to carry back to Malachi, to cynically relate. (Slight raising of the brow, a knowing laugh, oh yes oh yes that's perfect Turner. I can see it now.)

It's some kind of emblem, I bet: of this place, this preposterous Institute. Perhaps I should ask this woman here, absurd stick-legged creature signaling me to follow her.

—Yes, I'm coming, I'm coming.

Let's see: crimson beast of Lust driven off by champion of Purity? Or no, not quite. Struggle isn't lopsided enough; fleshly defender making too much threat of a comeback. Though that might be the point, mightn't it? Warning us. Be ever vigilant. Serpent lurking always just below. The blood-engorged snake. Hands above the sheets now boys and away from it.

Well, whatever. Turner's guide was circling back in a paroxysm of impatience. Rounding up her stray charge from the entryway. *The hall*, they would call it, New-Englanding the A. But my God, the way it's dominated by that awful Fibonaccian staircase, like some great pressed-concrete snailshell stuck up in a playground for kids to crawl up on and get lost in its never-never Escheresque regressions. Serve them right, little golden meanies.

"*Do* come now, young man"—five-ten, schoolmarmishly smiling—"or you will miss one of the most interesting experiences of your life."

Schubert in that moment abruptly ended. Snatched back by the scythe-bearer in mid-*adagio*. Perfect timing, a trademark.

Turner stepped away from the writhing symbols, his hands outspread. Harmless student routine. "Actually I was just . . ."

"I *know*, young man. You were just out for a drive and came upon the Institute by accident. Of *course*. But do come along, now. Please."

Turner, quite baffled now. Thin woman all in white beckoning like someone's nurse. Visiting hours almost over. Hurry now while she is still able to recognize you. Among all the orphans of the world.

"I don't have," he said, a loser's compromise, "a whole lot of time. I have to get off the mountain by dark." Then, surrendering, he followed the woman through the hallway underneath the swirling stair where a rivulet of light came down from a small cupola, grimy with ashes. They passed beaten-up bookshelves, lecterns, étagères, music stands—innumerable monuments—and doors giving off without symmetry left and right to dim-lit chambers of indeterminate size and function. Busts frowned down at him from corbels. Leaflets, stacked on a table by no particular door, gave off a faint whiff of Rosicrucianism. Nineteen Cases Suggestive of Reincarnation. What Is the Great Arcanum of the Ancients? Engraved on the Emerald Tablet—A Message for YOU.

"In here, please." The smiling nurse beckoned toward a door. Standing ajar. Yellow incandescence glowing cozily behind it.

No, not just yet. I wanna see, I wanna know. . . .

". . . *a story that Nature wants to tell.*"

It was not the nurse now but another voice, younger and less charitable. Filling the yellow room and spilling over. The unhappy student, fearing a limit to hospitality, nodded gravely and turned to face this odd next crossing, only a threshold but somehow intimidating. Fingers on his arm—the tall nurse touching, leading him inward. Deeper and deeper now.

In the ruined study—a large place clearly once dressed up and then, by subsequent owners, denuded—ashtrays sat on paint-stained analog speakers and half a dozen puffy armchairs hulked like bodyguards, squat-legged, unoccupied, around a coffee table being used right now as an armrest. Five, six, seven youths, years younger than Turner, sat cross-legged at attention, holding notebooks. Imagine it. Like some hallucinatory classroom, or child actors on a horror set, spellbound with money. Bright wide eyes staring up, unblurred by *cannabis.* Before them, at the focus of their parabola, her image cast upside-down on fourteen shiny retinas, was a stocky fiftyish woman Turner did not cotton to at all. Only she of everyone was seated in a chair. At her shoulder, less perfectly upright, stood a whiteboard across which spidered handwriting repeated the odd remark about Nature, a story She wants to tell, that we mistook for a fragment some few steps ago. And the air smelled faintly of mercurochrome.

My God I hope later I can describe all this.

The woman did not stop speaking but allowed her eyes in their sweeping, democratic passage back and forth across the audience, like water-sprinklers, to pore over Turner along with the five six seven others. (But who *were* they, these scentless archetypes, these children? Where did they sleep at night? What did they eat to make their upturned faces glow like that?) The woman was in the midst of saying:

"Now if we take *that*, my young friends, as our working definition of *immortality*, then we may consider three candidates for this status."

In the back of her throat she clucked a carriage-return.

"First, the melody of 'Greensleeves.'

"Second, a body of old stories you all will have heard, and which you may believe yourselves to have heard *enough* of, to which we refer rather indecisively as the Matter of Britain.

"And finally the face, just the *face* mind you, of Chief Administrator Rodarch, which resembles—among, probably, many other things—a certain comic-strip personality of the previous century; the leonine third of a mythic beast called the chimera, as depicted once in a classical dictionary *ringing* with homoerotic overtones; and the engravure of a coin circulated in the Western Empire and generally supposed to depict one Frederick Barbarossa."

Turner prayed for a tape recorder. Manifest yourself in my shirt pocket. Voice-activated and auto-compressing, otherwise I'll never get it all.

The woman, the Self-Realized Adept one supposed, pausing to make some slight adjustment to her facial set, regarded Turner just long enough an instant to permit the vaguest of categorizations. (University student, third year, unpromising.)

"Well," she resumed, "at any rate, there seems little enough doubt about 'Greensleeves.' The most astonishing feature of Mr Bennett's pleasant little tune is that no amount of assault by tone-deaf successors has really succeeded in altering the essential character of the melody. The notes, the phrasing, even the nuances of mood, have survived"—(break for air, then back with revivified conviction)—"drooling barroom panderers, tone-deaf labor balladeers, muzak-mongers frenzied with market research, orchestration for television, castration by twelve-tone evangelists, navel-gazing by the *ancien régime* of the New Age, and most recently, and most horribly, *processing* by mantic Neuros intent on removing the last vestige of humanity from this most seemingly slight—and more to the point, perishable—of cultural holdovers. All to no avail. 'Greensleeves' lilts on. This particular melody is, it appears, a kind of story. . . ."

Interrupting her well-rehearsed rhetoric, she turned to tap with a long nail the edge of the whiteboard. Even in this there was some dramatic effect; the nail was so long that the slightest lateral tension threatened to crack it.

"Nature itself," she emphasized, turning back. "Now our second case—the Matter of Britain—is a shade more ambiguous. I think perhaps the cleverest approach is that which regards the shadowy historical Arthur, the *dux bellorum*, as the embodiment, or so to speak the *incarnation*— which means the same thing, you know—of a much older, legendary, possibly godlike personage, on whose dharmic resumé the folk-mind has listed all manner of heroic and nationalistic accomplishments. There is, in other words, no need to search for an *actual* Lord of Camelot, or to yearn for a true Golden Age, since these are pathetic products of our racial imagination. Mirages, as it were, to sustain us on our journey through the Waste Land.

"This approach is probably the cleverest. But being clever does not necessarily mean that one is correct—though one might wish it were otherwise."

Turner felt very excited. It was a great idea, he now thought, to have driven up the mountain and turned at the swami-yellow sign. Because of it he was having an Experience, a genuine encounter with the world, of the kind that happens only in real life and not in the books where he spent most of his time, unhappily. By way of *being* there, of making of himself a character and not a dumb watcher of this drama, he shifted his weight forward (an actor's body language, preparing to upstage) and said ingenuously to the woman now pausing as though awaiting response:

"Surely you don't mean that we should take the romances as being literally true?" (The inflection didn't quite work there, but shove on anyway.) "I mean, all those deathless characters, the magical conundrums, the *quest del Saint Graal*. . . ."

The woman turned her water-sprinkler eyes around to gush full-force at him, and for a moment he wondered what he had gotten into. But her round pale face, no more healthy- or serene-looking than it ought to have been, after five decades or so of wear and tear, was not angry nor was it sanctimonious. It was a bit curious, was all, and the water-sprinklers themselves were a shade of green that was only interesting, not imbued with mysterious power; and the fingers that came up to attend to a mortal itching of the nose were short, white, and laden with no more jewelry than the occasion might have demanded: thin gold band and larger setting in silver of polished gemstones. Only the ridiculous sarong-thing wrapped around her like Scarlett's velvet curtains, but paisley, gave her an air of untasteful exotica. She was not at all fazed by his interruption.

"I don't *mean*," she said, "anything that can be so facilely summarized by schoolboys. What I would suggest, however, young man, is that a story which has endured for millions of years is likely to have a firmer purchase on Reality than petty-minded commentators who think they can explain it away."

"Millions of years?" Turner repeated. Smiling, for he was hugely enjoying this, and even sensed hopefully a certain advantage. "I didn't think there had been *people* for millions of years. Much less stories."

"Well you don't, I'm afraid, know much about natural history. For you yourself have lived for millions of years. Countless thousands of lifetimes. The experience of those lives is available to you, to aid you in *your own* holy quest. But you resist it. You refuse to learn. You don't believe that, do you?"

"No, I don't."

The young people at attention on the floor sniggered quietly—almost politely—but stopped when Turner looked down at them. Two of their seven faces sank deeply enough into his brain to find their way into later accounts of this episode: a boy fourteen or so, curly brown-haired, thin-necked, vaguely Greek or Levantine, and a girl a year more or less younger, who was certainly going to be beautiful one day and was quite possibly a blood relation of the woman on the chair. Fearless, with the same green eyes. Turner smiled at her, without really intending to. Connection. Precociously, or agelessly, the girl smiled back.

"For all *you* know," said the woman, following his gaze, "the two of you may have met many times before. You may have been brother and sister, in some very old and very beautiful life."

"No," said the girl. My God thirteen years old, shaking her head like a calm siren, immortal resident of these ancient rocks. "I don't remember it that way."

Turner said half sarcastically, "I don't remember it at all."

"Not brother and sister," the girl continued, thoughtful. "Something different."

Turner shifted his weight again. Reverting to his normal dramatic mode: Joycean, cowering backstage.

The woman sighed.

At this the nurse—that white-dressed stick-legged figure we had all but forgotten—advanced into the room as though the sigh were her special summons.

"Madame is very tired, children," she said, moving about with cheerful efficiency, sweeping them up before her. "She has been awake seventy-two hours. We should leave her now."

Turner was displaced, propelled backward by the general upwelling of young bodies around the room. He lost sight of the girl for several moments, brushed against instead by the warm-skinned boy who smiled timid and friendly but did not speak. A touch on his forearm came not lightly from the nurse but heavily, grippingly, from the saronged woman now processing toward the hall, going not gently into her seventy-third hour without sleep.

"Come spy on us again," she said, "another time. I think Maridel would like to meet you."

And Turner, tapping the side of his only tape recorder, wondered archly "Again?"

Childhood and youth

A stream of reradiant heat slipped endlessly away from the walls of the Institute of Science and Philosophy. September wind, arriving late, brought with it across the flawless lawn and around this two-story obstruction the first yellow auguries of fall: leaves of the stately tulip polar, *Liriodendron tulipifera*, whose broad soft faces were at first glance, by fading light, studies in perfect symmetry. Only by careful examination of the one that twisted up dust-devilishly toward his outreaching hand, beginning a second fall in the moment that he caught it, did Turner determine that for this leaf (as for everything else in the universe) the symmetry was an illusion. See, the right major lobe was wider and more rounded than the left. Each was a thoughtful portrait of the other, but artistically distorted. Warped by the subtle workings of supernal forces—gravity, the sputtering of the sun—on Nature's highly polished looking-glass.

For Nature abhors reflection. Symmetry is a fraud, perpetrated by anal-retentive mathematicians. The true thing, the state She prefers, is restless equipoise. A deteriorating standoff. Endless tugging by well-matched but ultimately unequal opponents. *Der Tod und das Mädchen*. Or the great columnar yews slowly dying at Sissinghurst. One of which would survive the others, by twenty years or so. Though they would all sink finally into the Sussex loam. Their molecules dispersing. Until the molecules themselves fell asunder. Deaths within deaths like Russian boxes on the screen, a much-used and still useful device, while the final credits rolled. Invisible worm burrowing at the core of Matter. *O Rose thou art sick*.

Turner let go of the leaf and watched it helicopter down the rocky jaw of the precipice. Beyond the handrail and sweet autumn clematis of the terrace there was nothing. Or almost nothing: the beginning members of an old long colonnade, beams of a grape-arbor one now only imagined, a perfectly consistent bit of classical pretention . . . and then the drop-off. End of the mountain. Where at some moment within this generation (for the earth hadn't yet thrown a leafy coverlet over its scar) an entire side of the summit had fallen cleanly away and crumbled into the valley. Right practically up to the Institute's back door. Which left the old building there as though bravely hanging on, and of course that was a fraud too; the place just sat there stupidly as it had always. Falling down, falling down.

It was hard to figure. Indeed impossible, one would have thought. Such geologic rebellion. Where the earth has not moved for millions of hypothetic lifetimes. But here it was—the evidence. Plain to behold by any who should arrive here, as Turner had, by a sort of willful error, a misstep unrepented, at the Institute's back door. Thinking not about the wasted plain laid out before him but the green and peaceful valley he had left, for the afternoon, behind. Where his books in a damp room rotted. And all their burdensome and unhelpful knowledge rotted with them.

Turner took the one step that was permissible down from the terrace, feeling already the rocky end of all things. He thought distantly of himself breathing that delicate air: the warmth slipping endlessly away, the coolness of autumn that would not for another week or two yet manage to arrive. And he felt, in that uneven moment, a sensation agonizing in its intensity of something he had not known for a very long time now, since childhood.

Fear it was. A very certain fear. Not to be home before nightfall. The evening coming down around him as he struggled to return, feeling lost though he knew perfectly where he was. A chill in the air so fresh and sharp and awful. The world made strange by growing darkness. Afraid of all things at once, of being worried about by others, and of not—of life being lived in warm yellow rooms without him. Forgotten by them all.

Them all, thought Turner now sadly. Where there is no one. Only drinkers, apartment philosophers, singers of mawkish songs. My own shabby Schubertians. Hardly worth calling a home, or going back to.

But these were nothing but thoughts: a gloss on the crust of awareness, the mind's vain effort to attribute that stab of pure sensation. That terrible brief moment in which an earlier Turner had returned.

It was leaving him behind now, dropping below its own horizon. Even the memory was weakening—first exponentially fast, then smoothing out, lingering in a fainter and fainter asymptotic vagueness. Never returning all the way to zero. Approaching and approaching it, but never . . . quite . . .

Even after death, though? Mustn't the curve end there? Did his own forever-gone childhood still exist somewhere, in some unfelt fundament? Were his memories immortal?

Nothing but thoughts, of course. Self-generating mood swings. Unanswerable questions. Pleasurable youthly despair. Something to carry back with him in the dark spirit-burner, comfort in his dangerous descent. Ought to rig up some kind of seatbelt in this thing, really. The curves were bad enough in daylight, when you could see what was coming.

Tomorrow, perhaps. Meantime we will just have to hang on.

2

Warmth, and light

Black Malachi Pantera's leasewarming party was entering its second week by the time Turner got back an hour after nightfall. The spirit-burner's bronchial wheeze drew no notice from the celebrants inside the Solar Temple, but Turner's irritable rap at the argon-filled superinsulated windows, a topic on which Black Malachi was especially hot, caused intruder lights to begin strobing over the parking lot, which in turn activated the energy-waste alarm, and this at last proved loud enough to get somebody's attention.

One story up, a pane of the greenhouse came open and a round head popped out, its hair a halo of frizzy umber.

"State you name," the head called cheerfully down. "Explain in brief your background and purpose. References are not required, but experience with heavy drugs is desirable."

"Malachi," said Turner. "Open the door. I've forgotten the combination again."

"Am I hearing the truth?" cried the guardian of the Temple. His voice fell into singsong declamation:

> "I want to be the wandering sailor,
> A silhouette by the light of the moon,
> Just waiting patiently by the window
> Watching seasons change—

Someday, you'll see,
My dreams will pull you through that garden door.

A song for you, Ashenden."

"Malachi," said Turner, unmoved, "send somebody down, would you? Why do you keep the doors locked, anyway?"

"Not unless you call me by my proper name," Black Malachi sniffed. "I went to a great deal of trouble choosing it."

"Damn it, I'll break a window."

"Oh, Ashenden." The haloed head hung down, its sentiments beyond hope of expression. "Whatever shall we do about this attitude? Truly, I despair. But hold still a minute, won't you? I'll try to work something out."

The pane dropped back into place and the intruder lights fell dark. A conspiratorial silence descended on the parking lot. Turner stood among expensive electric wagons and homemade horse-carts in the remnants of a compost heap, a compacted memorial to his efforts at gardening. He had ended up eating Malachi's vegetables, trucked up fresh twice weekly from town. By this means and others Turner's genial housemate contrived never to leave home except at exam time, and only then when more satisfactory arrangements could not be made.

"Continuous occupation," he had gravely explained, sometime during the now blurry opening weekend of the party: "that is the key to establishing squatter's rights. I have it all on the best legal authority."

Turner had smiled indulgently. "But I think"—aware here that he was only feeding straightlines into Malachi's inexhaustible comeback machine—"I'm pretty sure that sleeping someplace every night would qualify as 'continuous occupation.'"

"Certainly," the corpulent youth rolled onward, "but it would *not* qualify to deter the devious Goldaster."

This villian was, of course, the owner of the Solar Temple, which he had thoughtlessly called Hartfell Chalet.

"Let us suppose," Black Malachi urged his gathering audience, "that while I was away on some trivial outing—"

"Like classes," suggested Turner.

"—this greed-driven . . . this *rapacious* landholder, were to dispatch his hoard of lackeys to enter the house, cast out my few humble rooms of personal effects, and install a new set of door-combinations. Or indeed, actual new locks. I would be then, in effect, evicted."

"How poignant." (Straight man again.)

"*Driven*," Black Malachi emphasized, "to rent some miserable hovel, where I would be obliged in consequence to live like . . . like a common medical student!"

"Unthinkable."

"Quite"—at which the suppositionally homeless young man had smiled around at his circle of admirers. "But you see. My persistence has proven out. The verminous Goldaster, having failed both in his efforts to find me abroad and to locate within a radius of three hundred kilometers any governmental authority, elected or otherwise, willing to champion his cause—particularly in the way of enforcing a writ of eviction—and being at heart a reasonable man, though prone to these fits of possessiveness—in the end has been driven to acknowledge himself confronted by a superior will, and has granted me the concession of . . . a lease!"

Popping of corks; a theme was bestowed upon the party, which after a day and a half was already warming up nicely.

Money, you see, had turned out not to be the problem. Black Malachi was commonly held to be rich (though Turner had some doubts about the true extent of this). No, it was simpler than that, or more complicated, one or the other. The thing was, Black Malachi didn't like to move. He enjoyed activity around him, but preferred himself to remain at the calm center of his own storm. He was, about matters in general, and particularly about his choice of living accommodations, abundantly satisfied; and he wished that everything would roll right along as it was. And matters in general, where Malachi was concerned—as against Turner, with whom they constantly warred—seemed willing enough to oblige.

"Are you coming in?"

What?

Ah, I see. It was not the smiling self-satisfied youth of Turner's rumination who spoke, but a curious and conventionally pretty young woman of the here-and-now, standing in the doorway. Speaking again.

"You must be Turner."

"Mm. Did Malachi . . . are you a friend of Malachi's? Or something?"

"You mean Blackie?"—What narrow eyes she had. Opened just a

slit. The better to blink. And how tall. Gotten up in the standard University uniform of shapeless hand-me-downs. Saying, "I'm Cervina," now. "First-year anthro. I've never been to a party like this before, ever. It's like some, I don't know . . . pagan rite or something." She raised to her mouth a beaker of murky liquid in which something that made Turner think of a fetus, a tiny pig fetus, drifted in viscous suspension. From Cervina's intently focused expression, it was probably something else altogether. Through the door around her drifted a miasma of smoke and warm bodies.

Home again home again, jiggedy jig. Turner stepped inside and Cervina let the door double-lock itself shut behind him. She slipped an arm through his, moving along with him into the dim jungle of banana trees in the open foyer. First-year anthro indeed. Seventeenth-year city-girl more like it. Sent out here for safekeeping by a daddy too busy to look out for her back East. Something about this Cervina, anyway, made Turner feel not quite up to her level—callow and tongue-tied while the big girl flowed beside him like oil.

"Want some of this drink?" she offered companionably.

"What's in it?"

"It's called a gibson, I think. It's good with chips."

"Mm. Where's Malachi?"

"Who? Oh, gosh—I'm lost again. How are you supposed to find your way around in here?"

Turner smiled—a wistful showing, at best—and tried to restrain an eager coil of *Passiflora incarnata* that Cervina, turning unproductively, had run afoul of. Mother-of-pearl moonlight drifted down through stems and flowers, sprinkler tubes, banana leaves so large you thought you were dreaming them, from the exposed struts of the far-above glassy temple-top—rather mockingly, Turner had always thought—to fall at last on the genuine south-of-some-forgotten-border gleaming and slippery suntile whose surface at night was merely black, though so is the sky despite the infinitudes there. Someone was singing quietly a room or two over; and softer still, confused with the drip of a leaky sprinker, came the gentle finger-sounds of a harp. The walls had completely vanished, mere abstractions, behind it all.

"Things invisible to see," murmured Turner; for the two of them had come to a stop and been standing there for half a minute, mysteriously quiet.

"He did it on purpose, I bet."

The girl faced Turner in the dimness, her narrow eyes betraying, or feigning, a cautious intelligence. She added: "Blackie did, didn't he. It seems like him."

Yeah. Turner nodded and pulled the vine off her. [We liked her better then, didn't we? Though she no less intimidated us.]

"It's like a maze," he said—instructing, complaining—"the way he's got the plants laid out. It wasn't like this when we moved in. The main thing is, don't waste your time going *that* way, even though you know that's where the stairs are."

"I didn't know that."

"Ah. Well. But see, the quickest way is to act like you're heading back *out*, which means you turn either hard left or right."

Making the choice himself, Turner led her withershins through the maze. Cervina raised and lowered her beaker at his side. After several steps the harp-sounds grew louder, unnaturally. We weren't going *that* fast, no matter what-all might have come later.

"Wow," said Cervina, only stating it, as though from politeness. "What's all this?"

They emerged from the banana jungle into what must once have been a formal dining room—straight-walled, rectangular, lit by a nebula of tiny bulbs laid in whorls across the twenty-foot ceiling, where each bulb spent most of its life in darkness, firing only at long intervals for several seconds, in a manner that may or may not have been independent of the rest. Turner had watched the process for many hours in various states of consciousness without figuring that one out—though he had been assured by one Vincent Hawkmoth, leader of the house band, that the pattern broke down under cryptographic analysis to reveal a thirty-seven-day cycle based upon permutations of the notes in *Time's Encomium*. The effect was something like an invasion of cosmic fireflies.

"What's what?" said Turner.

"This, I don't know . . . electrical stuff. And the, like, chemistry lab." Cervina led him a few steps into the room, at which point *this*, whatever it was, pretty well surrounded them. Three relaxed-looking fellows in their indeterminate twenties moved in no great hurry around banks of equipment on a long oaken table.

"Hi, Turner," a tall one said.

"Partner, this is Cervina," he said—as much asking as telling, though Partner only smiled. Back to Cervina he explained: "Partner Trefoil is one of the house musicians. I mean, he's a member of this band that, or who, more or less live here these days. They're based in the dining room."

Partner offered no objection to any of this, or to the young lady. He was laying out biaxial cable in a serpentine path along the floor. As elsewhere, the odd humors of alternating current were regarded with due awe in the Solar Temple. Turner stepped carefully across, out of a lifelong habit of avoiding entanglement.

Cervina said, "You guys are a *band?*"

Partner shrugged; his cable-laying carried him slowly across the room. After further sampling the contents of her beaker Cervina wondered: "So where are their instruments? What do they *play?*"

Turner frowned. How to explain this. Which made little enough sense to him in the first place.

"Well," he said, to begin with, "they've sort of evolved beyond regular instruments, in a way." He pointed across the tea-stained surface of a sequence-analyzer. "Vinny, see, who's the leader . . . well, they *used* to be more into actually playing music than they are right now, but then Vinny started getting interested in simulation. Or he calls it, explication. And right now he's trying to make a, ah, Stradivarius."

Cervina blinked. "Can you just, *do* that?"

"That depends," said a new voice. Tricky acoustics: it took a few seconds to trace this to a short and dark-haired fellow moving carefully between racks of glowing tubes.

"Ah," said Turner, relieved somewhat. "Vinny, this is—"

The short man winked. "It depends on how you feel about information. Whether it's being stored up by the universe, or just, as we like to say, *averaged out of existence*. You know. Like warmth, and light."

Cervina frowned and gave a short, endearingly girlish shiver.

"If it *is*," Vinny continued, "like we think, being constantly accumulated, rolled up in the fabric of space-time, then it should just be a matter of squeezing it back out again."

As he spoke, a new series of harp-notes began. The acoustics of the situation were indecipherable; each pluck seemed to come from a slightly different place.

"There are quartz pulsers in the floor," Vinny explained. He ran his hand down a rice-paper panel. "And these screens are part of a damping and enhancement system, to eliminate spurious waveforms. Right now we're just trying to get the strings right. Then we'll go on to the bow. You know—one thing at a time."

Pluck pluck. Ghostly notes descending. Plunk. Ploomp.

Cervina raised a finger, the whole arm levitating with it. Remember the end of *Death in Venice*? Tadzio like a sexless angel pointing out to sea, into the blinding future? Like that.

"Oh, that's for later," said Vinny, and whether Turner grasped it or not he was talking about the tiny refinery of heatproof flasks and tubing, copper condensing coils, a methane burner, a spectrograph.

[You know I was following it, damn you. I think in places this is a little, you know—coy.]

"At some point," said Vinny, "we're going to have to figure out the transformations in the wood. We think, from what we've read, that we're talking in terms of kiln-drying followed by chemical interaction with goat's urine, followed by this long gradual oxidation."

Cervina said thoughtfully, seriously, "Goat's urine."

This was one of Turner's favorite parts of the Party Tour. He said, "Only—tell her Vinny—only they haven't found a goat yet. So they've got this *laboratory animal*."

Cervina said, "You mean a hamster or something?"

Hawkmoth's dark eyes sparkled. Cupping his hands he bellowed, kitchenward:

"Cagliostro!"

Some delay.

Then through a doorway murky with smoke and under the table scampered the happy victim of these strange experiments. Friskily it lapped at Vinny's well-remembered friendly hand, empty this time. Cervina laughed in surprise.

"He's a Jack Russell terrier," Vinny explained. "They're really smart and cooperative. Besides, it's a lot easier taking the samples right in here, and not have to go chasing goats across a pasture or something."

Shrugging off his shaky grasp of animal husbandry, Vinny nodded at the row of little yellow beakers that lined the back of the lab table.

"Of course *Malachi*," Turner felt moved, in the spirit of perfect accuracy, to point out, "says this is all a bunch of shit. He says he just likes having a band around the house."

Vinny, secure in the turret of his latter twenties, gave a chuckle.

"Yes," he acknowledged. "We've reached a philosophical parting of the ways. Our friend Pantera takes a rather dark view of the fate of human knowledge. He tells me I just think my music is so incredibly brilliant that I can't bear the thought that it's all going to disappear."

You could hear, thought Turner, the dismissive sneer in Vinny's paraphrase. We were rather in awe, in fact, of his ability to take it all so blithely.

Cervina set her own beaker, empty now, beside the others on the table. "I'm not sure I understand," she said, "what the point of all this is."

Vinny shrugged: okay, you did or you didn't. In the background, Partner Trefoil tightened a connection, producing sparks. Beneath a mountain in Wales, an old lightning god named Beli muttered and rolled over in bed. Somewhere in the Solar Temple a door was slammed, then opened, then slammed again. Above the harp-sounds in the dining room could be heard something like a small riot just getting started.

Cervina looked up worriedly, but Turner (imitating the guys in the band) made a point of looking undisturbed.

"Well," the tall girl said, edging back, "maybe I ought to go look for Blackie. Does anybody know where his room is? I've looked all over the place, but all I keep running into is like, one crazy thing after another."

The small riot seemed to be getting larger. There was a sound of glass shattering, a boy's frightened shout. Without waiting for a reply, Cervina began edging her way toward the dining room door. The party extended itself, amoeba-like, to encompass her. Her head was visible among others for a minute, then gone. Catching Turner's eye, Vinny Hawkmoth sympathetically shrugged.

"No," Turner said, feeling some need to explain. "She's not . . . I mean, she's just here with Malachi, I think. Or something."

Vinny good-naturedly, and so relaxed, as always, said, "Well, aren't we all?"

Übermensch, shouted from the barricades

A party is raging here. A raging party. Students who left the battlefront during the week—I don't know, to go to classes maybe—have rejoined the campaign; they're crammed like something a snake has swallowed into a narrow breezeway between the courtyard and the lawn, an important crossing, linking the bedroom wing to the left-hand loop of the maze. Malachi, who has named everything, calls this the Bug Walk because its tubs of tender *nymphaceae* breed mosquitoes. Already tonight Turner's been bitten twice. He swats late and loses his balance, bumping into a woman a couple years older than himself who is straining to see over the dark wall of bodies. Up ahead a tall guy is, like, *declaiming* something between a poem and a ransom note. Somebody else has begun a sympathetic thumping on a glass wall. The bodies murmur and sway.

"I wonder why the lights are out," the woman next to Turner says, her voice very nasal. "Don't these people have enough money to buy electricity?"

Turner thinks he remembers her from Philology, though he remembers very little about Philology.

"We generate it ourselves," he tells her, before catching the irony, the bitterness, in her voice. *Don't these people* . . . The woman turns to stare at him.

"You're Ashen," she says.

He misunderstands, glances away.

"The friend of Goldaster's," she goes on. Sounding perhaps accusatory. "Am I right?"

"Excuse me," says Turner, trying to press ahead. The crowd in the Bug Walk is unyielding. "Does anybody know what's going on?"

"They're reading the Manifesto," the woman tells him.

"Ah." Turner tries the insider bit. "Thank God I got here in time."

She regards him strangely. (Was "God" a mistake?) She says, "I thought . . ." but the speaker up ahead, lost in shadows, pretty well drowns her out. Turner catches odd phrases: *a pattern of systematic redomiciling . . . flatten the curve of economic . . . the dispossessors in their lair.*

"Wow," says the young woman. "That really spells it out, doesn't it?"

Her name is on the tip of Turner's tongue. Or maybe, you know, the base of his glottis or something. It's the voice he remembers, really: all stuffed up, as though she never managed to shake one of those winter-long childhood colds. *Stentorian* is the word that comes to mind, but he doesn't think that's right.

"Are you Blanche?" he asks her.

"No," she says, "my name is Dinder. Blanche is somebody else, I think."

"Well hey, listen, Dinder, do you know who these people are? Because, I mean, I'd really like to get up to my bedroom. If I could just get through here."

She watches him with dark eyes set back in a puffy, off-white face. "Forget it," she says. "They've blocked the hall."

I can see that, he thinks. But don't press her; she seems to know what's going on.

"You live in this place, right?" (She says this disapprovingly.) "So what's the problem, can't you hear? It's all in the Manifesto."

All Turner can make out of the Manifesto is certain clusters of words that sound like slogans: *the New Reason . . . reclaim our rightful heritage . . . crimes of the Old Souls*. He loosens his mental filter, letting in more of the noise, the thumping on glass, the muttering crowd. To his surprise he discovers that someone is addressing him: a boy with a little curly beard, like a goat.

". . . asking about you all day," the goat-boy is saying. "Where have you been?" Without waiting to hear, he places a wooden object carved like some kind of fertility symbol into Turner's hand.

"No thanks," says Turner. Who has enough biochemical confusion to contend with, without that. Plus, the symbolism is all screwed up. See, you've got this bowl which is clearly a receptacle, a form-giver, but then you've got this long phallic shaft discharging smoke: clearly, this is deranged. He tries to pass the thing, but nobody wants it. The goat-boy doesn't seem to remember who he was talking to.

Submit to the Chief Administrator . . . the Manifesto rumbles on, gaining intensity. *Additional areas chosen for camps . . . until personally certified by. . . .*

"Did he say," Turner starts to ask, but he cannot hear himself. The party is getting a little crazy. Nervously, reflexively, he brings the pipe to his mouth. It tastes like, maybe, coriander. He turns to Dinder, who's looking very pleased, and shouts, "Did he—did the Manifesto—say something about Rodarch?"

Dinder fires him a look. "Who do you think?" she says, only just failing to add, *stupid*.

Stupidly, Turner wants to explain. "It's just . . . it's kind of a coincidence, see, because just this afternoon—"

All of a sudden the crowd starts breaking up. I mean, like shrapnel. People are running past us with wild expressions, waving us out of their way, and Dinder is tugging at Turner's sleeve.

"What?" he says.

"They're going to blow the house up," she says very clearly, which proves that even a nasal voice can be loud and penetrating. Maybe *that's* what stentorian means.

Turner does not understand. "They're, ah. . . ."

"If anybody tries to get past them. They've blocked the stairway, see, to cut off the living quarters." She's following the crowd now, leaving Turner stranded. Over her shoulder she yells: "Didn't you hear the Manifesto?"

Turner responds to confusion, to danger, in all cases by continuing to do whatever he happens to be doing at the time. (In this instance, taking another hit on the rudely carved pipe.) This is a variant of the more common practice of freezing solid, only it involves a suspension not of motion but of *change*: a form of inertia. It is often mistaken, by onlookers, for preternatural bravery, or at least indifference to physical harm. People will recount, later in the leasewarming party, how Turner Ashenden just stood there in the middle of the Bug Walk sucking casually on this, like, smoking cock, while a couple of yards away this *time bomb* or something is about to go off. And how he very slowly started to turn (like, why do you think they call him *Turner*, the ad hoc historian will jest) until he was looking up the hall that everybody else had batted ass out of.

They won't know the half of it. You have to be standing where Turner is—halfway down the Bug Walk, blinking like an idiot—to see what's going on at the distant end, where the back staircase begins, leading up to (among other things) Turner's bedroom. Where at this moment, two guys in blue coveralls are busy fiddling with something down on the floor. Something about the size of an unabridged dictionary, Turner irrelevantly thinks; though at such a moment, any idea that occurred to him would pretty much have to be irrelevant. It's how his mind works. The two guys are propping this object up against a closet door, the closet where Turner keeps the fuel for his spirit-burner, in little glass jars, despite Malachi's warnings about such things.

Now talk about your peculiar mental states. It hits Turner—as the crowd is pulling up hushed and expectant several yards behind him, and the first and second puffs of something that tastes like coriander are just kicking in—it hits him that *if the house blows up now, Malachi will say it's because I didn't listen to him about the fuel*.

Perhaps only Turner would find such a thing worth worrying about. The two guys at the end of the hall are clearly thinking about bigger things, like making sure the fuse is lit, or the clock is ticking, or the little handle you push down is moving smoothly. Who knows? They're standing up now, brushing their hands off, making themselves at home.

"What do *you* want?" one of them asks Turner, in a distinctly hostile tone. But you know how irritable you can get when you're trying to concentrate on something. For Turner, the world has slipped into some high-ratio gear. He steps forward uncertainly, like a tourist, just a little turned around, nothing to worry about, let's ask these guys up here.

"What kind of bomb is it?" he politely inquires.

The guys look at each other. Their coveralls are an attractive Newport blue, which Turner recognizes now as the uniform of the Settling Out Camps. Oh yeah. They were hired, he remembers, as cooks or bartenders or something. On the theory that, being from the East and all, they'd probably be glad to get the money. Obviously this theory did not take into account certain important facts.

"A heavy one," one of them says—sweating, smiling, a little joke. They obviously can't believe Turner is really saying this, really standing here, which makes three of us. [Only three?] Perhaps like pure-hearted revolutionaries they are concerned for our well-being. Perhaps they will lift us by the narrow shoulders and carry us out of harm's way.

Not a chance. The second guy, tall and nervous-looking, glances quickly into Turner's eyes and then away. He shifts his weight. "This'll teach you greedy assholes," he says loudly, as though adding a little codicil to the Manifesto, "this'll teach you to try to keep us out of your precious valley. And you can tell your friend Goldaster, and all the other Souls—

this is only the beginning, Rodarch is going to force you out of *everywhere*, every place you've built with your stolen riches, before this is over."

It bothers Turner that this tall fellow seems unable to make eye contact while speaking. Also, there is a stiffness, a machinelike quality about his demeanor. This is not the way to behave at a party. Beside the closet door, the dictionary-sized box is inconspicuous, like a piece of forgotten luggage. Little strands of household wiring, diverted from a raceway along the floor, stick out like mouse-tails from its side.

"I was just thinking," says Turner (a lie, though probably okay under the circumstances), "that like, if you guys need a place to stay or something, maybe you should just go talk to Harvey. That's what *we* did. I mean, I'm sure he's got some other house, or. . . ."

He means this to be, you know, just an idea, an effort to clarify things, but it comes out like a smart-ass remark. Turner can't help it. It's something in his voice.

The tall guy, evidently tired of talking, raises an arm. Before Turner can focus on what's happening, a black-and-yellow flash of pain propels him sideways. He slams into a window, which yields ominously but does not shatter. Instead, like a joint being dislocated, the glass panel pops out of its frame and wags crazily, caught by a rubber seal, just above the place where Turner has landed. He lies there stunned but lucid. The energy-waste alarm, originally inspired by a passage in upper strings from *Vertigo*, starts to shriek.

"What the hell is that?" says the guy who decked Turner.

He and his companion look from the dislocated window to the box that very well might contain a bomb. They are trying to take this philosophically. The second guy says, "Maybe we should put something in our ears." You get the idea they're planning to be around for a while.

Turner stands up, but they've forgotten him now. They are pawing around in their pockets. Moving quickly and quietly, he steps past them to the staircase, climbs a step or two, then halts. The coverall-clad Settlers look around at him.

"You've fucked up now," he tells them.

After long and sad experience, he's finally got the timing down. Just as the tall guy takes a step to follow him, the household computer wraps up its thirty-second effort to close the broken window. It decides, as it always decides, to isolate the region where the leak has occurred. Electrical power is diverted from this section of the house, and—a final satisfaction—insulated partitions drop into place at both ends of the Bug Walk. One of these deprives the crowd of further appreciation of Turner's heroism; the other nearly deprives the tall Settler of his nose.

Turner stands in the darkness of the stairwell. There is a pounding, not yet frantic, from the other side of the partition. Naturally this is useless; the Solar Temple is a real brick shithouse. Well, thinks Turner. I guess you can't lose them all.

Far from the madding

In the center of his private second-floor suite Black Malachi Pantera, a colorful eminence, high priest of the Solar Temple, stood thoughtfully on the cross-members of a scaffolding he had erected earlier that night, from which to achieve a better perspective on his latest work of art. This great canvas lay inclined at a princely angle seven feet beneath him. Acrylic dyes from the hot quadrant of the color-wheel swirled around it in watery curves, though the greater part of the canvas was as yet only gessoed. Black Malachi's gaze upon it showed traces of pride, apprehension and gentle amusement. We have intruded on a private moment, it seems. Sounds of the party below enter with us, and the pneumatic glissando of a climate-control door.

Black Malachi looks up. A portly youth, alarmingly hirsute and worldly for his eighteen years, he waits with Buddha-like self-possession for the footsteps in the hallway to elaborate themselves into the edgy, angular form of his friend Turner Ashenden.

"For God's sake, Malachi. Do you know what's going on down there?"

Black Malachi, in a benign mood since approximately sunset, his diurnal pattern of some dependability, casts down upon his friend a kindly smile, tracing out with the tip of a number six brush the form of a five-sided star: Wiccan ritual of protection.

"There is a theory," he says, "that if one is allowed or encouraged to paint for a length of time, without restriction as to style or content, then one eventually winds up painting mandalas. In fact, all of one's paintings may be laid out chronologically—in evolutionary order, so to say—and it will be seen that one's creative development has been in the direction of more mandala-like forms, with some hypothetic ideal mandala hanging out there, like a mathematical limit, just out of reach. Do you agree with this?"

Turner squinted through the bottom struts of the scaffolding, trying to make out the pattern. He said, "But that would, ah, seem to require a state of innocence on the painter's part. Whereas you. . . . But listen, no kidding—there are these two guys who were trying to *blow up the house*."

The stout youth became thoughtful; he gazed at us like some sharp-eyed latter-day critic, spying the first-person behind the third. After a moment he declared: "I can't imagine such a thing. Now tell me what you mean, exactly, by 'whereas you.' "

Turner felt dazed. Also, however, a bit relieved. Malachi's congenital incapacity to worry about anything had a tonic effect on him. "I mean," he said, struggling to reorient his thoughts, "that, ah, if somebody knew they were supposed to be painting a mandala, they'd probably go ahead and paint one. Or else they wouldn't, just to be different. Is this for some art class?"

"Certainly not. And you are abusing the personal pronoun. I take it you do not consider me sufficiently innocent to be a viable experimental subject."

"It seems kind of late for that."

"Ha! What you mean to say is, I am totally corrupt. True. But corruption and innocence are not mutually exclusive. Indeed, I feel that by my perfect corruption, by having left no desire ungratified, no domain of sensual experience unexplored, I have protected my inner self from the ruinous influence of temptation. I have remained, if you will, in my deepest nature, a meta-virgin. Thus I am arguably the *only* ideal subject for an experiment of this type."

Turner drew closer to the painting that was indirectly under discussion. "It looks like a giant cunt," he remarked.

"How nice of you to say. I rather had hoped to develop an aspect of *enclosure*."

We laughed honestly then. "How long," Turner tried to say sternly, "is this party going to go on? There are *terrorists* down there. And I swear to God I saw somebody wearing nothing but a snake."

Black Malachi tapped with the paintbrush handle on his teeth. "Yes, that would be Lucette. Delightful girl. Someone's sister, I believe."

"Maybe we should call the police."

"Oh Turner, Turner. Sometimes I feel that you are not even *trying* to understand. There has been no meaningful law enforcement authority in this valley since . . . I mean, that's why we *live* here, isn't it?"

Turner shook his head. "I can't believe you're just going to ignore this. They talked like they were working for the Chief Administrator."

"Ah! Praise be to the Stainless Steel Savior!" Black Malachi genuflected, leaned over the scaffolding, and spat. His mood showed signs of brittleness. "*I* can't believe," he said, "that *you* feel threatened by someone with a title as bland as 'Chief Administrator.' Where did you disappear to today?"

"Yesterday," said Turner dryly, holding up his watch.

"Ah." A smile returned to the round priestly face.

"It's an unbelievable story," said Turner, who at the same moment realized that he no longer felt like telling it. "I wish my room was empty."

"Oh, don't stand on ceremony. We allow fucking in the halls here. Or for that matter, you're welcome to use one of my closets."

Turner tightened his lip muscles, cross. "Damn it, Malachi. Why is it impossible to just *talk* to you? Why does it always have to be this . . . this *contest* or something?"

The implausible teenager set the implements of his art in a solvent solution and came down comically from the scaffold. He laid a soft hand on Turner's shoulder, smiling up from a four-inch deficit that comforted no one. "How about a nice cup of fungus?" he proposed. "I know *I* feel like one.

"You know"—not waiting for Turner's demurral—"you can be quite disagreeable, too, in your own fashion. That may be too strong. Irksome, let's say. Your refusal, for example—"

Turner followed him, damn it, across the broad diffusely lit room. Black Malachi paused before an awfully impressive ebony lowboy, six thousand no sweat, plus bribes to get it here from the coast, across which were accoutered all the necessary, much of the optional and a good deal of the highly superfluous equipage of a pre-homeopathy candidate's crude investigations. He resumed speaking, neatly picking up again the dropped nuance of petulance, after choosing and agitating a stoppered phial.

"—to address me by either my chosen or my ancestral name. Only by the one that my mother liked, Lug rest her, which I care for least of the three."

"Your *chosen* name," said Turner, still closely following in all senses. "What gives you the right to pick a name for yourself, when the rest of us are stuck . . . and what kind of name is 'Pantera,' anyway? I mean, you don't look Hispanic or Italian or anything like that. As a matter of fact you look like a fat Dutchman. I can see you with a clay pipe in some, um, Vermeer."

"I presume you mean Brueghel." Malachi paused, relishing the image. "No in fact," he admitted, "I am none of the above. My parents' surname was Kildare—but that need not detain us. Now, now," waving aside Turner's *then why* expression, "my *true* ancestry, you see, was unearthed, and I believe that is not putting it inexactly, only after considerable research. The first definitely recorded Pantera, please pay attention, was mentioned in a rabbinical tract that *may* have been the source of certain ugly rumors, almost certainly accurate, put about by Celsus, the mean-mouthed Platonist. Stop me if you hear the ringing of a bell."

Turner nodded, ignoring what was probably, was almost certainly some sort of goad. "Go on—I've got to hear this."

"Yes, I suppose somebody ought to. You see this Pantera or Panthera, a Roman soldier, was reported by the rabbi and subsequently by Celsus—who by the way was quite the role model for Para-ditto—and I do not speak here of any poodle—"

"My *God*, Malachi, can't you stick to one obscure allusion at a time?"

"Funny you should say that," said Black Malachi. He raised a demitasse dose of brown potion to his mouth. Muttered a make-believe invocation. Drank. "Ah, happy host! The thing is, this particular Pantera fucked the brains out of one unmarried or at least unconsummated, to date, Jewish girl you will have heard of, who thereafter gave birth to a magician of some historical moment."

"I think I get this, Malachi, and it isn't funny."

Set the phial down. Breathe in then out quickly. Focus. "They found his grave," he announced.

Whose grave, Turner resolutely *did not ask*.

"Pantera's," replied the relentless Black M.P. "Somewhere in the northern reaches of the Empire. The only archaeological evidence, I am not kidding you now Ashenden, for the existence of the Holy Family."

"I see," said Turner testily. "So you claim divine ancestry for yourself, that's the point of all this."

"Oh no." The furry head shook in grave misunderstood-ness. "You are not listening carefully at all. I am but the latest offshoot of a very tall tree of *begetters* of gods, you see. Provokers of miraculous births. We Panteras, as a song or saying goes, love 'em and leave 'em—generally dying, ourselves, an ignominious death somewhere, while some *angel* gets all the credit. Did you know—just to seize upon another example—that the great Myrddin, before being renamed to avoid scatological puns across the channel, was said to have been conceived in just the same way?"

"Wonderful," declared the humorless housemate. "So whose father are you going to be? A new messiah? Or just some unusually glib politician?"

Black Malachi stroked his spottily bearded cheek, blinking. "Goodness, this stuff really kicks in fast. Ashenden, I believe I should go to bed."

We became concerned, a bit, just then, as was our unhelpable nature. "Will you be all right?" Turner wondered.

"I need silence. Silence and dark. And Cervina. Have you met her, Ashenden? Quite the little unit, hey? Would you go find her, my shining example? Say that her poor Blackie—"

Turner would not let go of it, though, just yet. "Is she the one?" he demanded, almost convinced. "Is she who you're going to beget your little Goddie on?"

Black Malachi smiled blandly (Jesus what a decoction that must have been) like the down-and-out denizen of a Settling Out Camp. "Study your pronouns," he said at last, "if you ever hope to understand who you are. No, my dear boy—it is not a god we are speaking of, but more precisely a hero. You know about heroes, don't you? Or do you. You shall someday, I hope. For you see, Ashenden . . ."

He drifted nearer. Remarkably light on his feet, stealthy as a spirit. His hand on my sleeve was barely material, his voice in my ears hot and damp. As he whispered.

"It's *you*, Turner. *You* that my secret seed shall someday make whole."

We just about stopped breathing then. While that self-satisfied bastard, drawing back, had the gall to stand there and nod. Smiling narrow-eyed. Knowingly. As one bastard to another.

"Now, now," the red-eyed begetter said, "don't get all in a huff. It is nothing to me, what your mother did. And I should say, it ought to be nothing to you."

He backed off, let go Turner's sleeve. At once becoming distant, even perturbed, as though by the thought of something, he said from a certain psychologic distance: "But the hour, you see, has not arrived. I need a bit more time yet. T-Time to—"

Stammering, shooing Turner toward the door. Then blatting out with remarkable clarity: "—to *forge in the smithy of my loins the uncreated consciousness of my roommate.*"

Oh, Malachi. You were so, just *so* chock-full of yourself.

Omphalos

Dawnlight breaking. It is the day after next. The unhappy student finds a terraformed bed, new contours of an old mattress, his bladder a burning center of the swami yellow world. God what sun. Do they pipe it here direct, avoid the UV rake-off at the port? Rolling over, a hot sound of expanding metal . . . KRMMNNMM . . . filling the ears, head swelling with fluid pressure, skullplates stretching, membranes, easy now. Feel better when you're standing up whether you believe it this moment or not.

In the bathroom Turner found a young man, God a boy really, where do they all come from, passed out naked in the shower—never an unclothed girl, of course, in *my* room—which allows us to economize on water if I just climb in on top of him. But haven't the heart: that blissful unknowing face. And look, his drink here still unfinished, clear and pink. With borage blossoms, Malachi's touch, to cool the blood. Turner sniffed it: hair of the goat manqué. Down at a gulp.

Daylight more orange now, the color they should never have let into rosebuds. It's another *mestiza* sunrise. Queer spirits, we begin to fear, at work. Just splash a bit of water here, keep this monologue going while I make my way downstairs through the post-party wreckage to the kitchen; maybe catch the Tuesday morning vegetable drop before the other survivors awake to savage the tomatoes, gnaw with dripping fangs the corn and groundnuts, coat their ravaged stomachs with okra-ooze. Oh what a beautiful morning.

Turner's room gave off on a narrow mezzanine open at the center to the roofdeck above and banana-court below. Other doors stood wide or closed adjacent. Through the former, one glimpsed rooms in an advanced state of randomization, clothing strewn, bottles, naked limbs, pages torn from books, pillow feathers, a head cocked back on an ottoman, antique memphis chairs reduced to rusty props for a coffee table, never more functional, a white wall hung with an old calendar, year not mentioned, depicting endangered wildlife, long since probably extinct, the bright floral colors faded to pastel, and surprise, an immaculate croquet set. We made our way to the *other* staircase—the one the guys with the bomb had apparently overlooked—and glanced down at the broad-leaved jungle. Good to take one's bearings now, above banana-level, or we may end up stumbling into something indigestible at this hour—dueling at first light in the parlor, fornication in the morning room, strange sacraments being spoken low over a woodstove—the legendary stuff of Malachi's endless *soirées*. It was a magic place, the Solar Temple. Sort of dangerous, when you thought about it, poking around like this. Run into any kind of trouble and there's no one awake to help you. *He vanished while on a lonely quest for fresh vegetables.*

But he shall return. We Await Silent Tristin's Empire. Study your pronouns, you chuckled, padding down the stair.

Now what the Christ—feet on the suntile, contacting again the primal Gaian energy, we discover that someone has rearranged all the plants. Paths among them have disappeared, or changed direction. Careful job: no trace of the old order discernible. Not the same as true *disorder*, though; you could still hope to follow the workings of the fiendish post-midnight mind. Turner intuited *left* then *left* again, then plunged through the bananas and look—it's the kitchen! Already, not eight o'clock in the morning, an accomplishment.

He came into a place of gleaming steel counters, rose- and sand-colored tiles, blush pink painted cabinets, and glacial white, 5000° Kelvin fluorescent tubes. Odd how decorative Malachi has become about this place; and how fastidious. Love among the ruins. Must have been down sometime before dawn, tidying up.

It was a near-perfect circle, this innermost sanctum of the maze, around which corridors bent in a contemplative architectural *asana*, deflecting the five energies inward toward the great black Aga, Malachi's pride and joy. Solar plexus of the Solar Temple. Left burning eternally. Touch it and you're toast.

Turner cleared a see-through occlusion—a system of hooks and rods from which depended breadpans, omelet pans, waffle irons, egg whisks, tortilla presses, colanders, sifters, rollers, graters, and Malachi's soft beige cooking shoes—and across the room saw Vinny Hawkmoth, seated at a work island, enjoying the week's first peach. Bales and baskets lay around him. Very well-rested Vinny looked up from a week's worth of University dailies and, with that effortless smile, "Good morning, Turner," he said.

"Ah, hi." Turner stared dismally at a peck of nectarines. Coming face-to-face with these hundred pounds of organic produce made him feel spiritually unclean—as though his body required a few days of purgation to become worthy of B-vitamins again.

"So, um . . ." Vinny sat comfortably fiddling with his pit. *He* was in no hurry to do or prove or change anything. "I understand you saved us all from certain detour."

And Turner, surprising himself more than Hawkmoth, said quite readily, "Sometimes I think I don't really want to live here anymore."

"Ah, well."

Yes, well; but why is he reaching into that drawer, and what is that red leather pouch all about?

"Before you pack your bags," Vinny said, "here's a little present for you. Pantera left it off a couple of hours ago. When does that guy *sleep?* Well, actually it's for Harvey Goldaster."

He tossed the little bag into the open space between them, presumably for the pleasure of hearing it drop solidly onto the floor and sit there, a compact and well-weighted bundle. A tag, comically hand-lettered in Malachi's bright acrylics, flew like a pennant from its cord. TO HIS GRACE KING HARVEY, it said. IN TRIBUTE, FROM HIS LEAST VASSALS.

"The first month's rent," Vinny explained. "Real money, not credit

notes. Pantera said to ask you *politely* to take it to Upper Moat Farm, if
you happened to be going out today."

And he added, quoting with clear enjoyment: " 'Where neither drug
nor sex doth corrupt, nor politicians break through and steal.' "

Turner could not help smiling, albeit wanly. "I guess I better go
before class, then," he said. Not quite willing, despite his consistent and
widely known record, to admit that the week would probably end without
him attending a single lecture. At which rate he would not be a student,
unhappy or otherwise, very long. He stared at his dull red burden, thinking,
And then what. And then what.

A climatic misunderstanding

Muscular, subtropical lindens overcrowded a tract of low-slung houses just
past the receding hedgelines of the University, near the statue of a triumphant amazon, understood to have some local historic significance, that
Malachi called the Grim Dyke. The last residents of this place had felt
pretty good, as they used to say, about getting in on the ground floor of
the development. Now their words were playing tricks on them: the "development" was clearly just that—a happening, an advent, shrugged off
by a subsequent century—and the lucky residents were in on a ground
floor they would not climb out of. Their timber and stucco houses still
stood, no longer imposingly, all but rolled over by the hardwood forest
that was Nature's first choice of landscaping styles around here. Turner
loved to drive through these ruined neighborhoods, to breathe slowly the
air of an imaginary past. *Beauty and Sadness*, he thought. A likely title
for the Ashenden autobiography, on the off-chance that I ever do anything
worth writing about. He much preferred this place—its beauty *and* its
sadness—to the countryside at large, whose every contour seemed scientifically calibrated as though it had been refined over centuries by a dynasty
of Capability Browns. Nonetheless it was to the countryside that he was
heading: the white-picketed netherland where the Goldasters and a few of

the other landholding families someone lately had started calling the Old Souls, or simply the Souls, lived in houses no one else could have afforded even to heat; not even now, at this breezy end of September.

Increasingly, after the recent wet summer, the spirit-burner was having a hard time of it. Saplings rattled against its undercarriage, rising in a resilient strip along the center of the roadway. *Memento mori*, thought Turner. (Speaking to the roadway now.) He held the steering-lever hard over, negotiating a turn into what remained of a rose-lined allée. Where whoever once lived had done a better job of paving than had the civic authorities; and of planting too. The eighty- or ninety-year-old shrubs were still represented by a buxom 'Madame Hardy' here and there, the blooming tip of an 'Iceberg,' blush-pink mounds of 'The Fairy' and half a dozen endlessly patient, all-enduring 'Penelopes.'

But what's this now? A bunch of people gathered ahead of him, fifty yards or so, and a couple of big utility vehicles, clumsily blocking the road. Turner eased off the throttle, let the spirit-burner purge its feedlines in a great soughing gasp. At the end of the drive, where the roses yielded to mutated, topiarily trimmed . . . well, they looked like cows now, but probably, Turner guessed, originally dogs . . . right up there before the sparkling ruins of a greenhouse, a work crew in Newport-blue coveralls was badly handling the upper struts of a windmill. A windmill. Are you listening? I mean, *here*, in the low hills above the University, where not even metaphoric winds (of change, of war, et cetera) had kicked up much dust for decades. Where, anyway, the damned thing would have to be a hundred and fifty feet tall to be sure of clearing the oaks that grew so lustily, now that they were spared the kindness of lawn-lovers and other killers of plants. And *this*, much to the diminutive, was just one of those kit jobbies you could get through the mail, at least in theory, during those months when the mail was running. Eighty feet we'll call it, tops. Less than that by the time this gang has finished warping its longitudinal struts. The two-foiled blade itself, perfectly appropriate for those gusts that scoured the wasted cornfields only a thousand or so miles from here, lay on the ground amid some cardboard refuse, presently being stepped on. Someone carrying a clipboard, impersonating a supervisor, faced the wrong direction—Turner's direction, that is—scratching her knee and smoking a cigarette. Someone else was shouting instructions: the left, goddamn it, no, the *other* left.

This could mean, Turner was pretty certain, Only One Thing.

Glancing around now, he noticed not far to one side a sign he might have seen earlier, on the way up the drive, had it not been nailed up backwards.

Camp Crane Lake
ESTABLISHED UNDER THE
Settling Out Act,
G. Rodarch, Administrator

Above the sign, nailed to a pole, an azure pennant, unfaded by the sun, waggled in the scanty breeze. The color of ancient swimming pools. Mutely proclaiming Be Reasonable, Be Calm—*here*, where wildness reshaped the sad allée like some soft-spoken gardener gone mad.

Well.

Turner (a great respecter of symbols and portents in all their diversely occurring forms, and also something of a coward) put the spirit-burner into reverse. The thing about this abandoned neighborhood, you see, this *double entendre* development, was that no one ever came here. No one knew about the place. It was like a monument to some quiet victory that only he, only Turner, who loved roses better than roads, understood. Or so he regularly congratulated himself. But the cool blue pennant—more so, somehow, than the work crew or even the flat-out sign—was proof that, as one should have suspected, Turner didn't know what the hell he was talking about. His secret monument crumbled in the sun.

Now as Turner, not so good with crowds, eased off the clutch, there came a stirring among opportunistic locust trees. Shadows wove like wind-blown branches. He reached under the console to touch the shockgun. Engine bubbling. Fingers groping for the latch.

Two sudden steps away, appearing head-and-chest above a rosebush, garden fork held forward, blustery, defensive: a young man Turner's age from some parallel science-fiction universe. His skin was both darker and warmer-toned than the blue of his uniform. His eyes shone black beneath a sweaty headband. As he stared at the badly surprised and still unsuccessfully groping intruder.

Turner, recognizing an instant later that the other young man was rather frightened, also, of him, abandoned his quest for a weapon. Now say something, Turner. (But:)

The dark-skinned youth swung smartly the action end of his fork, smacking Turner's fingers away from the steering-lever and moving inward with a sort of athletic stealth, as though ready for God knows what other menace or subterfuge. And calling out:

"Hey, man! There's some guy here trying to steal a truck!"

While Turner only sat dumbly, trying to work things out.

Um, hey buddy, let's get this straight here. I was just heading up toward the hills, see, and I mean I'm just passing *through* here. And what, stealing a truck? B-But, this is nothing but a spirit-burner, and anyway it's *my* spirit-burner. So like if you're moving in here that's fine, welcome to the neighborhood, I'll just turn around . . . see, I've already got it in reverse, okay? And, hey . . .

Yow!

Turner Ashenden. Tapped on the neck by the square tines of a garden fork. Clutching what feels like, my God, a *busted artery to the brain*, Jesus, you can *die* from this can't you? And the guy who's done this to him—smirking, of all things, despite the blood splattering his coveralls—pressing in with the goddamned fork held down like a *cattle-prod* or something, the little prick, so that Turner forgets for a moment his mortal wound and makes a move like he's climbing down from his seat, reaching up meanwhile under the console.

And there's the latch.

And here's a *shockgun*, you son of a bitch.

Dark-skinned young man ready to stab with the fork but stops himself, you wouldn't really *shoot* me he thinks, probably figures Turner is a snobby wimp like all the other University types, you can see his brain work behind the dark brown irises, and just as he's about to decide No, and Turner's about to decide Yes, down the drive from the hopeless windmill come not two or three but *nineteen more guys just like him*.

And Jesus. With them—not Yeshua ben Pantera, that was just a device, a biographer's gimmick—no, but a young thin woman who exclaimed in a nasal voice:

"Ashen! You've got a lot of nerve coming here, after what you pulled last night. What're you doing with that rifle?"

Um, being badly misunderstood, right now, and bleeding pretty heavily. Of all times remembering names. Turner blubbered, "Dinder, thank God. Listen, you've got to help me. This guy . . . see, I was trying to turn around. . . ."

"Back off, everybody." Dinder stepped forward and for some reason the crowd of wiry young men did as she told them. She leaned into the spirit-burner, sliding her hands expertly into the usual hiding places. A tag on her breast said STUDENT VOLUNTEER. She ignored Turner's shockgun as though really, this late in the game, it couldn't possibly matter. "Ashen, this could be trouble. They're pretty sensitive about people coming in here with weapons. They've had a lot of problems, you know. Where did you get this truck?"

It's not a *truck*, damn it. Don't you people know anything?

"I was just delivering, ah, something—"

"I see." Dinder jimmied open the secret, Turner had thought, storage box under the floorplates. In her hand was a dull red bundle, its surface a homey backdrop for the bright acrylic letters that seemed to leap, then tangle, clumsy ballerinas, in Turner's eyes. Dinder spent a long time examining this.

"From his least vassals, eh?" she said, looking up.

Look, I know what you're thinking, some part of him tried to say; but it's only, it's not. . . .

"This looks bad, Ashen," said Dinder's faint, ever fainter image.

And from somewhere else, a dark figure dressed in stylish Newport blue: "Should we kill him?"

Then Turner Ashenden, bleeding from the neck, blacked out and presumably fell sideways. We fuzzily see light slanting yellow through a metal frame (the windshield?) and sense ourselves pressing skin, or leather, and our shared memory shuts down for a while. A little death, uninvited, entering for the countless-thousandth time.

Into the life of our hero.

3

Übermensch, at home

A tent.

Turner Ashenden wakes up and finds himself inside this tent. Big thing. Ten yards tall at the center-post—that's *yards*, man—and wide enough to conduct your average bullfight in relative ease and comfort. But still. I mean, why a tent? Just for starters, if you were traveling, say, and you had enough domestic help to set up Circus City here—hey, you could pretty well take your pick of all the abandoned houses from here out to what they used to call the Coast, I bet.

Only, are we totally sure what we mean by "here"? Turner Ashenden, see, was last remarked upon in a marginally conscious and perhaps fatally indisposed situation. Indeed the phrase *kill him* was somewhere distinctly mentioned. So is Turner's mind now getting revved up again, or is this just some form of crypto-consciousness being run in a simulator some-where, a narrative system imitating awareness by making these references to itself? Hmm. Search for clues. How about this: the machine seems to have forgotten what it was talking about . . . remembers all of a sudden, like, and with even greater startlement, that *I'm in this gigantic tent. Holy shit.*

Turner sat up without the usual pounding head or blurred vision you often get at moments like this. In fact he felt quite rested. The tent was carpeted with an interesting roll-out canvas floorcloth that someone had painted in a pattern of spirals or circles (it was hard to tell from up here in the, what, hammock) which actually were unmistakably mandala-like, though still well short of the Ideal, the perfect limit, as though in proof that it all does mean something, life's architectonic insanities really do connect up, there's this one great pattern, see . . . but please try to concentrate. Your neck is a little stiff, now that you think of it, and maybe you're dizzy from loss of blood.

Why am I in a tent? Who would have a *tent* this big?

Then from twenty yards sideways there came a sort of wind-generated drumroll; canvas shuddered as a current of air moved up its sunlaced seams toward the broken hexagon of blue sky up there nearly straight above the hammock; and in a wonderfully stagey follow-through, a heretofore unnoticed door-flap parted in both directions and a tall black-haired man—tall even from this distance—stepped through. The drumroll petered out. The man walked straight toward Turner without bothering to pause to adjust his eyesight. And in the way you know things sometimes because you just know them, Turner knew this was Chief Administrator Rodarch. He made a ridiculous project of standing up from the hammock, which though not at all difficult is always a tiny bit trickier than it looks.

"Look," said the impressive Chief Administrator, "you don't have to stand up for me. I just want to talk to you, if you feel up to it, and then you can leave. It won't take much time. Does your neck still hurt? Did they bring you anything to eat? I think there's some fish around here somewhere."

Now at last, under this deluge of plain talk, Turner felt wide awake and bewildered. He touched the bandaid below his ear. The skin underneath felt numb and stubbly.

"Um," he said. "I guess—"

Rodarch pulled up the sort of chair that is always available to be pulled up and sat down beside him. He mentioned Turner back into the hammock. Often when you sit down in a hammock your feet come off the floor at first and you begin to swing.

"Well, you look okay," said the Chief Administrator.

An ordinary person, it came to Turner then. That was the picture. All these plain-sounding words were part of a mask, a persona, that declared *I am just like you. No one is different from anyone else.*

"I'm confused, mostly, I guess," Turner decided, letting the ordinary person in on this. "I mean, I don't even remember where I am."

"Oh, no. They didn't want you to know. I think they gave you some kind of medicine—you've been asleep since yesterday. You must have been very tired."

If you only knew, Turner thought, as the classical countenance peered kindly down at him. There is a pattern here. It is my eternal destiny to be kindly gazed down at. Well, what the hell.

"And now you expect me," he said on a rare whim, "to just sit here after you've had me drugged and robbed and, a-and kidnapped, and *chat* with you?"

He wasn't really rebellious and had no feelings one way or the other about your higher-level functionaries, but there was something just not *real* about all this.

"Yes," though, said a convincingly lifelike facsimile of the Chief Administrator. Having strong wide shoulders makes you look very relaxed and comfortable when you're sitting down leaning forward a little bit. Of course Turner had never seen a comic book or he would have counted on this. He waggled his shoulders, trying to puff up his own bony physique.

"I'd have thought," said Rodarch, "you would *want* to talk. Isn't it true that you were driving an unregistered vehicle on a government preserve, and carrying a weapon, and in possession of a substantial sum of money?"

"B-But, it was only a shockgun. Everybody's got one—you know, times being what they are. And it was just a *spirit-burner*, for God's sake."

"Your bag," the Chief Administrator pointed out (mildly, as though speaking to a child), "contained an illegal form of currency. And from its label it was clearly intended for someone. . . ."

"Oh, I get it. This is about Harvey Goldaster, isn't it? You've got some kind of war going on against the Souls, and I'm like, caught in the middle of it. Right? That's why you sent those guys to b-blow the Temple up."

The wide gray eyes became sharper for an instant, professorial. "The individual you mention," Rodarch said carefully, "has been closely linked to illegal business activities. If I were you, Turner—if I had been caught delivering illegal currency to such a person—I'd be eager to talk things over."

"It was just the rent," said Turner miserably. His shoulders collapsed. "All right. I mean, okay, sure—let's talk. Am I in big trouble?"

The Chief Administrator smiled, all avuncular now. Uncle Rodarch. "As it happens, Turner, I do believe you. You're apparently just a normal student who's made some unfortunate associations. And you've gotten involved in something serious. More serious than you seem to realize. That's a bad situation, and I'd want to avoid such situations in the future; but of course it's up to you."

Turner nodded feebly. Just a normal student. Well, it was hardly the unkindest thing he'd ever thought of himself.

"Here's *my* situation, though," the big soft-spoken man went on. "I'm sure you've heard of the Settling Out Laws. They are badly misunderstood, in my experience, but most people seem to have some idea of their general provisions, and I'm sure you do, too. Well, it's my responsibility to enforce them, you see, and at present I'm concentrating my efforts in the Population 50-to-75-Percent Below Carrying Capacity region. That includes a rather wide geographic belt, to which this valley is a sort of transition zone. If you will, a gateway. Now. My problem . . ."

He paused and looked at Turner with a momentary intensity, as though some hint of feeling or irony was about to present itself behind the aluminum-alloy eyes. It occurred to Turner to ask the great man, the Stainless Steel Savior, what was wrong. Like, is anything the matter, have you been hurt somehow? Can I help?

Wow. Insane, right? But Turner's mouth was open, even, before he realized how absurd it was, which just goes to show. How close, for a moment there, we really came. Then the normal student broke eye-contact, and Uncle Rodarch vanished behind his two-dimensional persona, and the Fates settled down in front of the tube with their crochet kits again.

"One of my more serious problems," the Chief Administrator said, leaving only this clue as to what the stillborn emotion might have been, "at the moment, is the resistance of local authorities to this important piece of legislation."

"Authorities?" said Turner, intrigued by such a concept. "You mean just Goldaster, or the Souls in general?"

Rodarch never blinked. He made efficient use of these interruptions to dispose of such concerns as the recurrent need to breathe.

"How close," he said smoothly, "have you and Harvey Goldaster become? Does he trust you, would you say?"

Turner sensed that the conversation had taken some twist, some new direction. "I'm not sure I, ah . . . ."

"You visit him frequently." The Chief Administrator's voice was a good analogue of his body, relaxed but overpowering, which gave you an idea of how he must dominate meetings of sleepy bureaucrats. "That's what I'm told. And Goldaster listens to you. He has agreed, it seems, to most of your requests. So what I'd like, Turner, when you leave here, and after you've thought things over, is for you to pay him another visit, and make a request for *me*."

"That silly bitch"—it was almost a game now, try to freak out the cool gray machine—"that's who told you, isn't it? Well look, she doesn't know me, she doesn't know anything. If she ever took the coke-spoon out of her nose her brains would run down and drip off her pointy chin."

Rodarch smiled, but it was a fake. He said, "This doesn't sound much like how I would have imagined a young University man to talk. I suppose you're doing this to try to offend me."

So he wasn't unperceptive, Turner realized. Just . . . *flat*. "I'm sorry," he said. "You're right. But really, I hardly know Harvey Goldaster at all. What did she tell you?"

"Why don't you have a little something to eat," the big man suggested, "and try to get your strength back? You really do look pale."

From beneath the hammock, or somewhere—I don't know, it couldn't have just popped into his hand—he produced a tray of crackers with some kind of spread on them. Turner picked one up and regarded it with a kind of superstitious awe. Food. The tray seemed to float effortlessly between Rodarch's large fingers, though it must have been heavy as lead. Or actually heavy as polished silver, which is what it was.

"The thing is, Turner," he said, snapping us back, "I've come out here to establish a precedent of systematic enforcement of the Settling Out Laws. And I do intend as soon as possible to have the situation under control. I can't afford to spend all my time on it, but I think I have enough time and enough material support to make things uncomfortable for anyone engaging in active resistance to my program. There's also the possibility that our appropriation level will improve in the out-years, and in that case it could become *very* uncomfortable for the kind of people I'm talking about. Now I don't mean you, Turner. But I think you understand who

I do mean. And I think you're rational enough to want to do whatever *you* can to make this whole Settling Out process go smoothly."

Rational? Turner, his mouth full of the dry and weirdly salty cracker, stood up again. "Look, I've never . . ." He tried to swallow. "I mean, really, I'm not a troublemaker. *I've* got no problem with the law. If people want to come Settle Out here, then I say, let them Settle. But, see, I've just got no influence at *all* with Goldaster, or any of the rest of the Souls. I don't know where the hell she got that idea. You ought to be more careful who you listen to."

Rodarch stood, too, which pretty much drowned out whatever statement Turner's five-eleven body was trying to make. He said, "I listen to whomever will talk to me. I'm grateful that *you* have been willing to talk to me, Turner. I trust that you will be equally willing to talk to your, ah, passing acquaintance, Harvey Goldaster."

But no, but hold on just a minute there . . . wait, I wasn't done eating . . . and when do I get my *money* back?

The Chief Administrator did not wait for a fortuitous updraft to rattle the canvas before striding toward the door-flaps. He moved amazingly fast for a man of his size. Of course Turner would have expected that, too, if only he'd done his research. If only he'd known.

True dimensions

Out now, in the hard light, hungry (for the silver tray was no longer, no, anywhere to be found) and foot-weary (for the spirit-burner was, yes, gone from him forever), with the bland words and flat heroic face of Chief Administrator Rodarch pressed into the skin of his memory, Turner began to recognize the true dimensions of his plight.

When he stepped out of the tent he found himself waited for by two unhelpful, um, civil servants, he had figured, though just *servants* might better convey the sense Turner quickly acquired that they were driven by a will besides their own.

"How's it going?" plucky Turner tried.

Neither blue-shirted man deemed this worth replying to. They mentioned instead by a communicative, if mute, movement of the shoulders that he might wish to precede them down a path outside the tent-flaps and not make any trouble about it. Finest kind, guys. Let's just take a look around here and see where we are, okay? What kind of place this is you guys have brought me to.

The big tent, from outside, looked surprisingly unimportant. It sloped up toward a dry and empty sky. Beside it, and built to scale, were the largest machines Turner had ever seen: antique farm equipment was probably a pretty good guess, though it would take more energy to run the things than you'd ever get back in food, from the look of them. Turner was truly impressed, though, which was possibly the point. Under the great cleated treads were steamrolled remains of what looked like a bunch of "modern" buildings, in the architectural time-sense. One of those executive away-from-the-stress-of-the-city conference centers, maybe; or the headquarters of some back-to-nature cult. Not that there was much left of Nature herself around here. Rolling away on all sides was a typical degenerative farmland: nitrite-blasted fields stitched together by the roots of locusts, lawngrass gone berserk and patented no-till nurse crops—with a few drifts of actual native species left here and there, bluestems and coneflowers and joe-pye weeds, to give a sense of locality (dry, shallow-soiled uplands). There was not much time to appreciate even this consolation prize, for the two escorts, real chatterboxes, didn't slow their stride, and the felt pressure of their closing bodies kept Turner moving a few steps-per-minute faster than his mind could parse the new world's stimuli.

West, was all he could make of it. The land he had stared at, the sunset-land, from the top of the godless mountain. He glanced at the path they hurried him along: yellow sawdust-covered, sloping down. It was packed hard, for what was basically wasteland, from which Turner extrapolated lots and lots of feet thumping this way. Going where? Overhead, disheartened ravens banked southward into an unexpectedly hot September sun: it's still technically summer, earthlings, until that astronomical instant you make such a fuss over, harvest rites grim reaping et al., which would be about next Tuesday, wouldn't it?

"Pretty warm one, huh?" was what Turner distilled this to.

This time to our surprise the left-hand man spoke up. "Past that big rock up ahead," he said—city-talk for schist deposit exposed by the gullying of a trench—"you'll find a little timber road that *may* get you back where you came from. Now don't waste time sneaking back to spy on us, because we're not up to anything and if you do, you won't make it *anywhere* by dark."

Turner's escorts halted, reverting to body language. Now get lost, their eyebrows chorused.

"Hey, next time I'm buying," Turner said with a generous flourish of the hand. He followed through on this, tennis-style, and got himself off to a puzzled, angry, energetic start, before the greater realization of his dilemma slowed him down and he came to a halt at the junction of the logging trail, sizing up.

Another country. Not just the landscape, scarecrow trees framing vistas of mountains he'd never seen this side of, but the inner contours of his life were different all at once; the old Turner Ashenden was a tiny figure in a dream-gray pre-Dissolution landscape. Go ahead, call out to him, he'll barely hear you, and you'll never make out his reply. *You're out here alone.* There were no assurances—not even the threadbare blandishment that every road leads Someplace. These days most of them did not; nor did they lead precisely Noplace, either. There was this growing indefiniteness spreading across the countryside, the land reverting to something less satisfying than wilderness, like maybe pages of rotting books, which are no longer read nor even readable, but which will never quite get back to being just part of a tree again. Some ultimate corruption engulfs them. And the characters that once laughed and drank and brooded in their pages—yes, and wandered lost, and copulated, and murdered one another—were never again going to be simply unexpressed ideas. The kindest fate available to them now was being mentioned or alluded to, their traits passed on to the heroes and villains of a less exalted era. And maybe a blessed few, exceptional creations, might spring back to life wholly formed in spruced-up or spaced-out retellings of the same old stories.

[But forget them, Turner. Here you were, alone in the scorched-out highlands. What did you do then?—*you*, I mean, not some reincarnated archetype.]

Basically, Turner ambled. Set a steady, strength-conserving pace. Sighted in on the most distinctive feature of that undifferentiated landscape, which was a lowish mountain whose western shoulder, turned to face him, lay open in broad igneous gouges, as though streaked by ungodly fingernails. And just kept walking that way, moving from one path to another as new branches sprouted off the old trunk, maintaining as best he could his chosen track-line. An arbitrary one, but they say any decision is better than none, and at least this way he was doing *something*, which meant he had not yet surrendered, not yet lost. And thus, just incidentally, he learned about himself the important fact, for future reference, that such things deeply mattered.

[But God I was thirsty. That single cracker Rodarch gave me, before he did whatever he did with the tray, must have dried up my mouth and then kept right on working, down in my gut, pulling water out of everywhere. Or maybe I just hadn't drunk anything for a while. Asleep since yesterday, they tell me. And no way of knowing, of course, how much blood I'd lost. It made me feel lighter, somehow, physically less substantial, all that depletion of vital humors. Maybe the æther rushes in then, to the vacuum. Or maybe . . .]

After some time, wandering that way, the flora began to thicken up a bit. New micro-climate here. Deeper soil, or more precipitation, up this slope. Beeches rose with uninitialed trunks to block Turner's view of the mountain ahead, cutting him off from what he hoped was his destination, if not his Destiny. A certain sense of charm or brightness in the air gave hint of water nearby, and by thrashing his way down imaginary isobars he found an arm-wide diamond-bright runlet. From across it, a raccoon gazed in astonishment at the first human it had ever encountered. I intimidate no one at all, Turner mused. The water shattered between his fingers. It entered him with a sharp sensation, a feeling of clarity, and clung to his two-day earth-toned beard. For an indeterminate while, kneeling before some dime-a-dozen naiad's shrine, he felt strong and whole and invincible. The water played its well-known pink-noise plainsong—the first lesson in Hawkmoth's Introduction to Synthesis seminar—and for the first time ever, Turner's mind soared in counterpoint. The Lady of the Lake popped her window open, just to smile. Out on her beleaguered hero.

Well, it's still legal to imagine things, right?

Then Turner stood and climbed back to the roadway and was just a poor traveler again. A *normal student*. Lost in the Waste Land, alone on an empty road. The earth rolled underneath him, heedless; lifted him on its great stony waves; plunged him into sunless troughs. Suffering him to stay afloat, though, at least for the moment. At least until dark.

Mountains never get any closer, is the problem. They've got them on these big underground rollers and they just keep pulling them back, keeping them this sneaky distance away so you think you're coming up on them, then MMRRMMMM the pulleys engage and they slide back again. And it's now, I guess, three-thirty in the afternoon, no daylight savings in *this* place, so I can cover let's say, three times four miles, if I don't collapse from exhaustion that is, before nightfall when all the beasties come out and there's another human sacrifice to mark the approaching equinox.

To keep himself hopeful, more or less, Turner started thinking *If I ever get back*. You know: If I ever get back I'll never leave the Solar Temple again. Except to go to class, of course, which I'll do *every day*, I promise. Or at least, frequently.

If I ever get back, I'm going to tell Malachi to deliver his own damned rent money. And never mention the name of Harvey Goldaster again. And if anybody wants to talk about politics, the Settling Out Laws or any of that, I'll use Malachi's line—*Hail the Stainless Steel Savior*—which all of a sudden seems pretty appropriate. Which means of course that Malachi was right again, but we can't let that dishearten us. Not right now.

If I ever get back I'm going back up to Bad Winters Institute and tell Madame What's-Her-Name she's right about Rodarch's face.

If I ever get back, I'm going to *murder* that asshole Dinder.

And more than anything else, if I ever get back—after what, three sweaty afternoons already—I'm going to take a long hot shower. Naked bodies in the bathtub or no.

Turner's legs moved carelessly beneath him, wobbling a bit, but things had gotten beyond the point where you would worry about such things. The unhappy student, the *normal* student, gave a perfectly normal, alone-in-the-world, lost and frightened and confused, but what else is new, self-pitying sigh.

The Solar Temple now was a dream-bright glassy fantasy. Filled with organic produce, laughter of partygoers, exotic flowers, a dog called Cagliostro living on weeds, can you imagine it? And me out here alone on a godless mountain road. Summer without mercy drawing to a close and the day about to go down.

If I ever get back. I'm going to sit down with candles and linen tablecloth (this is after the shower but before the slaying of Dinder) and have a civilized meal. I'll have, let's see . . .

But wait, I say *wait* just a doggone minute. Did some displaced portion of Turner's mind think "godless mountain road"?

Stopping now at last to look around. And seeing little change in the recently prevalent style of landscape (ostrich ferns banked along the roadside slope, under hemlocks). Turner wonders what had tapped the memory-key that called up that curious word-choice, godless mountain. Some subliminal impression, no doubt. An unbalanced momentary placement of the feet, or the scent of a roadside flower. Smell you know they say is the most evocative emotion. Because you can't wear it out by remembering it too hard.

Exhaustion, I guess, is like being crazy after a while. Or like those things Malachi has growing in the greenhouse that make your brain talk back to itself. But of course Jodorowski has already taken note of this. Cinematic geomancy: stay up partying three nights in a row and then go scouting locations. Turner sighed. Even *in extremis* I can't think of anything new.

The unoriginal hungry student moved onto thriving slopes, passing from the gloomy pre-Dissolution landscape back another century and a half to the glowing afternoon of Luminism. The last sunlight of the day spilled through great trees and seemed to acquire some of their lack of definition; around the shadows of oak limbs appeared a sort of penumbra or aura, as though the life-force were acting as a gravitational lens. *Reality wraps itself around us.* Had somebody said that, or was it just a line from some book? Surely Turner hadn't made it up himself. Anything but that. With the alertness engendered by hunger, the descendent of hunter-gatherers witnessed life flicking by all around him, migratory birds on a farewell forage, squirrels chippering, sleepy predators sniffing the air, trees infolded dreaming the heart of their great brown mystery. Life, a planet-wide conspiracy. Of which we are, the many of us, part.

Turner Ashenden, the part's first party, moved from one leg to another up the shadowy path he had not chosen to follow, sensing in some typically inarticulate way, not for the first time, but at last for a moment almost clearly, the real and true dimensions of his life.

Identities

What are hackles, Turner wondered. I mean, if you were thinking, for example—as in fact Turner was thinking just now—*the hackles rose*, which is a pretty common expression, then just what, precisely, were you thinking about?

The hackles rose on his neck.

So weary that it no longer occurred to him to believe or disbelieve in anything, Turner stood on the side of a godless mountain, watching quite stupidly as the sun dug a big orange hole behind the ailanthus fringing the roadway. And with raised hackles, whatever they were, he laid a hand to rest on a wooden sign-post. Inclining his head to the purple letters that hovered before us over a backdrop of swami yellow. Bad Winters Institute. Madame Gwendola, Co-Founder and what the hell is a Self-Realized Adept? If you don't mind my asking. Open 9 to 5 weekdays, though here it is unfortunately at the very least quarter-past-six. Becoming earnestly dark.

But the thing is, old man, the thing on which to focus here is that we've arrived by some impossible round-the-elbow route right back where we've stood once before. Or rather driven. The identical upsloping driveway. Deeply shadowed now by the same great-leaved rhododendrons. Not déjà vu, but something. *He retraced his footsteps.* Though properly speaking I left no footsteps to retrace, besides which I'm not quite certain how I got all the way up the mountain this time. As tired as God knows I must be.

At this most improbably opportune moment, Turner remembered an invitation to dinner. Come back and spy on us sometime. I think Maridel would like to meet you.

All right damn you Madame Self-Realized. I believe I will.

Trudging up, then, the rutted drive, Turner Ashenden came a second time in view of the old unbalanced manor. Its angles, pediments, half-blind overlooks seemed if anything more ridiculous by end-of-daylight, as all things were stripped to their essential selves before being dressed again, more flatteringly, for the evening. At his feet the lawn lay out like a warm dark carpet. Dying boxwoods sagged beside the path. The woods, a black and mutinous hedge, crept up to the retaining wall and huddled there, brooding in wind-whispers and owl-calls. Weary SPIRITS, said the little sign. Turner picked up his step just a bit until the parchment-yellow glow of the porchlight, outlawed where there were still laws, reached down to touch from a high angle his narrow handsome face, giving us all a preview of the wrinkles that would one day settle there, if Turner made it that far. Which seemed then only half likely, times being what they were. The air had grown rapidly almost autumnally cold.

But where were the roaring lion door-knockers? Or Pan-heads, or great brass griffins? Turner scanned the tall doors for these predictable trimmings, but found only a plastic bell-button, dirty and almost certainly nonfunctional. He pushed it anyway. After too brief an interval—only human, after all—he pushed it again, twice. He thought of the officious stick-figure, the nurse, scuttling fretfully down the hall, Who can that be at this hour, Madame is not expecting . . .

Um, hey—

Silently the left-hand door had fallen open, trapping Turner by surprise in his incorrect version of events. Before him smiling up, her expression arch but comradely like she'd caught a shy brother, maybe, naked in the shower, stood the youngest and most unsettling of the folks he'd seen here the first time around. Who wanted to meet him.

Ah, hi, I'm—

"You're rather early."

She stood aside primly, still doing the sister bit, as though the shy brother should be ashamed of himself.

"Dinner's not till eight," she went on, motioning briskly inward, "but I don't think you're ready to sit down yet anyway, do you?"

Are young girls imitating someone when they talk like that—characters maybe from storybooks—or does it somehow come to them naturally? Turner stepped forward, into the yellow light, out of the cold shower, feeling queerly exposed and unsure of himself, among other things because he had not quite figured out how to talk to young kids. I mean, *children*, sure, he could . . . but not like . . . I mean, how old was she, anyway?

Maridel firmly closed the door.

"This way," she said: up the grim Fibonaccian spiral of the stair twenty-seven steps, no less, to an upper landing surprisingly warmed by a pink woolen floorpad, made cozy by twin cherrywood pie-safes flanking a doorjamb of stenciled wood. Nouveauesque roses. A tall washbasin whose fittings glowed of brass. Yards of bleached muslin swagged over doors leading out to a black balcony. "Hurry," said Maridel, "wash up. You don't have to pee, do you?"

Turner regarded her. From her businesslike expression, she would have supervised that also. He turned experimentally a tap, let the cool sweet water stain with dirt off his fingertips; shook his head. He was actually dehydrated. As a helpless dreamer, trying and failing to awake, lets his head back slowly to the pillow, Turner lowered himself into the position suggested for facewashing. The water had turned as warm as beer. Soap that smelled precisely of green apples went squishy in his palm.

"God," he said, more comfortably. "I never thought I'd be clean, ever again."

"You don't smell very good," observed Maridel, "but we shall overlook that, I suppose. Mother will be *too* annoyed if I don't entertain you properly."

Wondering very much, of course, what he had come into, here among the cool rooms of this house, he followed her out of that most memorable of all the bathrooms he had known and farther down the hall, not toward the stair now, but deeper and deeper along some corridor, its precise orientation never quite clear to him, diagonal somehow, defiant of the otherwise unyielding symmetry. At a certain moment Maridel surprisingly laid a girl's thin-wristed perfect hand across his forearm, and the two of them entered together, both accordingly escorted, into a wide and formal yet somehow clearly *family* upstairs drawing room. You really needed, Turner thought, a grasp of both architecture and etiquette to follow this.

The room was empty, or seemed so at first. Turner's eyes passed over green-glazed walls, smoky bookshelves, the faded chintz peonies of a couch, a tall arched mirror bearing his own reflection back to him, warm flames cheerfully wasting wood in a wide stone fireplace—all terribly Colefax & Fowler, though its aging had been less artfully supervised—

until the Turner in the mirror made some twitch that the other Turner, the point-of-view character at present, had not initiated. We stepped back in a moment of sheer unreasoning panic, before coming to understand that the tall arched mirror was a *door*, of course it was, and the slender figure standing there was not our own spitting image but a split one, the curly-headed fourteen-year-old boy we had noticed here the first time around.

Hm, thought Turner. The same two. Rather implausible, isn't it? I wouldn't have done it this way.

But the unseen director did not appear to acknowledge this criticism, and Turner was left to follow Maridel to the center of the room, where there was a nice warm rose-colored rug, soft and cottony, whose simple pattern of knots did *not* resemble a mandala, thank you, and in the middle of which there was some kind of toy-set or game.

"If you'll take off your shoes," said Maridel, aiming a finger downward to reinforce this courteous command, "you can join us. We were just playing Identities."

Turner sank to the floor with a considerable feeling of gratitude. His shoes were utilitarian enough, but nothing he possessed, including his barely formed philosophy, was fit for an outing like this. Worried about of all things, at such a time, the strong likelihood of foot odor, he tucked his feet beneath him at the edge of the rug. Maridel and the olive-skinned boy sat down diametrically, the former frankly regarding him as the latter glanced bashfully away. Turner for his part was in a definitive state of bewilderment which no degree of social uncertainty could have made worse; but for all that, how *was* one expected to act, under such circumstances? I mean, did one meet the forthright gaze of this girl, this soap-smelling porcelain-skinned child, head on? Did one admire her perfect new-gold hair, her grass-green eyes, the faint blush of mauve in her dry, slightly pouting lips? Or was it wrong to notice, even to perceive such things?

Maridel, arbiter of conduct for the occasion, pointed sternly to an object at the center of the rug. It was a joystick of some kind: cheap metallic rod sticking out of a plastic casing, with wires trailing away. The wires ducked out of sight into a fine box of polished and ornamented holly-wood.

"First," she instructed him, "the subject takes the handle. Then someone else asks a series of questions. It's most often the same questions over and over again, though variations are possible."

Turner nodded uncertainly, waiting for her to go on. She only stared.

"What, um . . ." he began.

"Oh, you don't have to tell the truth," she said, as though that's what he was worried about. "The system doesn't care about *that*. It doesn't care whether you say anything at all."

"No, but, what I mean is—like, what are we trying to accomplish? What's the object of the game?"

Maridel's mouth turned up, the pale lips growing pinker, rather pleased it seemed, as though such ignorance were an interesting new variation. "Oh, it isn't a *game*, really. It's . . . well, you see my father invented it. He was *very* intelligent. And this is a kind of, of *modeling* device actually, which he intended for much more serious purposes. But we use it as a kind of—"

She stopped herself as though she had been about to give something away. Beside her the boy fidgeted nervously, which made Turner nervous too, in natural empathy, which in turn caused Maridel to throw a stern glance over the two of us.

"I'll tell you what we'll do," she decided: a ruling. To one then the other, Turner first, she said, "We'll give you something to drink, to tide you over till dinner, and then we'll let *you* show him how it works."

The boy—whose name we ought, oughtn't we, to know by now?—made as though to stand up. Maridel firmly and efficiently prevented this, using nothing Turner could see but a simple head-shake, though the boy looked as chastened as though she'd kicked him under an imaginary table.

"She's *bringing* it," the girl said primly. "Now . . ."

The boy's brown eyes went wide with an unknowable emotion; then, hesitant, he reached out and took the cheap-looking handle of the thing that was not intended as a game.

Right then, that very moment, something peculiar happened to the air of the drawing room. Turner sucked his breath in, astonished, as things went dark and bright and dark again. A faint whine creased his ears, bringing up shivers. Just past the rose-colored rug there seemed to be a pair of tall black doors. Only of course he understood they weren't really there at all—not just intellectually, as he knew right along that nothing had changed *that* much—but also in their proper substantive essence, they were simply not meant to fool you into thinking they were real, that you could stand up and reach out and touch them. But even within the limits of their unreality they were somehow, Turner felt, compelling. They drew your attention the way the sky does, at night, at least if you're high enough: pulling you and pulling you, making you feel not anchored safely at all to any planet, tiny and afloat in all that nothingness.

Maridel touched lightly the back of his hand, which made him start.

"It's only because it's *seen* him," she explained, speaking low. "The projection wouldn't come up like this, already, except that he's already in the matrix. It already knows who he is."

This did not make things much clearer, and certainly did not make Turner feel reassured. The curly-haired boy, from what a quick glance could tell, wasn't enjoying it very much either.

"All right," said Maridel. She faced not Turner nor the boy but squarely into the black immaterial portico, the vast deep center of the illusion. "Come out," she told it.

At once the night-black doors came apart, swinging soundlessly back into themselves. Turner drew his breath—but there was nothing behind them. Nothing mysterious at all. Only the opposite wall of the drawing room, the couch with its faded peonies, and the slender fourteen-year-old boy whose name, we knew at last, was Tristin.

"Come on," urged Maridel.

And not before then—the boy's first halting step into the space where the doors had been—did Turner understand that Tristin himself was still sitting there, plainly uncomfortable now, beside him on the rose-colored rug. Squirming wretchedly, yet unable to look away, as horribly fascinated as Turner himself, while his own perfect *doppelgänger* strolled calmly and sadly into the room.

"Tell us about yourself," Maridel commanded.

The voice of the image was pure and ghostly, emanating from no-where.

I'm lonely, it said. *There is no one who loves me, and I don't know why I am here. I believe I have lived on this mountain all my life. I don't remember coming to this house, or going away. I think Madame Gwendola is the smartest person in the world, and Maridel is my only friend, but she is cruel to me. I'm afraid I will never be allowed to die, that I'll be like—*

"For God's sake, stop it," said Turner. He forced his eyes away, turning to the poor miserable boy, Tristin in real flesh and blood, in whose eyes tears had started to form.

Maridel, shrugging, leaned forward and unwrapped the boy's hands, which seemed to have lost connection with their own motor controls, from the sinister gleaming handle, one finger at a time.

"How can you," Turner asked her, as a big brother maybe would, "how can you be so insensitive? To just sit there and let it say such awful embarrassing things about him?"

Maridel watched him dispassionately. "You don't understand," she said, shaking her head. "I'm not *letting* it do anything. That's just what the system is *about*. That's why we call it Identities."

As Turner continued to stare at her, and Tristin looked numbly at his toes, she laid it out more plainly.

"You see, all those things are simply *true*. No one loves him. He's terribly afraid of me. He's in awe of my mother. That's what my father invented the system for: to know people, to *render* them, exactly the way they are."

Turner scowled. "There are kinder ways," he said, "of getting to know things about someone. You could just *ask*, for starters."

"Not in this case," said Maridel simply. "Tristin doesn't talk."

For the next few seconds they stared at the boy—Turner as guilty as Maridel—with the scrutiny one might give a laboratory animal. Tristin, apparently accustomed to such treatment, suffered their gaze in stillness and resignation. Only after a moment or two had passed, he gave a soft and somehow eloquent sigh.

"My God," murmured the unhappy student. Having come to know at last, in that comfortable drawing room, someone far more unhappy than himself.

Maridel gave him the smile of a succubus. "Here," she said. "Your wine has come."

The tall stick-legged nurse, her white dress made a notch more expressive today by a scarf of tasteful lavender, stood beside him, leaning down, proffering a tulip glass filled with claret. Turner took this with purely autonomic eagerness. By firelight, it was the color of a substance he had recently lost quite a lot of. The nurse was already in retreat by the time he raised it with shaking hands.

"Don't drink it too fast," Maridel warned him. "And be careful of the carpet. The handle may tingle a little, but don't worry—you won't get shocked."

Turner took a second sip (warm, spicy . . . magnificent) before he figured out what she meant.

"Come on," she said impatiently. Her perfect golden child's finger wagged down at the metal-and-plastic contraption in the center of the rug. Smiling innocently, radiantly, she commanded:

"Go ahead and grab it. It's your turn now."

Turner looked dumbly back. (No, silently. How brutal one's casual thoughts can be.)

Identities, he thought, as the wine crept into his blood. Well, it was something we had always wanted to know. And there were other considerations. Courtesy, if that quaint worldly concept were operable here, on this mountaintop. And sympathy, comradeship, already felt in a subterranean way for the sad and kind-spirited boy. We took another swallow, tremblingly.

"All right," said Turner. "What do I do?"

Maridel pursed her lips. "I *told* you that," she said.

So she had. Turner set the wine glass, almost empty, at the edge of the rug. Reached out. Touched, then resolutely grasped, the shaft still warm from Tristan's fingers. And looked up to meet Maridel's pleased and precociously ironic little smile.

Well, so now what?

Whatever Turner had expected, there was none of it. He sat there inclined uncomfortably forward, feeling nothing but a little foolish, and the wine running rampant in his head.

"What's your name?" Maridel asked.

Ah: the questioning.

"Turner Ashenden."

"Where do you live?"

"In the Solar Temple . . . in a house, down in the valley."

"Are you a virgin?"

Turner did look up, but was past amazement by now. "That's none of your business," he said.

"Hm." Maridel frowned not at Turner but sideways at the wooden box, the nexus of this menacing little toy. She murmured: "Something seems to be . . . um, let's try . . . Have you ever killed anyone?"

"No." (Almost, almost enjoying this. Turner glanced sideways at Tristin, but the boy was looking away.)

"Is your mother alive?"

"No."

"How about your father?"

The capillaries in the underlayer of Turner's skin were already dilated, from the wine, which explains the rush of color into his face.

"Ah," said Maridel, gratified. "Mysterious parentage."

Some quiet vibration emerged from the holly-wood box. Maridel ran a finger over its carved face, with an attitude of impolite secretiveness. Of course we were unkindly disposed toward her just then.

"It's ready," she announced, looking straight in Turner's eye. "It knows who you are."

He stuck a nervous hand out, reaching for the wineglass, but Maridel gave him the Tristin treatment: a firm shake of her aristocratic young head.

"*Both* hands," she emphasized, "on the handle."

She tapped lightly on the box, and then we all sat back waiting for the great revelation.

Finer detail, this time, as things weren't so astonishingly new: we noticed the slight buzzing that continued to come from the little box, and a crackling sensation in the air, as though a flood of ions were sweeping past us. We noticed too that Tristin and Maridel were sitting more perfectly upright than before, their spines straight, the girl's swaying slightly, making you think the whole performance might be some kind of religious or meditative rite.

And about the doors. The tall black panels themselves, when they appeared again before us, were more perceptibly *nothing*, if that makes any sense, than they had been the first time, when we thought for a while they were *something*, even though the something was illusory. But no. They were simply planes of air, or not even that—of space—and what gave them that peculiar quality of pulling you in, of absorbing you, was that they appeared to be doing exactly that: they soaked in all the light, the images, the energy that happened to enter that particular rectangle of the room. Maybe that's where the power came from, to run the complex simulation. Turner didn't know enough to guess. But anyway. There were the doors.

"Very good," said Maridel. "Come out, now."

And as before, the black panels falling open. Collapsing within themselves, our view of the room returning.

And as before, nothing unusual. Only the air, the light, the chintz peonies. The warming fire. Only that.

Only that. Do you get it? There was *no* Turner. Or alternatively, if Maridel was correct, and the purpose of the system was to know, to understand and remember, then Turner *was* there, his innermost identity displayed for all to see, and it was . . .

But Turner hadn't gotten this far; the awkwardness of the moment was too great for rational analysis, or even irrational analysis. To break the terrible silence he said, "So, um, what . . . is it not working or something?"

"Oh, no," said Maridel. "It always works."

Turner felt a slight warmth, a pressure, around his fingers, and looked down to see that the boy Tristin was removing—in a pretty big hurry—Turner's hands from the warm metal hilt. Funny, how numb they had gotten. He raised them before his eyes, flexed the fingers, relieved that everything still moved, and nodded his thanks to the boy, who was silently (of course silently) watching him. The strength of Tristin's gaze, a new attribute, caught his attention. Brown eyes grown dark with a private, unfathomable passion. Seeming to drink like the black magical doors the very essence of Turner, the hapless houseguest, whose image had been no image at all. And then at last—because Turner was damned if *he* was going to be the first to break eye-contact *this* time—turning away with the faintest, most secret of smiles.

The new voice in the room seemed all the more loud and startling for coming from a distance: the first sound in how much time, we couldn't have guessed, to come from anywhere beyond the rose-colored rug, our charmed circle.

"Come along, children," Madame Gwendola called from the inner doorway. "Maridel, ask Mr Ashenden if he will join us in the dining room. The soup is already on the table."

A civilized meal

Here were the candles and here was the linen tablecloth. Here was the priceless setting of blue-and-white china, the famous willow pattern, two hundred years old if I'm a day, chipped barely enough, its glazing webbed with tiny cracks, to make you feel nervous using it. And here before us, by the bowl of chard-and-barley soup, was the tulip glass of salmon-tinted wine. Thinner than before, and cooler, with a slightly acrid nose, the warm spicy blood diluted now with other humors, what were they called? Black bile, yellow bile, phlegm, or wait—Turner Ashenden, rather befuddled just now, sat twiddling the stem of the tulip glass between his fingers.

"You don't seem," Madame Gwendola noted, "to be enjoying your soup."

"It's very good," Turner said. He really meant it, but, "I just . . . gosh, I don't know, I was pretty hungry there a little while ago. I guess I'm just tired."

Tired and out-of-balance—phlegm clogging up his head, melancholy dimming his vision, choler making his limbs feel like Play-Doh—Turner sat two seats down from Maridel, she on his left, with Tristin cater-cornered across from him, also leftward, and Gwendola herself seated distantly in the opposite direction, at the head of the table. Which could easily have seated twelve. An efficient arrangement, if the idea was to leave Turner suspended where they could examine him patiently, a new specimen, from all angles at once. Thank God we remembered from somewhere, some life before the Solar Temple, our table manners.

"This is quite a remarkable room," he said—again really meaning it, though the words came out like the tritest of courtesies. Making things worse, he gestured around at the four great columns, painted bone white, from which the plaster-cast finials had mostly crumbled, that stood like sarsen stones around the table.

"There's a bandage on your neck," noted Maridel from her new point of view. Her tone, her entire stern persona softened with concern. "Were you hurt?"

"Actually, um . . ." Turner glanced around the table, trying to get his own persona in focus. Things were complicated by the strongly felt presence of Gwendola, behind his back if he turned too far toward the girl. He said at last, from the left side of his mouth: "I was kidnapped."

Across the table, Tristin brought his head up. Madame Gwendola lifted a white finger, ringed by gemstones, in reprobation.

"You are *certainly* mistaken," she said grandly, as though this were giving Turner the benefit of some doubt. "It is impossible for one to be kidnapped, for one can never be taken against one's will. One can only be taken *by* one's will." She made swimming motions with her hand, displacing a copper bracelet. "You must learn to *flow* in your dharmic chreode. You must stop climbing out of it, trying to enter modes of being that are alien to you. . . ."

"Oh, good heavens, Mother." Maridel tapped a soupspoon testily against her age-old bowl. "Can't you see he's had a hard day? Surely you can wait till after dinner to . . . enlighten him."

Turner smiled meekly aside, from one hostess to the other. Gwendola adjusted three tourmaline necklaces strung deep in the cleft of her bosom. As though some slight asynchrony had been set right by this, she faced Turner again, more companionably. *Vibes*, he thought. *She's switched vibes on me*.

"Was it highwaymen?" she inquired, emitting vibes now much closer to those of normal table-talk. "I do hope you weren't carrying anything of value. One shouldn't, these days. Though, perhaps if they truly needed it . . . Tristin, give Mr Ashenden some more wine."

God, did we really need that? The silent boy reached for a decanter.

"No," Turner said, meeting Tristin halfway with the tulip glass. "Thank you. I mean, no—actually it was the, ah, Chief Administrator."

Gwendola consulted, with a frown, her strong-minded daughter, as though expecting some clarification from that quarter. It was hard to see without obviously looking, but Turner thought the girl gave a sort of shrug.

Gwendola flexed her forearms. "That's hard to believe," she pronounced.

Not an excessively feminine person, really: a layer of grace imperfectly concealed a layer of what might even be brutality. Well, at least the grace was there. Turner's wine went down, dry and bitter, and from it he drew a modest sense of resolve.

"The Chief Administrator," he said, "looks exactly like you said he would."

Gwendola acknowledged this with the barest of nods. It was a curious gesture—as though he had responded correctly to some challenge, some quiz.

"Yes," she said, glancing past him, toward the kitchen, with what seemed an absent-minded nod. "It is an unmistakable face, an important part of the pattern. I am glad that you have recognized it. *If* indeed you have. Such things are often more complex, young man, than we believe."

—No shit, Turner imagined himself elaborating, hours later, to Black Malachi. That's exactly how she talks. As if there's always this big *mystery* or something, out there, just on the other side. . . .

And Malachi nodding happily.—What happened next, old man? This is quite good, really.

Well just then, responding to what turned out to be a summons, Gwendola's unseen audience appeared in the person of—

—*Nurse Tawdry*, Malachi would declare, pouncing on the image.

Turner laughed. Really laughed right there at the dinner table, drawing odd looks from those seated around him, as an oven-fresh perfect soufflé was brought in by the stick-figure he could now only think of as . . .

"Thank you," said Gwendola—never addressing the poor woman by a name, when you thought about it, so it was up for grabs anyway.

There's something very odd about this house, Turner once and for all decided. Something . . . out of place. The soufflé, however, looked wonderfully good. Heaped on the plate airily, inviting the fork. Tempting one like fairy food. Which of course, if you eat it, does something, changes you in some way. Turner could not just then remember the details. But even if it makes you sleep a hundred years, for instance, that would be perfectly acceptable. Likewise trapping one for a decade or so in front of this glass of salmon-colored wine. Through which one espied, tipping it penultimately toward one's nose, Maridel's kind gaze uptable, even that tender despot rendered now benevolent. Yes: something *very* out of place. Though also oddly agreeable. About the house and likewise its occupants. But God it's good to be sitting at a table again. Enjoying—just as we promised ourselves, though little believing at the time—a civilized meal.

And as our ultimate gulp drained down the old hand-blown slope of the glass toward our upturned mouth, some interesting trick of refraction caused, from one side of the tulip, the image of the girl Maridel to slide, inscrutably watching us, down toward the stem; while from the opposite direction Tristin, the tragically silent boy, slid also on a collision course, his eyes weirdly widened by some goldfish-bowl effect, thoroughly written up in the literature I'm sure, so that his expression grew even more intense, the brown eyes hungrier than before, as he sat there not eating at all and getting even skinnier while his image and the girl's blurred together, the glass reached the horizontal, and the once and future dinner guest closed his eyes for one brief, enchanted moment, as eventful in its own peculiar way as your basic garden-variety hundred years.

Come back

Climbing out of the Institute's ancient carriage, Turner looked back a final time to thank his driver, to say goodbye and perhaps find some other appropriate sentiment, some remotely accurate summation of the countless ideas stacked up in his mind. But in the moment of turning he realized he had forgotten exactly who the driver was. . . . Nurse Tawdry? But no, that wasn't right; it must, of course, be Madame Gwendola; she wouldn't have entrusted the carriage to anyone else. Yet even as Turner formed the more cautious words this memory demanded, he knew it wasn't Gwendola in the carriage after all—that would have made him too uncomfortable —which really narrowed down the field.

You'd think, wouldn't you, that Turner would just glance discreetly back inside the car, make out Tristin's melancholy features in the blue light of the console. . . . But it couldn't be Tristin. Turner would have remembered that—being chauffeured by a boy so young. And surely they wouldn't have let *her* drive.

Turner was perspiring now, the sweat a fine chill halo on his brow. Somebody was inside the goddamned car and he was standing outside the Solar Temple like an idiot, prolonging beyond all reason the simple stupid goodbye. Not that "goodbye" was exactly what he would have said; in fact it was the choice of words that got him into this. This confusion. This rising panic.

Panic, see, because all at once Turner understood that, far beyond not remembering who had driven him here, he couldn't remember the drive in the ancient motorcar *at all*. He couldn't even remember leaving Bad Winters Institute. He couldn't remember what he had eaten for fucking *dessert*.

Man, I'm in bad shape.

He felt trembly, full of the darkness outside him, out there between the cool blue glow of the console and the warmth of the Solar Temple. Out there alone.

But wait a minute, now. The Solar Temple. . . .

No, thought Turner, prayed Turner, out there in the silence, don't let it get worse.

The Solar Temple . . . why can't we turn our eyes and *look* at it? Don't we believe anymore that it's really there? That we can get control of ourselves and walk across the parking lot and try to remember the goddamn combination to the door, the *door*, damn it, which is really right over, somewhere, thirty feet or so, *please* let it be there.

The ancient carriage waited patiently, its driver in no hurry, for Turner to say whatever he was going to say, to have this great revelation, to understand what he was doing. Out here all alone.

Meanwhile, inside the tulip glass

Turner was feeling distinctly odd. There were these people looking in at him, their faces blurred together, and the aftertaste of watered-down blood on his tongue felt more or less a hundred years old, depending on how you counted.

"I don't like forcing him," someone was saying. A woman's very old voice; or a girl's. "You can't make somebody be another person, if he's perfectly happy. . . . It just doesn't seem fair."

"We are not speaking of *another person*," a second, less charitable voice said. "You know perfectly well who we're speaking of. And who we're dealing with. You can see that *tent*, for heaven's sake, from the balcony. And you are hardly the one to talk about forcing things. It was *you* who wanted to play Identities. But you were right: there is no time to just let things happen."

I've got the time, thought Turner, while some lurker in the back of his mind wondered what the hell he was thinking about. Believe me, the thought ran on: I've got the time.

"But I don't *feel* the same, this way," said the first voice, extremely youthful now.

"That doesn't matter," said Lack-of-Charity.

"Then what does?" demanded his comrade, his ancient ally. "That's *all* that matters."

Dismissively: "You're too young to understand."

Ha.—Turner could hear her thinking it.

(Wow!)

"I felt something just then."

There was a tone in her voice, a quality, that Turner began to recognize. Familiar wave-forms. Sound, the pure product of events occurring in time. A very old song came back to him: from some time, the emberglow of memory.

"I don't know . . . singing or something. I . . ."

—!

: a gasp. The girl's or Turner's, afterward. In bliss backing down from some impossible breathless height. Rapid breathing, God I'm going to suffocate inside this tulip glass.

There it was, Mother. It was there, really. I think he's started to . . .

Moving away from the glass now. Getting larger, filling this chair, the glass growing small as it sank to the table. Turner blinked his eyes, trying to remember something, equally trying to forget. There was no particular reason to be surprised at the girl, Maridel, sitting primly, silk-sleeved, at his left, or the brown eyes of the boy with an inward-looking sadness staring down the table at the half-collapsed soufflé. Only . . .

"What a *memorable* dinner," said Gwendola, as she said things, overdramatically, rotating with unthinking thumb-twitches the gemstones in their silver band.

Turner just then remembered he was so godawfully tired. Such a long day, a long and still unfinished journey. Stumbling into this odd, this disturbingly out-of-place old house, as before, by implausible happenchance. And pausing here, briefly, to dine, maybe on fairy food, before setting off again, soon he hoped, toward someplace that no longer felt, for some reason, quite so much like home.

Come back

"Goodbye," said Turner gratefully, easing shut the door of the Institute's ancient motorcar.

And Madame Gwendola, her politeness all but used up, said—

Come back

"Goodbye," said Turner gratefully, easing shut the door of the Institute's ancient motorcar.

And Maridel, who shouldn't really have been allowed to drive, leaning over to take Turner's hand before it left the door, parting her dry lips and smiling ambivalently, said—

Come back

"Goodbye," said Turner gratefully, easing shut the door of the Institute's ancient motorcar.

And Tristin, who had never been allowed to leave the Institute before, twisting uncomfortably as though struggling to subdue some long-sequestered urge, opened his mouth and agonizingly strained to say—

4

Morning afterthoughts

Turner Ashenden stepped quietly into the Morning Room, an ironically named second-story alcove whose expanse of argon-filled windows was angled and overhung so as to ensure that the sun could not possibly creep in, this time of year, two days before the equinox, one moment before twelve-fifteen. There he found Black Malachi curled pensively in a Cherokee red bathrobe, sipping amber liquid through a neatly severed pipette and perusing a volume of neo-Celtic holography. The sunlight made the heavy-stock reproductions seem to shimmer and float, ghostly images fleeing the confinement of fixed dimensions. With a fluttering of page leaves, Black Malachi gave a sigh.

"Days like this, Ashenden," he said without looking up, "one is led to contemplate the impermanence of all things."

Days like this. Days *like* this? Has there ever, anywhere, been a day remotely similar to this one?

Turner stepped closer. The sun lay warm across his feet. Ingenuously on a hot-tray a lab flask of amber beverage sat steaming. From the walls around them, the sonic sculpture Malachi had installed the previous winter, consolation for the drop-off in party attendance during midterms, made a faint wind-chimey tinkle, occasionally plunging to shudder at the threshold of audibility like a distant gong, as the sculptor's moody algorithms responded to whatever was in the air. To me, thought Turner uncomfortably. Careful not to rattle the gestalt any harder, he lowered himself into a barrel chair.

"Care for some of this?" said Malachi, gesturing toward the flask. "Take your mind off."

Turner wondered why it was that some people could just, like, *be* there—turn and speak and raise the cynical brow—without any undue agitating of the energy waves in a room; whereas he, Turner, couldn't scratch a goddamned *eyelid* without his entire body making a big production out of it, feet turning insecurely inward, fingers twitching, peculiar sensations in the groin . . . The sonic sculpture, all too mindful of this, began an annoying sine-wavy ululation.

Malachi smiled surmisively. "Something on your mind?"

Turner nodded. Relieved to just be sitting here. As afternoon sun streamed gaily into the Morning Room. And the sculpture quieted down again. Waiting to see.

"Malachi," he said, "do you believe in . . . I mean, spirits or mind-reading or . . . or reincarnation, or things like that?"

Amenable, the stout youth gathered his bathrobe around him and closed his book. "I hope this is by way of offering some explanation for these mysterious trips you've been taking lately. Your unannounced departures, followed *days* thereafter by precipitous, to say the least, returns. Do you have any notion, Ashenden, what you looked like last night?"

He paused for another sip of restorative, one must gather, beverage. Then exclaimed almost gleefully: "It's a woman, isn't it? You've taken up with some slinky little spiritualist, and now you're afraid of being haunted by the ghost of her vengeful grandmother."

Turner failed to rise to this. "What's that stuff you're drinking? Maybe I could use a little lift."

"Ah." Black Malachi, happy to be helpful, poured a cup. "*Camellia sinensis,* laced with *Monarda didyma.* Or for your more perfect understanding, Earl Gray tea. Do you take milk, or are you a philistine?"

Turner sighed. "Whatever you say, Malachi. It's really complicated. First I was driving up to Goldaster's with the rent money, and then I was captured and drugged and woke up in this *tent,* and the Chief Administrator was there. I mean, himself. And we talked. And after that I wound up at this weird place, this Institute, where I'd been before, only with these . . . people . . . and something happened there but . . . Well, for example, I can't remember who it was that took me home. Or anything. But I have this real funny feeling that something, like, *big* is going on. And the thing is, now I've lost the rent money and the spirit-burner, and Rodarch wants me to talk to Goldaster, and I don't know what the hell I'm going to do."

He paused, absent further inspiration, for a sip of tea. The sonic sculpture had fallen perfectly quiet, dubious, or eager for more. To placate it Turner said, "This doesn't make any sense, I suppose."

Black Malachi slapped the tea table: an emphatic sound, surprising us.

"By God, Ashenden," he declared, "I'm proud of you. Truly I am. After all these months of moping around the house, fretting about how you're not going to classes, you're not getting laid, you're growing old and wasting your life away—why, all of a sudden you've *woken up*. You've had a bit of misadventure, and look: you're scared shitless!"

He turned aside and waved a stubby hand, *voilà*, showing off his housemate to the sonic sculpture, which clattered its applause, as though the state of scared-shitlessness were a sought-after and, indeed, wholly admirable condition.

"Tell me," he said, "all about it, at once."

What I need now, thought Turner, is a biographer. To get all the details right. [Nonetheless I bumbled through without you, creditably well—at least up to the part about Identities, the rose-colored rug, Maridel saying *It's your turn*, and the stick-figure, the nurse, walking in, officiously bearing wine. . . .]

"Ha!" exclaimed Black Malachi. "A nurse, quite! Nurse—"

"Don't say it," Turner warned. Holding a hand up, helpless to impede the onrush of inevitability.

The portly youth gave him a look. "I was merely going to suggest," he sniffed, "a nickname," feigning a social wound. "To name a ghost is to lay it. You want to lay a ghost someday, don't you Ashenden?"

Not that one. "What kind of nickname?" we ventured cautiously.

"I've forgotten now."

"Ah." (Is not to know better?)

But, to go on. The murky part then about the tall black doors, sitting dreamily at the dinner table, an odd conversation we may or not have heard—and Maridel's voice again, we were sure it was Maridel's, *There it was Mother, I think he's starting to . . .*

"Drink your tea," said Black Malachi.

Turner looked up, startled, What? Was I dozing off or something?

"You are becoming *caught up*," his roommate sternly pronounced. "You are losing your famous detachment. What's happened to you, Ashenden? I've never seen you quite this way."

The lordly teenager rose, taking it upon himself personally to refresh our teacup, even stirring the milk in—an unprecedented gesture of concern. As he placed it in our hands he gave a smile one might have called actually gentle, saying: "Well, whatever it is, I believe I like it. Truly I do. That old Ashenden air of untouchability could be so . . . wearying."

God, had he really thought that? In spite of everything we nodded, surrendering to the medical student's bedside manner.

"Now pay attention," he said, bending very near us in the barrel chair, "and will you please finish your tea? Very good. Ashenden, I'm going to tell you *exactly* what to do."

The way things were

The old University sat on hills beside the time-lost town of Candlemas. It had stone walls and thick boxwood hedges, very popular in these parts two hundred years ago, so there you had the basis already—the bones, as gardeners say—of a defensive perimeter. There were also buildings, hard to date, architectural Januses, that stood at the boundary itself, the Zero Lot Line, with small windows facing out on *the other side* (a code-phrase) like those of the caretaker's house in an ancient cemetery Turner had visited once when much smaller, his mother beside him never relaxing her grip on the heavy volume always in her hand, the spawning ground and final resting place of somebody unnamed, maybe Turner himself, deep down South.

What, the book or the cemetery? I'm sorry; you can't go back anymore. The story continues the way *you* understand it. Its mystery must persist. Its ambiguity. A problem in scholarship like who the hell all those pronouns in Malory refer to. *Which* knight got his head chopped off? Which one mounted the great steed and rode off to make sport with some maiden, and isn't that really a code-phrase too, a christianized or just innocently corrupted memory of the pagan courtesy of offering up the warm person of one's wife, one's choicest daughter, to the ceremonial king who's going to take it on the chin, anyway, this coming May? (But how did *she* feel about it?

Anything I can do for the Cause, Dad. The improvement of the racial stock is paramount.)

Turner adjusted his trousers uncomfortably. Unlike most people, who could walk down a public street and no big deal, Turner tended to get hung up on questions like how to move the body, how extensively the hips should be involved in the transfer of body weight, just how far forward the arms should swing so as to be properly outgoing without an unseemly display of extroversion. It was confusing. If you thought hard enough you would end up staring at your feet, your pace would become uncertain, an adjustable limp, result of some vaguely remembered injury. *For he had been wounded through both his thighs.* Well, we know what *that* really meant. So what about a wound on the neck, then? Did that mean your brain had been emasculated, your mental potency lopped off?

Across from a row of stores, thriving little businesses, the University opened on a broad lawn bounded by various revivals or survivals of historical sentimentality: the greekish colonnade, colonial brickworks, a bogus Bauhaus cafeteria, a war memorial whose attention-grabbing obelisk invoked the wrong deity, driver of the blinding chariot, the son-of-a-bitch who'd claimed all those young lives in the first place. More recent structures, too late on the scene for a shot at the best real estate, clamored for attention in New Century sunglasses, reflective Maya Lin slickers, Jefferson caps. The view was spoiled only by barbed wire, unspooled carelessly along the street—the University's chastity belt, guarding the womb of knowledge against penetrations of commerce, assaults on its political virginity. At least making the salesmen and pamphleteers walk around the corner to the grand-arched official entryway, where there was some pretense of controlling the passage of characters on and off the grounds. Even here, after all—even in this chaste and indolent valley—things were the way they were.

The way things were was more conspicuously in evidence along the row of storefronts across the street. Turner's destination, as it turns out. Here one caught glimpses—whole eyefuls if you want to know—of conspicuous thugs retained by the Souls, rumor had it, or somebody, to keep an eye on what passed in Candlemas for a town square. A "pedestrian mall." There was an odd term, now. A concept. You couldn't "drive your car" here. (Get it? It's like, *très* pre-Dissolution.) Florists, chemical-vendors, news-hacks, a butcher's stall and various people- and mail-carriers had set up shop in the slots once reserved for "motor vehicles," see? Oh, you lover of lost causes you.

Turner passed the little piazzo, gaining the crowded main sidewalk and getting ignored, as ever, by the hunched-over guardians of the gate. He slowed his pace, enjoying the locale, the wares on display, the whole operation. KNOWLEDGE SHOP, Several Media Represented, catered to students of course, and hangers-on up from the valley still interested enough. Which maybe Turner would turn into, any week now. When were grades due out? Here was the food-seller with whom Malachi had his dealings, and you could see the current offerings, *Weekly Specials!*, left boldly out on a table, a certain level of pilferage being anticipated, welcomed in the interest of publicity, the price adjusted accordingly, Malachi cheerfully signing a voucher when the invoice arrived. Turner paused to examine grapefruits, Jenny Lind melons, a small early pumpkin whose informative label explained that it represented "an historical variety long thought to be extinct." (Was that right, *an historical?* And how about this "extinct variety" business? Sure, you'd lose a little genetic information, but *extinct?*)

Turner kept on. Blithely past clothing merchants, the Healing Center, and a small gallery selling local crafts, mostly, though a few of its wares stood at the threshold of *the other side*, the shadow-world of Art. He paused to examine a lump of black crystal, perhaps a sculpture, that looked like it was forming again after a meltdown, a transubstantiation. Exceedingly Rare, said the tag. Nothing can tempt you when you haven't got any money. Which brought us by the sort of cruel but natural irony the world is famous for to our actual destination. Whose sign only stated, all dignity, BANK.

Turner entered at a self-confident saunter, returning the stare of the, ahem, *doorman*, with, by way of interest, a smart-aleck, student-in-goodstanding smile. (I'm going to get a better job than *you've* got the minute I walk out of here, you cretin.) Right away—as soon as he saw the look of resigned desolation in the man's eye—Turner regretted this unkind imposture; he wanted to turn back and say, Look, the only one I'm kidding is myself, I'll never get a job, I'll never even graduate, I don't know how to do *anything*. . . .

Quickly the moment passed for soul-baring. Turner stepped, not sauntered, past sundry usurers and collection agents to the "teller cage" (what an image, the prisoners were all outside) upon whose smooth pine countertop he tapped to summon attention. A slight, moustachioed young man looked up wearily—like, wouldn't you know it just when I was about to go to *lunch*—but Turner's gaze seemed to surprise him. Fixed as it was.

"How can I help you?" (Arm twitching, fingertip reaching somewhere low for a secret button, death-ray control, what.)

"I've, um, got to see Harvey Goldaster."

"Who?" The young man smiled, then dropped it. "I'm afraid Mr Goldaster no longer has any relationship with this institution."

"I'll put you in a fucking institution," reciting Malachi's script here, "if you don't let me through that back door right now."

The young man smiled mincingly. "We don't really want trouble, now, do we?"

"Harvey's not going to like it very much," don't worry, just say it word for word, "if some asshole like you causes him to lose a lot of money, just because you *don't know who I am*." Turner added this emphasis himself.

The young man looked irritated now; he swapped glances with someone off-screen. The death-ray finger twitched, irresolute, while the narrow mouth said:

"And just who *are* you?"

Turner swallowed. A familiar dilemma threatened to present itself. Malachi must have covered this obvious eventuality, though.

"Um, Turner Ashenden"—his mind blank, temporizing.

In the teller cage the young man lowered a single eyebrow, his gaze clicking in, as though hearing something very faint from one side. Turner glanced around, up at the pastel ceiling, wondering where the death-ray would strike from, then he looked back to find everything magically changed, the young man smiling deferentially, a purring sound at the back of the room and a narrow door swinging open.

"I'm terribly sorry, Mr Ashenden." God, it could make you paranoid—"If you'll just step this way. . . ."

Turner passed through the door feeling unworthy, mistaken for someone else . . . mistaken for *someone* . . . while the door breathed shut behind him. No turning around now. No drifting back to sleep. As a further door, an invisible door, the door adduced by metaphorists everywhere, came open a crack. And somewhere else, incredibly distant, an island of apple trees, some bird or another twibbled the opening bars, the most it could manage, of a certain undying melody. "Greensleeves," isn't it? Oh what the fuck, thought Turner. It's show-time, folks!

M.F.H.

The horse had his number. Everybody else in the known universe could probably have sat up here and sort of gone with the flow—you know they could—but Turner Ashenden was terrified, and motion-sick, and he didn't care who knew it. He suffered himself to be bumped and dragged at alarming speed down the hill, the large gray animal snorting happily underneath him, as hounds bayed ahead and wind blew in his face and Harvey Goldaster, reaching in to give him a little help with the reins, shouted companionably:

"Have another drink, here, Ashenden!"

Turner's mare slowed down, which mainly served to remind him how *extremely high off the ground* he was. He accepted helplessly the flask Goldaster thrust into his hand—flask hell, it was a whole fucking bottle —and in one gulp drained about two days' rent worth of single-malt scotch, brown and peaty, unobtainable even at that ungodly price by the common run of poor horsemen. Cheered by this thought, though he hadn't really the taste for whisky, Turner took another slug of the stuff and handed the bottle back to his host, his tormentor, no poor horseman in any sense. Master of Fox Hounds, in fact. Harvey Goldaster, M.F.H.—what fun Malachi would have with that. The *H* being the only point in question.

"You figure that'll hold you?" The M.F.H. grinned sportingly. His teeth were perfectly even and white.

"I believe so," said Turner, who believed nothing.

Goldaster handed the bottle back. His skin was perfect, too. Tan and crinkled with smile lines at the corners of the eyes. Only the thinning hair, mostly hidden now by a red riding cap, gave some assurance of normality. It made his nose, which was not really too large, seem a wee bit overly prominent. Though there was scant comfort in that.

"Thanks," said Turner, taking the bottle. "Listen, Mr Goldaster, are we going to get a chance to talk? There're a few things . . . I mean, like about the rent . . ."

"Harvey," grinned the M.F.H. "Call me Harvey. What about the rent? What's your friend Pantera got up his sleeve this time?"

"It's not Malachi, it's—"

"Ho!"

Harvey Goldaster dropped the mare's reins, forgetting Turner, forgetting even the very expensive scotch. The dogs had taken a scent, it looked like, and the huntsman some hundred yards ahead was tooting his bugle.

"To the hounds!" Goldaster bellowed, and as with so much else in society, so many forms of ritualized behavior, the words themselves were of no consequence; the field of riders, hunters, partygoers, whatever they were, was already crashing off leftward across the screen, bounding through yellow fields, hurtling fences, scattering piles of hay—ungraceful in the extreme, it seemed to Turner, regardless of what one might have been led to expect by one's life spent in novels. At that moment *he* expected to die. Goldaster urged his own huge gelding off calmly, genteelly, and Turner's mare fell behind him into a mild-mannered trot, taking it easy on the poor horseman, the normal student, or maybe the scotch was already working. Some people actually enjoy this, you know. Only pity the damned fox.

The hunt, and you may capitalize that if you like, proceeded from Upper Moat Farm across the green and yellow postcard, A Traditional Fox Hunt in the Valley (photo courtesy Bureau of Tourism) whose imported *bocage* of fields, stout fences and hedgerows had been imposed upon a landscape whose native contours were once quite different. The forgery was innocent, though; there was a common feeling, at least among certain racial types, that *this is what the world ought to look like*. At the very worst, it was a sort of Neolithic nostalgia.

The farm itself, Upper Moat, where the postcard picture was snapped from, YOU ARE HERE on our poor horseman's tourist map, was another

story. It wore its symbols as jauntily as the M.F.H. wore his Mighty Fancy
Hat. And the most ridiculous of these (thought Turner) was, there really
was a moat. And it was, yes, an *upper* moat, at least in the sense that it
was much too high up the hillside to masquerade as any sort of natural
water formation. The most generous assumption you could make was that
maybe it was a drainage ditch, part of some scheme to keep the vineyard
above from getting waterlogged. Though you wouldn't think this if you
knew anything about rootstocks or soil types; and anyway the assumption
would have to break down when you cleared the row of outbuildings—
the stable, an equipment barn, a granary—and came in view at last of the
preposterous Tudor (more or less) mansion squatting up there smugly so
high on the hill that it caught every little puff of winter wind, which proved
only that neither an engineer nor a geomancer had been consulted in its
placement. But of course that was the M.F.H. again. Master of this Foolish
House.

The hounds changed course, racing into a pocket of wetland that
narrowed like a funnel between mirror-image stands of oaks. Brambles,
imported berry plants gone wild, multiflora roses, every kind of thorny
undergrowth you could think of snagged at Turner's city-boy pants as the
mare plunged onward. The breeze was cool and damp, sweet-smelling
despite the billions of airborne bacteria. At the center of the bog was a
pond as dark and blue as cobalt glass. Twin chimneys rose beyond it,
where a house had been torched as the digital calendar turned, an anti-
climactic millennium that mostly fizzled, another nail in the public coffer.
And off in the distance—there, moving slowly along the opposite hill-
line—was that another hunting party, footborne, former University guys
out clomping after some deer, or . . . or do you think it could be a band
of Settlers, armed and determined young men in blue coveralls who would
love nothing better than to ambush a bunch of wealthy riders like this,
this down-at-the-hooves horsey set that passed for a local gentry, with some
asshole student tossed in for shits and grins?

Face it, Turner: the fresh air, the exercise, the high-quality booze—
it was getting to you.

"Come along, Ashenden!" yelled Harvey Goldaster, halfway around
the pond. He spun about, waving theatrically from his great black gelding:
equestrian performance-art. Mullah of the Fabulous Hunt. He added,
"You don't want to get left behind!"

Turner nodded gamely, miserably, and did something that only confused the mare, caused her to veer a bit leftward, getting bogged down in some cattails. Goldaster made a faint motion with his riding-crop, and half a dozen faceless riders fell back a little, letting Turner overtake them. He blushed at this, felt furious. We didn't want to be hand-held. Damn it, we didn't want to be *out here* at all. We came to deliver a message, have a little heart-to-heart talk, and instead we were being dragged through mud and catching our death of, of *futility*, all to let the Maestro of Frenetic Horsemanship prove that he was the one who called the shots. That he, Harvey Goldaster, and no one else, was the bloody king of the valley.

About those faceless riders, though . . .

It occurred to Turner somewhat belatedly, as his horse trudged out of the cattails and things got moving again, that there was something, um, *uniform* about this bunch of guys who had fallen back to keep him company. I mean, if you were to have made a little prediction, based on the sort of people you'd met here on your earlier trips out, you'd have guessed that there would be a larger proportion of women in this hunting party, an older median age, a good bit more yelling and cutting-up in the ranks. But there, did you hear that? "Ranks"—see, the military analogy just suggested itself. These guys weren't really faceless, you now realized; each one had a face, but it was the same face for everybody. It was an emotionless . . . a *fixed* sort of face. Like a living statue. Like, to be specific about this, a certain oolite head, once painted crimson, discovered in Gloucestershire at the site of an Iron Age excavation, a fortified hillock. . . .

Okay, Turner. Let's keep it together here.

These guys, we decided, feeling quite sober all at once, are not hunters at all. Not the postcard kind. They are soldiers. Vigilantes, mercenaries, something. They are here to protect Goldaster & Co.; to protect *us*. A bunch of Mounted Faceless Henchmen.

Well, well.

There's no telling what a fox is going to do. Dogs on the other hand are fairly predictable. Harvey Goldaster, lowering something from his eyes—looks like a pattern-seeking optic enhancer there, folks—gives a new signal with his riding crop and gallops off up the right-hand hill. The pack of armed horsemen sets off in disordered array behind him. The few guys straggling back to cover Turner's ass exchange looks of (we figure) mild irritation. And Turner, pretty irritated himself now, thanks, takes out the scotch, helps himself to a decent swallow, and gives his horse a thunk on the . . . the big rear muscular area, with the bottle. His mare gets the idea despite Turner's lapse of equine vocabulary, and suddenly we are *storming up the slope*, overtaking Goldaster, leaving the Faceless Brigade to get its shit together behind us.

Tally ho, guys, thinks Turner.

From the top of the hill, emerging between half-clad sycamores, you could see for miles across the valley. There were pastures, clusters of empty-looking homes, the remnants of a train track. The notion of *richness* impresses itself upon you. Our particular point of interest, though, lay in the middleground: a farmhouse from whose stovepipe drifted a wispy cloud of white smoke, rising against the deep green matte painting of distant mountains. It's inevitable, this stylization; it's just what the memory does. Call it transcription error. With a neat, baton-like angling of his crop, Harvey Goldaster plunged for all he was worth down the open slope of the hill, while the huntsman blew frantically to call the hounds off whatever they had been chasing. The fox hunt was turning into something different; Turner couldn't tell what and didn't like to think about it, but his attention was definitely caught. The mare seemed to sense this, to approve of it, because she carried Turner at a respectable pace hard on Goldaster's heels, right down into the middle of all that scenery.

We closed rapidly on the farmhouse. To someone sitting lazily up ahead, rocking on the porch, it might have seemed that a cavalry charge was in full swing. No one was sitting there, however. The farmhouse had a locked-up air about it, despite the rising smoke. It was a simple two-up/two-down structure, with the usual additions out back, now turned away from us, under the shade of some sunburned maples that were probably a lot happier when they were first planted here, before the climate changed. From the driveway, just around the corner of the house, a bit of movement caught Turner's eye. He glanced sideways, looking for a clue—like, does Harvey know these people here? Are we expected?—then snapped his head back as a fresh perception made it through the fuzzy membranes of his mind, the layers of habit and familiarity that filter out a lot of the stuff we don't expect to be there. In this case, a sky-blue pennant, flapping from a patriotic aluminum stick in the front of the house, above the stoop. *Sky-blue*, dinged a bell somewhere in Turner's right hemisphere, as a certain dire pattern was invoked. He reined in the mare, at more or less the same moment that the rest of the party was also slowing down and falling into a kind of loose formation, just far enough from the house that you couldn't quite make out the floral print on the curtains, though you could see them lightly flutter.

Goldaster rode briskly along the suddenly formed phalanx of horsemen. He came right over to Turner, hauling up a couple of yards away and motioning with a forty-pushup arm.

"How about some of that whiskey?" he asked with a team-captain's energetic smile.

"Harvey, listen." Turner clutched the bottle, using it to gesture. The tricky fluid dynamics caused his arm-motions to appear tremulous, uncertain. "I really ought to tell you . . . I mean, if there's going to be trouble here . . . See, I've got this message for you. It's f-from Rodarch. The Chief Administrator."

Bad timing, as usual. The door of the house came open and a single figure appeared. From this distance, you would have to guess a young man maybe Turner's age. He yelled something, waving. He wore badly fitting coveralls of Newport blue.

Harvey wouldn't be rushed. He urged his horse closer to Turner's, slipping the whiskey from our helpless hand.

"Arrogant little prick," he muttered. He peered keenly into Turner's eyes, gauging or confirming something, ending with a nod. He said, "Well I've got a message for Mr Rodarch, too"—then spun about and clopped a dozen yards closer to the farmhouse.

"All right, you," he shouted ahead. "It's time to go. You've had your little romp in the fresh air, now I think you'd better get the hell back to the reservation."

The young man on the porch was brave enough, you had to give him that. He stepped down to the ground, and once Turner adjusted to the clipped Eastern accent he found he could hear him pretty well.

"This *is* where we belong," the young man said loud and evenly. "Nobody was here, man, and we need a place to stay. We *deserve* a place. We're not bothering anybody, man. So why don't you just leave us alone? What's it to you, anyway?"

Harvey's Army came forward. Turner was forced to do likewise, or he would lose his front-row seat. All of them, including the guy on the porch, were circling inward, zeroing in on something whose shape seemed oddly clear, already somehow form-fitted to Turner's mind.

"What it is to *me*," said Goldaster, more lordly now, "is that I *own* this house. And I own quite a few of the other houses you and your friends have broken into and trashed and looted around here."

"You can't prove anything, man. And I bet your troopers there don't have permits for those guns."

Ping, went Turner's brain again. What it was this time was rather more clear: the feckless, fearless youth standing practically toe-to-toe with Harvey Goldaster, Minister of the Fertile Homeland, adducing a bunch of irrelevant, or worse than that, completely meaningless, points of law. It was a moment of recognition.

The M.F.H., sizing things up, said, "You don't know where the hell you are, do you, boy?"

Sneeringly the young man replied, "Give it up, Goldaster. Your day is over."

And Turner, whose recognition was of a more personal sort, kicked his mare in the flanks and, trotting into the no-man's-land before the porch, demanded:

"Where's my spirit-burner, you asshole?"

As though he had been expecting this, expecting Turner to show up sooner or later, the young man slipped a hand into his Newport-blue coveralls and brought out something small, golfball-sized, which—in the instant that he dropped it, gently lobbing it forward as he spun with a familiar athletic stealth back toward the door—some dim corner of Turner's mind, little used since his much earlier boyhood, Armed Conflict Through the Ages, Knights in Shining Armor, Cowboys a-and . . . that part of his mind duly identified as *a concussion grenade*. And then

THOOMP

—the air like a firm hand pressing outward from the house

—a *very* surprised Harvey Goldaster ass-over-teakettle tumbling from the saddle

—the Faceless Brigade pushed back, unhorsed, demoralized, and of everyone in the hunting party only

—Turner Ashenden, forewarned by one critical half-second, already turning, flung forward but hanging on in the saddle, pounding the mare's ribs by way of reassurance, *this way* damn it, rounding the corner of the house, and coming onto the scene of a pretty well premediated getaway. Out the back door, momentum unbroken, burst the guy, the guy from the front porch, who had once a few days ago wielded a garden fork, now sporting a smart-looking shockgun, where could *that* have come from, crossing the porch, and leaping into the blood-stained driver's seat of a humble spirit-burner once mistaken for a truck. Of all the stupid mistakes. Where his comrades, three of them, were already waiting, keeping the well-remembered temperamental engine warm. So all the guy had to do was, like, slap the lever down, and off he went.

For Turner the situation was more complicated. The mare was still in a blind panic, and this was clearly not the best of times to practice precision horsemanship. Plus, the guy was aiming the shockgun at us over his shoulder, building up speed down the dusty driveway, and time was working against us.

Phzipp, phzipp, the weapon sputtered. Threads of yellow-white energy trailed behind Turner's beloved, dilapidated vehicle. They faded well short of the heaving mare. It was a pretty sad spectacle, when you took everything into account. On top of that, Turner's rear end was getting sore.

Well, the hell with it, he thought.

Rising one final little half-foot or so to the occasion, he hefted Harvey's priceless, fluid-dynamically unstable bottle of scotch, decided it would be ridiculous to take aim, and let it go in a brilliant, unerring, epoch-making toss that caught the fleeing young Settler behind the ear, knocked him forward into the wheel, and sent the spirit-burner into an unrecoverable skid. It took out two fenceposts and a ruined chicken coop before meeting at last something firmly planted enough to overcome its mulish momentum: a well-house made of fieldstone. The spirit-burner, as though astonished, sat in a heap for several seconds, hissing its vapor out, and then turned into a blinding, unbelievable fireball.

Turner was thrown off the exhausted mare at last, but in the grand scheme of things this wasn't much to complain about. The young men in Newport blue were just then quite painfully dying. Harvey Goldaster was bending low at Turner's side, but maybe this was later; maybe some time, an hour or more, had passed.

"Well, Ashenden," said the Mender of Fallen Heroes. His clear amber eyes, the color of good whiskey, gleamed down with something you could easily mistake for enjoyment. "I guess we've got time to talk, now."

Turner made as though to sit up, but various odd sensations from the lower seven eighths of his body suggested that this might not be a timely idea.

"So," said Harvey, "what was the message from Rodarch, anyway?"

Turner tried to cough, in surprise, or something, but that didn't work too well either. He said carefully, "It was, like, words to the effect of, *Give it up, Goldaster. Your day is over.*"

And very smoothly, very happily, the M.F.H. stretched his mouth all the way wide, showing off both rows of perfect teeth, and gave a quiet, victorious chuckle.

"Are you happy in school, Mr Ashenden?" he asked after a few moments. "Are you learning anything there?"

It was as painful to think as to speak, so Turner just shook his head.

Harvey nodded, thoughtful. "I wonder, then—would you like to have a job?"

Hold your head up

Turner groaned as Black Malachi laid what had promised to be a companionable clasp on his upper arm. The clasp tightened into something sinister, a mad chiropractor's Vulcan death grip. Rays of *qi* fired upward from his shoulder blade, a couple of them scoring bull's-eyes on the vertebrae in his neck. The back of his head went numb, then began to tingle.

"The healing touch," he muttered through clenched teeth.

"You see, Ashenden," Black Malachi explained, as the treatment proceeded around his back and onto the opposite forearm, "all a king has got to worry about is functional gonads. How many children does Goldaster have?"

Turner frowned. It did seem like there was always a pack of kids around the house.

"Of course your kings are purely ceremonial. Whereas your actual leaders, your generals and field commanders and whatnot, have got to worry about *keeping their backs perfectly straight.*"

He lowered a single finger, punctuation point, to touch some minor energy-nexus in Turner's spine. A sound like a cat would make came out of the patient's mouth.

"Wonderful, wonderful." Black Malachi stood back, regarded the slouched and agonizing form of his housemate as though it were a sculpture-in-progress.

"What I'd like to know," said Turner, propping himself up on the divan in Malachi's dressing room; everything began hurting all at once, but this was not qualitatively different, only worse, than the usual barrage of distractions that attended Turner's efforts to speak—"what I'd like to know is, what does all this have to do with helping you study for your homeopathy test? That's what you wanted me for, right?"

The young practitioner made a clucking noise. "I am thinking of switching fields," he said, "to faith-healing. The laying on of hands. Particularly with reference to gynecologic disorders. Open your mouth."

Turner reflected, as a sweet-tasting yellow powder was sprinkled over his tongue, that people were forever offering him things to eat and drink, and that no good ever seemed to come of it. Though actually this particular treatment was rather pleasant. "What was that?" he asked.

"You must understand," said Black Malachi, constitutionally incapable of a direct reply, turning toward the window and then back again with great rhetorical flourish, "you must appreciate, Ashenden, that homeopathy is the only branch of medicine in which one seeks to cure by *poetic license.* Consider the jargon of the field. We speak of simile, of correspondence, of cycles and balance and natural progression, the transmutation of signs, reaching the inner person—in sum, the achievement of a cure is spoken of in the same terms as the perfection of a work of poetry. Organic wholes, Ashenden: we are speaking of fully realized, æsthetically satisfying patterns."

Turner at this point no longer cared so much about the yellow powder, which had a sickly aftertaste. Sensing which, probably, Black Malachi added, "Oh, it was just a bit of *Trillium.* A striking plant, Ashenden— the shape of a slender human form, that of an ascetic perhaps, only with no head inside the cowl. Exceedingly erect of stem, however, and aphrodisiacal to boot. Quite the horticultural metaphor, if you ask me, for the subject at hand."

Turner ran his tongue around the inside of his mouth.

"The *point* is," our medical theorist rambled on, "there is no such thing as a general remedy. One must proceed with particular attention to the *esse*, if you will, the individual *beingness* of the patient. A physician can only assist, only stimulate and strengthen, those properties which are already present. It is a great mistake to introduce anything new."

"So, no head?" said Turner. "An ascetic with no head?"—not surprised, exactly, but still a little aghast at the bald audacity of it.

Black Malachi smiled.

"A fixed level of resources," he pronounced, as though citing some famous authority. "There is a concept for you. Have you read the paper lately, Ashenden? You've created quite a stir, you know. SETTLING OUT PLANS SCUTTLED. Chief Admin Cites 'Fixed Level of Resources.' — Not enough money to build Camps and fight a popular uprising, too, is what he means. That's you, Ashenden: a popular uprising. Tell that to your pecker. No, but a useful concept, isn't it, for all that? Only so *much* and no more. So much money, so much energy, so much time. So much and counting down, too: that's the unspoken corollary. What a bleak view of things one simple phrase can imply! And an accurate one, despite what that idiot Hawkmoth has to say."

Turner shook his head. "I don't know what you're talking about," he lied. "It wasn't my fault. I only went up there to give Goldaster your message . . . I mean, Rodarch's . . . A-And, I *would* have, but he was already on his damned horse when I got there, but he *said* there'd be time to talk."

The fuzzy head shook earnestly. "Oh no, Ashenden—you misunderstand me. Everything went wonderfully well, I think. Don't you? You were so much better, so much more *efficient* than I could have dreamed. Now things are really starting to happen. I don't suppose you've been to town, have you? And seen the barricades? No, well, I haven't either, to tell the absolute truth. But I hear things, you know. Little voices."

Damn it, Malachi. Turner stood up, feeling lighter and somehow more self-assured. High on *qi*, maybe; tingling with *Trillium*. He said, "B-but, I was just . . . I recognized that guy, and there he was, driving away in my own spirit-burner, shooting at me with my own shockgun . . ."

"Yes, exactly—so you killed him." Black Malachi nodded in well-meant appreciation. "A master stroke. Really it was. Something we physicians strive for, so seldom with any success: the single dose, the pressure brought to bear at the precise location, the prophylaxis applied in the nick of time. I mean to say—one paltry multiple homicide, and look. The Stainless Steel Savior orders his flock to stay in their pens. The Horse King declares everything west of the Grim Dyke off-limits to migrants. And he puts *you* on his payroll. We are all *breathless*, Turner, to see what it is he expects you to do. We don't for a minute believe, do we, that 'just keep your ears open around town' nonsense. Whatever you may be, Ashenden, you are no common spy. No, I sense that this is the beginning of something grand—that your great work lies ahead of you!"

W-Wait a minute . . . work? The beginning? "Not for me," vowed Turner, terrified to ask what Malachi could possibly be talking about. "It's just a job. You know—for money. Since I'm probably about to get kicked out of school."

"Ha!" Happily nodding. "That's the spirit, old man. 'Just a job.' Ha!"

Malachi stepped closer, clapped us again—more gently this time—high on the arm. His grip was calming, now; maybe this was all part of getting ready for the test.

"We'll continue with *Trillium* for a week," he said, his manner brisk, the waiting room's full you know, see my nurse for an appointment. "Now, do be mindful of your posture. It is all-important, truly. The face, the expression, mean nothing, but for Lug's sake hold your fucking head up. It will make all the difference. But just wait, Ashenden. You'll find that I have a way of being right."

Out here

Some sort of party in progress. The music room filled with happy students, musicians, hangers-on. A banner displaying Malachi's Motto of the Month draped grandly from a wall of amplifying panels.

"ALL YOU WANT TO DO
IS BLATHER AND SMOKE."
(Attrib. to Capt Beefheart)

Vinny Hawkmoth, leader of the house band, had arrayed his equipment and his fellow performers—whose roles were at present reduced to checking connections and psychoanalyzing the software—for a demonstration of his latest synthetic acquisition, the horsehair bow.

"There's still only one instrument, of course," he explained, smiling apologetically, as though anyone were actually paying attention. Well, Turner may have been, halfheartedly. "It's not *quite* a violin yet. We've diddled with the waveforms to give you a sense of timbre differentiation—something cello-like, something viola-like—and then we've doubled up the original to make a quartet. They won't *quite* all play at the same time—you know, by a few thousandths of a second or so. We think this is important in building up the sonic image. But you'll see."

Black Malachi stepped forward, stubby arms pumping, on with the show, saying, "Fine, fine, thank you, thank you. Just tell them what they need to hear."

Hawkmoth smiled at Malachi like a father regarding his irksome but lovable progeny.

"The first item on the program," he said, "is the *Andante cantabile* from Tchaikowsky's famous quartet. The lyrics are by Pantera."

Oh come on, though Turner. Not lyrics, not really. He can't have . . .

The room was immediately filled with sound. Lush, believably string-and-bow-like chords from four invisible instruments. The most obvious problem was in fact its very flawlessness: the lack of tone color, the way the notes so cleanly saturated every corner of the listening space. Not bad work, though, for a couple of months. Turner began humming along, swaying. Lah dee dah dee dumm dumm . . . Very autumnal, wasn't it? The gushing emotions perhaps too *out there*, on-the-sleeve, as Nabokov had complained; but who cared about that in October?

Malachi paced through the opening bars, like a competitor warming up for, say, a pole vault. Then without warning he commandeered a chair, leapt on top of it, and sang with loud and precise intonation, as the melody began to repeat:

> Ashenden's our hero,
> Lend me your ear-o!
> I am his da-a-ddy, he's my boy.
>
> Ashenden's our agent,
> Cunning and pa-tient.
> I am so glad, he's our helpless toy.

Turner blanched. All the partygoers were reaching into their pockets, pulling out something . . . program bills? Sheet music? As Turner shrank, mortified, into the farthermost corner—not far enough, by half a mile or so—Vinny's instruments slid smoothly into the countertheme, and don't be paranoid about this but *the entire roomful of people began to sing along*.

> Don't worry 'bout
> Settling Out, Camps—
> Pass him the buck,
> Rodarch is fucked,
> Oh, wow!
>
> Don't argue for
> Social or-der—
> Goldaster's rich,
> Life is a bitch,
> And how!

Oh my God. The horrified student, the helpless toy, got the hell out of this bad dream as fast as his slow-motion limbs would ooze him through the crowd, even as Black Malachi's clear voice began another solo (*Ashenden's a cherry / Come girls, be merry . . .*) and the further amazing thing was, nobody paid the slightest attention to his departure. The band played on. Turner's physical being, what he had always naively thought of as his "real" self, was neither here nor there to these people. They were having it off with their memory of Turner Ashenden, the *idea* of him, the snowballing legend of the Headless Housemate, into whose cranial void uncaring narrators poured their plots.

All of it—laughter, music, party streamers, paper crumpled, pipes passed from hand to hand, new chapters in Turner's saga being written and sung even as he staggered down the hallway and into the maze of banana plants—all of that faded slowly from earshot, dissolving into incredibility. Perhaps, probably, it had never really happened at all. Almost certainly it hadn't. Malachi had slipped some arcane *extractum* into the punchbowl, and everyone was enjoying a collective third-eye slide slow.

Nearly breathless, Turner reached the kitchen and found (further proof of the hallucinatory nature of these events) the *omphalos* was empty. I mean, that was *really* fictitious, right? A party going on, and nobody in the kitchen.

Oh . . . except for.

"Hi, Turner," said a tall, sheep-eyed girl—a walk-on from an earlier show, some parallel drama running at the same theater, more naturalistic than *The Headless Housemate*.

"Oh. Hi." Turner paused before the work-island. "Cervina."

There, he thought, addressing the hidden playwright. *Hear that?* He had even, he was pretty sure, gotten the name right. The tall girl and Turner exchanged smiles: surprised, rather pleased at the dimensional crossover that enabled them to perceive each other, made it possible for their characters to speak. (Glance quickly toward the curtain, though. We don't want the audience in on this.)

Cervina stepped away from the huge refrigerator—a separate room, practically. MAINTAIN GRADIENTS: an earlier monthly dictum. Life itself, Malachi believed, depended on lively distinctions.

It flashed on Turner, all of a sudden, that he wasn't acting right, something was expected of him here that he wasn't coming up with. Like, a cue had been given but he wasn't stammering out his lines. Cervina stood uncomfortably in the middle of the room, the center of the elaborate set.

"Well," she said, "I guess I'll . . ."

"Cervina," said Turner. Oh, giving it a little too much emphasis, taking too hasty a step into the lights; but the big girl exhaled gratefully, looked at him with the sheep-eyes as wide as they ever got, I guess. We blinked at each other. "So, um . . . what are you doing? In the kitchen, I mean."

She looked away; Turner took a breath; we got our vibes a little better in sync.

"Quite a party, huh?" he said now more smoothly.

"Aren't they all?" She smiled. "Blackie really knows how to throw them."

"Yeah. He really does."

Something barely perceptible was flickering, some shutter opening and closing a couple hundred times a second, a rate of vibration which according to laboratory experiment only schizophrenics can perceive. It was the natural movement of the eye: the ceaseless oscillation without which there would be no vision, necessary to prevent blurring, retinal burn-in. Pretty weird. The cool sharp light of the kitchen bulbs made the features of Cervina's face seem too angular, too clearly delineated. It did flatter, though, her sand-toned skin. Her eyebrows were thin and naturally arching, without being plucked.

They came a bit closer together, following a subconscious prompt, a primordial memory of clearing or cave, distance across the fire on the old savannah, our long-lost home, until they were close enough to (for example) pass a shank-bone of the week's unlucky mastodon. Thank heavens you don't normally have to think about this.

"Turner," Cervina said seriously, "I don't know if I can stand it anymore."

He nodded. He actually understood.

"God, I—" She turned away. She was holding, why hadn't we noticed before, a plate and a cup.

"No, don't . . ." Turner stepped around her, not really getting closer but coming more definitely into her egg-shaped node of personal space. With a bit of good-natured roughness, elbowing camaraderie, he said, "What's *this*, now—raiding the cookie jar?"

She smiled through damp eyes. Arms raised slowly, exhibiting their loot. "Oh, I know it's silly. But I just . . . you know, milk and brownies, somehow . . ."

In some plane of meaning they nodded, shared a laugh at it. In Black Malachi's province, the gleaming kitchen, they each took another edgewise step to face the dark back-stairs door.

"Is it cold out?" Turner wondered. "I mean, I wonder if it's too cold to sit out on the roofdeck."

Cervina nodded, thoughtful, grateful for a decision to ponder. "We could try, I guess," she said after a moment.

It was very cold, of course. October. Turner, afraid to break the spell, was out of breath because he had felt the need to *run* to his room for a blanket, and back. A miracle, Cervina was still sitting there, hugging her arms, and Reality did not seem to have moved very much.

"Thanks," she said. Seeming older now. Tucking the blanket around her. Delicate fingers, long slender arms. Her profile by starlight, diffused windowlight, enhanced by memory and something else we didn't want directly to think about, took on classical or archetypal contours. The nose was almost regal, when you looked at it close by. The eyes not so much small as, as languid. Yeah. With swooping lashes.

"You can have some of this," she said, meaning the blanket. Lifting an edge of it. As we drew nearer in our adjacent chairs, dragged up next to the railing where we could look down at such lights as there still were, those days, along the road to Candlemas. Somewhere down there was the University: never truly a home, but at least, for a year or two, something solid, a thing to hold onto. Now that too was slipping away, falling into the darkness of the past.

Turner pointed at something, nothing much. "It all looks so tiny from up here."

Cervina passed him a cookie. She said, "I know it really sounds . . . trite. But I don't know. Sometimes I feel like all I want in the world is for things to be just, normal and like, *ordinary*. You know, like I always thought they were supposed to be. I mean, I love Blackie and I love the University, and all this . . ." She gestured around, encompassing many things, the world above and the world below; kindly though, bless her, sparing Turner. She turned to look at him, urging upon him some agreement, some pact. "But sometimes, I mean, it just seems so . . . *weird*."

Turner, of course, agreed so profoundly that he couldn't begin to talk about it. He felt as though Cervina had just reached a lower plateau of the mountain on whose top he'd been stranded for years now. They sat in moody silence for a while, their bodies under the blanket forgotten, while the stale smell of charcoal and the sound of something down in the valley, people-noises, a faint chiming bell, reminded them of an imaginary home. They shared the milk glass: brother and sister sitting in the back yard long past bedtime, wishing someone would come looking for them, discover them gone from their rooms, shoo them inside where they belong.

"But it's not going to happen, is it?" Cervina said, just as though Turner had spoken, which maybe . . . She said, "We're really just *out here*, aren't we? Out here by ourselves."

Turner, the older brother, the hero, in silent dignity nodded. He said, "But it's okay."

She nodded back. She wanted to believe him. He understood that. He took her hand.

They went back to Turner's room and undressed in absolute silence. Twining wistfully, they made love until very late, each lost in private wishes, tangled in unfamiliar arms.

STANDING
UP

1

Not ready for daytime

Walking in cool light
Turner alone in forests of winter
Exhaling frost
Pass softly through these halls of boxwood
Around him dark
Footsteps
Dry on cobbles, white then brown
So many of my lost countrymen

Gray seasons move around
(Tulips, he thinks
Red—), turning
Wake me out of this, this slow

And after the cold remembers
Deep ground dead robins watch fobs c-
Coats and,
Meadows slumping off to streambanks
Someone waits for him down there
Cervina . . .
No, it's—

Over the bent grass
Thin limbs, palely

Wrapped in the merest fabric
Desire
Maridel
Coming to him
Think of a sound, any word, dissuade her
Gosh hey you're so young, you're only

. . . then, like, Turner remembers it's only this dream, see? He squeezes his eyes back tight and his cock is standing up, swelling to fill the space between them, him and the girl, and what the hell, he draws her closer, her warm hair flows around him, he embraces the dreamsoft skin of her breasts, small loaves, presses himself between tender thighs. She moves to him, blends with him, the girl-smell of her like something green, drifts down against the earth, draws him down to her falling and falling, till he can somehow circle her while embracing, watching, kissing her the while. Her pubis lightly furred and innocent, pretty, like it was nothing *sexual*, see, only Turner's blood is pounding in his ear and his eyes are getting blurred, his hunger falling across her like a net . . .

Turner. Please, I—

Whoops, too late. Can't stop now.

As his ejaculation gushes away, draining him of illusion, Turner realizes that he has been lying, in the dream, and I mean at the *very end* of it, with the naked gold-skinned boy Tristin. He takes a panicky gasp of air, pushes him away, stupid brutal attack against his pillow, disgusted, as tears form in Tristin's eyes. . . .

A mountain, maybe

Somewhere we could stand and look down from. The old house mean and impervious behind us; all the world, a green valley, so neatly spread out below. Spring, sailing through the high branches of the tulip poplars. It was only in spring that the real, the unbearable part started. That is not over now, even now, no matter how far you've gone.

We can see the whole thing from here. This valley and the next, the life we were leading and all the others. The endurance, and the fragility. We see westward, the wasted plains; eastward the crumbled cities. There is Candlemas, cradled between them, its venerable University standing, hanging on, like a great inturning creature without eyes, without reason or fear. Only memory. Damp corridors echo with a million remembered footsteps—even, Turner, your own. A trail in the dust, leading back.

We were creatures out of the past, then: our lives, our struggles, were pieces of that ancient pattern. The crazy-quilt. Poetry of ages threaded our brains together, pulled thin by now, unraveling. But it was our only language; we could not think but in those old incantations. We could only sing the songs we knew. Somewhere along the path, the urge to create, to bring forth the new, had died in us. Look at me, if you doubt it. Your redactor.

Song-names, place-names, person-names, everything alluded, nothing anymore was only itself. They curled, they interpenetrated, each began where some other had left, or been torn, off. Spirals overlapped spirals; the way in jumbled with the way out. (Think of Black Malachi's never-quite-realized "mandala." A *feeling of enclosure*, he said.) All the tunes we knew ran together like the confused, deafening, heartfelt and in its own blurry way, heartbreaking drink-up chorus in a crowded bar. And everything, every image, each allusion, every breath and syllable of the poem, dangled somewhere, tenuous, no longer bright, its colors bleeding into the others—and receiving their blood in turn, but fainter and weaker now—along that fraying thread.

Listen again, though. Listen back: you must hear it now. A rumbling. Up the great double-belts, the old routes of commerce, the miles of broken paving stone—a low sound, a throb, the very earth rising and falling beneath it—there was a new thing moving in the world. I was not a historian; none of us then were. We were History, I think, or its captives: unreflective, unselfconscious, whatever else you might have thought. The greater thing of which Rodarch was only the front-man, the embodiment, was little known and barely comprehensible to us. Even its names, its slogans, most of which I've forgotten, told us nothing, for they were woven of some unfamiliar fiber, a new synthetic, that might as well have come from an alien star. "The New Reason," we would mouth aloud, and our poor patterned minds would leap to *Reason for what? To live? To buy government paper?* But of course that wasn't the point at all. It was a self-sufficient formula, something none of us were used to: a concept without association. We preferred "The Stainless Steel Savior" because it made sense to us; it sprang from our commonly held ideas, our abundant store of memories; we thought it ironic, or witty. Anyway it was part of the pattern, *our* pattern, our culture—ourselves—tired and mean and worn-to-death, maybe, but still. The stuff our brains were made of.

Rodarch himself, though, was . . .

Well, a problem. For you, Turner, more than anyone. You felt you *knew* him, that he was recognizable somehow, while everyone else—those who looked to him as a champion, and those who found him an impediment, even an enemy—everyone at least agreed that his coming, after the decades of Dissolution, was a turning point. Which is to say, something new. A new puzzle-piece to be fit somehow into our old, old pattern. Everyone thought that but you. And of course me, who knew nothing, who barely mattered.

But standing up now. And looking down. From our windswept vantage, our metaphoric mountaintop. Side-by-side, mind-upon-mind, two-against-Time—losing badly, of course, but still hanging on—I am sorry, but I mean to press this. We can get the sense of things more accurately from up here; at any rate more distinctly. All the gradients are preserved. We see smoke hanging in the northern sky, bloody great clouds of it, from where the riots had come, for once, in autumn, the time of least hope. We feel the snow, blown by a careless wind to lie in drifts along the barricades. We smell the fear of people called, absurdly, "ordinary"—fear of the chaos, the refugees . . . but equally fear of the new order. The New Reason. The blue-clad bringers of law. And fear of their ponderous, plain-spoken Superman, who thought people were "ordinary," and that he was ordinary too, and who had been given, or given himself, that most ridiculously drab honorific, Chief Administrator—a *token*, Turner, listen to me, of the colorless, allusionless, self-sufficient, calm, and above all *rational* language that was right then, that very winter (while you worried and partied and slept through your final morning classes), being forged.

But I know, you doubt that. As you doubted everything. As you doubted, even, while you stood up with your eyes wide open and looked around at what was happening to your life, or stared into your mirror, that you were really *there*. As though you, the deepest Turner, were your own, your only, ghost.

Laying plans

Turner stepped cautiously through the door of his bathroom. I mean, you could never really be sure, could you? He stood in the shower, looking at the soap for a moment as though awaiting instructions. His stomach smelled of sperm. A headless ascetic, he thought. Flow the bounteous water. Cleanse me, for I have been impure. Give me a fucking break.

While out there, *out here*, in the jolly wide world, even as we splashed and quietly, cautiously, began singing a little tune, plans were being made for us. The twisty little path leading out toward our future was being dusted off. A few yellow bricks were being inserted beside the native sickly pink ones—just to encourage us, you know. While we blithely, like a perfect idiot, crooned:

> "I think it's just about time
> You realized
> That we're not gonna make it alo-one.
> You've got to

[snare drum]

> "Change your mind
> And compromise

[synth. strings]

> "Or at least pick up the pho-one,

[ensemble]

> "Or at least *pick up the phone*."

Now there was an interesting problem or question here, which is whether Turner, who had never heard a telephone ring, though the Solar Temple had at least ten of them, each believed to be in working order, could really (as a singer, an interpreter) bring the proper tension to any line that invoked this instrument. Could he manage to convey, for example, the sense of irritation with which an earlier generation had infused the phrase "pick up the phone"? This question was the very thing that Turner was thinking about as he walked (unsuspectingly, a bit later) into Malachi's bedchamber, while simultaneously digging around in his left ear to determine the cause of this really strange itching that was going on there, possibly due to water having gotten in as a result of the little canals opening up while he sang in the shower. In some part of his mind he was wondering about this, too. From the mountaintop, one is omniscient; *we know these things.*

So Turner.

"So Turner," said Black Malachi [*You see?*], looking up from a desk that Turner had never noticed before, a desk he would have sworn had been dragged in not five minutes ago, plopped into its conspicuous location—centered before a large east-facing window, from which the sunshine had long departed, leaving behind a nice long-shot of the University, the Medical College in fact, a picturesque tickler-file—and covered at due speed, yet still in keeping with Malachi's distinctive spirit of Tidiness Despite It All, with stacks of papers and notebooks and medical tomes, writing implements pigeonholed in slots, a gram-to-ounce conversion chart, the *Quik-Reference Materia Medica*, and a priceless and unbelievable, guaranteed 100 percent accurate, limited-edition bootleg copy of the final Homeopathy exam.

"So Turner," Black Malachi said, his eyes floating innocently above all this, while Turner paused with the first seeds of disbelief germinating in the dampness of his ear canals—"just the person I've been looking for!"

"Malachi," said Turner. Captain of his soul, et al. "Where did that desk come from?"

"Hm?" The studious teenager, his face just the right shape to model as a cherub, except for all that hair, frowned distractedly. "Oh, it's um . . . been here. But listen, Turner. If you're going to be out running errands for Goldaster today, there is something I need you to do."

"Malachi—" Turner circled, taking in this alarming new sight with minute attentiveness "—is that a copy of the *final Homeopathy exam?*"

The hairy cherub glanced down. "Why, bless me. I believe it is. And just in time for Beltaine. Ashenden, would you quit stalking about like that? You are giving me vertigo. Here: try that chair by the window."

Turner flopped down, so perplexed he failed to notice that the chair was also new, factory fresh, even smelled of the chemicals used to tan its leather. But who paid any attention to chairs, really. Black Malachi directed a round-hand pen at his housemate.

"But there's a rub," he said. "You see, I have not yet managed to arrange for all aspects of the examination—the written, the oral, and the practical—to be administered to me specially here in the safety of my home."

"Oh for God's sake, Malachi."

"Please! Do not make light of this. It is extremely important, you see, that I become a certified practitioner as soon as may be. One never knows when the need for a physician might arise."

"And you don't think you can just, like, go to class and take the test the way everybody else does?"

"Ashenden, your lack of sensitivity surprises me. Truly it does. But I shall overlook it, as always, in light of my high expectations for you. Now pay attention, please. I shall outline my plan."

Turner paid attention, mainly because he was still curious about the desk, and all. There were no clues to be had, though, from Malachi's careful laying-out of the most ridiculous proposition Turner had ever heard.

"That's the most ridiculous—" he started to say.

Black Malachi dismissed any and all objections by belching loudly, leaning back from the desk, and scratching his belly. "There only remains," he said, "the task of obtaining the explosives and planting the charge. We will then *swoop* to the scene, utilizing the large motor vehicle which you will, as I have mentioned, obtain, and transport the dazed and bleeding but not *too* terribly bunged-up members of the Examining Board here, to our own modest facilities. Whereupon I shall employ the latest methodology to set them all, within hours, aright. I shall then accept the certificate which will be offered by acclamation, and my patients shall be discharged. As a fallback measure, however, you must remember to arrange for an extra-large delivery of food and drugs, both therapeutic and recreational, in case there should be a, shall we say, protracted inpatient visit."

Turner was even more than usually aghast. "You don't mean you would actually hold them *hostage*. A-And I mean, *drug* them, and—"

"Pish-tosh." Black Malachi wagged his hand, as though shaking something off of it. "We will see that they are all quite comfortable, and that they arrive as quickly as possible at an unprejudiced decision. Very well, then—let us move on to logistics."

Turner shook his head. "No. I mean, forget it." He made for the door, impressed with his own unusual firmness. Reaching it, he paused. Malachi said nothing; still said nothing. Turner dared to glance back across his shoulder. The stout youth sat placidly, pawing through a stack of books on his desktop.

"There's no way," said Turner, beginning to wonder if his voice were actually audible.

Black Malachi smiled. "Ah, here you are," he said, which gave Turner the idea that maybe he had blinked out of existence for a moment there, but his jolly housemate went on: "So tell me, Ashenden—have you seen your friends at the Bad Dinners Institute lately?"

Turner scowled. As a matter of fact he had managed to put all that out of his mind. At least until an embarrassing but thank God private episode half an hour ago. He shook his head. Then firmly, since Malachi did not seem to be paying attention, he said, "No, I haven't."

"Well, then," said Malachi, pulling a book from the heap on his desk, "let me give you this. Just something light, you know—to refresh you between courses of *Miss Mackintosh*, or whatever starchy thing it is you're reading these days."

It was a narrow, black-bound volume, much more battered than Malachi's medical texts. Turner came hesitantly forward, feeling that he was being lured into something, seduced . . .

GRAILNET USERS MANUAL, the cover said. Sic.

"You may find," said Malachi, "that you can't put it down."

Suspecting a dumb and obvious trick, Turner tried putting it down right away. It sat looking drab, all bent up at the corners, on Malachi's desk. Oh, all right. He picked it up again.

"I'll be straight with you," he tried to say very firmly. "Book or no book, I'm not going to help you kidnap a bunch of medical professors. No matter what."

"You'll be *straight with me?*" The small eyes like a bird's—a Pantera family trait—shone up in delight. "Why, how delightfully idiomatic! Where did you learn that one, Ashenden? It is so rich in associations, and all of them inappropriate."

Turner squeezed the USERS MANUAL and turned tail out of the room. *Turned tail*, he thought with chargrin. Thank God he can't read my mind. On second thought, glancing back a last time furtively from the doorway, he fretted *Though you can't be too sure*. . . .

Black Malachi, up to something, sat behind his desk smiling narrow-eyed, peacefully, as though his work for the morning was done.

Not to mention daffodils

"Well, here it is," said Harvey Goldaster.

He juggled a walking stick from one hand to the other, patting alternate pockets of his coat. Aprils around here have been too warm for tweed, really, since all this greenhouse business got started, but some people insist on dressing like the folks in the pictures. You know, *H. Tyrone Goldaster, Founding President* on the clubhouse wall, that sort of thing. Turner's mind was racing in idle as he tried not to concentrate on the hand (muscular, maybe from squeezing tennis balls) now pulling a crinkly lump of paper from an inside pocket, near the heart, where H. Tyrone had probably kept his "checkbook."

"Here," said Harvey Goldaster. "Look at this."

Turner did not look.

Leaning over, Harvey unfolded the paper in a series of dry crackles on the grassy hill. Aprils around here are too breezy for this sort of thing; the wind kept hiking it up at the edges.

"So what do you think?" said Harvey. Still companionable, not yet catching on.

Turner was staring away, anywhere, up at the grape arbor, down at the neatly managed woods that someone else might have called a Deer Park. Unlike Black Malachi, Harvey had no interest in naming things. He simply wanted to own them.

Turner said, "The redbuds are already coming out, isn't that ridiculous? I mean, by May there's going to be nothing left."

"What's the matter?" said Harvey. Peering quizzically. "You look a little spaced-out today. Has Pantera been slipping something in your lemonade?"

Oh no. Turner was spaced-out, for sure, but it went back much farther than that. He shook his head.

The thing was, he already knew what was printed on the crinkly piece of paper. The *poster*, if we're going to be specific. He had seen it and studied it and memorized it, pixel by pixel, this poster and its thousandfold clones, since they started popping up on trees and abandoned buildings and rusted-out railway cars. You could even see them behind the fences of the Settling Out Camps.

There was going to be a rally, the posters said.

It was scheduled for the first of May. Now talk about your flaming symbols: here you had at least two distinct sets to choose from, each with its blurry pile of historico-political overlays.

It was going to be sponsored by an organization called Students Against Superstition (an odd, Hubbardite usage, from L. *superstitio*, "that which stands over"—you're supposed to imagine something that casts a shadow over the present day, as for instance an old-fashioned habit or belief).

And it was going—this is the real pisser—it was going to be the first appearance in the valley, the first public appearance, of Chief Administrator Rodarch. (From the pictures they'd seen, everybody figured Rodarch must have a terrific public presence, real charisma, but nobody could remember having seen or heard him, in person, before. So he was invited, had been invited over and over again, and finally on May Day he was going to show up.)

Turner—remember?—was shaking his head. He said, "I know all about it."

"Ah, good," said Harvey Goldaster. He raised his riding boot, freeing the poster to float like a G.E.V. down the hill. In this age of broken and dying machines, we look to mechanical things for our poetry. Harvey said, "So you've had a chance to give the matter some thought."

"Fuck no," said the poet of the shower stall. Kicking at the poster now out of reach, well on its way to reunion with the pines from which it came. "I haven't thought about it, and I'm not going to."

He faced Harvey with the closest thing to ferocity he could manage. "I don't know where you all got this idea that I'm this . . . this kind of, rabble-rouser or something. But like I keep telling everybody, I've got nothing against Mr Rodarch. I mean, I've actually *met* the guy, and he's just sort of . . ."

Well, you couldn't say "ordinary," really, could you? Was there such a thing as "superordinary?"

Harvey smiled and nodded. If he were Malachi, he would have clapped us on the shoulder. Instead, like the old team-captain, he said, "It's good to see you standing up for yourself, young man. It's about damned time."

He took a step in the direction of the manor, but not by way of actually going anyplace. He struck a far-seeing pose—staring off into the valley, *his* valley, over the pale green shoots of meadow grasses, the wrinkly stigmata of dogwoods. You can read the past there (one could imagine him thinking): you can read the future. Quick, somebody, call a sculptor.

"Actually, Turner," he said, "all I wanted was to ask your opinion. You've been a great help to me, these last few months—you really seem to understand the point-of-view of the average student."

Sure, thought Turner. From years of successful imitation.

"So I was wondering. Perhaps you could give me the benefit of your thoughts. How do you suppose Rodarch will be received by the people at the University? What will he say to them? How will they respond? Will there be, do you think, some kind of . . . of call to arms?"

Turner squinted, trying to see through the various layers of the Machiavellian onion-peel. What was in the middle, he had no idea.

"Look, Mr Goldaster," he said. "I'm sorry I snapped at you there. But see, I really don't know much about politics. I mean . . ."

Harvey was listening courteously, watching him, nodding—the Debate Team, that's what he would be the captain of. *Keep talking*, said his whiskey-colored eyes.

"Well," said Turner, "I guess basically, people are sympathetic about all the problems back in the, um . . . the places where the Settlers come from. Overcrowding and residual toxicity and all that. On the other hand I think most of them—students, I mean—are from *out here*, from the valley, you know, or farther west. So they tend to be worried, also, about the fate of your farmers and your small property owners and like that, who've been living here all along and basically haven't done anything wrong. With all this Settling Out. The sudden displacement, and all. I mean, some people, I guess a lot of people, really *like* it that there's no real law out here, that things just pretty much happen the way they happen. So they're a little suspicious because . . . well, it's the Settling Out *Laws*, right? Which kind of implies certain things."

Harvey Goldaster—evidently in the mood to be unpredictable—reached down among the moist pulpy grass stems and snatched a buttercup. He held it close, in front of his nose, crossing his eyes to look at it. He said, "It sounds like a tough audience to work. For Rodarch, that is."

Turner cleared his throat. "Yeah, but."

The two men stared at the flower. It was pure chromatic yellow, almost startling in its clarity. When they still made weed-killers, you didn't see too many buttercups, especially on this side of the valley.

Turner [What the hell—he asked me] finished his sentence. "Yeah, but they don't like *you* much, either. I mean, or any of the Old Souls. And if it comes down to a choice between Rodarch taking over the valley, or the Souls hanging on—which *is* what it might come down to, right? —then, see, at least the Settling Out Laws represent an honest effort to do something, to start dealing with all these problems. To, like, get things organized again."

Harvey Goldaster let the buttercup slip from his hands, forgotten. "That's the problem, then, is it?"

Turner nodded.

"People hate us," Harvey said.

"I don't . . . Not *hate*, I don't think. But let's say, you're hard to sympathize with. People don't mind thinking that, you know, Harvey Goldaster is going to lose his bank, or those people from the East are going to be crawling all over his horse farm."

"But damn it, there's more *to* it than that. It's a complicated system, we're just a little part of it. It's an ecology—an economic ecology—with interconnections, complicated relationships, that have evolved over a long period of time. You can't just charge in, no matter *what* your intentions are—"

Turner said, "Don't tell me." Shrugging. "Like I said, I'm not much into politics."

"It's not *politics*. It's a question of social evolution. Of natural law."

"It may be," said Turner, who was beginning to think you could learn to like this standing-up-for-yourself business, once you got the hang of it, "but still. I mean, let's face it. People like to see rich people unhappy."

Harvey Goldaster opened his eyes—like, They do?

Turner went on, "So the way I see it, as long as it comes down to this High Noon thing, between you and Rodarch, *you've* got problems."

Harvey nodded, very slowly. You could hear the tumblers dropping in some locked cabinet of his mind.

"Ashenden," he said, back to the team-captain routine, "I think you're absolutely right."

I am? Turner felt all of a sudden uncomfortable.

Harvey dipped his head, as though he had just called the team into a huddle. "Okay," he said, with a special smile for his favorite athlete, his star performer, "let's think about this May Day thing, then. Maybe there's something we can do."

"No," said Turner. "I mean, no sir. I mean, I've enjoyed working for you and you've been very generous, but I don't want to get involved in this."

The team captain nodded. *Sure, kid,* his winning smile said. *We all get the jitters before a big game.*

"I'm not kidding," said Turner. But he felt weak, like, and a little dizzy, as though all this standing up for himself was wearing him down.

A room of one zone

Turner's apprehension became concentrated into a neuromuscular knot somewhere in his upper intestines. It was something like the dread and impatience you feel before asking somebody for a date. Something like that; but did people really ask one another for "dates" anymore, or was this just another cultural stand-over (a *superstition*, see?) that had gotten into Turner's head from some book? You couldn't really be sure.

He stayed at home, which helped a little. But spring is a time when things are in the air. News of the preparations underway in Candlemas drifted west to the Solar Temple: bleachers being erected on the lawn, more barbed wire rolled out, aging janitors drilled in the use of firearms. Turner's stomach got worse and worse as the day, May Day, drew nearer. Maybe he should have done History instead of Literature. Some History professor, Turner heard at a party, was minimizing the importance of the Chief Administrator, placing him "in perspective." Turner's own perspective was badly skewed. Maybe he was developing an ulcer from drinking Malachi's homemade beer. As April dragged on, new posters were placed on top of old ones. A topic was announced: *Toward an Orderly Future*. Turner thought about the gigantic empty tent, hammock strung from its centerposts, floorcloth painted in spirals. A salty taste seemed to linger on his tongue. Windows popped open all over the Solar Temple, temperature-activated, but Turner continued to sweat. Alone in his room, beneath a photograph of Mike Harrison, a famous mountain-climber, he curled up in bed and started to read everything within arm's distance, at once.

He read *South Wind*, a fantasy. It moved very slowly while Turner's mind wanted to move very fast. The effect might have been therapeutic, but he couldn't get into it. He cut out the yellowing art deco illustrations to pin on the wall, then mislaid them.

He read *Gravity's Rainbow*, and "alternate history" type of book. It made him wish he were a polyglot, a world-traveler. But he was nobody. But at least he understood that better now.

He read *Ada*, a science-fictional novel set on a planet called Antiterra, where there is no electricity. Imagine that. Early on, there is a great sex scene. Later the plot loses energy, or the characters turn into metaphors, or something. Turner put it at the bottom of the stack, to try again.

At last he picked up GRAILNET USERS MANUAL. The writing was very bad. It told about some imaginary system or network whereby you could be sitting in your room in, say, Ladoga (an actual town), and you could plug somehow into this "real time experiential matrix" where you would encounter, um, "virtual personalities" which were generated by "a holologic, cross-inferential sampling of observable traits" . . . but wait, that was only the beginning:

> The user may compare this to the encoding/decoding process utilized in such analog digital media as 8 mm tapes wherein the originating signal is sampled at a high rate with the resulting

stream of data bits being stored on the media for later reprocessing and playback. Important features to note are—

• There is *no interpretation or out-selection* involved in the initial encoding phase. Data is gathered across the entire sampling range without regard to substantive content.

• There *may be inadvertent coloration* of the data during the decoding phase, analogous to the digital to analog (playback) process wherein the outgoing data stream is subject to sampling error or other hardware or software-related bias, or to further distortion by projection equipment. In this respect the system is not different in kind, from the results often obtained from normal entertainment media.

For this reason, we strongly recommend that only the standard configured terminal available from GRAILNET be utilized in these sessions, as we have found it to be bias free within the normal range of human perceptibility. If you're "amazed at the friends you're having on your trip" then you better check your equipment.

Turner flipped pages. Certain passages seemed to have been drafted by a different hand.

It has been a dream of generations of Psychic Explorers. To walk a mile in another's footsteps! To see ourselves as others see us! Simply by joining in good faith and open heart with our fellows through GRAILNET, we can all become participants in the drama of the collective consciousness, exploring the Great Mystery together, watching from our front-row seat as the myriad divergent *onta*—each operating within the comforting illusion of "personality"—meld into the one true Identity.

Hmm. Something odd about that last bit . . . familiar, you know? . . . but this was a pretty ordinary feeling these days and Turner just tucked it away somewhere, maybe the same place he'd tucked the art deco illustrations. He kept flipping the pages of the MANUAL. He learned about band widths and sampling rates, about conference jumping and system protocols. He browsed transcripts and examined fuzzy black-and-whites of "typical online gestalts." Through it all he felt he was missing some subtle but crucial linkage that would tie it all together, make it *mean* something. He got to the end of the MANUAL and hadn't found it, so he started over from about midway through, where the style began to change. He thought, I may never punctuate properly again.

In one of the photographs two men stood close together in a murky room. They were dressed in period costumes of about forty years ago. *Eye-to-eye*, Turner thought at first glance, but when he looked more closely it appeared that in fact they were looking slightly past each other, each man staring at something out of range of the camera, their lines of sight crisscrossing in the middleground. This symmetrical oddity—the two figures standing so close, yet seeming to ignore one another—gave Turner an uncomfortable sensation, a sense of things being out of place, and even *that* felt uncomfortably familiar. The caption under the photograph read:

Prof. Drode, developer of the GRAILNET hardware, appears online with a System user. Can *you* tell which is the onta?

Turner scowled. Enough of this shit is enough. He flipped to the back of the MANUAL, to the Glossary. Naturally *onta*, the key to everything, was not listed. *Online* was discussed at great length, as for some reason was *ontology* ("The study of the possible existence of numinous entities"—???). He extracted his finger from the Glossary and was about to do likewise with the thumb that was holding his place at the picture, and possibly toss the book out the temperature-activated window, when some faint impulse—we're talking about the tiniest squiggle of a thought, here—caused him to look one last time at the photograph. And this time he saw something.

It was in the immediate foreground, the very bottom of the picture, nearly cropped into oblivion. It was part of someone's hand, the hint of an uncaptioned third person, throwing the mirror image off-balance. Turner strained his eyes. The fingertips seemed to be holding something, pulling or squeezing some . . .

But of course. It was a joystick. Its cheap glimmery handle shone between the thumb and index finger of the ghostly hand. Recognition caused a faint electric tingle to buzz in Turner's palm, the wisdom of the body, a memory more sure than any yet managed by the mind. Turner rolled over, bringing the book closer to the reading lamp.

Meld into the one true Identity, his mind played back.

And in a different voice, multi-tracked over the first: *We call it Identities*.

Well, what do you know, he thought. Malachi was right again. I can't put the goddamned thing down.

A face in the crowd

Oh, all right. All right. But only for a minute.

Early on May Day afternoon, a little past the starting time of the rally, Turner managed to kid himself for *just long enough* that if he stepped out the door of the Solar Temple, like maybe for a breath of fresh air—as though anything blowing in from the Poison Belt could compete with Malachi's greenhouses and negative-ion pumps—then maybe he would just stroll through the garden or something, not succumb to this dire attraction that was tugging at him, urging him down the hill toward the green open sward of the University. Toward an Orderly Future.

But you know how it is. In a minute there is time. Turner threaded his way outward from the living quarters (by habit now avoiding the Bug Walk) through the banana jungle and out the double-locked front door. Where he could hear the public address system pumping waves into the spring air—which did feel fresh, even if it had had the oxygen kicked out of it—and then of course it was too late. His feet followed the thumping of Destiny's drum. The best he could manage was to distract himself with passing scenery.

You saw so much more, walking. Overgrown orchards choked with broomsedge ran up the hills, their fences knocked down, their arthritic apple trees nobby and hunched. Gray cottages hunkered down in mounds of honeysuckle, porches crammed with the trash of student squatters. From a field, half-wild horses watched Turner pass, placid but wary. Did they sense something? Turner looked down, at the furrow of grass between tire-ruts, where cowslips and dandelions bloomed in complementary tones of yellow. What cowslips were doing here, on this side of the ocean, Turner couldn't have told you. Unless maybe they had escaped from the pages of, say, *Jude the Obscure*, a real Ashenden theme-book, and gotten naturalized. It could happen, couldn't it? At the gate of the University, he slipped through the gamut of opposing security forces—the Newport blue and the lumberjack plaid—without being noticed at all, without even being *ignored*, which was convenient under the circumstances but awfully disheartening. I mean, suppose I were an assassin or something.

But you're not, don't you remember? You're—

All right, damn it. Turner the Obscure made his way through the sparse crowd just inside the grounds, students holiday-eyed, waving wine bottles, tossing wadded-up leaflets, laughing in the sun, so innocent, so much younger than I've felt for a couple of years now. He bent to retrieve a fallen paper ball . . . unrolled it . . . and there was the classical profile. The dignified chin-line. Roman nose. Eyes blurred a bit in this cheap reproduction, but you could imagine them there: zinc-gray, unblinking, steady as machinery. From over a wall, bouncing off adjacent buildings, a voice that seemed eager to reassure, like the operation was successful ma'am, your son will be fine, spoke casually to the multitudes.

". . . should be remembered," the voice said, "that personnel detailed to permanent or semipermanent billets in districts classified as unpacified enjoy the full protection of regional or broader-scale law. Thus all reports . . ." (a few words here and there lost to multipath interference) ". . . in local-area scenarios will be investigated fully, and consequent actions directed toward ensuring nonrecurrence. Where instigation or exacerbation by local-area authorities is suspected . . ."

Turner stared at the dull green leaves of an azalea, clinging to the last rose-flushed petals of its flowering. The ground beneath was carpeted in pink, dirty trudged-over pink, like the bathroom of an abandoned cottage. He thought, Is Rodarch really saying these things? I mean, is he actually standing there, somewhere on the other side of the wall, and *talking* like this? Or is this just a speech—hashed out by a committee, run off on blue-gray paper—which he's dutifully regurgitating?

". . . indices of activity by the local business community," the voice droned on, "will naturally be monitored for compliance." (Had the subject changed? Was there a subject at all? What does it mean, Uncle Rodarch, *Toward an Orderly Future?*) "During the implementation period, there may also be certain controlled classes of vehicular activity, and although this may necessitate a reconfiguration of area transportation patterns, it is strongly believed that the resulting enhancement . . ."

Turner moved past a row of administrative outbuildings toward the worn-out edge of the lawn. The crowd of students, farmers, novelty-seekers grew thicker. Despite the long cryptic phrases, and the echo-chamber effect of old brick walls, it seemed to Turner that there was nothing especially distinctive about the Chief Administrator's voice—nothing to set it off from the random chatter around it. But maybe that was the idea, the symbolic message. The flat and archetypal face was just another among the couple thousand faces in the crowd. His words were no more interesting; his message no more profound; his whole *presence* here no more important (or so the message read) than that of the students throwing paper balls around, stepping on azalea blossoms, asking one another for "dates." Or bobbing up and down like idiots, looking for a larger-than-life Chief Administrator, when all there was was this Ordinary Person, reciting bureaucratic nostrums about "increasing levels of societal coherence" and "progressively de-sharpening contours of economic influence." All of which meant probably very little more than Rodarch had told us back in the tent. *You may have heard of the Settling Out Laws*, he had said. *Well, it is my job to enforce them.*

At the dense center of the rally, the grounds sloped down in wide terraces toward . . . but hey, let's not get ahead of ourselves. The first thing Turner noticed was, like, a barometric drop in crowd-pressure. He stopped: it was like the dearth of wind, a troubled stillness, that comes before a thunderstorm. Or not exactly; not a real, physical calm. With so many people, under such a warm sun, you naturally had a certain amount of crosstalk, shuffling, popping of corks. But even so, the crowd was strangely attentive, even hushed, and Turner couldn't have been the only one who sensed it. Lots of eyes were staring at the speaker's platform, as though that's where the silence was coming from.

But silence, a negative quality, can't *come from* anywhere, can it? And God knows this speech wasn't the sort of thing to draw your attention. So it was all fairly mysterious.

The voice, no louder from where Turner now stood, nor more vivid than a sun-brightened gray, mentioned something about inappropriate concentrations of wealth. In a kind of afterthought—since he, of everyone on the lawn, was *not* curious about what Rodarch looked like—Turner squinted his eyes to see the stage. He saw the ice-blue gonfalons, strung from the limbs of an ash tree. He saw the modest wooden deck. And he saw (quite clearly, despite the hundred yards between them) the dark-haired Chief Administrator, standing alone with his hands held calmly at his sides.

A-And then, it hit me.

I mean, there he *was*. The Stainless Steel Savior. Preaching in mono-tone the Gospel according to some bureaucracy. And like, holding us, the whole crowd, in his palm. Snaring us with nuances we hadn't heard before. Fixing us with his sincerity. Really shaking us, right where we stood, with the bright energy of his passion. It was all so striking that I didn't even wonder—not until much later—Wait a minute: *what* passion?

"I want to be very clear about one thing," said Rodarch, his voice falling onto the crowd as though from heaven, or booming up from the Underworld. He's changed his tune, Turner thought; now he's talking more plainly or directly, like in the tent.

"I want to assure those of you who are my friends," the voice said very clearly, very carefully, "that *you will not be forgotten*."

The sun had all of a sudden grown hotter. Turner loosened his . . . well, there was nothing especially to loosen, so he just turned and began moving through the crowd, outward he thought, though for some reason the people ahead of him were just as tightly packed as the people behind. He looked around, but from his position on the crowded lawn there were no points of reference. All the ash trees were hung with blue streamers. The sun was *there*, but where had it been a moment ago? The voice went on, without pause:

"And to those of you who may choose to resist these actions, who may take up roles of active opposition, let me say this. Wherever you may go, wherever you may hide, *you will be found*."

Turner was feeling pressed-in and panicky. All around him the crowd of onlookers stood listening blankly, as before, as though Rodarch hadn't changed tone at all, or as though they had been lulled by so many drab and colorless sentences that they were no longer quite capable of hearing anything. Turner felt himself gasping for breath. He brought his hand to his windpipe, worried less about suffocating than about making a spectacle of himself. But naturally nobody was paying him the slightest attention.

He was alone with the Voice. He stumbled onward, in no direction at all, across the lawn.

"I hope this is perfectly clear," the Voice intoned. "I hope that *you* understand."

Actually, you know, it seems probable that Turner was imagining at least some of this, at least the nuance of *directedness* that couldn't really have been coming through a public address system, broadcast to everyone in sight. He forced himself to stop walking, to breathe deeply and slowly like you're supposed to, really fill the lungs, expand the shoulders—get that blood to the brain, man—and was rather surprised to notice all these Newport-blue coveralls around him. He seemed to have wandered into a different place, a different crowd. The wooden stage stood twenty feet away, surrounded by what must have been the Chief Administrator's retinue. For a couple of seconds Turner entertained certain colorful fantasies about being recognized, set upon, That's him, That's the one that killed . . . but of course such thoughts were lacking a necessary verisimilitude, owing to his inability to give them his full attention. There was still the Voice, you see. The Voice that no one seemed to hear but Turner.

"Hello, Mr Ashenden," said a voice at his side.

Turner's skin got up and calmly strolled right off his body. But no, it was just *a* voice, okay? It didn't thunder with passion. It was just, like, ordinary. Slipping back into his skin, Turner looked around to see who had recognized him.

There beside him, not at all overpowering—smiling shyly, if you want to know—stood the tall black-haired figure of the Chief Administrator. He was holding something that looked like a microphone.

"I had rather hoped to run into you," Rodarch said pleasantly. "Hasn't it turned out to be a nice day?"

"Um," trying to catch up with all this, "I guess. Hi. I mean, yeah, it's real nice and sunny. Are you, um, taking a break or something?"

The Chief Administrator continued to give him this funny shy smile, the sort of look you might wear if you were . . . well, caught backstage, say. "Not exactly," he said.

Turner had a feeling he had committed some monumental faux pas, the implications of which would be pondered by etiquette columnists for generations. "Gosh," he said, "I didn't mean to interrupt you, or anything."

Rodarch seized his wrist.

"I'm not sure about that," he said. His voice was reposeful, though he was exerting about ninety pounds per square inch on Turner's wrist. "I'm not sure," he said, "about *you*, Mr. Ashenden."

Pain they say clarifies the mind. Turner felt more clear-headed than he had since—to seize an example—the afternoon he'd spent wandering through the wasteland. He realized immediately that the quiet, faintly ominous voice now addressing him was not the same as the Voice that boomed from the stage. He noticed, in fact, that the Voice itself was still booming—right this second, while Rodarch stood bodily before us, clutching the microphone.

But hold on. While we're realizing things, how about taking note of the fact that the shiny rod in Rodarch's hand isn't a microphone at all? How about a little mention of the wires trailing away from it, falling to the ground, disappearing like mouse-tails into a small box of polished holly-wood?

"Wow," said Turner. Beginning to understand. As he glanced up at the stage, where the image of the Chief Administrator faced the crowd, radiating a passion Turner had never seen in him before. A passion which Rodarch—the real, the *ordinary* Rodarch—could not possibly have expressed.

The pressure on his wrist slacked off, replaced by a tingly sensation, like blood returning to his hand. But when he flexed his fingers he realized that the tingle was caused by a metal rod, inserted into his palm. He tried to shake it loose, but Rodarch—the ordinary Rodarch—closed his own large hand around Turner's, pressing it into the surface of the rod.

"So let's see, Mr Ashenden," the big man murmured, "who you really are."

Up on the stage, at the focus of the crowd's attention, the Chief Administrator hesitated in his address. He turned, as though some movement had caught his eye. It was nothing, probably: a shadow cast by an ice-blue gonfalon. He began speaking again.

"I could have told you," Turner hissed. "This Identity thing doesn't work with me. You're only going to get—"

The crowd drew its collective breath. From the podium, Rodarch was staring at an angular young man who had somehow eluded the security forces and appeared on the stage. The young man came forward in an impulsive, half-limping kind of stride, like he wasn't sure what had gotten into him but didn't have the presence of mind to admit his mistake. (You could tell this, somehow, just by looking. You could see right through him.) Two arm-lengths from the Chief Administrator, the young man stopped.

Jeez, what an idiot. Look: his mouth is open, but he doesn't have the slightest idea what he wants to say. Before him, the Chief Administrator stood calmly, palms open—*typical fucking martyr*—while the young man looked wildly around, seeking guidance. You could feel how baffled he was, and how terrified; in this game of Identities, such things were embarrassingly clear.

This is it, thought Turner, addressing his shadow self. What now, sport?

Rodarch must have wondered the same thing. His hand tightened around Turner's on the metal rod. Their *doppelgängers* tottered for a moment on stage, as though the wooden planks were shifting beneath them.

Turner got this funny idea, almost a certainty, that some reckoning had just been made, a no-man's-land crossed. On the stage, his look-alike seemed to grow taller. Actually he was just, at last, standing up straight. Holding his head up. And waving, in two shaky hands, this long club-headed thing. . . . What the fuck, Turner thought. Through the crowd there passed a slight, hesitant titter.

"It's a croquet mallet!" yelled someone in the audience.

Ah, of course. A nice red-tipped mallet we remembered from the Solar Temple, as a matter of fact. Which might be a clue as to how this Identity business operated, if anyone is keeping track of such things.

The mallet drooped like a flagging erection. Laughter spread through the crowd, a collective release of tension. Turner was mortified. Before the astonished gaze of two or three thousand people, many of whom must have begun to recognize him by now, the Ashenden understudy began to demonstrate your five most common errors in present-day croquet.

#1, you clutch the mallet too far up the shaft. This causes you to lose your balance when (#2) you draw the thing back like a golf club. Then, in a vain effort to compensate, you shift your stance in mid-swing (#3) and bring the mallet forward in a wild, underhand swoop (#4).

But everything thus far—though the crowd was enjoying it, and even the Chief Administrator cracked a stern sort of smile—all this was *nothing* compared to the fifth and most egregious mistake, which is likely to get your present-day croquet player banished forever from the wide green lawn.

Turner Ashenden, failed student and unpromising competitor, threw every ounce of strength and fervor he could gather from the dustbins of his being into the stroke that whooshed through the air at center-stage, narrowly missed the podium, grazed the wooden deck, and jerked his wobbly figure forward in a slapstick follow-through. The hilarity reached its peak when the nature of error #5 became plain: our bumbling cro-queteer was *aiming at the wrong balls*.

Chief Administrator Rodarch still stood with his hands out martyr-style as the wooden head of the mallet rounded the arc and flew upward. It was too late by then, anyway. But the Chief Administrator made no move. His eyes did not close, his body did not crumple as the mallet-head struck with a muffled thump that was the most viscerally horrifying sound Turner could right then imagine. For a couple of moments the only other noise came not from the stage, nor from the badly shocked audience, but from somewhere beneath the ash tree, where a metal rod clunked onto the ground and a tall man gave a slow, mournful kind of sigh, as though from disappointment.

Turner didn't stick around to hear more. Feeling like a fish about to be snared by a Newport-blue net, he plunged singlemindedly toward the teeming safety of the lawn. By the time the security forces fanned out from the empty stage, he was only a face in the crowd.

It's been fun

"The Delirious Blow," pronounced Black Malachi, lowering the freshly delivered University daily. "That's what they're calling it. Who is *writing* this atrocious stuff, is what I should like to know."

Turner Ashenden continued to sling clothing, books, oddments of food more or less at random into a canvas sack. The portrait of the famous mountain-climber gazed down on this, looking perhaps a trifle embittered.

"You could at least proceed," said Black Malachi, "in an orderly fashion. There is the question of money, among other things. Are you quite certain you are not overreacting?"

"Don't ever mention," Turner said, "that word to me again."

Malachi frowned. Facing the window, he pointed vaguely northward, up the valley. "For instance," he said, "there's Harvey Goldaster. Have you thought of that?"

Turner said testily, "Thought of what? I can't understand you, anymore, and you jolly damned well can't understand me. For all I know, you tricked me into going out there. You knew something was going to happen, didn't you? Like, what was it you said—*your great work is ahead of you.*"

"Ah. And so it is." Black Malachi shook his head, grew solemn. "But prophecy is an imperfect instrument. Consider the telescope. One sees certain things with acuity, and other things less well, but all at the expense of context, of perspective. Again, though: have you thought about underwear? About socks?"

"You should be thanking me," said Turner. "If I hang around here, Rodarch'll have his stormtroopers swarming all over this place by noon tomorrow."

Black Malachi rustled his newspaper. "Oh, I don't know. One rather suspects that if the Great Excommunicator had any stormtroopers to begin with, they would have been in evidence by now. No, if anything, he should send you a thank-you note, for providing an occasion to do what he fully intended to do in the first place."

Turner looked up dumbly from his bag, caught between taking inventory and wondering what Malachi was trying to say.

"Do you have any money?" he said at last. A sort of compromise.

"Look here." As always, answering the wrong question, Black Malachi laid out the paper for Turner's inspection. CLASSES SUSPENDED, ran the banner head. From there it got worse: Chief Admin Proclaims 'Festival of Renewal.' Travel Restrictions Announced. Shops to Close for Summer. (Details p. 4)

Oh, shit, was all we could think to say about this.

"But don't worry about money," Malachi said brightly. "I'm sure Harvey will see to that."

"You're crazy," said Turner, fed up. He started zipping his bag, then tossed in, as an important afterthought, GRAILNET USERS MANUAL. The whole thing came to about seventeen pounds, which was pretty pitiful when you thought about it.

From far below came a boisterous thump on the front door.

"Relax," said Malachi quickly. "If there were such a thing as storm-troopers, they would *storm in*, don't you think?"

Turner shouldered his bag, stepped out to the balustrade. The thumping below continued.

"Cervina!" Malachi shouted into banana leaves. "Vinny! Why doesn't somebody see who it is?"

They had all probably gone out, Turner guessed. Escaped to spring-time. Only a madman would lock himself inside like this. As he stood with Malachi looking down, footsteps sounded on the dark glazed tile, and without further prelude the tanned face of Harvey Goldaster appeared in a frame of sprinkler pipes.

"Pantera!" he exclaimed. "You should change the combination of that lock. Elementary precaution, you know. Ah, Ashenden, there you are!"

What, hadn't he seen me before? Am I translucent or something?

"Here I am," agreed Turner.

Goldaster's face assumed a considered seriousness, like a father trying to act fatherly. "Got a bit carried away out there yesterday, don't you think? When I mentioned, you know, a *mild disruption*, I wasn't really thinking of anything quite so . . ."

"Personal?" suggested Turner, sourly.

Goldaster lifted an eyebrow. "Now don't get me wrong: I appreciate what you were trying to do. And naturally I'm prepared to pay you every cent I promised—every cent and then some. In fact, I've been thinking this over, and it occurs to me that it might be just as well for you to stay, you know, out of sight for just a little while. Until things begin to calm down. In fact I've come to offer you a ride out of the valley. And of course some money. Some *real* money. To keep you on your feet, if you know what I mean."

Turner shook his head in dismay. "But you don't . . . I mean, the thing yesterday, see, it wasn't—"

Malachi did one of those things with his thumb and index finger. "Take the fucking money," he whispered. "And say thank you."

"Um, thank you," Turner called down, weakly. "It was nothing. Actually I've just finished packing my bags. Bag."

Harvey nodded, pleased that they were seeing eye-to-eye. "I wouldn't mind getting away for a while," he said, more candidly, "but it looks like I'll have a few little things to attend to. I've never *seen* so many blue uniforms before. Rodarch must have been bringing them in all night. And there are roadblocks going up—had you heard? I suppose we really ought to get moving. Which way would you like to go? Not east, I hope."

Turner looked at Malachi, whom he'd decided to try and keep out of this. He told Harvey, "Maybe we should talk outside."

At the foot of the back staircase, he nodded at his plump erstwhile housemate. "Well. It's been fun, I guess."

"It has been perfectly dreamy," said Black Malachi, with a different kind of affectation than Turner had expected—the kind that makes you suspect there *is* something there. "I am so sorry to see you go."

Well, there were two schools of thought about this, even back then. The landlord bustled us along to the front door, though he clearly would have enjoyed a more complete inspection of the property.

"Was that a chemistry lab?" he wondered, just before they left the banana court for good.

"No," said Turner. "It's a bandstand. I guess I am going to miss the place, after all."

The car stood tan and gleaming before them, the color of Harvey's favorite horse.

"Take a left at the fork," said Turner, climbing in. "And just head on up toward the mountains."

2

Find me

Aglaze, the schist banks heaped at the foot of the sunset had two layers of color—orange on black—or maybe these were the genuine earth tones, a pale sienna brushed lightly across deep umbra—but as Turner looked down and the sun cut more sharply through the mixed gases and particulate debris above the plains . . . after he took a few slow breaths . . . the orange part started to drift, as though it weren't attached to the rock banks at all. Or maybe this was a numinous experience, the first distinct one in Turner's personal history. Maybe the phosphorescent aura above the rocks was the shiny forehead of some minor-league deva, way down the waiting list for a goat-path in Tibet. Maybe thinking about auras was a bit like pondering the red sunrise after a whole night up taking drugs. You know, grasping for portents. Surrendering, out of philosophic exhaustion, the perquisite of mapping things out for yourself.

Let's play the game anyway. Let's say the orange glow was caused by escaping mineral wastes, radon and horrible shit like that, refugee gases that will colonize the atmosphere after all the oxygen has sailed off to ash-gray havens. If that's too rococo for you, let's say it was fleeting pain, like sunburn, headache, a punch in the groin. The nerve-ends of the earth flared up for a while until the analgesics kicked in. For a few moments the mountainside shuddered, trees flapped, weary travelers fell into gorges until the gods of pain were propitiated, then the lights went out at last and the earth got a few hours of shut-eye, recouped all but a smidgen of the day's loss. Death draws closer unnoticeably like that, one hangover at a time, until in the end you're sick of the taste of aspirin anyway. Turner had figured this out while lying in bed.

You couldn't help wondering, though, what was *out there*. Staring west. As a faint wind made wave-patterns in the native grasses and gonzo hybrid grains that had dropped from the rear ends of birds getting the hell out of Dodge during previous decades, when these interesting dust-storms full of residual poisons had made dunes out of farming towns and caused Candlemas to look like an up-and-coming community once again, despite the fact that for two hundred and fifty years it had been quite scenically down-and-post-coitally-depressed.

You could get to like it, though. Turner was going to miss his room, Black Malachi's jibing, periodic visits to class to see what he had lost out on. He wondered if money would make up for that. He wondered, in fact, if money would do him any good at all, where he was going. He did *not* wonder where he was going, for at such a time this line of thinking was inadmissible. There were still plans to carry out. Hidden agendas. There was the faint motive of revenge.

When it finally got just dark enough not to see quite where his feet were about to fall, Turner stood up from the little outcrop where he had planted himself after climbing from Harvey Goldaster's car, a number of hours ago. He covered the last few hundred yards of roadway as fast as he could walk, pausing for breath beside the sign that glowed now more white than swami yellow. Here, where the mountaintop was shaved, it was unexpectedly bright, and Turner wondered if he should recalculate. But if he waited much longer there was the likelihood of stumbling around and announcing himself, which was not to be discounted anyway, so he got moving again for the third time up the sloping driveway, this time with neither hunger nor curiosity to distract him.

The thing was, the windows were mostly too small and too high on the walls to really worry about. To see out from one, a person would have to be practically standing in it, staring out deliberately, even in daytime. This late, Turner didn't bother to keep to the shadowy underskirts of conifers but strolled brazenly out onto the perfect lawn, which might as well have been floodlit, there was such a contrast. It occurred to him, like a private joke, that this might actually be a *croquet field*. If there was such a thing. The grass was short and the underlying dirt so level, he got the peculiar sense of being suspended, moving his legs but not going anywhere, each footstep falling on the same cushioned spot it had just left. As with delusions in general, you just had to wait for this one to dissipate. The ugly old manor swelled up, but imperceptibly, so that by the time Turner reached the path that swerved around it he had forgotten the ridiculous idea this moment might have served to refute.

His plan was to wait on the back porch, the place where he had stood once for several minutes, not quite by accident. He didn't care especially if he had to wait all night; his level of energy and fixity of intent showed no signs of losing their edge, and he had *no* concern for anyone or anything. This was a new sensation for Turner, a lifelong worrier. It lightened the feet that carried him by small blind increments along the wall of the house, still warm with the memory of sunshine, under the windows filled with silhouetted geraniums, to the clematis-covered railing that stood between Turner and the great invisible drop-off, felt now before him as the same kind of emptiness that had grown to occupy his future.

It helps to remember, too, that I was twenty years old, an age often given to self-dramatization.

On the porch beside the back door of the Bad Winters Institute—the spot where, had this been run like the Solar Temple, there would have sat instead a compost pot—Turner Ashenden made himself comfortable. You couldn't say *at home*. But reasonably at ease with all this. Internal exile et cetera. Behind his head, felt more than heard through the stone of the wall, a thump of maybe footsteps moved right-to-left, then fell quiet. New lights came on behind old curtains. *In the velvet darkness . . .*

There were roadblocks going up, Harvey had said. And hey: even on the roads leading out, to the barren fields and the mountains, we nearly ran into two of them. Back East, some adjustment must have been made—numbers shifted from one column to another, budgets increased. A new fiscal quarter, several hundred warm bodies measured for Newport-blue coveralls, placed on transports headed west.

Turner figured he must be a Famous Outlaw, now. Quite a change from his earlier incarnations as Unhappy Student, Headless Housemate, Idiot Bastard Son. Progress, you might say. For at least we now have a definite identity; to our name there is fitted a fixed and widely recognized face, which for all we know by this time tomorrow may be staring out from posters offering a reward for information leading. Did they still do that sort of thing? Turner's ignorance of the customs and orders of his own age was an endless astonishment; all the more disappointing seeing how dependent we are. On these scatterbrained remembrances, this testimony.

[You're not doing badly, though. I mean, taking all things into account. But could we get back to the porch?]

. . . And the value of identity of course is that so often with it comes purpose. Our purpose now in life is to remain *at large*—to elude our blue-shirted pursuers, find our way in the world, arrange things so that we may sleep and eat in relative comfort and never come face-to-face with the Chief Administrator again.

This purpose being clear, it has been Turner's chief preoccupation for a full day now to shuffle out from under it, just as he had shuffled out from under an earlier and essentially heartfelt ambition to do well at the University. Which is why, we believe, contrary to all indications, he was to be found at such a time at such a place as this.

After an hour or so of hearing nothing, no movements or voices, Turner got up and moved cautiously to a window. Through it he saw the shadow of a Biedermeier table cast halfway down the length of a hallway by a wall-mounted swivel lamp, hung too low. On the floor coming out of the shadow was a runner made of Navaho rugs sewn end-to-end, sand-painting motifs done up in threadbare wool. Naturally the compass orientation was all bunged up, spirit barriers open to the east which was *precisely* where the danger was coming from. God, it was a cultural landfill, all this wealth lying around in disregarded objects. Nothing moved over the runner or beyond it, into the light, in the five slow minutes Turner stood there, so he moved disconsolately to a window set higher than the first, thinking probably he ought to have stolen a watch.

Other people's houses, he thought. And then he saw Nurse Tawdry.

From somewhere offscreen she entered a small chamber fitted out like a scullery: lots of horizontal surface area, and great washtubs. The lighting was cool-white fluorescent, imparting an ambience of sterility in which the tall woman looked very much at home. Turner slunk down a bit outside the window, troubled by the idea that these schoolmarmish types have eyes peeking back through their hairbuns. Nurse Tawdry went about her business, though. She dumped something from a pot into a stainless steel sink and opened both valvecocks. There was a good deal of steam. While the soaking or rinsing proceeded, she removed from the drawer of a metal cabinet a pair of green plastic gloves which she tugged on carefully, with special attention to the lower parts covering the wrists. Then she opened a high cabinet and stood back, scanning its contents. Through curtains of steam, Turner saw containers with bright labels of red and orange and blue, tiny gray hand-print, rubber stoppers the color of hot water bottles.

This is no scullery, he thought: it's a pharmacy.

Nurse Tawdry selected a larger-than-average flask full of something clear as water and produced from a white pocket a phial which she filled to *just there*. The flask went back in the cabinet, the valvecocks were singly shut off and Nurse Tawdry still carrying the spoon or phial walked briskly without spilling a bit, touched a switch, and left the room and the small patch of terrace outside it in indigo darkness, through which for several moments her bustling image still seemed to swirl.

Turner looked around at the last gloomy colors of sunset. It was like half a conversation, he thought. You really didn't know how much weight to give anything. He felt lonely and, for some reason, frustrated. The latter was hard to make sense of, until he figured out after minutes of reflection and in total darkness by now—the wall lamps in the corridor having gone the way of the cool-whites—who it was that he had really been hoping to spy doing something secret or revealing in a tiny room. And when he got all that figured out he had to wonder a little about his real reason for coming here in the first place, to this strange old house, and about the little voice that kept whining like a child in the back of his mind, high-pitched and miserable—

Find me.

Flash

Q. Why would anybody want to lock up a house at the top of a god-damned mountain?

A. So people like *you* can't stroll right in in the middle of the night. I mean, you're an outlaw, right?

Q. I'll ask the questions, if you don't mind. So how the hell am I going to get in?

A. Try that small hatch that looks like the cover of a root cellar.

Q. God, how bizarre. Are these *ashes* in here? I'm all covered in something, and it smells sort of like . . . old cheese?

A. At least you're inside.

Q. Yeah, maybe. But inside where?

A. (. . .)

Q. Ah: here's some kind of ladder. I guess this must be a pantry or something like that. Well. —Where was that room, that upstairs parlor or whatever?

A. You might look upstairs.

Q. Smart-ass. It was pretty strange, I remember, the last time, and I wasn't even really paying all that much attention. But like, sort of diagonal or something, that hall running past the bathroom. Wait, is this a staircase?

A. Sure looks like it.

Q. That was rhetorical. Twenty-seven steps. Moonlight through tall black windows. Antique rugs galore here so you don't have to worry about making any noise. My God, this hall just goes on forever. Which room do you think is Maridel's?

A. Why do you ask?

Q. (. . .)

A. Here—you've found your drawing room.

Q. Drawing room, that's it. It's awfully goddamned dark in here. Anyway, I guess it's ridiculous to think they'd just leave the thing lying around, on top of everything. There was a rug, I think. . . . What's this?

A. It's amazing how things work out sometimes.

Q. God, I can tell just by touching it. Remember that carved box, the
    curly sort of designs in white wood?
A. Holly-wood.

Q. Right. I mean, like all these sort of celtic swirls and knots and so
    forth.
A. Like a mandala?

Q. I don't have to answer that. It's pretty crazy to be talking to yourself,
    basically. Is there some way to get this thing open?
A. Maybe you should pick up the joystick and follow the wires back.

Q. Ha! Fat chance I'm ever going to touch *that* thing again. Here we
    go—some kind of latch or hook or something. I wonder maybe if I
    just pull up on the lid here . . .
A. *FLASH*.

Turner Ashenden

Morning sun pranced happily through the bedroom wing of the Bad Winters Institute of Science and Philosophy. All the rooms were arranged so
as to get lots of eastern light, as though the architect had wanted to be
real sure nobody would waste a minute of life's most precious commodity:
the part of the morning when you weren't really expected to be doing
anything yet. Or maybe it was just an early venture in passive solar design.
Either way, all those foot-candles made Turner's head hurt like a son of
a bitch even before he was awake enough to realize where he was; and it
got about six times worse when he sat up all at once, panicky, like someone
running late, and found Maridel sitting calm and pretty on a Craftsman
daybed across the room, dressed in a schoolgirl uniform, beside the sloppy
pile of every item of Turner's clothes.

"Would you like something for your head?" she said. Without smiling.

"What?"

Maybe if an ocean liner came lumbering up the valley and moored beside you, you would be as astonished as this.

"Your *head*," Maridel repeated. "You must have the worst headache ever. Or at least you must think you do. Actually it's happened before, for your information."

Turner felt old, trodden, indecent. He said, "What was it? I feel like I'm going to die."

Maridel turned her head: girl character in a Victorian fantasy, set chiefly in gardens. Everything fresh and morning-like about the room seemed to emanate from her, while everything else—headaches, bad smells, etc.—was attributable to Turner. Besides which, he was self-consciously naked under the sheet.

"Well, here." The girl rose from the daybed, bringing something across the room. "It's like aspirin only better."

All it was was a small open phial, filled with something liquid and clear, its surface conforming precisely to an etched fill-mark. This might have given one pause; but we are speaking here of Turner Ashenden.

"Thanks," he said, and gulped it. There was no taste to speak of. The sheet lay around his thin but out-of-shape abdomen, which Maridel indifferently looked at. After half a minute, caring less and genuinely amazed, he said, "I feel better already."

"Yes," said Maridel. (Sweetly? Or was that a side-effect?) "You will."

"Now," she went on, giving it a bit more time, "you must come down to the kitchen as soon as you can. Tristin will bring you clean clothes."

Out the door, yellow shirt, tan trousers, ragged underwear, Malachi's hiking shoes (a sort of final bequest) and prim little schoolgirl whisked together in a purposeful blur, while Turner enjoyed a headache remedy that was causing him to devote much of his cognitive effort to remembering who the hell he was, waking up in an unfamiliar room and feeling so good.

. . . Meet Turner Ashenden

He was standing naked by the window when Tristin walked in. It was embarrassing—not that Turner realized it. He just turned around blinking, smiling sheepishly, like a little kid caught doing something not really bad, just boyish, a minor sin of the caliber of getting one's hands dirty before lunch. Tristin paused shyly inside the door, stared for a few moments despite himself, remembering the real concern, the in-it-togetherness, right up to the threshold of actual friendship, he had felt in Turner the last time around. His own feelings were different today—less gushy, but just as excited and even more afraid—as he saw in the older youth before him a kind of summation of several possibilities. He was sixteen years old, and had had a lot of time to wonder.

"Hey," said Turner. Wide-eyed, slightly crazy-looking, but no more than you'd expect. "You're, ah, Tristin. Right?"

The boy came closer, which took more courage than anyone would realize. He began laying out the uniform, the carefully measured pieces of cotton serge, in neat mounds on the bed. His fingers shook considerably. Turner was fascinated.

"Wow," he said. "What an odd design. Nice colors, though."

There was that innocence in him, then. How had he held on to that, when I had been incapable for years now of anything even close?

[I believe I will let that "I"—a slip—stand. It is too late now, I think. And anyway, that morning did mark the beginning of a kind of coming-out for me.]

"Hey, I'm sorry," Turner said, after silent moments had passed. "I didn't remember . . . I mean, about you not talking, and all."

He looked so ashamed and seemed to feel so awful, it might have been perfectly appropriate to embrace him, just for reassurance. *No, it's all right*, the gesture would have meant. *It's not like that—not as bad as you think*. He wouldn't have known the difference, probably. He was in the mood to be accepting of things.

Responding to some clue, I think, in my own eyes, Turner began piece by piece to put the new clothes on. It was a transformation I could not feel good about. Still, it would make things easier. I exhaled silently as he tucked himself in place.

That done, I led him like a new puppy along the hallway, down the servants' stairs and out into the big warm kitchen, where the rest of them had assembled. They were doing their usual canny imitation of A Family Gathered for Breakfast. Of course the imitation had its bizarre twists, the least of which was the hovering, fussy presence of . . . of "Nurse Tawdry," as Turner would teach me to say. Already, in unintended directions, our mutual education had begun.

Maridel must have said something along the lines of We thought you'd never get here, and Madame Gwendola probably smiled and hushed her daughter and asked Turner if he'd care for coffee. I don't remember. I don't want to remember. The only thing that mattered to me, then or ever, was the look on Turner's face as he drew himself up to the long narrow table and glanced across at a figure he'd met once or twice already, but without *quite* the same shock of recognition. This time, the shock (or at any rate, the recognition) was slow in coming. But that was no doubt due to the famous "headache cure."

Turner stared ingenuously at first and then with a kind of hesitant horror (like the story he told once, later, about a fire starting in the Solar Temple when everyone was so high on one thing or another, they didn't quite fathom for a while that *the house was burning down*)—his eyes getting wider a millimeter at a time, with little glances around—at me, especially—as if for confirmation. They let him go for an awfully long time. Just sitting there with their muffins and their marmalade. Then, just before I would have given it away by twitching or laying my head down —which I'm sure they could sense too—Madame Gwendola fixed him with a businesslike kind of stare and said:

"I'd like you to meet Turner Ashenden."

The late sleeper

You don't get used to this kind of thing, ever. But you develop, maybe, some attitude whereby you can get through the next half minute, and then the half minute after that, without the shrieking or the rending of hair that would feel more appropriate than just sitting there and cataleptically watching other folks eat. And by that time, though your mood hasn't improved one iota, you're sort of halfway paying attention to the bland niceties being mouthed around the table, and absent-mindedly your hand goes out to see if the corn muffins are still warm or the coffee hot, and somehow by the second or third minute the morning normalcy of the thing has seduced you, and there you are having breakfast with four other people, including yourself. Or make that, your self. A distinct concept. Implying possession, at least, if not sameness. Though the facsimile doesn't seem to be hungry and is rather avoiding your eye; fiddling with the seams of last night's clothing.

They've scoped you out, all right.

Bland niceties—

"The children will be here soon," says Nurse Tawdry, a fretful thought, ignored by everybody.

"I told him," says Maridel, "that he *mustn't* play in the tulip beds. But boys can be so stubborn."

And Gwendola: "This may be the last sack of coffee, if those travel restrictions are actually enforced. Unless Mr Ashenden knows of a way . . ."

Nurse Tawdry: "Madame, you ought to be getting ready. They'll be anxious, you know, to meet their new instructor."

"But *so*," Maridel insists, "later I found him way back in the azaleas, all by himself. I don't know what he could have been doing. He's been acting like this for weeks now."

"Who do you mean?" says the person introduced as Turner Ashenden.

"Just tell them," Madame Gwendola says—in a definitive tone as though handing down some ruling—"that Mr Ashenden is a late sleeper."

Tristin by this time goes all wide-eyed, and though nobody else seems to notice, they all must have heard it as clearly as he had. The sparkly conversation falters for just a moment.

Turner says: "I'm, ah . . . did I say something?"

Nurse Tawdry stands peremptorily and begins clearing away the bread plates. Gwendola gazes into the distance, thoughtful. Only Maridel, pivoting deftly at the narrow waist without otherwise altering her posture, deigns to reply:

"That's the whole point, you see. You *did* say something."

Holy shit, you think, as by now the thing has cut through even the miracle headache cure, and you join the others in regarding the prodigal table-partner. However hard this is conceptually for a late sleeper to grasp at not quite eight in the morning, you've got to strive to *realize* this. Because the fact is, someone who looks and sounds startlir.gly like Turner Ashenden has just joined in the happy breakfast chatter. While *you*, the last guy known to have held the position, are still sitting there with your thumb up your ass and a lot of neurochemical pollutants in your brain, trying to find the bubble. I mean, get serious, Ashenden. Who's it gonna be, here?

"How . . ." you attempt to say. A beginning, at least.

"I'm sorry," he says, this Turner-figure, looking bashfully at you. "I *know* . . . But maybe they'll, like, fix it or something."

Tristin regards you sympathetically, and by way of comfort you slip for a moment into his gaze. There's something about this kid, you think. For the first time in your career you are grateful for the signs of a headache creeping back.

"This is crazy," you tell your likeness across the table. Then, speaking at large: "If *he* wants to stick around, that's fine by me. But *I'm* getting out of here. As soon as somebody will tell me what the hell is going on. I mean, like starting *way* back, with this whole Identity business."

The balance shifts. Glances slide around the room, down at the marble floor, up at the whitewashed timbers; like those diagrams of how a telescope works, the broken lines bouncing this way and that, as though the energy were going outward, smacking into the target, instead of reflecting in. Only in this case the target, the late sleeper, is avoided by all lines-of-sight. Amidst the general furtiveness, Nurse Tawdry plucks your half-full coffee mug out from under your nose.

"Not so goddamned fast," says Turner. The first-person Turner. Snatching it back and raising it to his lips. We'll battle this headache in the time-honored fashion, thank you. And did the fake Turner, the projection or whatever it was, just crack a holographic smile?

"Is he—" you gesture with your butter knife "—is he really *there*? I mean, can you touch him?"

"We don't really know much . . ." Maridel begins.

"Mr Ashenden," says Gwendola, "you are behaving as though it is we who owe you some explanation. Whereas in *fact*, you are the one who woke us all up in the middle of the night, and whom we found unaccountably lying in the middle of our drawing room. While *that*—" (she means the counter-Turner) "—was poking around in people's bedrooms quite as though it were *looking* for someone. Don't you think you might offer us a word of apology?"

Off the bat, Turner says, "Where are my things?" He's just remembered the GRAILNET USERS MANUAL. "Let me go look for my stuff, and I'll offer you more than that."

You really have to work to get Madame Gwendola's attention, but it's possible. Turner is up, bumping around in pantries, looking for a way out of the kitchen, until Maridel, sighing, points him through an archway obscured by bunches of dessicated herbs. The regime here is much different than back at the Solar Temple, where Malachi makes his extracts fast and fresh. Sunlight bouncing off the brown plains rises toward him through a row of French doors.

The canvas sack lies undisturbed on the porch.

"What were you doing out here?" wonders Maridel, following at a cautious distance. "Nobody ever comes here, it isn't safe. Nobody but Tristin."

"Look." Turner holds up the ungrammatical MANUAL, which she squints at. "It's all about—"

"Oh, sure." She stops him with the simplest of shrugs. "That's my father's book. I mean, partly. It was printed right here, you know. We've got *hundreds* of them."

As Turner looks at the girl, the distance between them seems to shrink. He thinks of her for no apparent reason as a comrade, someone he can talk to. He says, "Then you can tell me what happened. How long is this split personality thing going to last?"

She steps near to him. The wheat-colored hair blows forward around her face, in front of her leaf-green eyes. She's gotten a little older since his last visit out, six or seven months, which can be a big deal at certain times of your life, but in general she still has that air of being ageless. Studying her perfect smooth face thus poses a kind of mathematical problem, like whether one infinity can have more things in it than another one. Or, can someone ageless grow up?

"I tried to tell you," she says seriously. "We really don't know. We don't understand that much. It was my father's invention, and he's dead. Everyone is dead that had anything to do with it. Or, mostly."

"Then what are you doing letting that thing, that box, just lie around? I mean, it could be dangerous, couldn't it? Somebody could, like . . ."

Maridel takes his hand, a gesture that puzzles him until he senses, in the shadow that falls over her eyes, the presence of Madame Gwendola on the porch behind them. For another full second—a long time under such circumstances—the ageless girl presses warmth from her palm into his thin, page-turner's fingers. Even the manner of her letting go has the character of a signal.

"Like I said," she says brightly (*Yes, but when—and what had she said, exactly?*): "It's happened before."

The stand-in

Close cousins of Maridel's schoolgirl costume lay pressed and neat against six, seven, eight slender bosoms, differing solely but intriguingly in the swirled needlepoint insignia at each upper left breast, which seemed to be personalized. The occupants of these uniforms were only slightly more individuated, forming a small troop at the foot of the spiral stair, where they stood barely whispering. It all had the air of a ritual, something to be gotten through in good order.

What now? Turner regarded the youngsters balefully from across the hall, where Madame Gwendola detained him. Only Tristin was missing from the gang he'd once seen here sitting saucer-eyed on the floor, and there were one or two extra. Also absent was Turner's double, unglimpsed for at least an hour. He *wanted* to wish that the thing had disappeared, been reabsorbed by whatever etheric clay it had sprung from; yet he held back from hoping so. Gwendola had wrapped herself up in one of those sari things, paisley printed on silk, that made her look like a cheap medium, and she smelled of something old and dry.

"All right Mr Ashenden," she said at a moment that seemed to have nothing particular about it, which Turner supposed was in the nature of good timing, a mysterious faculty. She gestured for him to proceed with her, then moved out across the tiled floor. Like the kids he went along with it, just to see.

"Good morning, children," Gwendola grandly said, sweeping a hand sideways in a manner that seemed to implicate Turner in the thought, as though she were speaking for the two of them.

The "children"—a loose-jointed term, straining a bit to embrace the older ones, as big as Tristin, and the youngest, a tiny girl half hidden behind Maridel's skirt—answered readily yet, one felt, withholding commitment. Something was different this morning, it was clear. Some news seemed to hang just below the high tin ceiling: an announcement, like a banner to be unfurled. Gwendola let the moment float. She smiled around the little group of her disciples then unexpectedly exclaimed, as though the idea had surprised her: "Let us go quickly, children, and sit upon the lawn!"

Comically, the kids tromped out, probably well accustomed to Gwendola's marching orders. Turner remembered going in and out of the small sideroom, his first time here, with the paint-stained speakers. Gwendola had at least a wide choice of stage-sets in this old house, and evidently enjoyed to use them. The sun was out, and there were sheets of muslin laid in a wide U on the lawn, open to the east, repeating the error of the Navaho rugs. An easy breeze was blowing. Without being told to, the kids sat down around two adjacent sides, leaving Turner and Gwendola with ten yards or so of cotton to divide between them. An early blossom had appeared on the yellow rambler rose, pale against the backdrop of rhododendrons.

"Now, children"—as Turner was just stooping to take his seat—"you must say hello to Mr Turner Ashenden, who has come to us here at the Institute."

The kids said nothing, though their pairs of earnest young eyes fell quickly upon him. Turner straightened hastily, but never quite got back the sense of having his posture straight. She had that timing.

"Mr Ashenden," Gwendola said (proudly, one felt: possessively), "is a *very great man*, children. He has returned to the earthly plane after a long absence, and will be staying with us here in order to learn more— as we all are learning, aren't we?—about his own special destiny."

She posed like the fairy godmother in some vapid wish-fulfilling fable, beaming out at the audience as though expecting maybe gasps of joy at the good news she's sprung: got these tickets to the Ball off a scalper, stiffed the asshole with a bad check, now you can make it with the Prince. Turner, for one, wasn't buying it.

The eyes upon him turned openly curious. Waiting to see, I guess, what the Very Great Man had to say for himself.

He cleared his throat.

"Well," he said, "gosh. Thanks for the kind words and all that. But, um, actually . . ."

"Mr Ashenden," cutting him off, showing the old velvet-gloved brutality, "had a fateful accident during the night. While wandering in the darkness, he *most* carelessly touched the Identity terminal with his own hand, and *this* is what resulted."

Oh, come on. Turner might as well have been a cardboard dummy, Gwendola tapping his flat chest to demonstrate the basic principles of safe somnambulism. He caught a smirk, he thought, in the eyes of the oldest boys—but not an unfeeling one, as though they had all taken their turns as Dummy of the Day.

Just then, though, the merry eyes turned away from him to stare at something over his shoulder. There was a ratcheting sound, a crunching of gravel. Quickly the eyes got wider. Turner followed them back to the underskirts of the house, where double doors opened to a storage shed. Out of this came a small group . . . let's see, Tristin and Nurse Tawdry a-and, oh Christ . . . dragging a large and awkward but apparently not very massive object, mounted on wheels and wrapped in a loose tarp.

The procession gained speed and assurance as it came nearer, towing its odd-shaped burden up the drive. Leading the pack, Turner's *doppelgänger* hummed a banal little tune.

[Hey, wait. It was Rochberg's *Variations*, wasn't it? Not the ideal choice for the occasion; but "banal"?]

As they jostled along, the tarp came loose and began slipping down to one side. You could see pieces of something white underneath, long thin bones covered in a skin of taut fabric.

"You have all heard," Gwendola said loudly, failing to draw the young eyes away from this remarkable advent, "you have heard me speak of the

Akashic Other. Well here, children, is the Akashic Other of Mr Ashenden, brought down into the material dimensions as a result of last night's mis-adventure."

The shadow-Turner seemed to know he was being talked about: his motions became—in classic Ashenden style—awkward and self-conscious. His foot got caught in the slipping tarp, pulling it the rest of the way to the ground.

"How long is it going to be around?" asked one of the older kids, as though he disapproved of this bizarre complication.

"It is difficult to know," said Gwendola.

Then Turner—interrupting *her*, for once—said, "Isn't that some kind of aircraft?"

It was not entirely a question; the general nature of the object was plain from its broad wings folded like a bat's, accordion-style, and its tapered wood-and-laminate body. What Turner really wanted here was an expla-nation: whether the thing actually worked, or had ever done so, and what in God's name it was doing here.

Gwendola, for her part, was happy to ignore him. She lectured: "The appearance of the Akashic Other is, as we know, normally restricted to very brief sessions when we interact with the Identity matrix in the intended manner. On such occasions its event-field is a very weak and delicate one. Situations of *this* type have been quite rare, especially since the death of my late husband. All we know at present is that Mr Ashenden's Other appears to have gathered unto itself an elemental vortex of considerable strength."

How could anybody listen to such drivel? Turner stared as Tristin, assisted by Nurse Tawdry and hindered slightly by the fumbling good intentions of the A.O., unfolded first one wing then another, joints creak-ing and sailcloth snapping in the wind, until the insubstantial aircraft stretched out over an area of lawn where half a croquet match would have fit. Only the bulk of something matte-black at its center—an engine, I bet—kept it from rising on gusts of air and soaring away.

"Th-That thing looks like it could really *fly*," Turner exclaimed.

Gwendola granted him a smile. "That is exactly right, Mr Ashenden."

"Well that's perfect!" He stepped forward, exultant—then halted, as this brought him closer to his shadow self, which made him at the very least uncomfortable. "I can use this to—I mean, if I could borrow it . . ."

Gwendola touched his arm. It was the closest she would ever come to gentleness. "I am sorry, Mr Ashenden. Really, I am. But for the time being you musn't go anywhere. And certainly not anywhere far away."

He looked back at her hopelessly.

She said, "This has happened before. The manifestation of the Other. It surprised us, just as it surprises you. We sensed a certain danger, as well as the obvious awkwardness. . . . But my husband was dead, and we could only guess what to do. And as it happens, we guessed incorrectly. We sent the *real person* away—it was an old, dear friend of the family—and kept the Other here among us. For safety, as we believed."

Turner caught a faint whiff of where this was heading.

"Instead of losing strength," (her tone detached, the rote sound of an often-repeated narrative) "the Other actually became more *present*. Like someone material. Someone alive. In due course we learned that the poor woman herself—who had fallen badly ill, it develops, as soon as she left here—soon thereafter died."

What happened to th— Turner stopped himself. Either he knew enough already, or he decided just for the present not to add one more item to his list of things to deal with. Besides, there was the real possibility that Gwendola was flat-out lying.

"So, what?" he asked her sourly. "What are you saying we should do?"

"Mr Ashenden"—this to the troop of schoolkids, who had gotten an eyeful of the old aircraft by now—"is going to honor us here with his presence, and instruct us on the many wonderful things he has learned in his years at the University. He is *especially* well versed in Mythology."

Is this a joke? wondered wry, unhappy Turner.

"While his Other," she went on, her gaze minutely sharpening, "will go away from us. Out into the wide and dangerous world. So that we may learn—for Mr Ashenden's benefit, and for ours—something of what Nature intends for him. Perhaps we may even learn the reason She has chosen again, after so many centuries, to awaken her late sleeper."

The kids seemed to reflect upon this, and God knows Turner did some quick thinking himself. "You mean you're going to send h-him— send it, the Other—*out there?* But what if, like, he just goes *phhtt?* Isn't that kind of a waste?"

Of a perfectly good aircraft, he meant.

Gwendola: "Well of course we shan't send him alone. One of us must go along, so as to record everything that happens. It is *such* an opportunity."

For an instant Turner experienced a mental image both nonsensical and sharp: in it, Maridel was waving goodbye from the aircraft's small passenger-box, sailing off into the wild blue with this Ashenden knockoff, clutching frightfully, ecstatically, at his arm. . . .

In the next moment there began a kind of slow-motion screening of this fantasy's final cut. Somewhere in post-production, a stuntman had been thrown in to replace the lead actress, whose life was after all too valuable to risk for some flashy, spur-of-the-moment effect. The stand-in was now boarding the plane, joining the actor chosen to portray Turner Ashenden, Fortune's Child. He looked back a last time wistfully, his brown curls puffing in the breeze and his eyes, wide to begin with, getting bigger as they filled with that mysterious, artistic element, *screen presence* they used to call it, a light that burns brighter than life, while beside him, rocking as the aircraft turned into the breeze, the leading man seemed to grow pale and diminish. It was an odd sort of reversal: Turner found that he was much less interested in this edited version of himself than in the poor boy being sacrificed, as it seemed, to some queer notion of Destiny. For a few moments—and then for many years, afterward—he wished it were he himself, the flesh-and-blood Turner, gaining speed across the emerald lawn, rising first tentatively and then with sudden, soaring confidence into the sky, flying off though it be to certain doom with Tristin on that bright May morning so far away, so long ago.

COMING
DOWN

1

Our own shadow

"We'll have to come down eventually," was what he finally said.

It was an anticipatory remark; answer to no question. But by being said it made many questions unneedful. First among them, what to think, how much to expect of the tall thin figure—shivering, wearing clothes he had borrowed from another life, clutching the hand-straps with fingers that at certain angles of the sun were perceptibly translucent—beside me in the belly of the Moth. As we flew on and on, low in the deepening sky.

"We could land in somebody's beanfield, I guess. Or look for a road." His own voice seemed to bring him to life. The eyes became more definite, irises deepening to almost purple. "Or we could keep flying all night. I wonder if I'm going to get tired, like this."

I could have told him.

"Maybe like this I'm not even . . . you know, myself, anymore."

He smiled at the convolutions of that. The pinkish skin of his face looked firm enough to touch, now. But you must know how afraid I was.

He said: "Maybe I'm immortal."

—In the west, I told him, there's a place where they've got a religion, a cult of two or three generations' standing, that places great emphasis on the ability to avoid physical entanglement. You know, they walk through walls and so on. You could probably make a name for yourself there.

He laughed and (as I now imagine it) looked at me fondly. Nothing about my ability to communicate seemed to surprise him. I suppose at some level, the *akasha* or wherever such things are possible, he had known it, had always perfectly understood me. As Black Malachi had known Turner: the older soul embracing the younger.

After a while he said, "No. No, I've got work to do."

And of course I agreed with him. As I had my own work. And Gwendola, and Maridel. Each of us the servant of a hydra-headed god.

"I want to go down," he told me, as the sun touched the most distant mountain. He gestured across the hills that rippled like waves, flowing southward. "You know, I've just got this feeling that Turner belongs down there. In the world."

—I want to stay up, I told him simply.

Yet it was my hand that guided the Moth in a slow plummet through the penumbra and into the cool first stirrings of twilight, until some minutes afterward, while it was still bright enough, we touched lightly upon our own shadow.

Wine Barrens

They took us naturally enough for a trader and his young account-keeper; knight and page. Fittingly I did carry a record book—this one, in its most artless version. Turner carried his canvas sack. Had he been the sort of person robbers or government monitors were interested in, our burdens would have been reversed, and the sack would have been made of finer cloth. Therefore the field crew appraised us only briefly, named a fee within reason for keeping the Moth, and showed us the road leading down the hill to the larger and cheaper of the two hotels that together comprised the main *raison d'être* of Wine Barrens, at least for the time being, until somebody figured out how to breed a tougher grape. The present feeble stock of chardonnay had proved no match, apparently, for the latest raise in the UV stakes, and was being pillaged by some tribe of wandering viruses. Things were worse, they told us, farther south. They told us this much without our asking, so you know how much it was worth.

—Ask them who owns the vineyards, I suggested.

Turner blinked, signaling that he had heard. I was thinking of this other-self already as "Turner," and as a matter of literary convenience I think I shall go on calling him so.

"Oh, the Quoins," said the big man by the toolshed, after Turner had translated the question into the kind of waves normal ears are attuned to. "The family still owns it, I guess. But they're mostly gone now. The regional administrator from up the Bay comes down and looks things over now and then, takes whatever they've got. Not much these days, of course."

Turner counted out some money, careful to let show only the government notes. The real thing would come out later, as the occasion required. Meanwhile we took a very small room at the Barrens Plaza and thought about how to handle dinner.

"Well, *I* can't eat anything," he said. "At least . . . can I?"

I told him no. Then maybe.—Drink some water, I proposed, and see what happens.

Whatever this body was made of (and we are all, aren't we, only patterns of energy, connected more or less porously?) it was solid enough to contain the water as canvas does: allowing it to permeate little by little, until his shirt and pants were evenly dampened. Ectoplasmic osmosis. All this was entered dutifully into my book before we proceeded—it was about eight o'clock now—around to the dining room.

It was becoming an adventure. I was terrified.

The hotel was of the old sort, an enfilade of rooms opening onto cracked paving that was sprouting with green things Turner someday might tell me the names of. From the edge of this, one looked down across the lower hillsides where once, I suppose, had been fields of grapes or pastures picturesquely sauntered in by cattle. We had not flown very far south— three hundred miles, I guess—but the impact of Dissolution had been much greater here than in our own, better-protected valley. Whatever had grown here, grasses or grapes, had been swept away and the soil beneath stripped to bare shale, which was now covered in lawn-sized patches by the scaly growth we called moon lichen. This was visible now, in the last stage of twilight, as an almost luminescent blanket over the dead black ground.

—We're not going to find much here, I told Turner; but the words were really an expression of something else, a greater desolation.

This Turner, though, was not one for fatalism. He shrugged with a kind of phlegmatic equanimity (perhaps the *akasha* is where they store the humors one's material self is short of) and said, "Well, at least we'll pick up some local gossip."

Yes, well. As we turned back to the whitewashed stucco hotel, he seemed to have a new notion about this; and with a sudden sharpness in his voice he asked me, "What do *you* know about Wine Barrens?"

I knew rather much, as it developed, about a lot of things. I had spent two thirds of my life being schooled energetically; preparing, as it now seemed, for this expedition. Quickly I ran through it—the story of a once-booming region in decline for much of the century; then an uptick, as the latest government showed itself more paternal than the last, or even (though this was beyond my personal recollection) the short-lived and ill-tempered one before that, and installed a trade emissary in the more costly of the two hotels, to invest in local produce. —Now, I said, people come here. Traders and tourists and owners of failing farms. People like that. And people like us, whose business one can only guess at.

This was an invitation, but Turner failed to acknowledge it. He listened instead, nodding, prompting me with questions of a conventional sort. An exam in Geography: Principal export crop, wine grapes. Primary land use, cultivation of same. Populace uneducated, declining in number, quiescent. Infant mortality no worse than anywhere else. Local militia, inactive. Relations between government and local gentry, cordial. —Yes, I said (sensing a certain edge in Turner's voice), there are a few Settling Out Camps. This is about the southernmost extent of them. No, as far as I know, there has been no trouble.

"I wonder why," he said. ". . . Well. Let's go in."

I did not ask *him* anything. I did not, for example (though it may seem quite natural to have done so) inquire at any time what it was he planned to do here. My purpose, as I perceived it, was simply to follow Turner and to observe him, being careful neither to guide nor to obstruct, helping him only insofar as he requested it. What was important, I thought, was to learn what *he* would do. Not what we, the two of us, might do together.

But still. Stepping down into the chrome-fitted, glass-walled restaurant at the Barrens Plaza, where the lighting was a shade too bright for any feeling of comfort, it was hard to believe that we were not in this as a team, a partnership; that only I in any real sense was here at all; that everything else was a complex sort of shadow-play. A dharmic illusion.

Turner chose a table near the center, from which we could eavesdrop on a maximum number of conversations. The place was only a third full. Our fellow patrons were older, on the whole, and less well clothed than the two of us, but this did not seem to make us conspicuous. A waiter stood by without speaking while Turner finished looking down the menu-board.

"I won't be eating," he declared at last, as though this were a sudden decision. "Bring a bowl of stew for the boy. And some half-strength wine."

The message seemed to be, *I am in charge here, this young man will do as I say and ask no questions.* Which was right enough; but for whose benefit?

At a table near us sat two men and one woman, older than Turner by a couple of years, dressed in Newport-blue coveralls. They had finished eating and were now drinking wine from a jug, splashing it about from glass to glass and talking loudly.

"It's just so *extreme*," was the first remark from over there that I took note of. The woman was speaking. Turner sat very quietly with his eyes pointing at a crack in the cheap tableware, which probably meant that he was a couple of sentences ahead of me.

"And the music," said one of the men, "that's just as bad."

"But what I *can't* get used to" (the woman again) "is how the idiot farmers just stand there along the walls staring at you, like it was a, um . . ."

"Cattle auction?"

"Mm. Or you know, a village dance or something. Waiting for someone to just step over, and—"

The three of them broke into laughter, and Turner tightened his mouth.

"Face it, though," the second man said, more seriously, "you've got to get used to it. It's what there is, from now on."

"No." The woman made a face that was no doubt meant to be resolute, but the wine had gone around too many times. (My own wine, even watered down, was as strong as anything I'd ever had at Bad Winters.) Her expression was merely sad, and bitter. "I'll never get used to it. I hate it here. I hate the things we have to do."

"What do you mean?" The first man, a joker, feigned astonishment. "You don't like treating people like shit?"

"I don't like watching *you* treat people like shit," she said quickly and coolly. "I don't know how you can behave like that."

There was a silence at their table, which for a moment seemed to be amplified by the silence at our own; I was afraid our listening in would be noticed, and busied myself fussing with my stew bowl. Turner did nothing, and of course no one in the room had taken the slightest interest in us, one way or another.

When they began speaking again the subject had changed, perhaps by unspoken agreement. There was a prolonged and indifferent consideration of the likelihood of rain in the morning; the nuisance caused by bandits along the highway; unspecified scheduling problems. Turner said quite clearly, as though he didn't care if anybody heard:

"Well, isn't that interesting? Even the invaders are discontent. I guess it's like they say—you know, *the wages of sin . . .* however it goes."

This might have been thrilling, such audacity, but it was quite clear from the beginning that the three people at the next table were not listening and did not care. They went on about the local climate: evidently it rained more here than wherever they had come from, and of course they didn't like that at all.

Turner said, "It's surprising that the people don't just rise up against them. Like they're doing up north there, what's that place called? Candlemas."

—They aren't paying attention, I told him, thinking perhaps that from where he was sitting, a different angle than my own, he didn't realize. I added, as neutrally as possible (since it seemed reasonable, at least, that I should know what was going on): —Are you trying to start a fight?

Turner replied, for the first time, in an undertone: "I know *they* aren't listening." He leaned back a bit, and concluded more loudly, "The idiots."

I tethered my eyes. —Who, then?

Turner made a motion toward the parking lot, as though to say I should drink up, he was tired of this place, we were going. He pulled out a couple of coins—real coins—and laid them in plain view on the table. *Thank you,* he nodded to the waiter. We stepped to the door.

For a second or two I felt an immense pressure on our backs, as though great hands were about to seize us from behind, angrily detain us.

But Turner swung the door open and, unimpeded, we stepped into the sullen evening air.

"Now," he said, as we dodged the cracks in the paving-stones. "We'll see what kind of place this Wine Barrens is."

Our first night

We did not undress. We did not do anything in particular, back in the room, but walk from there to here, leaning against the walls, staring through the window and at one another and at nothing, then at one another again. There was nothing but a mattress on the floor, which we weren't ready for yet, an electric lamp, two books left behind by someone, towels and soap in a neat stack outside the washroom, and a small bench you could sit on or use as a table. Turner stepped over to this bench after a while and looked down at it, as though unsure whether or how such a thing might relate to his *ad hoc* body.

"Tell me about myself," he said abruptly.

"Tell me," he went on, coming toward me, imposing himself as it were on my attention, "tell me about *this*. Like, what's happened to me. And how long's it going to last. And is it . . . like, is this really *me*, or what?"

I nodded, remembering that Maridel and Gwendola always avoided such questions, determined that I wasn't going to be like that. —It's really you, I told him. —It is part of you, anyway. Madame Gwendola believes it is a kind of energy field that your body produces, or that produces your body."

"Madame Gwendola is full of shit," he said.

—Well, there, I said. —Do you hear that? The normal Turner would not, would he, have said that. He might *think* that, and he might someday *decide* that, after considering it for a long time, but the ordinary Turner, the one back at Bad Winters, would almost certainly have been too . . .

"Chicken," he said.

—Well. Perhaps. Or simply polite. But you see, this Turner is different. It's really you . . . it *feels* like you, doesn't it? . . . but at the same time it represents an extreme version of what you are, or an outer limit of what you might be. The sum of all your tendencies. The final, the ultimate Turner. (I paused here; resuming cautiously—) Gwendola calls this an extrapolated self, a projected self . . . as though the forces that drive you to be what you are, what you are becoming, were brought into physical existence, translated from hazy potentialities into actual forms.

"And that's what the Identity machine does? Makes forms out of, out of nothing?"

—No, out of something. Out of what people call the aura, maybe. Madame Gwendola thinks so. Her husband, Maridel's father, thought something different. A field, he called it. An event-field. A matrix of subtle energies. In other words, something essentially physical, though hard to apprehend. Maybe it all comes to the same thing, but the two of them argued about it. I was very young, but I remember.

[Did I pause here? Did I stare moodily, stupidly, into some misty childhood landscape? Perhaps Turner can tell us, who was watching me so closely.]

—*He* used to say, I went on, that the field was connected to ordinary matter through the motion of the molecules, the DNA. *She* used to say it was not connected at all. That it existed before the DNA, long before conception. That it had always been there, waiting. That it somehow predestined the chemical vibrations, the molecular dance, and shaped the Self to its own pattern. She believed in archetypes, you see. The primacy of the Idea. Idea, Identity: a kind of equation for her. The Doctor, her husband, said that ideas are simply human constructs, a natural result of our habit of observation, our desire to impose pattern upon randomness. That was their one, constant argument.

"What about you?" he said.

This forceful new Turner, a concentrated essence of himself, looked at me, straight into my eyes; and though the same qualities were there as always—the compassion, the concern—there was also a hardness, the obsessive center of him, the part he himself had seldom glimpsed and could scarcely even have guessed at—and he wanted to know

What about you? He demanded it. His eyes pressed into mine, and I was quite sure he didn't mean what did I believe, which of the two points of view did I agree with. He meant, in the most fundamental way, *what about me*. How did I account for myself? What manner of being was at the dark center of Tristin, that presumed to know the dark center of Turner?

I was sixteen years old and looked younger and was usually shy. But I was thoughtful enough to know these things, and other things, and to foresee possible outcomes. I saw that Turner and I were about to pass a dangerous line, a border, whether or not we particularly liked the other side of it.

—You know about me already, I told him, as evenly as I could. You know everything about me. You've *seen* me.

This may have surprised him. But *Yes*, you could feel him thinking. *I have seen him*. There in the drawing room, clutching the metal rod: stripped bare in a way for which mere physical nakedness is only a metaphor. Though in this case a fitting one. It embarrassed me, that memory, as it continued to enlighten Turner, in retrospect. Yes, he nodded, with narrow eyes: I saw. I see. I understand now.

"I'm sorry," he said. "Gosh, I didn't . . ."

A blush spread across the features of the half-substantial ghost. The truest Turner.

I looked away.

"I mean," as always, unable to leave it alone, he stammered on, "I don't mean I'm sorry that, that you feel . . . but like, I don't—"

Was I about to reply? I looked back at him, I remember. I thought of all the things I might never again have a chance to say. It was not *really* Turner, after all.

Then the door, a rusted metal thing, blew open.

The electric bulb shattered into blackness, leaving only a smell of smoke, scorched metal. Moonlight.

Into the room came three, four, many people, carrying firearms. They were dressed in dark clothing, loosely fitted, still showing wrinkles as though just an hour ago, for this special occasion, it had been unpacked.

"Don't move," said one of them. I was startled to recognize the voice of a woman.

Turner made no motion at all except a slight twist of the head: from my face to that of the person who had spoken.

"Don't do *anything*," she said. There was a note of something, desperation? in her voice.

Turner was remarkably calm. Because I could not help it, following his lead, I remained calm as well. The people crowded in the doorway seemed to find this all very disturbing.

"*We know who you are*," said someone to the woman's right.

She looked sideways—pale skin, silvered hair just discernible in the foggy light around the door—and said, "There's no need to tell him that. There's no need for any of you to talk. Just bring him along."

She was gone; you could not quite follow her movements. The other people in the room grew larger, closing in around us. It was Turner they were after, and Turner they were afraid of. Almost offhandedly, paying little attention, someone grabbed me by the wrists, someone unaccustomed to doing such things.

Around Turner there was confusion. Two or three people had laid their hands on him, on his shoulders and neck and clothing, but for reasons none of them understood—including Turner, I'm sure—they could not manage to move him toward the door. The harder they shoved at him, the more solidly he stood there, covering whatever surprise he may have felt beneath a kind of apathetic mask, a look of annoyance. For an instant, he sought my eye in the shadows.

"No one," he said (trying the concept out, I think), "no one can move me but myself."

They had pulled me halfway out the door, but everything within me was trying to cling to him, to stand by him through this baffling crisis.

"If you'll take your fucking hands off me," his voice went on (I was gone; I could not see him any longer), "I'll be glad to follow you. And take your hands off *him*, too."

There was silence after that, then the sound of footsteps. Beside me in the parking lot, the light-haired woman caught her breath as Turner stepped finally from the room, our own room, into the crowded night.

The end of the line

"I don't know why you came here," Nicola Quoin told us, "but I'd really appreciate it if you'd get your things together and just leave. There's really no sense in you hanging around acting like a teenager and throwing *money* around. With all the trouble you're in already. I really can't see any sense in that at all."

For effect, or out of exasperation, she tossed down onto the threadbare Persian carpet a coin, one of the very coins I suppose that Turner had paid for dinner with. It glinted under the lights. It rolled a couple of yards, still on the carpet, and came to rest having covered barely half the distance between us, a golden space too wide for normal conversation. Which was okay with Nicola, who seemed perfectly comfortable shouting.

"Look," she said, on a new tack, "if all you want is attention, like to distract the government from wherever it is you're going, then fine. Why don't you start a couple of fires and move on? The point is, why just check into a hotel and talk a little too loudly in a restaurant? Why be *subtle* about anything? Why do you have to do this to *me?*"

Turner, at last, taking up a large glass of brandy, said, "Ah. I see."

"No," she said, "not *Ah*. Not like that. Don't make me out to be this . . . to be not sympathetic or just this selfish little bitch or anything. You *don't* see."

She was standing, stepping around things. An ottoman. A teapoy. Turner was sitting deep in the compacted down of a loveseat. I was somewhere off to one side, seated too, but it plainly didn't much matter. I was a witness only; a third person. The ceiling was high, the walls mirrored and covered with linen scrim. The fabric was sagging, a trellis pattern, with faded roses. We had been brought to a very large, expensive and badly maintained private house. It was the home of the Quoins, the great family of Wine Barrens. Nicola was the last of them, the last Quoin, and though energetic, and only a few years older than Turner, she looked remarkably tired. We had come to the end of a line.

"You don't see," she told Turner, steadying her bright, worldly, turquoise-tinted eyes, "anything at all."

Pretty eyes, I thought. As opposed to beauty, which is always present, if only inside us, prettiness was something you didn't see much of, those days.

"Thank you for the brandy," said Turner, putting his glass down.

"Don't thank-you-for-the-brandy *me*." She stared, and Turner stared back at her. On each face was the predawn lightening of a smile.

"Well," said Turner, "it was pretty good, though. As if I would know."

"Yeah, well—thank you. It's old, from our winery." She raised a slender finger, pointing, warning, don't get off the subject. "Who the hell are you?" she said. "And what are you doing here? What are you doing *here*, for God's sake? I've got enough problems."

"I'm sorry," he said.

Which, you know, had been among his last words to me, to me alone, back in our room. The true Turner, always apologizing.

Nicola looked at him with those very pretty, very pale eyes (they seemed to be lacking something, an element that must once have run stronger, earlier in the line), and within her stare a new thing took shape. She drew nearer. Her long arms, tan and somewhat leathery, a horse-woman's arms, extended from a black silk blouse. I shifted in my seat. We were closing in on something.

"Of course we were thrilled," she said, "when we heard about it. Really, when we saw the picture—you there on the deck, the stage, whatever it was, standing over our friend Mr Rodarch, holding that . . . What was that thing you hit him with?"

Turner smiled. At last he smiled. Nicola went on, gesturing with her hands, dangling some invisible proof of sincerity:

"Really, we were all just dreadfully excited. But naturally Rodarch *lived*, that's the thing, you busted his balls and got your picture in the paper, but for what? Now things are worse than ever, up there, probably. They must be. He's even taken back some of his people from here, from Wine Barrens. To hunt for *you*, I bet."

At times, such as her final short *e*, a soft regional accent would surface in Nicola's speech, making her seem for that moment more girlish, more gentle. She was a tough one, though—with which, because she had gotten that way so young, I briefly empathized.

Turner startled us both by rising and stretching his muscles, in an upward spiral, as though he were unfolding before us. The dark-clothed men stepped closer, but Nicola waved them off. From his eyes came a look of remarkable clarity and purpose—so strong, in fact, that I worried whether it might be getting implausible, like the unmovable figure in the hotel room. Nicola looked ready to shrink from him, but equally—my God, where had I left my record book?—ready to drop into his arms. So I worried about that too. The gilt-edged room seemed to sparkle with possibilities.

Nicola ended it. She turned away, masking her thoughts with a show of hospitality.

"More brandy?" she murmured, gathering his glass before her. Her movements, her speech seemed part of some highly developed social instinct.

Turner said nothing. Nicola took a few steps away, toward a wet bar, but paused well short of getting there. Paused, posed.

"The thing is," she said not looking around, confident of his attention, "we've worked *really* hard to get where we are—to the point where we don't have them constantly snooping around, prying into our books, blocking our roads, putting their Camps right down *smack* in the middle of town, or the vineyards, or—" (turning only her head) "—or posting spies in the restaurants. It's really been hard for us."

She finished her stroll to the bar, this time giving herself time to refill Turner's glass, and another one. On the return trip she said, "But you know, times have been worse for us than for you. We're nearer the coast than you are. The ports, the cities. We don't have the mountains to protect us. We're under much more pressure here. It's so easy for them to make things difficult. All they've got to do is open the highways, and refugees just *come*. The Camps, we can handle those. But not *that*. So for now we want to just keep things—for the moment, is all I'm saying—right where they are."

As Turner accepted the second brandy, it struck me to wonder what had become of the first. Had he drunk it, actually? Had he kept it in, or was he sweating, bleeding away the precious liquid? I ought to be taking note of all this.

Turner said, "Do you know Harvey Goldaster?"

Nicola was a little startled, but self-assured enough not to bother hiding it. "Harvey," she said. She raised her glass so that the yellow beams of a wall sconce shot through its contents. It occurred to no one, I suppose, that I might like a drink myself. "I know Harvey," Nicola went on absently. "Yes. From very long ago, for a very long time."

"Harvey's having some trouble these days, himself," Turner told her.

"I shouldn't wonder, with you waving the red flag in front of Rodarch, right in his own back yard." Nicola moved her head from side to side, once, as though watching some memory go by. "I've wondered about him. We never see him anymore."

Borne by this thought, she moved in fluid steps across the carpet and came to light on the vacant half of the loveseat, just beyond Turner's cocked-back arm. She did not look at Turner. Somewhere out there, past the walls of the slightly tarnished room, a bridge formed between Nicola and Harvey, a bridge of remembrance. Perhaps in his sleep, at Upper Moat Farm, the king of the valley genially smiled.

"Harvey often spoke of you," Turner said.

—She can tell you're lying, I warned him.

But, "We used to drive down there all the time," said Nicola blithely, still staring away. "There were all those people. And the riding, and the parties. Those silly afternoon games, with everybody drunk by the end of them. That was when you could travel, of course. I mean, you could buy *gas* then. And he would call us at home, and tell us jokes over the telephone!"

She must have been perfectly sincere. A restfulness came over her face, into her turquoise eyes. She even said—extending the bounds of her own theatricality— "What's *happened* since then? What's gone wrong?"

Turner said, "I don't remember telephones. I never heard one ring. But Harvey says he still gets a call now and then. From somewhere. And of course there's GRAILNET."

"He's still on GRAILNET?"

It might have been too much. Nicola turned to look at him, trying to gauge this. She could not quite believe he was telling the truth; yet neither could she look into those eyes, clear and unblinking—the truest Turner, you know—and believe that he was lying.

Turner said, "Harvey's very careful, naturally. But he's managed to use it now and then to arrange a shipment, to contact his agents on the coast. The main problem is keeping it repaired, of course, now that nobody . . ."

Nicola straightened up. "What kind of problems is he having?" she said, becoming businesslike. "Is there anything I can do?"

Turner frowned. "Well, yes. Maybe. I mean, I hope there is. See, Harvey's been going it alone for quite some time now. He's been doing all right, I guess, compared to some people, but still. It's wearing him down. And now that Rodarch has come to Candlemas . . ."

Nicola nodded. Yes, yes, she understood.

It's the eyes, I thought. The power seems most concentrated there. A word used in books, in love stories, came into my head, into this new context: *captivated*. Turner has captivated her.

". . . the reason I've come here," he was saying, improvising I suppose, but expertly, motioning with his glass. "And of course there would be some expense involved. But Harvey is ready to cover that. There's plenty more," nodding at the coin lying bright, disregarded, on the worn-out rug, "where that came from."

"But what—" Nicola twisted around in the loveseat, eager for more. "I'm not sure I understand. What does Harvey want? What do *I* have to do with any of this?"

Turner paused for the briefest instant, choosing just the right tone; then said casually, as though surprised that she hadn't caught on:

"Oh. Harvey thinks it's time for a meeting of the Old Souls. You know. A gathering of the clans. Can you arrange that, do you think?"

Light, and coolness

I have a theory that light, whatever its immediate source (and from there in the large and over-bright room we could hear generators throbbing in some far chamber), comes only and always in the first place from the Sun. Or if not, then from another sun more or less identical. And thus it is connected, always, to the great cycles. It has seasons, in other words: periods. It wanes and waxes, gains strength and loses it; and as with everything else in nature, everything cyclical, we make a dangerous mistake when we bend the periods of light to our own convenience—when we try to shut it out, or unnaturally prolong it.

Well, to be quite honest I had never thought these things before, and I am not sure I believe them any longer. (I am scribbling by candlelight.) But there in the wide glittering parlor of Nicola Quoin's house, where Turner sat beside our hostess, with me across the room looking on, the light that came from table lamps and wall sconces seemed to change, to change in its very essence, as the hours drew on and drew on. As the night got older and deeper. The light became lurid, its rays harsh and somehow brittle. They could hurt you, I thought, if you stared too long at them, or too hard. The material objects in the room—and among these I would count ourselves, our own bodies—began to blur somewhat, to melt and drift, and after a while it seemed that nothing was entirely solid after all, except our own shadows. But that was right: it was the shadow-world, the proper world of night, creeping in to claim its own dominion, and there was nothing we could or ought to have done to interfere. We should have turned the lights off right away— only keeping if we must stay awake longer—and if moonlight were not enough—a bulb lit here or there, beside the loveseat, or a log burning in the grate—or just sat whispering in the darkness. We should have done that; or what we *should* have done was just go to bed, and let the nighttime alone.

But Nicola would not hear of that. It was two o'clock or it was three, and she and Turner sat thick and close on the down cushions of the loveseat, only getting up to pour more brandy, or to pee. (We had become informal by then, let down our hair; I am only reporting.) They spoke of Harvey and of others whose names I have written down elsewhere, the patriarchs and matriarchs of several clans, Old Souls, who had not yet been killed or co-opted by some government somewhere, and who might yet be able to summon forth some spirit of resistance to the Chief Administrator. After a while of this Nicola offered me a brandy glass myself, asked me oblivious of my age if I would like to join them: probably so that they could afterward ignore me all the more peaceably and completely.

—Sure, I said (a Turnerism), nodding so that she would understand me. Why not?

Summon forth, I'm sure they said that. Turner said it first, I think.

Honestly, there are a few things from very late, from three o'clock or four, that I no longer perfectly remember. I am not, for God's sake, a true historian. Only a survivor.

Who can still summon forth some spirit, he must have said, or something very like it.

The Ashenden look-alike (another Turnerism, I hadn't known I had already acquired so many), a shadowy figure, a creature of the night if ever there was one, drank his brandy and somehow, in his warm and believably fleshly body, he metabolized it. He became slowly drunk. I became drunk, owing to my size, more quickly. Nicola seemed not to grow drunk at all, but merely to become impetuous. Her arms went this way and that; her eyes became a deeper and more luminous blue, and flashed; her speech was more thickly interspersed with *really*'s.

Really, she didn't know what to do.

Really, did Harvey say that?

Do you really think this will do any good?

So it really isn't too late, after all?

They were making plans. They were speaking, slow and solemn, self-deluding conspirators, of halting the trend of history. Of recapturing some, just some, of the territory that had been lost. Of reasserting the traditional, natural order of things—which to many people seemed no order at all, or no more than the order of the wild. Do you know what that means? That means that the two of them were drunk enough to believe that time's flow could be halted, or even momentarily reversed; that some golden age that had never been, some delusory Camelot, could be brought again into being; that from our place at the edge of the precipice, with the great landslide of History roaring down on all sides, we could contrive somehow to hang on. Which, however young and drunk *I* may have been, I understood full well was impossible.

At any rate, Nicola believed it. She wanted to believe it, and Turner allowed her to. What *his* role in all this was, what he was trying to achieve in Wine Barrens, in the home of this desperate heiress, I did not understand for a while; and ironically it was very late, when I could not follow their eyes or their sentences any longer, that it came clear to me. Not a realization, but a memory.

Madame Gwendola sitting awake on a night like this. The lights of a chandelier staring down, piercing, boring into us. It was a habit of hers, staying up all night. And keeping us, her young charges, around her. In case some insight, some pre-dawn hallucination, should need witnessing, remembering, writing down.

There was music. Schubert, Hovannis, Harry Partch; and beyond them, *Black Angels*, *The Pavillion of Dreams*, slivers of Glass, grains of Sanders. A typical nighttime succession. Even we, young and clearheaded, would come to feel strung-out on it: on the cold light, and shadows, and desolate chords. At some point, or many discontinuous points, Gwendola was talking, and I think it might have been possible to make sense of it (I was old enough) except that the ideas were not sequential, and there was no prelude. Maybe, at last, I know the prelude now.

"The Defender will go out among them," she murmured dreamily. "He will unite them, and they will know victories, for a time. For a time they will remain united, and he will live. Then he will leave them again."

Homemade instruments pounded, tooted, clunked. It was up-cycle music, not yet midnight. The summit almost visible. Already, hints of the long decline to come. *And on the seventh day petals fell in Petaluma*.

"Errors creep in through redaction."

Gwendola stood and looked around at the whiteboard. Something was there, what, circles? Natal diagrams? A flow-chart?

"Here and here and here we find references to a hidden source, an unknown first storyteller. They drank from beakers, introduced beakers to the island. Not Joseph, not a cup of blood. Cups *and* blood. An invasion. Genocide. The oldest war."

Besides me there was always Maridel, and the others who would come and go. They had families somewhere, I suppose. People with odd ideas, eyes set on a new age. When they understood that Gwendola lived not in that new age at all—nor even in a recent age, the age just ending, but in something older and rather more bizarre—the kids would disappear. Back to Candlemas, to the mountains in the north, to besieged enclaves on the coast. There were always other schools, other refuges. Eternal hope of parents, and eternal dread. Soon, always, other children would arrive.

"Essentially"—Gwendola was most rational-seeming at a certain distance from dawn—"essentially, the Arthurian struggle is a racist one.

Preserve the neighborhoods. Maintain the purity of the line. There is nothing heroic, nothing moral, nothing grand in it, anywhere. It is useful to remember that."

Somewhere tapes were changed, by unseen hands resolved into something close to flesh by now; around us a minimalist landscape unwound in whispers and spare brushstrokes.

Distantly, in her parlor, Nicola's face fell in slow motion toward Turner's warm, slightly sunburned (from the Moth) and brown-haired neck. The table lights glared, astonished, indignant.

In the long-ago sitting room, near and visible only to me, children moved their cramped and restless limbs below the coffee table. Gwendola had not spoken for some time, perhaps an hour, and for the past several minutes we had even run out of music. The most remarkable thing, sometimes—as though we *did* feel something, as though we really believed the things she said—was just that we continued to sit in that room during all those nights.

"Do you hear?" Gwendola whispered, once upon a time. "Do you hear him now? I think . . ."

Turner's breath, his *prana*, flowed in and out of the lungs of this creature on the loveseat, this possibly living thing, and into the lungs of Nicola Quoin, a lonely mortal. Tristin, forgotten Tristin, who had no role in this drama or the other, only sat and listened, sat and watched. Maridel at least occasionally made some comment, some objection.

But then, she did have a role, didn't she? A speaking part. Or so she believed; so Gwendola had told her.

"I don't know what you're talking about, Mother," said Maridel petulantly. I guess, nine or ten years old.

"*Listen,*" said Gwendola, whispering loudly. A stage whisper, do they call it? "He is coming now, coming to us. Waking up in the world again. Soon, perhaps soon, he will climb this mountain."

She looked at her daughter. Nodding: "You will know him, then. You will remember him. At last—the Defender abroad in the world. The Invader before him. The Betrayer behind."

Something stirred within me, a feeling almost of rebellion. Or no, of having lost, having been robbed of something so close, that had come so very near, I had almost . . . I don't know, I was a child, I was drunk, I am misremembering, not a historian after all. Only, after all that has happened, all that has come and gone, a survivor. Still alive, and still alone. In the sitting room, legs curled underneath the table—

At the closed door of Nicola's bedchamber, watching the light of dawn approach from the ends of the hall—

In this small warm sphere of candlelight—

In the cool rooms of my house.

The tear-streaked sky

—So you're here again, I told him.

Here in the hotel. In our own room.

He wore a look of abstraction, or dreaminess, or confusion. I knew him well enough, almost well enough, to let him sit there on the bench, unmolested. There was a little mess from the night before; the door was ruined, was the worst of it; but beyond this there was no sign of the revolution, the great wheel turning and returning in the night. Our room faced east, over dead fields, and the sun stood warm at the window.

—You understand now, don't you?

I could not quite leave it alone: somehow, I had to touch him. *Feel him out*, they used to say.

—You know, I said, what you've done?

Turner looked at me, not with indifference, but not caring the way I cared, the way I hoped.

"She was crazy," he remarked at length. "That woman is really crazy. I'm sorry I left you out there in the hall."

Well.

"I guess we're through in Wine Barrens," he said. "I was hoping she'd be able to tell me more—like, what's going on, other places—but it seems like she's really pretty much out here by herself."

He stood up. For some reason, this morning—maybe the sunlight —I did not think of him as "Turner" quite so much anymore. I was conscious now of some important difference. My feelings toward him were attenuated.

—The meeting of the Souls, I reminded him. —What's that all about?

"Ha." He stretched. "God, I'd forgotten. You know, I have no idea what made me say that."

This seems important, don't you think? I touched my record book, lightly, as though it were some reassuring icon. —Did something *make* you say it?

The Akashic Other was evidently not so much given to introspection as was his worldly precursor. He gave me a bored look for a couple of seconds, then shrugged.

"Just a figure of speech," he said. "Look, are you hungry?"

—Are you?

"Not really. But I think I could, you know, do it. I'm pretty sure. I mean, I was able to . . . you know, last night, all that brandy."

Oh, it was egoistic, I suppose. But there was a taste of gratification in the fact that this almost-perfect likeness of Turner Ashenden had no *desire* to feed his flesh—though clearly he could go through the motions.

"I don't think I saw coffee on the menu last night," he said, gathering himself up to go. "I'll have to remember to mention it to Harvey. There ought to be a great market down here."

That's how it was going to be, then: we were to go around to the dining room and sit there like any other patrons—like the people in blue-gray suits, for example—making the blandest sort of conversation.

—You'll have to have *Turner* mention it to Harvey, I corrected him. —Harvey will be able to tell you apart.

"Ah. Do you think so?"

I should have been friendlier to him, I think. We were probably, right then, right now, scribbling notes in the *akasha* that will be part of the story, the cycle, in all its subsequent turns. Well, but that's done.

"Come to think of it," said Turner, "I'll have to remember to tell Harvey that Nicola—did you catch all that?—about Nicola's contacts up north? It's no wonder she gets along so well with the government."

He went on, warming to this topic, bringing forth tatters of last night's incandescent talk. Trying them on for size, like. Laying them out in the sun.

But I tell you, such things are dangerous: the bringing of light into the realm of darkness, and equally of darkness into light. The shadow-creature passed through the broken door, into the sunshine, leaving me to follow with the canvas sack. I thought of suggesting a walk, a bit of fresh air, while I worked up an appetite; but before I had a chance to do so Turner seemed to take interest in something in the direction of the landing field. He started off that way at an easy gait that soon became something different, a kind of glide. His body passed over the crumbled parking lot so fast that he rapidly outdistanced me, but at the same time his legs scarcely appeared to exert themselves. His frame sagged somewhat as he gained speed, as though he were falling asleep at a dead run.

No—it was not his body that sagged, but only his clothes. The same clothes Turner had worn, the real Turner, to the top of the mountain. They were drooping—slipping off, in fact—because the body of the Other was losing solidity, was becoming too insubstantial to support them. For several horrifying seconds one could see (anyone could have, but I was alone in the parking lot) the angular body, gone translucent now, like a holographic projection, emerge from the layer of cotton—the shoulders, the skinny legs—and then the clothing flopped down among the stubble of spring weeds. The body itself, no more than a ghostly outline, bearing little resemblance now to Turner Ashenden, continued to float away from me like a balloon, or a cartoon fairy, swooping low, strafing the Island of Lost Boys. Go ahead, clap your hands, little bastards. He is gone.

Perhaps, for an instant, the face turned back to stare—perhaps the eyes were wide with fear, perhaps the mouth rounded upon an inaudible cry . . . or probably not. At such a moment one would have thought larger issues than a set of used clothing might be on one's mind; but my first reaction and only immediate concern was to retrieve that pile of sweaty cotton. Only then, having done so, and heading back to the room, did I pause to stare up into the glare of the sun, searching the tear-streaked sky for any last traces of Nicola's lover.

2

Days

Turner Ashenden, unhappy teacher, spent his days trying to remember what he had meant to do when he left the University and went out into the real world, seeing as how it looked like he had basically gotten there. After a while it came to him that he hadn't really meant to do much. If he'd imagined anything at all, lifewise, it was maybe a vague form of eminence—a degree of knowledge or accomplishment in some undemanding field which, once acquired, you would basically sit around and get paid for. Figuring this out was a relief, and a surprise—a glimpse in an unexpected mirror—since his routine at the Bad Winters Institute sure didn't seem much like a job. Mostly, he lay in bed. Otherwise he wandered in and out of the rooms of the old house (now that they had him here, nobody seemed awfully interested in what he did with himself) stumbling over things: musical instruments, bits of machinery, priceless books being used as doorstops, the costumes of half a dozen eras, notepads covered with energetic writing, much of which sadly consisted of mathematical symbols or musical notation, occasionally both, and—as Maridel had promised—at least a hundred copies of GRAILNET USERS MANUAL. In several places around the house, seemingly random locations (a trestle desk in an upstairs hallway, for one), there were duplicates of the Identity machine that had lately deprived Turner of his akashic half, or more exactly *fifth*, if you subscribed as Gwendola evidently did (or thought the Hindus might, or something) to the theory of the Quintessence, element number five, Yesod, the lunar sphere of the Qabala, who the fuck knows. Not me. That's why I'm a teacher.

In his spare time, or what seemed like it, Turner sat in front of a roomful of school kids trying to think of something to talk about.

Nights

At night Turner thought mostly about the previous day, reliving in considerable depth the embarrassment of sitting there at the front of the room, feeling dumb, looking dumb (no doubt), and answering well-meant (basically) questions about life at the University, how it felt to be a famous outlaw, and the intrusion of mythic resonances into everyday life. The kids were smart, and these were subjects that Turner was believed, unaccountably, to have something to say about.

What made the whole thing embarrassing, though, was not the questions—which if nothing else he could bullshit his way through—he had once been a smart kid himself—nor the necessity of sitting there and being looked at by all those bright and unblurred eyes. No, it was a specific . . . um, one particular . . .

Actually it was Maridel.

I mean, Maridel was a school kid too, you know. She was, what had we decided, fourteen? Fourteen or so years old, a child essentially, unformed, innocent. Virginal, to put a pencil-point on it. And there she sat in the room with seven eight nine (it varied) other kids looking up at him. All those eyes. Small thin bodies twitching under the table. Identical uniforms, except for the breast insignia. And yet.

And yet. A certain image came to Turner, sometimes in the night: out on the perfect lawn, wind and sunlight, a movement of people: slow, like the extras in 8½, step and pause, stare forward, keep your place in line. Only, in all of that, one figure standing out, walking slowly away from her place in the column of actors. White blouse billowing. Turning her head . . . so distantly . . . away from the thing, the sight, whatever she was supposed to be looking at, moving her eyes in no hurry around to stare at Turner. For only a moment. Then off: shadows like blankets thrown against the nearby peaks the sun had drained away from.

It had really happened. Turner believed the moment had really occurred, though the context, the rest of the afternoon, had come loose. He could not explain, for example, how there had come to be so many people out on the emerald lawn, or what he himself had been doing there. The little epiphany had detached itself—as Maridel had, within it—and stuck somewhere in his memory while the other, more ordinary creatures of the day kept their places in line, stepping slowly toward the shadows. Out of sight out of mind. Fallen from the mountaintop.

Maridel's look, he only remembered. The eyes as cool and still as new leaves. Far away, coming nearer. Across some boundless divide. A moment, packed with infinity, expanding, exploding, rushing out to swallow Turner and hurling him backwards, rolling over him, and then gone. Maridel's head turning, returning, to stare obediently forward. Turner's head fucked up beyond all recognition.

Parallel narrative

It seems only fair to mention that Tristin, forgotten Tristin, was going through hell in a handbasket right about now.

One day

Like a leaf blowing in, a small roadster whipped up the sloping drive and out of it stepped Cervina. Dust hung behind her like a bridal train, motionless in the late June heat. Turner stared right through the tall sheep-eyed girl and down the mountain and into the Solar Temple and saw Black Malachi behind this, as behind everything always: inescapable.

Cervina came forward, glancing without much interest at the Institute beyond. What a weird old house, she must have thought; then looked away. Her high forehead was shiny with perspiration. She had caught Turner doing his usual afternoon thing, or basically nothing. Just sitting out on the perfect lawn surrounded by things he had meant to read, back in his now blurry existence as a student. We cannot reconstruct that afternoon exactly, but let us imagine, say, a stack of *Confessions:—of an English Opium Eater,—of a Child of the Century* (the Thomas Rogers version), and of course Augustine's, though probably not Rousseau's. Reason, as a philosophical category, was sucking hind tit this summer.

"Turner," said Cervina, "you've lost your spark."

Wha—?

"You know. You always had that, like, special thing. Like you were going to be somebody, or do something great. Like you were just waiting for the right time. Then you were going to *stand up*, you know? And show us who you really are. Now look. You're just sitting here. Like you're waiting for the cosmic broom to come and sweep you away."

[I recognize that quotation. But did she really say these things, right out? Turner swears so.]

"It's like you're . . . I don't know. *Missing* something. You know? Whatever it was that made you so . . ."

Turner and Cervina exchanged a blush, remembering the night they had never exactly talked about since it happened, and which in fact had stood like a subtle barrier between them, but which had established a lingering correlation, kept their spin-states perpetually in phase. Like that EPR fiasco, another setback for Reason. Action at a distance. Or as we say on the mountaintop, instant karma.

Cervina pulled up a piece of lawn and folded her limbs like landing-gear. "Listen, is there anything to drink around here? Or do you all just, like, keep yourselves cool by secret cerebral processes?"

"That sounds like Malachi."

Turner knew without looking up that Nurse Tawdry was already coming along with, let's see now, lemonade. An ice bucket, a plastic tray. Cervina accepted her tall glass without surprise. Sleeping with a prophet, you get used to such things.

"I'll level with you," she said. "Blackie asked me to come and see how you were doing. He misses you. No, he didn't say that. He said he hoped the little bitch was keeping it greasy. But you know Blackie."

"What else did he say?"

There was no wind now, and the sweat gleamed at Cervina's temples rather becomingly, like ephemeral jewels. She held her head straight up, the way Black Malachi was always saying to. Turner looked at her with a quiet affection that cost very little and meant nothing. Hey, I was entitled, right?

"He's been so preoccupied lately. Since you left, and especially since they came looking for you."

". . . ?"

"You know. The guys with blue trousers. That awful girl, what was her name? Dinder, was with them. She kept saying *here's* where he *slept*, and *here's* where he whatever, in this real sneer. Or maybe she can't help it, it's just that voice she's got. So they followed her all around the Solar Temple, looking behind furniture and things like that, which was pretty funny. I mean, like they thought you might be hiding under a coffee table! Only, they didn't know it, but they really only got about halfway into the maze, and then you know how you keep thinking you're going in but you're actually coming out again? Well, they kept winding up in the music room, and Vinny kept sicking Cagliostro on them to keep them away from his equipment. God, it was so funny. These big muscular guys with overalls on like some construction crew, and this little terrier nipping at their feet till they were jumping around like a bunch of overweight ballet dancers. I mean, they never even made it to the *kitchen*. Blackie finally felt sorry for them or something, and he came down and gave them all this kind of lecture."

". . ."

"Yeah. It was weird. He was like, *The Stainless Steel Savior shall win no battle until the final one, and that will destroy him*, and on and on. You can probably picture it better than I can remember. The guys from the Settling Out Camps—'Blue Boys,' is what Blackie calls them—they were totally brain-wiped, they didn't know what to make of anything, they just stood around and now and then one of them would pull out some kind of weapon and wave it around.

"—Ha, said Blackie. You don't think you can hurt *me*, do you? I am secure beneath the benign aegis of the Castrating Angel, the Freudian-Fear-Made-Flesh. *You* are the ones who should be scurrying for cover. Hasn't Ashenden already popped off three or four of you? And scrambled the eggs of the Savior Himself? Truly, I would not fuck around like this. I would be slinking back east and circulating my resumé among the contaminant clean-up crews. A *much* safer line of work.

"By then the Blue Boys were really pissed off, and one of them did something with his big long weapon—can they really set them to STUN, or is that just in like fairy tales?—and Dinder was shouting *No don't shoot him you idiot, we can torture him till he's ready to talk*, but when the guy pointed his gun at Blackie, something, um, really . . . I don't know how to describe it. But it was like, Blackie must have had this recording of you or something, like on a tape. A projection. Because all of a sudden, this sort of Turner Ashenden hologram pops up in the middle of the hall—we were down in the foyer, near the sprinkling machine—and without saying a word (which I figure is because Blackie hasn't got the sound hooked up) this picture . . . God, it was really lifelike, even Vinny looked like he had seen a ghost. But this thing—this, like, *you*—walked over to the Blue Boy who was pointing the gun and just—"

". . . ??"

Cervina looked at us pityingly, which made no sense at all; then she murmured like an apology:

"I don't know, Turner. I mean, the guy was just, all of a sudden, *dead*. He dropped down on the floor, and the other guys got scared as shit, and they didn't know whether to even bend down and look at him or just get the hell out. Blackie turned around, real slow like, and walked up to his room. I didn't even understand what had happened for a couple of minutes, until Vinny started saying how it must've been a heart attack, like from being startled and so forth. And oh, the projection of you had gone away. Or I mean, it just *stopped*, like I guess Blackie turned the machine off or something. Anyway, that's the last time any Blue Boys have come to the Solar Temple, even though Dinder was shouting the whole way out about how we were going to pay for this, that we would spend the rest of our lives in some work camp. You can see them watching us, though. They keep a wagon parked a ways up the road. Just sitting there.

"But what happened then was, Blackie didn't come downstairs for two whole days. I don't know *what* Vinny did with the body. There was a party that weekend, and like *everyone* showed up, I guess just to hear how Blackie would tell the story. Vinny had written some new verses to that song, 'Ashenden's Our Hero,' and they all liked that. But Blackie just stayed up in his room, painting, and finally he told me I ought to come up here and see how you were getting along. See if you were *all there*, is how he put it. So."

She gave him a new look, deliberating. "Are you all here?"

Turner felt shaken and pale, as though suddenly grown anemic. "I've lost my spark," he reminded her.

"Oh." She frowned at her lemonade glass, which was nearly full. "I thought that was supposed to be just a figure of speech. I mean, when he told me to say it."

Turner nodded, feeling vindicated but grim. "Yeah, well. Did he tell you to say anything else? Any messages?"

"Just one other thing." Cervina set her lemonade down, for good. Twitching, readying her limbs for flight, she recited: "*For the love of Lug remember to keep your pronouns straight. If the little slit is too tight for you, send her down for a quick professional adjustment.*"

She stood up. Courteously, or from lack of courage—as though the mountaintop were no longer quite safe—Turner followed her. Nurse Tawdry appeared on the horizon, like a white cloud rising above the lawn.

Cervina said, "That last thing was supposed to be a joke, I think."

"I guess so."

What was the use of standing around? The roadster spurted down the driveway like a hare. Or—to polish up the simile—like a hare that's seen a ghost.

One night

In GRAILNET USERS MANUAL there's a section called "Hints & Reminders." A funny title, Turner thought; as though the book contained rules for some role-playing game, and this was where to look if you got confused during the campaign, forgot who you were supposed to be. A couple of days had gone by since Cervina's visit, and if ever Turner had felt like the sort of person "Hints & Reminders" might apply to, the moment arrived shortly past the middle of this particular night. In fact it was a clock striking twelve somewhere below, in an unlighted corridor, that made him think of the MANUAL in the first place. He remembered Hint (or Reminder) number, what was it, 27 or 28.

28 (we'll call it). The Black Body is purest around midnight. Plan your sessions now if you want to avoid the immanence of the day ahead, or other resonances with the future. Spirits, contrary to reports, have no preference for this hour, therefore you may venture forth without fear. Try asking for HELP if you need it.

Fucking A, thought Turner. He sat up in bed. His copy of the MANUAL, as he remembered, was lying on a table in the library—a typical misnomer for what was really a disused ballroom, down on the first floor, filled now with white-draped furniture and piles of dusty books. He had left it there beside an Identity machine, or GRAILNET terminal, or whatever you call a cheap little joystick hooked up to a holly-wood box.

He wouldn't have slept tonight anyway. There was something the matter; something in the air. Yeah, that sounds dumb and portentous. But I swear, after living on top of a mountain for a while the state of the air becomes much more important, more palpable, to you. It's like how the Inuit had two dozen words that all meant *snow*. (How are the Inuit doing these days? Are they thriving, now that the Big Chill has come? Or do they miss their satellite TV?)

But about this air. Turner didn't have a word for it, yet, but there was something heavy, something *present*, that was keeping him awake, so he figured he might as well stroll down to the library and take another look at Hint #28 (as we're calling it) and maybe give some thought to this pronoun business. Seeing as how at this particular hour there was nothing much else on his mind. Except, of course, the usual. He tightened the cord of his nightshirt, trying to remember how long he had felt this way, how many nights lying sleepless in his room, and on further thought pulled some socks on. The floors of the Institute were mostly stone, silent as a goddamned crypt and just about as cold, even smack in the middle of summer.

[My God, could this have been Midsummer Night? *Mid*-Midsummer Night? Probably not, but still. It's a good thing I didn't think of that at the time.]

Turner padded carelessly into the library, née ballroom, where there was a fair amount of light from the moon coming through huge windows high on the wall. One summer long ago, someone had swathed the tables and paintings and chandeliers in ice-white linen gauze, filmy as mosquito netting, in a ritual known as Summer Dress. Autumn had come, but something must have happened, for the linen was never taken down, and now, at least a generation later, it hung limply like the skin of so many aging cartoon ghosts. Out of familiarity, Turner no longer found this place in the least spooky, though you are perfectly free to feel otherwise. Indeed, we encourage it. From some discreetly placed sanitary station or wetbar came a chilly dripping of water, and outside the great windows night-things turned their heads, on the prowl. Books lay dark and secretive everywhere, stacked head-high, or knocked sprawling. It was a proper enough place for a pronoun hunt. Turner took a seat with his back toward the distant entrance. Fearless. Branches fluttered, and shadows moved around him like black cats.

My sister, do you still recall?

But this was no Night of the Burning Barn. It was not even Midsummer Night, probably, if the truth will ever be known; and this is not a play-within-a-play, nor a tale of incest-for-art's-sake, nor even a quest for the Great Golden Symbol. It is a much humbler thing, the Legend of the Headless Housemate, and not even all of that: only fragments, views from different windows. The windows of the former ballroom faced mainly north, where the pole star hovered like a steadicam. Gyroscopes whining. The great cycles spinning toward a simultaneous nadir. Antecedents soundly asleep, and pronouns rising translucently from the grave.

Watch, now. Turner opens the MANUAL even though there is not light enough to read. Just to look at the words there, linear stains on the page. Hints & Reminders. Some of them he's got by heart.

> #11. Be careful of unfinished business. Lots of things tend to
>   sit quietly in the back of our minds until they are given

a chance to come forward. Be sure you're ready to remember, because it's much harder after an on-line gestalt
to ever forget again.

＊ #24. Touch the MONITOR DISABLE coil if you don't want to
see your own *onta*.

#32. Do not under *any circumstances* touch the black rock.

Hm. Was this the same as the Black Body? Turner guessed so. At
least two writers had taken a whack at this thing. Or one poor slob split
into two parts.

#38. Those who have tried in vain for a generation or more
to design interface technology to emulate GRAILNET have
often proceeded from the unfounded assumption that
the linkage must be made through some type of hardware. If they only looked with their eyes instead of their
computer models, they would find the "wiring diagram"
everywhere. Trace out the serpent of your desires, friend.

Well, fine. But what about #28—"asking for HELP"? What coil do
you touch for that? This goddamned machine doesn't have anything at
all that looks like a dial or a switch—or a coil either—you could use to
change settings. There's only this shiny handle, which I'm not about to
grab a hold of, and this little box covered with spirals and celtic knots,
and there's no way I'm about to open *that* again. So maybe some crucial
part is missing. Maybe there's a master unit somewhere, locked up in
some closet. Or maybe it's all done with magic. Magic words. Midnight
invocations. *Try asking for HELP.*

"All right, goddamn it," said Turner, alone in the library. "HELP."

"That's easy enough," said Maridel.

[A bit more emphasis, please. You must allow for our startlement.
THAT'S EASY ENOUGH.]

Turner jumped. "What . . . Maridel . . . my God, you scared
the—"

She moved around him, circling the chair. The light in her smile
must have come from the moon (and hence as Tristin would argue ultimately from the sun) but it had much of the fixity of the pole star, which

could only have made an infinitesimal contribution. Those green cat's eyes surveyed him, waiting him out, impenetrable. The shit had been scared out of Turner, all right, and this creepiness was doing nothing to put it back again.

"Jesus," he said, "I wish you'd quit walking around like that. Are you going to say anything, or not?"

"I said something," she pointed out. "I said, 'That's easy enough.' You asked for help, and I said—"

"Right." Turner swiveled in his chair, tracking the moving target. She stepped like an Egyptian dancer, sideways, the head held perfectly straight. She was wearing some kind of black nightie, down to her lower thighs. Her feet on the dusty floor were bare and white.

"So," she said, "do you want it, or not?"

He checked his robe. What kind of question was that?

"HELP," she said impatiently. "Do you want me to show you?"

He didn't know what to say, exactly, but managed an uncertain nod. Being awake in the middle of the night is different from being awake in the daytime.

Maridel seemed quite comfortable; very much at home. (Well, naturally.) She slipped in next to Turner, lightly touching him at certain points, which was necessary in order to reach the gleaming joystick. This without hesitation she took firmly in both slender hands. Her fingers interwove around it, and her eyes locked with equal firmness on the wooden box.

"Watch, now," she told him: an utterly needless instruction. Turner had time for one or two breaths of girl-warmth, then the great blackness fell around them.

It really grabbed you. If anything it was more striking in the darkness—you could tell then how different a thing it was from a simple absence of light. You've heard about this before, I know. But like the cliché about art (and this was art, someone's art, some secret master), each time he saw it Turner noticed something new.

This time, the cold. A deep icy cold, the all-devouring blankness of the void. That was how the thing felt to him—not the *thing*, though, but the no-thing, the Black Body. The lifeless and deathless Black Body, out of which the *onta* arose. See, you don't have to understand a thing to sound like an expert. Just memorize the buzzwords.

Now we must confess to some avidity here: a standing desire to see Maridel—to *see* Maridel, as Tristin would emphasize—in her truest or plainest or most revealing guise. Turner did not exactly quiver with anticipation, but it was close. He lost the sense of her standing beside him, pressed against his forearm, and felt instead only the draining of awareness into the matrix, the event-field, how's that for snazzy lingo, until the moment when a pale finger, vaguely perceived, reached over and stroked the coils engraved in holly-wood.

Two steps in front of him, Maridel stood in her schoolgirl skirt and white blouse, feet spread a bit apart, shoulders half-turned, as though interrupted at light calisthenics. She glanced at the table, the USERS MANUAL, then up at Turner's face. Her own features, lit by something much brighter than moonlight, showed an immense and vexatious understanding. *She looked right through me*, said the cliché-quoter in Turner's mind. *She cut me dead*.

Maridel. Ageless Maridel. Moving slowly, continuing the turnabout in which she had been interrupted. But how oddly: you couldn't tell, though she never ceased to turn, whether she was moving toward you, unfolding, opening her arms, or exactly the opposite—drawing into herself, turning wordlessly away. Turner stared for what seemed like a long time, long enough anyway, but he couldn't figure it out. It was like a dream, the way a dream sometimes freezes in your mind, endlessly cycling, trapping you no matter how devotedly you strive to move forward, out of it, into the light. *The light of Reason*, quoth the cliché-meister. Well, there was no Reason and little enough light in this ballroom.

The dream thing, though—that should have been a warning. Because if the clear image of Maridel in front of him was acting like a character in a dream, then it couldn't have been just the Identity machine that was doing it. Could it? No—there must have been some collusion by Turner's awareness. People have been writing and singing and filming dream-sequences for centuries now, and they *never* get it right—unless you decide to go along. Maridel must surely turn herself in one direction or the other, any millisecond now: she must come to face primly and girlishly in Turner's direction, or turn like a miffed vixen the other way. And maybe (thought Turner, with the inarguable certainty of the dreamer), maybe it's up to me. All I've got to do is, like, *get into it*. Go with the flow.

Maridel, the dream-Maridel, smiled at him. He knew that smile. She held out a hand, and he knew that too. It was the same warm hand, the same sharing-a-secret smile, she had given him one sunny morning on the back porch. Pressing her energy into him. Holding him, for that long moment, as though she were not fourteen and he not twenty-one, but as though they were both incredibly older and had done this and many other things together, over and over, for a very long time.

"Turner," said the girl before him.

What? Yes?

"Come here." The hand came out, further, nearer. The smile clicked a notch, from friendly to the next thing up. The girl-image said, "If I'm going to help you, you're going to have to cooperate."

Who, m-me?

At the table, Turner felt himself shrink. Why did this frighten him? He had seen these phantasms before, had heard them speak, had even himself in some peculiar way become one. What was so different now?

Maridel touched the buttons of her cotton blouse, and without much fiddling they came apart. You could only dream this. There was nothing but moon-colored skin underneath it, as the blouse opened to the inner swelling of small breasts. Holy shit.

"M-Maridel," you said. "Wait. What are you . . ."

Your voice sounded like a pretty good imitation. Not really convincing, but at least feigning the proper gentlemanly concern.

"You must want this," she said simply. Her own voice so quiet. "Or it couldn't be happening."

No, but, yes, but—

The schoolgirl skirt slipped like a shadow down slim hips, long thighs, delicately jointed knees. Straightening, Maridel shrugged the blouse away from her childish shoulders. She stood unembarrassed, a ghost shaded with moondust, as though someone—in a classroom, say—had just called her name, and she was confident of her ability to respond.

The unhappy teacher, cowering at his desk, thought: *Thank God none of this is real*.

"It's real," said Maridel. Still that smile. The arm reaching out. "It's real enough. And besides that, it's *true*."

"No," someone told her, a voice almost like Turner's. "I'm not, I'm not going to—"

Beside him, felt but not seen, a slender hand took his, pressed it around a wand of warm metal.

Turner Ashenden—the *true* Turner Ashenden, not the weak-willed creature hiding behind the desk—stood before us. He blinked, as though he had just wakened from a nice refreshing nap, and gave us that diffident grin. Aw, shucks, ma'am. Here, let me give you a hand with that.

Hey— You opened your mouth, you tried to say something, honest, but somehow you couldn't quite get past the intention to speak. The two figures before you, the naked schoolgirl and the grinning University drop-out, back in town after seeing a bit of the world, were so much more believable than you, it was useless even to try to compete with them. Face it: they had that spark, and you had lost it.

Maridel's hand finally made it to what it had been reaching out for, and this as it developed was someplace that Hebrews had once clutched each other while exchanging solemn oaths. Turner, our truer-than-life protagonist, stopped grinning long enough to softly groan. Then he drew his complaisant partner inward, surrounding her with long but no-longer-awkward arms, running a hand down to one buttermilk buttock. The schoolgirl raised her face to his. Their breathing deepened, synchronized, and then, for a few moments, stopped.

You couldn't take it anymore. You tried to wrench your hand free of the metal shaft, but some other hand restrained it, and it was that other hand, not the shaft itself, that you finally couldn't let go.

So you were left in the end with nothing to do at all. Except to sit there watching this impermissible thing. Only thinking, in the last part of your mind that still held itself back from the midsummer midnight's dream:

—*Help.*

3

Innocence abroad

People speak often of the "real world," and it is not at all clear what they are talking about. I think most often they mean something like "the world as we mutually perceive it"; though sometimes there is a further connotation, born of a desire to appear sophisticated (or, we may better say, *worldly*), along the lines of: "the world I have come to know through long and bitter experience."

In contrast, the one thing people almost never mean, when they invoke this old formula, is "the world as it has been made clear to me, and to me alone." Yet this is the *only* real world, isn't it? Certainly it is the world that each of us inhabits. Probably it is the only world we can ever know. Thus when we talk about the real world we must be talking about our own world, our own imprisoned awareness—or else we are talking about nothing at all.

I bring this up because it occurs to me that among my readers (bright though overly cynical scholars, is how I imagine you—but what can I know?) there are probably not many who have been arrested, or interrogated, or raped, or rescued. Yet all those things happened to me within three days of my arrival in the desolate town of Wine Barrens. Thus, for me, the real world is inevitably a place where such things happen. Your own world may be otherwise.

But those were only three days, out of a life that has already gone on longer than I would once have wished. Before them had gone thousands of other days, some of which were equally dramatic; and after them came the most dramatic of all—days I have not yet spoken of, and days of which I will never tell you. The events of those days, too, have conditioned my view of the world. And beyond even that, I know that the *real* world, the objective world, must contain any number of things that are outside my personal experience, but that I believe are possible, nonetheless. Happiness, for example; and mutual love. I am careful to include such things in the world of which I think, and dream, and write.

Still, I know that my world is incomplete. It is fragmentary. Everything I have known plus everything I can imagine, taken together, are no more than fleeting glimpses of all that there really is. All my memories amount to no more than an unsorted collection of independent views, like photographs made by a faulty camera, which may obscure or exaggerate more than they truthfully record. To realize these things is to understand that one is *innocent*. Imagine that: innocent, after all! And that is a wonderful feeling. I thought I had lost it—that feeling, and innocence itself—lost it forever, one bright morning in Wine Barrens. But that was only one view; happily, a mistaken one.

And this is only another.

Alone

I left the room at the hotel, the room I had shared very briefly with the astral personality I am calling, for convenience, "Turner Ashenden," as soon as I had managed to collect myself and choose some tenable course of action. The most important thing, now that Turner was gone, seemed to be the Moth, which we had left tethered to creosoted posts up at the landing field. If I could get the Moth into the air, which was not at all certain, then I could get away from Wine Barrens, and with a suitable combination of luck and skill in navigation I might find my way back to the Institute.

The room had been paid for in advance, as had the keeping of the Moth, so I had no evident need of money. I took the bag of old coins Turner had gotten from Harvey Goldaster and wrapped them in a pair of socks and shoved them deep in the canvas sack. Then I struck out across the broken pavement, up the long incline toward the outskirts of town, without any real sense of either urgency or danger. In fact, the thought most on my mind was of how unfair it all was. This thought had several aspects, but most important was the resentment I felt toward Madame Gwendola. After all, it was she who had sent me out here. Sent me out in the company of, in essence, a ghost. And sent *me*, who was only sixteen years old, and looked younger, and was emotionally vulnerable at the time (as Gwendola should have known, though I did not), and who on top of everything else could not even *talk*. Sometime I must explain all that. Anyway, it was all very unfair, or so I continue to believe. And that's what I was thinking about.

The sentries at the landing field had all the time they needed to look me over as I approached, and I had no time at all to change my course, or to turn and flee. Suddenly they were there, confronting me. The world became a different place in that moment, desperate and gray. But there was no time to think of that, or anything. In all there were ten or twelve of them, coming from everywhere.

"That's the other one." The voice is all I remember here, gruff but obviously frightened.

"The other what?"

"There were two, like I said. This one's not the one . . ."

"We can see that."

I was grabbed and harried and all but thrown bodily across the landing field. I remember blue-gray sleeves rolled back, thick arms covered with hair, a stench of bodies. More vaguely I perceived other things—the Moth lying on its side, its sinewy wing-struts broken, and the canvas bag being disemboweled beside me, pieces of clothing strewn about as though the redistribution of my modest personal wealth as quickly as possible were these people's main objective. I saw the pair of socks in which the money was hidden thrown to the ground with everything else, and even in that dire moment I felt a tiny bit of triumph about that. Then things got dark and only gradually lighter, and the air was hot and dank, and I understood after a moment that I had been taken into a tent.

Tents, as you know, had achieved the status of symbols, signature-pieces of the Chief Administrator. The idea seemed to be that no matter how large and ostentatious a tent might be, and no matter how much labor was required to erect it, and no matter how long it should remain a fixture of the landscape, there was still something humble, something unassuming—folksy, if you will—about a shelter made of cloth. The implicit contrast was with the old and massive and usually pretentious homes still maintained here and there by the Souls, whose very permanence embodied, in the Chief Administrator's view, an objectionable thought: that the occupants of these old houses did not just live in them but *owned* them, owned the terrain they dominated (as they invariably did), and would continue to own and to control that land like modern-day fiefdoms until the stones themselves should fall asunder, if not the very molecules the stones were made of. I do not intend to write a political tract—I am hugely unqualified to pull off such a thing—but I am sure this is what the Chief Administrator believed, and that the surviving Souls were aware of it, and that conflict between them was practically preordained. On a hillside some distance from the landing field, more or less on a level with the tent, stood the home of Nicola Quoin. I have described that home to you, and tried to give you some idea of what it might represent, what it might *mean*; and now I am telling you about the tent. That is all.

It never occurred to Rodarch, I suppose, that his tent-symbol might allow for another line of interpretation. But the fact was, by its impermanence, by having been brought to its present location from somewhere else, and by being capable at any moment of being carried away again, a tent marked its owner as an *outsider*. Furthermore, an outsider who is accompanied by numbers of well-armed women and men—as of course Rodarch, for safety, always was—is indistinguishable from an *invader*. And thus anyone who stands against him is a *defender*, even a *patriot*. These are not terms in which the Chief Administrator would have thought. But the point of symbols, of course, is that they do not speak to us in the language of thought, or reason, but flash their meanings directly and immediately in the language of intuition. The Chief Administrator was a reasonable man. Which is as much as to say that he had none of the intuitive sharpness of, for example, Black Malachi Pantera; or even Nicola Quoin.

I don't know if Rodarch himself ever came to Wine Barrens. It does not matter especially. His symbols were here, his colors, his slogans, his Settling Out Camps. His orders. His laws. And I was now—where I stood in the hot and stinking tent, being stared at by a dozen blue-clad lawbringers—Rodarch's prisoner, though the man himself might have been a thousand miles away, soundly asleep, as innocent as the day he was born.

A wild boy

My interrogation began immediately. I will not tire you with the early stages, the formalities required by law, the initial misinterpretation of my silence. By the time we all got to know each other, I had acquired a few bruises, one of which made it painful to breathe. The gang of sentries who arrested me was replaced after an hour or so by a different group, evidently higher-ranking, who I must say were much better groomed and more hygienic than the first, though on the whole they were even less sympathetic. Their uniforms were the same—this was Rodarch's army, after all—but it was clear that I had been handed up a rung of some hierarchy.

No more than four or five of the new group were present at any time, and after a while—when it became evident what a feeble prisoner I was, indeed—the number dropped to two or even one. It was afternoon by now, I don't know how late. Heat radiated from the canvas like an orange haze. I was taken to the center of the tent, where murky light came down from a sort of smoke-hole, as in a teepee, and there I was placed beside a small table on which lay a pen and, of all things, my record book. This had been thumbed-up roughly, and several pages torn, but everything had subsequently been put back into fastidious order. Without doubt, every word had been carefully read. There were messages aplenty here, for all of us.

My chief interrogator at this point was a gentleman (this term occurred to me spontaneously, and seems quite appropriate) with a taut rectangular face, and nearly colorless eyes. The physical contrast between the two of us was so great that we might once have been said to belong to different "races." My own skin had a tan or olive-toned cast, deepening to mocha brown when (as rarely happened) I stayed much in the sunshine; and it was thin, so that in places you could see blue veins and the spectral silhouettes of bones. The skin of the interrogator was thick and plaster-white. He seemed, himself, to be struck by our dissimilarity, and just as quickly to perceive this as being to his own great advantage. For he wasted no time in ordering me to strip off all my clothes.

How can I describe my state of mind? I had always been greatly dissatisfied with my body. Though it has since proven itself to be a durable thing, it is so small and delicate-seeming that people have always taken me to be a good deal younger than I am. (Turner, you know, was off by two full years.) Puberty had come and gone without notable impact: my voice, though fuller, was still high and soft, and my physical proportions were those of a ten-year-old boy, all taken up with gangly limbs and skinny torso, with barely a moustache of hair above my pubis. The white-skinned interrogator surveyed all this with a dispassionate pleasure, surmising that he had visited upon me the ultimate humiliation. I have been told since that this is a fairly standard practice in questioning prisoners, but in my mind it was a torment invented especially for me.

"Why did he bring you?" the man said softly. "Why did he come here with *you?*" (Faint note of contempt here.) "Why wouldn't he have wanted to make his escape alone?"

He gestured toward the record book, at the same time turning partly away, indicating that I should write whatever I might have to say in reply, and not feel hurried about it. This too is probably a standard technique: intimations that the interrogator himself has nothing in greater abundance than time.

In that moment, if I could have done so, I would have cursed him in half a dozen languages. And then I would have cursed myself. I would have uttered those dark phrases that Maridel had used, when we were children, to frighten me: *enchantments*, she called them. I would have summoned forth every horrible spirit who would hear me, to deliver us and the tent and all of Wine Barrens to hell straightaway.

In truth, I could do no better than make a noise somewhere between a sigh and a whimper. The tall man looked down, well gratified. He smiled at me with a mouthful of immaculate teeth.

"It is very puzzling," he said. "Very puzzling indeed. That a notorious criminal—a murderer, many times over—a man who has dared to stand in open defiance of a great leader of the people—that such a person should choose as a companion such a pitiful thing as *you*."

If this was puzzling, he seemed to relish the puzzle very much. His eyes flashed, and he stepped back and forth beside the table, tapping the record book now and then as though to remind me of its presence. After a minute he resumed:

"Mind you, it's clear enough why you wished to travel with *him*. That stands out a mile, from every page. Every sentence."

It did? I trembled, though at the same time I could neither understand nor believe this. I had been most circumspect, I thought, in jotting down notes and recollections that would be meaningful only to me, with no reference to the overall context, lest just such a terrible misfortune as this should possibly occur. Nonetheless I was immediately filled with dread, and found the phrases of the record book spinning wildly through my mind.

The interrogator (I have no other name for him but that) was watching me closely. I wish I had known what he was trying to do—what in fact he was successfully doing. I cowered before him like a trapped, helpless beast; or like a wild boy of legend, caught and dragged in from the woods, facing for the very first time the terrors of civilization. Like the wild boy, knowing nothing better, I began to cry.

"Little wailing faggot," the interrogator muttered, possibly to himself. There was nothing—no color, no animosity—in his voice. It was simply a categorization. I was a specimen, and he was a scientist, examining me calmly, recording his observations.

Well. If nothing else, I understood now what he had learned from studying my notes, and it would be foolish to dispute it. Of course I was in love with Turner Ashenden. You have probably, a bright scholar, taken due note of that yourself. From my present standpoint it does not seem so alarming—something that must be *admitted*, rather than simply said —but at the time, in that awful tent, it was my great secret, the one thing I would never have revealed, no matter what sort of torture ensued. And this is not a vain claim to heroism. Rather, it is simply the case that I would not, could not have spoken of my feeling for Turner, because I had never dared to think directly about it—not even to myself. Until that wise, cruel, deliberate stranger, tapping on my notebook, informed me that I was a *little wailing faggot*, I had actually never known.

My world had just become a stranger and larger place, because I had just changed within it. Should I have thanked my interrogator for that?

The questioning continued. The interrogator came and went, sending in other men (always men; this rung of the hierarchy did not seem to involve women) in teams of two and three, then coming back himself to check their progress. What they wanted to know, of course, was what had become of Turner. But it is, I imagine, a feature of their art that they seldom put this question to me in any direct way. No, the interrogator had identified the point of weakness, the flaw in the stone, and it was from there—chipping, rather than hammering away full-force—that things proceeded. The general strategy in such cases must be to crack open the psyche like a nut, confident that everything of interest within will then be revealed.

I made no effort to resist, though neither exactly did I cooperate. In fact, early in the game I had virtually told them all that I knew: that Turner had never been in Wine Barrens at all, that their informant at the landing field had been deceived by a very convincing look-alike, that the real Turner had never boarded the Moth at all. For my frankness I was rewarded with numerous cuffs about the ribs (this having been determined to cause me a good deal of pain but no real injury) and a stream of vilification which was probably a good deal less effective than my questioners might have hoped. After all, there was little that could be said about me just now that I would not have believed. I heard each new epithet with a sort of philosophical sadness: the feeling that my eyes had been opened at last to the sorry state of my soul. Deeper than that, and than the bruises, those foul-mouthed men in the tent were unable to touch me.

They gave it up sometime very late that night, and left me to lie in exhaustion—too wrought-out really to sleep, which might have restored some of my clarity of mind—where I had cowered all day, in the center of the tent.

Very early, before dawn, the interrogator returned. He was not surprised to find me wallowing there, half-awake and crazy-eyed; nor, for that matter, was I surprised to find him alert, his clothing new and well pressed, his face close-shaven, his manners impeccable. It seemed an essential part of his approach to emphasize how greatly different, opposite in every way, we two were.

"Do you know," he said, "I have been thinking it over, and I don't believe anymore that you are unable to talk."

This captured my attention, which by then was not an easy thing to do.

"No," he said. He stood there smiling, as though this line of thought gave him much pleasure. "You aren't deaf, after all, and that's what one would normally expect. Nor do you seem to be impaired of mental function. As a matter of fact you are surprisingly intelligent."

This seemed to cause him a bit of regret. He tapped again, as was his habit, upon my notebook. This smallest of gestures had by now accreted a heavy load of association; which of course he knew.

"I think the reason you don't talk . . . that you *won't* talk, let me say . . . lies somewhere else. Some psychological ground, perhaps. A trauma, from your childhood . . ."

He let his voice hang there, in the stale air of the tent, which had only just begun to brighten with the new day. I suppose he was concerned that the sunrise might give me a sense of renewed hope, and had wanted to forestall that.

A trauma, from your childhood. I would never have thought to describe it that way. He was a brilliant man, I decided. This sharpened the hatred I felt for him. Of course I understand now that hatred is like nothing other than love in its ability to arouse one's fascination.

I lowered my eyes, partly because it hurt my head to stare upward like that, partly out of a reflexive need to absorb these new thoughts. The act of doing so, however, must have angered the interrogator, because he was suddenly upon me with a fury he had not shown before.

"Damn you," he said, "you wretched little bastard. What kind of thing *are* you? Where have you come from, to end up like this?"

He had dropped to his knees, nearly straddling me, and now seized me by my hair. My head shook loosely, as though it were barely attached.

"Look," he cried, "you're not even *made* like a human. You're just a bunch of bones slung together. You're like some—"

The power of language seemed to desert him. He released my head, then struck me hard on the chest, until despite myself I gasped and sobbed, and then he grabbed me by my shoulders, lifting me up, as though he wished to assure himself that I had not lost consciousness.

"Is there anyone *in there?*" he demanded. "Is there a *person* inside this stinking flesh?"

I think I know what it was that so enraged him: an aspect of my character, no more than that; a tendency to assume in the presence of stronger wills than my own (and they are everywhere) a nearly absolute passivity. I must have been born with at least an inclination toward this, but whatever potential had been granted me at birth had been nurtured and brought to perfection at Bad Winters.

This meant nothing to me at the time. Nothing did, but the overwhelming forcefulness of the interrogator. He began to shake me, first violently, by the upper arms, then more slowly, with great cruelty and calculation, timing his upward yanks so that my head should snap as far back as it would go, then forcing me down again, into the floor of the tent, with agonizing slowness, his strong fingers quivering where they pressed into me.

"God damn your soul," he said, his voice a kind of breathy chant. "I'll make you talk. I'll make you *beg.* You fucking animal."

I have told you what happened next. I do not much want to elaborate it. But I should say, at least, that in that horrible moment—because I was crazy with pain and sleeplessness, and because the tent was less than half light, and because the powerful man above me seemed to glow as pale as a spectre—I had no warning at all. Nor was I at all surprised. I had lost the sense of both the future and the past: the memory of how I had gotten to this moment, and the belief that I would ever go beyond it. I was suspended, as it were, in an eternal present. There are religious disciplines, I think, that try to teach this—rituals that are supposed to lead to such a detachment from the flow of time. I can attest that there is, or was for me, even there on the floor of the tent, a kind of serenity about it; though it may have been no more than the indifference of one who knows he is going to die.

The interrogator forced me over, face-down, by lifting rather than rolling, so that my naked bottom was hefted up against his thighs, and my weight was supported by one of his arms curled around my stomach. In this position he prepared to mount me. I sensed some fumbling from behind, an adjustment of posture, and in a certain blind way—though I thought and felt nothing about it, one way or another—I sensed the coming thrust.

History is made up of tiny quanta of time. The universe was created in one, and will cease to exist in another. Somewhere in between, my own universe, my real world, melted and reformed, and I swear it took no more time than the smallest measurable interval. This is precisely what happened:

Turner Ashenden came to me, walking hesitantly with that sort of sideways-turning gesture of his, entirely habitual, that makes him seem to wonder what he's doing there in the first place. In this case he was coming to save my life; and he did so, as he did all things, without making a big deal of it. He walked over until he was standing beside me in the dusty tent, looking down with worried eyes, glancing up and down the length of my body. I was looking away, of course—staring blindly at the ground-cloth—but somehow I could see clearly every movement of Turner's eyes, every nuance of expression.

—This guy's trying to fuck you, he said, sounding rather perplexed.

—Yes, I said. (My own voice was flattened, as befitted someone in my position.)

Turner frowned, scratched his head. He studied the situation at some length, trying to make sense of it. His foot brushed the ground beneath my chest, checking it for softness.

—Well, look, he finally suggested, why don't you roll over, at least. That way you'll be maybe a little more comfortable.

—Sure, I said, why not? I was grateful for the occasion to use this one last Turnerism.

He nodded, gave me a wistful little smile. Politely, then, he turned away, and made an awkward show of ambling toward the door. Halfway there, he vanished.

The interrogator bent me forward at the middle, lifting my bottom high in the air, then began roughly to force me down onto him.

I knew exactly what to do. With a smile that must have looked like one of pleasure (it was really one of gratitude for this piece of good advice) I forced myself upward with one leg, twisting around so that I was more or less face-up. The tall man was taken very much by surprise. When I was able to see him, looking down between my splayed legs, he was clutching himself in desperation, with a look of something like agony on his face. It was only lust, I think: an extremity of self-loathing and desire. In my inspired state, I did everything imaginable to stoke his consumptive passion, as though I knew that would destroy him. (I did not: I was merely following Turner's suggestion.) When he lowered himself against me, cursing hotly in my face while thrusting blindly, furiously below, I reached down and guided him to his target. Then—purely to lessen my own discomfort—I pulled my legs up, pressing my own sexual parts against his stomach, gripping my knees while he pushed and pushed inside me. It did not last long.

Of course it hurt terrifically, but what did I know of that? I was protected by my own insanity. From a great psychic distance I observed the interrogator pulling out of me, forcing himself brusquely back into some semblance of self-repair, and fairly running from the tent.

That was the end. The end of my life, I must have believed at the time. I closed my eyes against the pain that blared from my head and chest and bottom, and in a few moments I fell into one of the last sound sleeps of my life—for ever after I have been something of a night-owl, and an insomniac. I did not know it, but my interrogation was over. I was to be remanded to a local court for prosecution, on the charge of abetting a fugitive. There was nothing more to be gotten from me. I never saw my interrogator again.

.

After that

I opened my eyes, not in a tent—a room with whitewashed walls, the purring of machinery, calm light drifting through curtains, forgetfulness like salve laid across my mind—and closed them once more.

When I woke again, for good, I learned that I was in an Administration clinic, somewhere near the local Settling Out Camps. The people who came to look at me were all politeness, though they must have known I was a criminal. Their job was to care for me, to restore me to order, and they set about doing so without minding who I was or whether I really wanted to be put back in order or not.

It was my first encounter with what I now think of as "rational" medicine. There was equipment of various kinds, probes and tubes and monitors, things that were stuck into me or wrapped around or pressed against; each thing measured some parameter of my physical state, and the findings of each were duly noted on papers and charts, which regularly were consulted by one or another of the concerned professionals who came and went. There was something quaintly democratic about the process, as though the question of what was the matter with me was being decided by a tally of votes, each instrument casting a single one and the returns being counted and analysed by a team of experts, who concluded in the end that I was ill. Accordingly, I was fed and injected and urged to get up and walk now and then, across the room and back. Every few hours a fresh set of readings was taken, and my bodily wastes were gathered in a shallow pan and borne away.

Always at Bad Winters, when I did not feel well, I was attended to by Nurse Tawdry, though Gwendola chose the proper course of treatment. Her catch-all therapy was extract of echinacea taken every couple of hours, under the tongue, and three days of bed-rest. If a weakness of the liver was suspected (as it often was, with me) the remedy of choice changed to dandelion juice, and because this acts more slowly, my confinement was extended to one week. I cannot remember either treatment failing, ever.

There were many more remedies than those, of course, prescribed for other children at the Institute; and in fact an entire corpus of theory underlay their application. Here, as one looks more deeply, one begins to grasp the distinctive features of the healing arts as I had known them—in comparison with which, I am calling the sort of medicine practiced in the clinic "rational." Let me give you one example.

On certain mornings, chosen beforehand by Gwendola in consultation with a mechanical orrery, various herbals and an ephemeris, those of us who formed the Institute's inner circle were roused before dawn to join in a sweep of the herb gardens. These gardens were tucked into ledges and terraces all around the mountaintop, which permitted a variety of microclimates and compass orientations, and were strung together by a winding footpath. Our mission on these outings was the harvesting of a particular herb—the one whose planetary influences and cultural requirements reached an optimal confluence on that particular day. I must have gone on hundreds of those walks, and I can assure you—who may need assurance by this time—that if you find it ludicrous that rosemary should be gathered on a certain morning under Leo, while comfrey must be left alone until the first waning moon in November . . . well, I thought it was ludicrous, too. And so did Maridel. For (though I was a timid and impressionable child, and Maridel had her weird streak) neither of us was stupid.

Gwendola came along, when she felt like it, and on those mornings particularly Maridel let her doubts be known.

"This is so ridiculous, Mother," she would say—I am thinking of her at about the age of eleven. "It's just superstitious and dumb. The *plant* doesn't care when you cut it."

Gwendola either ignored her or, on very fine mornings, laughed. An act was only superstitious, she explained, if it was performed without reflection. As we were both very reflective children, this was not a danger. In any case, the effectiveness of ritual is *not* dependent upon belief, no matter what the anthropologists tell us; and moreover Maridel's concern for the opinions of the plant boded well for the success of our expedition!

In the whitewashed room of the clinic, time was quite different. I don't mean that the clinic represented a different era; it is my understanding that both strains of medical science—indeed, of human knowledge at large—have jostled together for quite a while. I mean that the nature of Time itself, the way in which events were related to one another, seemed altogether distinct. There were cycles and rituals here, as at the Institute, but they were driven by something apart from the whirlings of the cosmos: their gears meshed without regard even to the time of day. It must have been afternoon when I first opened my eyes in that room (I have recorded the impression of soft window-light), and I think when I really woke up it was well into the evening. At such an hour, at Bad Winters, I would have been out of luck. Night, for the invalid, was a time of compulsory darkness and solitude: even reading silently in bed would have been discouraged. But here at the clinic, I found the room as bright as though it were daytime, and plenty of courteous people willing to talk to me—even to discuss in detail my "condition." I will not go into all that, some of which made for uncomfortable conversation; but the most serious thing was an injury to the liver (aha!) together with an accumulation of blood. It appeared to the staff that I had been dealt with rather badly. Yet at no time did any of them ask me what had happened, or why. Gwendola would *never* have commenced a course of treatment without knowing that.

I lay awake all of that night, only slipping into an unsatisfying doze shortly before daybreak. Something that was being fed to me in little capsules made me perpetually woozy, yet also effectively interfered with the most restful kind of sleep. Thus when I greeted the third morning of my visit to Wine Barrens, I was feeling tired and muddle-headed, and generally unwell. They say that prisons are useful chiefly in producing a class of people called criminals, and it is probably also true that hospitals are most successful in the manufacture of invalids. Fortunately I did not spend much time learning to become one, and the habit has not stuck.

Now there occurred the fourth new life-event of those three days: my rescue.

As a measure of how dull-witted I had become, from the unfamiliar routine of the clinic, and the pain-reducing drugs, I did not even perceive at first that a rescue was in progress. What I did perceive was two black-cloaked figures who entered my room, smack in the middle of lunchtime, surprising an attendant whom they promptly smashed over the head and for all I know killed on the spot. He or she (honestly, I can't remember) fell down heavily enough, and lay there motionless. The only thing I could think was that—in defiance of all statistical likelihood—I was about to become the victim of some bizarre crime. I had no experience of criminal behavior, other than my own, though it was said to be quite common nowadays. I had read of outlaws, known as dacoits, who dressed and acted like this . . . or was that in another part of the world? But you see how confused I was.

The chief criminal—a third one, entering the room after the first two had cleared the way—stood before my bed and looked at me through pale eyes that glowed beneath a cowl. After no more than a glance, this fright-some individual complained:

"That's not *him*. Wasn't there another one?"

I was not surprised (though I could make no sense of it) to recognize the voice of Nicola Quoin.

One of her confederates began, "This is the room they—"

"Damn it!" The Princess of Outlaws drew her hood back. To me she said, "We thought you were . . . I mean, when I heard . . ."

I looked away, and we passed a moment of abashment, for everyone knew what she had thought. Nicola ended this by saying:

"Well, all right. Take him and let's go. Can you walk?"

I had crossed the room, and back again, just an hour ago. I motioned to the cupboard near the bed where the staff had packed away my things. Nicola opened the drawer to a pile of clothes from which all traces of the tent had been scrubbed away, and the battered record book.

"Oh," said Nicola. "Well—get dressed, then. Hurry, though."

She made no move to leave the room, and did not so much avert her eyes as stare pensively aside, reformulating. I did not care much. My own nakedness was of little interest to me now, and I supposed of little interest to anyone. It was harder than I had expected, getting dressed, and Nicola wound up helping me put my pants on.

"They really knocked you around," she observed—with, I thought, a stirring of sympathy. It was the first time she ever had seemed to notice me. I felt very frail, standing there leaning against her. She told the larger of her two henchmen, "I think we're going to have to carry him."

She drew her cowl up, and her companion hefted me like a sack of feed, slinging me across his shoulder. My view of the world outside the whitewashed room was thus even more than usually slanted and incomplete. I saw other outlaws, who held at bay with hand weapons the members of the clinic staff. What I saw most clearly, though, from my peculiar point of view, were the bodies dressed in Newport-blue coveralls who lay all about the floor. There was blood on some of them, and none so much as twitched as we scuttled by, and I guessed that every one of them was dead.

All my life I had been told of killing and dying, much of which— the dying as well as the killing—was being done by people who believed there were good reasons behind it. But this was the first time I had ever looked at death straight-on, and I am sure that it is only because I was still traumatized from my interrogation that the sight did not have a more profound effect on me. What effect it had was confined to my intellect— or as Turner would say, my Reason. I knew that I was witnessing at last that contest which Gwendola called "the oldest war." More surprisingly, I found that I myself had taken, or been taken up by, a particular side in it: the side known variously as the Old Souls, the Resistance, "local chieftains and their mercenary armies" (a newspaper term), the outlaws, the defenders, even the Home Team . . . but that was later; that was Malachi. As Gwendola had predicted, or rather recalled, there was nothing heroic or noble about the side I had fallen in with. Nor about the other one. The people whose remains lay scattered on the ground had been murdered quickly with sophisticated weapons. There was no sign that they had been given a chance to resist, or to surrender, or even that they had been carrying arms. (Though in fairness, it is likely that at least some of them were warriors themselves, and that their weapons had been scavenged by Nicola's people as a matter of course.) There is no telling how I would have felt about all this if my faculty of Feeling had been operative. Perhaps I would have been horrified. Or perhaps I would have thrown a cold glance across those bodies and felt glad that the outrage committed against my own body had been avenged. As things stood, I felt little more than relief at being taken from the clinic. I had already seen and done and felt too much, and I needed to rest.

There was a vehicle outside, under heavy guard, and weapon-fire being traded with someone farther up the roadway. The raid on the clinic had been timed (as I later deduced) to coincide with the weekly supply run—manufactured goods from the coast being ferried in to trade for Nicola's withering harvest of grapes and other small produce. Neither side of the bargain was much to get exercised about, but—as someone had said the other night at the restaurant—it was what there was. To protect it, the garrison at the Settling Out Camp had been siphoned off to guard the highway. The local administrator must have been alarmed by the rumors of a famous outlaw on the loose.

With Nicola at the wheel, we bumped and fought and jostled our way down into the valley, where our vehicle was hidden eventually among the rows of grapevines. From there we proceeded on foot—by the most tortuous route imaginable, so that if some segment of our trackline were later discovered, it would lead nowhere conclusively—among the poor plants that provided Nicola's diminishing livelihood. They were stubborn old things: fat, squatting stumps blackened with fungus, from which sprouted medusa's-heads of yellowish, chlorotic scions. Many plants bore no grapes at all, or tiny bunches clutched as tightly between the leaves as the testicles of a superannuated Cupid. I watched the grapes and the steel-blue sky and the pitted ground, in alternation, as I was shifted from shoulder to shoulder, from one set of arms to another; one more burden on these desperate farmers, to be shared as evenly as possible.

What an odd, pointless exercise! Such pains to hide our tracks, to conceal the identity and destination of my rescuers, when in all the land around Wine Barrens there was only one imaginable source of resistance to the Administration, and one haven for fugitives like ourselves. Even to Nicola, who seemed not at all a reflective sort, it must have been clear that the authorities knew what she had done, and where she had fled to, and that they could with minimal notice have mustered sufficient firepower to storm her house, and overwhelm her allies, and put an end to this nuisance once and for all. But Nicola must have sensed as well that, by making this absurdly transparent gesture, she was rendering herself safe. She was protecting that bare pretense, little more than a social nicety, which allowed the local administrator *not* to respond in force. And that was enough. No wave of blue-gray uniforms was going to swoop down on the home of the Quoins (as, indeed, it did not); and Nicola would be free, in the morning, to offer food and shelter and other humanitarian assistance to the victims of the mysterious raid (as, indeed, she did). The local administrator would coolly decline this offer, and would call within a day or so to ask some fairly sharp questions about Nicola's activities that morning; but within a fortnight he would be back sharply at six to take cocktails on the lawn, and would join Nicola and the other guests (tenant farmers, mostly, who looked quite presentable out of their black cloaks) in lamenting the lawlessness that prevailed here, so far from the ordered urbanity of the coast.

It was what is called an Accommodation. Neither Nicola nor the administrator was happy with the circumstances in Wine Barrens; but such as they were, these circumstances represented a kind of truce between them. Since neither side could lay claim (as yet) to full control of the territory—and neither side would accept a division such as Goldaster's staking-out of all the land beyond the Grim Dyke—both sides were allowed, under the terms of the Accommodation, to claim the whole thing. And each side was permitted in certain ways, under special conditions, to have its claim upheld. Arrangements of this kind—however unsatisfying it may seem to those who believe that things ought to "make sense," or insist on "being reasonable"—must have prevailed throughout history. Years later I would deduce that such arrangements are no less than Nature's way of achieving the equipoise she constantly seeks: the moment-to-moment balancing of great unstable forces, the building of equations that constantly shift and seethe, and which are at every instant being revised. It is called homeostasis, and it is one of the truly great laws. Turner knows all about it.

We reached Nicola's home at midafternoon. By then most of the farmers, her partners in crime, had left our party and gone back to their usual drudgery. There was only a small contingent of us left to enter the manor, and I was embarrassed at having been carried on other people's shoulders for so very long. As soon as I dared—which was not until we were in sight of the door—I insisted on being put down, and walked the last few yards myself.

The exertion of actually doing so, however, nearly undid me. I was dizzy and faint by the time we stepped into the sitting room, and landed all atumble on one of the very down-filled loveseats I remembered so well and so darkly from just two nights before. Nicola stood over me, peering down with what looked like part anxiety and part calculation.

"Well," she said. "Now that we've got you here . . . What were you in the clinic for, anyway?"

Her tone was brusque, but think about this: she must have wanted more than anything in the world to ask me something else, a question which at such a moment would have sounded callous, and might have caused me (as she no doubt intuited) a degree of unnecessary pain. So she held that question inside, and inquired instead about my own state of health. For a bit of brusqueness, I hope we can all forgive her.

I found my record book among the pile of robes and firearms and other items brought back from the clinic. Nicola handed me a pen—a beautiful old thing with an italic nib that was wasted on me. I wrote out, in my small back-slanting hand:

Something wrong with my liver.

Her expression became thoughtful. In daylight, softened by damask at the windows, this room seemed a different place than it had that other evening. One could see the real elegance, even beauty, of these furnishings—which the years had not done so badly by, after all—and one could appreciate the sort of cultivated life that once had been lived here. Seen in this deeper, more flattering context, one could appreciate too that Nicola Quoin was a lovely and even a gentle woman; though she was also a murderess, and probably the last of her line. A shadow lay across her suntanned features while she wondered, I suppose, what to do with me.

I set the pen to the record book again. Nicola's head moved, following along. Before I was quite finished she said:

"Oh, no"—eyes wide, fairly exclaiming it, as though I were proposing something very irregular. "But, I mean . . . it's only June. You can't dig up dandelions until . . ."

She paused, puzzled by the smile on my face.

I was remembering something: another thing about those pre-dawn strolls through the herb gardens, back home. When Maridel waxed particularly unpleasant, complaining about the hour or the cold or the silliness of the whole project—"Just consider," Gwendola would say, "that anyone who rises each morning at dawn, and goes out walking on a mountaintop, and touches the earth, and gives thanks for the healing gifts that Nature has given us . . . why, that person isn't very likely to become ill in the first place. Now is she?"

Nicola looked down at me. Relieved, no doubt, that I was smiling; but perhaps a bit worried about why. She smiled back, though: pleased and puzzled. Another innocent, abroad in the world.

A game

I thought that I should be the one to mention Turner. The occasion for doing so came quickly—at the end of a short and unintended nap, there on the loveseat—when I realized that Nicola was *doing* something. I'm not sure how to explain this. There was a quality at once furtive and purposeful about her activity: she came and went, sometimes carrying small bits of paper, and after a time she settled herself at a writing desk at the distant end of the room. I watched her from where I lay in a blurry state of uncertainty and exhaustion. Pages rustled beneath her hand, and faintly above the throb of the generators I heard the aqueous clack of a pen tapping an almost empty inkwell. She was writing a letter. Or, as it developed, many letters, all alike, one after another. The long summer afternoon grew late and dim.

—Nicola, I thought. (You know, just an experiment.)

"Do you want anything?" she called. "Some dinner? There's gazpacho." The perfect instinct of a naturally gracious hostess: she did not look up.

Again, I thought—Nicola. Here.

She raised her head. The oddness of this must finally have struck her. "You, um . . ." She lowered her pen and rose, with seeming reluctance, her thoughts not fully diverted, from the desk. "You and I really didn't get a chance to talk the other night, did we? Or I mean—"

She stood nearby now and blushed.

I smiled, meaning that it was all right, and she smiled back. We had reached some kind of accord, I suppose. We were comfortable with each other. Things in common, et al. I picked up the notebook and scribbled out, *Are you busy?*

"I was just writing," she said. "Sort of an invitation. You remember, the other night . . ."

I remembered everything about the other night, up to the moment of being left alone in a darkened hall. With a pen-stroke, I broke our mutual taboo.

> *Turner—the meeting of the Souls?*
> *About that?*
> ——*Are you really going to?*

Nicola gave me a studious look, a real examination. She said finally, "I'm doing what I said I was going to do. I'm trying to arrange a meeting. Did you think I was lying? I'm writing to some people I know . . . well, really everybody I can think of, who I still know how to get in touch with." She sat down beside me on the loveseat, and in this she seemed to indicate that there ought to be at least a little understanding between us. I got the message pretty well, I thought, even before she added solemnly:

"I promised him."

—How can you love him, I wanted to know, after only one night? While in the record book, more circumspectly, *The meeting, where?*

Nicola was still, at this stage, quite capable of surprising me—in this case with a very penetrating glance, and an answer to both questions at once.

"You tell *me*," she demanded, "since you know so damned much. You practically act like you own him. Tell *me* something, for a change. I don't mean to be mad at you, but I really wish for God's sake you'd stop screwing around like this. Playing some little psychological game with me. Like I'm a child or something. *You're* a child, you know. No matter what's happened to you. But since you *do* know so damned much, and you *don't* act like any other fifteen-year-old I've ever seen, why don't you tell me where Turner wants the damned meeting to be, so I can put it in the invitations?"

She raised a horsewoman's firm hand to her face to brush some strands of hair away, and you really had to give her credit.

I'm 16, I wrote. And then, for reasons Turner may have to explain —perhaps an intuition of my own, or a memory of something I had heard once, or perhaps just because the devil made me do it—I added on a clean page:

> *There's a place—"The Solar Temple"*
> *where Turner lived once. I think*
> *it's safe there. And I think he*
> *would come.*

Nicola frowned, but did not question this. "We'll need directions," she said.

Not sure, I replied. *Safer without? Let them find it?*

"Okay, sure," she said. "Why not? They might like that, really. Sort of a game to them. They like games."

I had little notion of who "they" were or what "they" might like, and in truth I was rather alarmed about this improbable gathering. A game to them, she said. Nicola walked back across the room and the wet clacking started again. Enunciating carefully, by phonemes, she said:

"The So-lar Tem-ple" . . . writing it out. "And would that be in Candlemas?"

—I've never been there.

She looked up at me, her pale eyes sharp as ice. So close, I thought. So nearly breaking through. Which would put her in the smallest club, probably, in the world. Nicola (almost); Turner's double; and Maridel (the enchantress, not the schoolgirl). As Turner would say, you never knew.

"We'll say Candlemas, then. We'll say: To Meet a Very Fa-mous Out-law."

—And play a game?

"Tristin," said Nicola, my own name the most startling thing I had heard during that long afternoon. "I get the feeling you don't approve of this."

I tried to stand up from the loveseat, but only managed to sit a little straighter, so she could see my shrug. It was twilight; she ought to have a writing lamp on.

—It isn't my place to approve of anything, I pointed out. (To myself, to myself.) I just want to go home. I want to get well. I want to see . . .

"I get this feeling," said Nicola, "like we're having a conversation. Only I'm not quite sure what we're talking about."

But yes she was.

I felt the slow ache of blood moving through wounded tissues, a visceral ledger of my lost innocence. Nicola stared at me opaquely for a while (which meant only that I was too tired now to divine what she was thinking about), then flipped on the desk lamp and went back to her writing, inviting all the Old Souls to Turner's party.

Coming to oneself

Nicola bought some bottles of dandelion juice from an old farmer and set about supervising my recovery. For a few days I felt steadily better, but it seems looking back that this was just the product of getting enough rest. Staying there in the Quoin house was like being fixed in time, some genteel time past, which was very different from being at Bad Winters, where one seemed to drift across the centuries. I suppose life at the Solar Temple must have been different still—an Eternal Weekend. After a week or so, my health reached a certain level of mild debility and stayed there. Nicola worried with me for a while, then stopped, or a least seemed to withdraw her attention. There was nothing else she could do.

I guess I became accustomed to the soothing rhythms of the farm. It *was* a farm, really, and even a modestly profitable one, which seemed almost a miracle in such a place, at such a time. Soon I was to learn a little more about that. But for the moment—during the second week of my stay there—I was content to rise early in the morning, drink tea with Nicola on a terrace where the sun was broken into slivers by ancient wisteria, and walk slowly through the ravaged pine gardens on the hill below the manor before settling into the loveseat for a long midday nap. It was not that there was nothing on my mind, or that I had nothing to do. In fact I was planning even then my next course of departure; only just now nothing seemed particularly urgent. The invitations had gone out, borne by traders and couriers and even Administration transports whose drivers were thoroughly bribed, but the date Nicola had named was still more than a month away, and a month of southern summer is a great slow crossing, a temporal sea. Anyway, I had little energy, and Nicola had lots, and it seemed all right that I should live *her* life for a while, as I had already lived a succession of others. If Tristin was to have a life of his own, it would not begin during this particular June.

One thing was important, and Nicola was as aware of it as I was. She stared at me in the evenings across the great sitting room (lit more suitably now with low-level bulbs, the harsher fixtures having been wrapped in silk for the summer) and a single question, the issue that bound and separated us, hung as plainly as though it were a physical object, real and palpable, suspended in the air. We let it hang there for a few nights. They ran together, anyway; the nights were part of one continuum, the mornings another, the afternoons . . . Finally, as though she were picking up on a conversation we had left off some other night (which was true enough), Nicola looked across the room at me and said:

"How are we going to let him know?"

Not *when*, you see. The asking of the question meant that the time had come. I thought about this and decided she was right. It had been two weeks, and then some, since my rescue from the clinic, and a few days more since I had last seen Turner—the *real* Turner, as opposed to the *true*—waving goodbye from the mountaintop. At the Institute, if I had the date right, they would be done with whatever observance they were making of the Solstice (the extremity of Gwendola's bent toward paganism varied from one year to the next) and would have drifted into the doldrums of midsummer. I was not sorry to be missing that. Maridel became restless and prone to fits of agitation at this time of year, and when Maridel was agitated . . . well, you never knew.

So I answered Nicola's question.

—GRAILNET. You've got a terminal somewhere, don't you? You must. You knew what Turner was talking about, when he mentioned it.

Now, Nicola did not really understand what I was "saying" at times like this. But it often seemed that I could make ideas occur to her. I gave her other clues as well—hand signals, facial expressions—and with the help of such hints she was able a remarkable amount of the time to seize directly upon the thought that I was trying to communicate. This was not, however, one of those times. She looked quizzically at my hands, which were wrapped around an imaginary joystick, and gave a nervous twitch of the eye as though she had formed God-knows-what misimpression.

—No, I said, pressing the issue. —The NET, the Identity machine. Look—

I stood up, running my hands along the contours of my body, as though to say *This is me*. Then, holding my hands in place, I stepped quickly to one side. —*Stepping outside myself*—get it?

Nicola got it. In fact she seemed to grow rather excited.

"God, I had forgotten all about that. But Turner . . . I remember now. He said that Harvey was still using it. Wow. I wonder if it's even working, still."

I was feeling pleased with myself as I followed Nicola up the stairs and down the hallways of her house—so tidy, so *logical*, compared to those of the Institute—until we reached a little boudoir that seemed to be a kind of repository of the things of girlhood. There were beautiful dresses in graduated sizes, embalmed in ancient, amber-hued plastic and hung in open armoires. There were hats and dolls and costume jewelry. There was a dressing table, hand-painted with roses and trimmed with lace. There was even a tiny mannikin, dressed as though for a ball—one of those preadolescent affairs where the boys and girls are not *quite* sure how to regard one another, and spend most of their time standing uneasily, on their best behavior, pondering the distant prospect of adulthood. I could not help noting that the mannikin's formal clothing would have been a perfect fit for Maridel. But what a thought *that* was. The precocious terror of my own childhood, wrapped in silk and chiffon and needlepoint lilies —*madonna* lilies—preening herself, affecting innocence, waiting for some shy youth with a cracking voice to ask her for a dance. Then, with a cloying smile, bending toward his red-flushed ear, and whispering—

"Here it is," said Nicola.

Just as well: I could never, in my wildest imaginings, do justice to Maridel. I left the imaginary boy one moment short of mortal embarrassment, and turned to a miniature bureau on which Nicola's GRAILNET terminal lay.

"It's really old," she said apologetically.

—They're *all* old. It doesn't matter.

I crossed the room and looked over the intricately carved control-box. It was fine: no dents or blemishes. That was the important part. The metal contact-rod was touched here and there with rust, but the wires were firmly connected and free of corrosion. I nodded, to signal that the apparatus had passed my inspection.

"So, um . . ." Nicola hung back, a couple of steps behind me. "So now what? Do you know how to work it?"

I must have frowned in impatience (*did I know how to work it?*), because her expression became a bit worried. I motioned her to come nearer. I was not about to go into this alone.

—Just stand here, I gestured. Just *stand* there, that's all.

Nicola's behavior was entirely normal and understandable, I'm sure: the way anyone would have acted who had not spent her life around these demonic little engines. She said, "Doesn't somebody have to, you know —grab it?

—Not yet. (I shook my head.) First we'll just see what's happening on the waves—you know, whether the air is clear.

She did not understand, of course, which was fine. One was not supposed to speak much of these matters, anyway. With a rapid and automatic movement of the hands, I grounded myself against Nicola's wrist and ran a finger down a coil on the near side of the box. She suppressed (I could feel her) an urge to yank her arm away, for the subtle current of the NET passed between us instantly, and the soft pink-noise hiss of the Black Body filled the air of the room. Nothing had changed, otherwise, that we could sense, and I spent a few moments slowing my breath, hoping that some of my own steady-state would resonate with Nicola. It was clear that she did not understand this at all.

As always, I began to experience some blurring at the corners of my eyes. My metabolism was still too high (I was being held up in beta-consciousness by my link with Nicola), but I could not wait very much longer, and anyway Nicola's state of mind would probably have deteriorated if I tried. So I turned to her and said, quite sternly:

—Just look, all right? Just watch. Don't do anything else.

Her eyes opened as wide as they would go. For the first time, without hints or prodding, she had understood me.

I took the handle. The room blinked from light to dark to light almost too quickly to register. I touched the SEARCH coil, and we waited. Images flickered around us, none lingering quite long enough to be examined. One had the sense of flying at impossible speed through a series of disconnected locations: railroad station, alleyway, immaculate kitchen, dusty attic (more than one of these), wheat-brown meadow, closet, corridor, ballroom stacked with books. There were other impressions as well, and these were even murkier—sounds and smells and textures, a feeling of air across one's skin, heat and cold and an oppressive thickness of must. The whole thing lasted about a minute and a half, and Nicola was trembling at the end of it. I mistook her reaction for alarm, though it turned out to be a more pleasurable kind of excitation. She squeezed my arm as though the two of us were on some kind of carnival ride.

"How did you *do* that?" she said—nearly squealing, like a little girl. "That was really amazing."

—It's clear, I told her.

"Clear? What do you mean? It didn't . . . Hey, and how come I can understand you?"

I shook my head. —There's nobody there, I mean. There's no *feeling*. No consciousness.

". . . ?"

—It's all right, I told her. It's good, in fact. We need it clear, so we can look for Turner. What time is it, do you know?

Nicola looked around for a clock, but the only timepiece in the little room (a cat's face, with hands instead of whiskers) had stopped running many years ago. It was late, I knew. Nicola was what is called a night person, and under her tutelage I was becoming one myself. I shrugged.

—I don't guess it matters too much. It's just that this is supposed to work best around . . .

At the same moment Nicola said, "Midnight."

We exchanged a look. My hand hovered above the holly-wood box. I had never done this before, but I knew the theory quite well. It was only necessary to remember, or to guess, what sequence of swirls and spirals would spell out, in that immemorial language, the pattern of energies that was called in a less precise tongue *Turner Ashenden*.

My fingers moved, lightly touching the old wood. Without being told to, Nicola moved closer to me, and tightened her grip on my hand.

In the next moment, we were somewhere else.

Nicola gasped. (Poor woman; it must have been a shock to her. It was startling enough, even to me.)

—*Damn*, I said. I can't believe it. I just can't—

"Who," stammered Nicola, "who *is* it?"

In the strange place we had come to—a ghostly realm, of moonlight and moondust, and white-draped shadows—we were not alone. Someone else had gotten here before us. A spectral figure stood half-turned away, smiling back, beckoning.

"Who is she?" Nicola demanded. "You know her, don't you?"

I sighed. —It's just Maridel. Someone I've know for a long time. Someone who knows Turner. I guess she's looking for him, too. Only she got here first, so we'll have to just sit and wait. And watch.

Nicola narrowed her eyes. She flared her nostrils. She looked like someone girding for a fight.

I could not have fought, then. I was enfeebled and dispirited. All my life I had walked a step or two behind Maridel, and now—as astonishing as it ought to have been, that we should come upon her this way, in the middle of this night—I was not surprised in the slightest. I was angry, a little; but what good does anger do when there is no hope of a confrontation? In this state of mind, I settled myself to watch Maridel's performance.

The performance itself, you have heard about. The enchantress slipping out of her schoolgirl costume, a parody of endangered innocence, and standing naked before us. The pale arm reaching out. The bewitching smile. I could have lunged forward, into that imaginary space, and strangled her. But then again, I was not really agitated enough for that. There was nothing here that I had not seen—with physical eyes, at the Institute—fifty times before.

Not so Nicola. She was disgusted and furious and fascinated, and probably many other things, and she did not bother to hide it. She began speaking in a low voice to the image before us—I only half listened, because sustaining the image required a fair amount of concentration—and then, in the moment that Turner appeared, she gave a shout.

I was surprised, too. There he stood before us: the very soul that the two of us, Nicola and I, had desperately hoped to see. Or at any rate, his perfect likeness. And despite his immediacy, his seeming nearness, we could not touch him. We could not speak to him. We could only watch—as I had warned Nicola, at the beginning—while the enchantress had her way.

"No," said Nicola. Her voice came out slowly, keeningly. "No . . . no . . . I can't stand to . . ."

—Yes you can, I told her. You have to. It's the only way. Because see, if Maridel gets tired, or if her attention falters, then we have to be ready—

Before us, Turner's look-alike gave a soft moan.

"My God," cried Nicola. "The little slut has grabbed him by the cock!"

I almost smiled. I thought, if you knew Maridel . . .

She was quite agitated; the wrist I was holding grew taut and began to shake. I worried that she might jerk herself away, and that we might lose our connection.

"Why does he," Nicola babbled, "why does he let her *do* it? Why doesn't he, just—"

And for a moment I wondered as well: Why does he? But the question frightened me, because it had only one answer. As Maridel had just told him, a million miles away, he must *want* this. Otherwise it couldn't happen.

—Damn you, Turner, I said. Damn you.

"Damn *her*," said Nicola.

Before us, a naked schoolgirl pressed herself into the arms of our hero.

And a million miles away, the poor mortal container into which the hero had been born drew down deeper in a dusty chair, and squeezing the metal handle (a critical point) uttered the single word—the magic word—*Help*.

Energy surged through my fingers. I reached into the NET with all the power I could summon, and all I could draw from Nicola. I felt Maridel's mind very near, and felt her recognition. Her hold on Turner, for just that instant, came loose.

And we had him.

4

Some consolation

So you've lost that spark.
So you've lost your sparkle.
At least they can't see you
In the darkle.

Don't find me

Turner got up early one airless summer day and decided to join the morning herb forage. Normally he didn't have the particular kind of energy you needed to traipse after Nurse Tawdry and Maridel and the couple of other kids who liked to go along, listening to Gwendola (if she was up that day) tell preposterous stories about the healing rites of native mound-builders, whoever they are, and getting his clothes slashed by multiflora roses. But today—who knew? Maybe the walk would do him some good, and he was awake anyway.

The mountain was an odd color, like something metal would corrode to. Maridel arranged things so that she was directly ahead of him in the little procession. He supposed that was so he could watch her ass closely as it moved back and forth beneath a layer of worn denim. He supposed he would watch, too, despite himself. Gwendola wasn't out today. Nurse

Tawdry was way up ahead with an energetic brown-skinned girl named Ewinda, and some smartass little prick from up north hung back with Turner, talking on and on about the major practical jokes he had planned and executed at the expense of the stupid Settlers, back home, until things got pretty hot for his daddy and the little prick was contracted out to Bad Winters for the duration of adolescence. Turner listened to all this without comment. He wondered how he had come to be a real grown-up, all of a sudden. He tried to remember himself as a child, but got only a blank screen. As far as he could tell, he had always been this Turner Ashenden. You know, the same container, with the same basic shape and feel to it, into which life poured from time to time a new mix of contents. Right now the container held, in a ratio yet to be measured to accurate laboratory standards, confusion, bitterness, pluck, detachment, resignation, stolidity, and—for seasoning—a dash of hope. You couldn't leave that out; he had read this someplace.

Maridel pointed away from the mountain.

"That's where you used to live, isn't it?" Her finger was pointing east, or slightly northeast, where a hot smudge was taking shape at the bottom of the sky. She stopped walking, and Turner nearly bumped into her, following her finger. He was really pissed at Maridel, he reminded himself, in keeping with a kind of New Month's Resolution he had made a while ago, after that night. . . .

What would Malachi have called *that?* It ought to have a name, for filing purposes if nothing else. Something like, maybe, the Astral Ball. Though the Chastity Ball would be more like it, seeing as how Turner's alter ego had turned its alter cheek and slunk back to the alter æther at the first sign of a willing tango partner. How had that happened, anyway? Turner remembered the bizarre affair—if that word was applicable—with a certain twinge of regret, which seemed the least any red-blooded empty container could do; but at the same time he *was* pissed at Maridel, and on the whole he was resigned to the fact that his psyche wasn't ready to handle the idea of pronging a fourteen-year-old chick, even an immaterial one, even one with his own immaterial hard-on in her immaterial hand. He didn't seem to be able to look quite straight at Maridel, either, since it had happened, or almost happened. Sure, there must be dark subconscious reasons for this, like probably she reminded him of his mother or something, and he couldn't confront his desire to stick it so far up her that her eyes bulged out—but there you had it. Maybe in a couple of months, or a couple of years, it would all shake out differently. Meanwhile he followed her finger, avoiding her eyes.

"Somewhere down there, yeah," he said. "Sort of, just off the main road down to Candlemas."

"My dad's got a warehouse in Candlemas," the little prick commented, barging up next to them. "They sell lots of stuff—let's see, *fuel oil*, and *turbine parts*, and—"

It was still dark; you couldn't see the other two ahead up the trail, and you could barely make out the expressions of the people beside you. Only of course in the case of Maridel, this sort of come-hither look was burned into the retina of Turner's third eye. He stared at it, and she winked at him.

"Not now," Turner said.

The little prick looked up. "What?"

"Not now, your dad's got a warehouse. Businesses have been shut down for the summer, haven't you heard? Nothing's coming in or out except what's shipped by the government, to supply the Settling Out Camps. It's the old squeeze play. If your father wants to stay in business around here, he cuts a deal with the Administration. Otherwise . . ."

How about that? Speaking in a detached and *ennui*-laden voice, listening to himself in moderate amazement, Turner felt very much the man-of-the-world. The sophisticate who understands how godawful life really is, but sets his alarm clock each night anyway. It was a trick you learned, being an unhappy teacher.

The other trick was, let the kids ask the stupid questions.

"What are we *looking* for?" the little prick basically whined. He was wearing short pants, Edwardian schoolboy-style, and had made a mess of his knees scratching some run-of-the-mill summer rash.

Maridel looked down her (small, perfectly molded) nose at him. In an instructional tone she said, "What would you *expect* to be looking for at the end of July? Don't you feel the oppressive heat? We are looking, of course, for *Borago officinalis*, the incomparable cooling agent. If you are a good boy, we may put some blossoms in your lemonade."

Well, that was news to Turner. He supposed that this *B.o.*, whatever it was, must grow somewhere on the east-facing slope, where the herb beds were at the greatest remove from the Institute, because their path had led them away from the well-tended grounds and down through the sumac and honeysuckle that choked the open space in the woods, the "approach," through which otherwise one could have stood on the front porch and enjoyed a pretty impressive view. Turner wondered if this were deliberate, the way it had gotten all overgrown: an urge toward concealment. Somewhere ahead of them Nurse Tawdry came to a halt; they heard her voice through the leaves and the twilight, presumably asking her charges to shake a tailfeather.

Turner thrashed ahead noisily. The path dropped down a couple of steps and came out from the underbrush, growing much wider. Only it turned out that what Turner was stepping into was not the path actually, but the godless mountain road itself, the one he'd followed two or three times on foot and otherwise. They were somewhere near the sign that glowed purple-on-swami-yellow, where the drive branched off but you couldn't yet get a look at the Institute. And as Turner realized, lastly, and too late, they were not alone there.

Further along the road, where his memory told him the sign ought to have been, there was some kind of transport vehicle, probably an electric one, because the engine gritted its teeth almost inaudibly. In front of this were half a dozen guys in dark coveralls that when the sun came up would probably turn Newport blue, and before Turner could even think of doing anything sensible, like slipping back to the trail or dropping into the shadows of the tree-line, the little prick shoved up behind him, nudging him farther onto the road, and a flashlight picked his face out of the shadows. Turner blinked; his heart pounded; there were footsteps on gravel coming near. If Turner hadn't lost his spark he might have made a run for it. As it was, he didn't really care that much. Nor was life so peachy at the Institute that he didn't halfway hope for something to blow him out of it. For sure, an arrest and public trial followed by unspeakable punishment without a prayer of clemency ought to accomplish that. Maybe this isn't quite what he was thinking at the time; but maybe it wasn't that much different. His heart slowed down, anyway, and the guy with the flashlight came over, rustling papers.

"Sorry to disturb you, sir," the guy said. "Are you in charge of these kids? We asked the lady there, and she said something about a teacher . . ."

Turner blinked his eyes, which the guy apparently took to be a complaint about the flashlight. The bulb clicked off. Everything was gray and smudgy pink, the color dawn was turning into, and the guy in front of him was just standing there, not even all that unfriendly.

"I am a teacher," Turner managed to claim.

"He's our History teacher," piped up the little prick. "He's from the University."

"Oh, yeah?" The guy with the light and the paper shot down one of those obligatory smiles at the little prick, then back to Turner: "From the University? So, maybe you can help us here. We're looking . . ."

The paper came out, unfolded. It was a memorable scene, a photograph, by now widely reproduced; even in distant Wine Barrens, Nicola Quoin had seen a copy. Turner's attention was drawn more to the big man half-crumpled on the platform, clutching his most private regions, than to the bold young criminal standing above him, holding high the club-headed weapon with which the Delirious Blow had been struck. A caption muttered something about *attempted assassination*.

"So maybe you were there that day," the guy was saying. It was like a prompt. "Maybe you remember. See, this is the person we're looking for—this young fellow here with the, ah, weapon in his hand. There were reports that he had left this area, turned up down south somewhere, but then there were other reports that the person down south was an impostor. Anyway, he's still on the loose. So if there's anything you could tell us, something funny you might have seen, any rumors . . ."

Turner had an odd and yet a familiar feeling here, like he had become invisible again—the guy with the flashlight was looking right at him but somehow looking through him, too. I mean, there was the picture, and here was the real thing, and yet for some reason he wasn't making the connection. Screwing up his audacity, Turner said:

"Could I take another look at that?"

The guy handed the photograph over, carefully, and Turner took it by the edges.

In a way, you could see what the problem was. Look here—the person in the photograph, who according to the caption was believed to be a psychologically disturbed student, had a kind of glow or gleam about him; you could tell somehow that he was *driven*, that he was a person with great, though possibly demented, strength of will. A "forceful personality." A leader, even, of sorts. You would say, taking the whole situation depicted in the photograph into account, that the young man belonged there—that he fit the role he was playing, up there on the stage, just as much as the Chief Administrator fit his own role. Stricken Dignitary and Would-

Be Assassin, the newpaper might have called them. Though Gwendola would have headlined it otherwise. In caps, though, one way or the other. Major roles, to be filled by your leading big-name actors.

Turner handed the picture back. "Nope," he said—glancing edgily, not sure how far to press this. "Haven't seen him around."

He stopped himself within a breath of adding, *lately*.

The guy nodded. You could begin to make out the blue of his coveralls, though perhaps only because you knew it would be there. So much of perception seems to depend on that. The guy placed the photograph in an envelope and turned back toward the transport.

"Well, we're sorry to interrupt you," he said, speaking more generally, to the kids as well as their weak-kneed teacher. "Having a little field trip here or something?"

"We're going to pick an *herb*," the little prick was happy to inform him. "You've got to do it at *dawn*, because of the *devas*."

The guy nodded politely. His attention was all but withdrawn now. "Well," he said over his shoulder, "we don't want to hold you up any longer."

Turner stood with Maridel behind him as the transport rolled up the roadway. Just to satisfy some lingering doubt, he walked on a few more paces, toward where the driveway ought to have started, and by the breaking light he was just able to make out two black-painted posts, 4 × 4's, set into the ground in concrete. There was no sign anymore between them. The lip of the driveway was thinly but effectively covered in a layer of honeysuckle, about one month's growth. You could have driven over it, but you'd have to know where to make the turn.

All of this seemed to confirm something. Turner could not have said what—he was still sorting out the implications of what had just happened, the transport, the photograph—but as though he really understood, as though the whole thing jibed neatly with the things he already knew, he solemnly nodded. It was another trick he had learned, being a teacher.

He was just wrapping up the nod when it really struck him: the central thing, the difference between the young man in the photograph, a major role-player, and the person of Turner Ashenden, who barely qualified as an extra. He nodded again, a different nod, a different audience. He swung his eyes to the open road.

The sun was rolling over in bed. Soon it would climb out, lay the hairy eyeball on things, and Turner figured it would be good to be some-

where before that. At least on the way. So that when the sun got around
to you, it would see only the top of your head, and your knees working,
and not your entire body laid out on somebody else's lawn re-reading
Tapping the Source. Maybe, this time around, the sun would pick somebody else to give skin cancer to. And you would escape for another day,
another roll of the statistics, by which time maybe you'd have found a
nice shady spot to hide in.

You would escape, though—that's the concept. That's basically all
Turner was thinking about as he heard the gravel crunching under his
heels—not even his own legs that were moving, or things like what he
was going to eat.

Maridel was calling something. His name. It seemed to come after
him from a great distance; or maybe it didn't seem exactly to apply to him
as much as to that other guy, the one in the picture, the one who hadn't
lost that spark. Or maybe it was Maridel herself that was funny: like, the
voice wasn't really the voice of a fourteen-year-old girl.

"You could stay," she said at that instant, clearly.

Turner stopped and looked at her. She stood behind him with her
hands on her hips, way up the road. Striking an attitude.

"You don't have to leave," she said.

Not, *Don't leave*. Just that he didn't have to. Like a review of available
options; a commentary on where his dharma was pointing, at this stage
of the game.

—I know, said Turner, silently, breathing it into the æther.

A breeze blew Maridel's pale hair forward, in front of her eyes, and
in the motion of pushing it back she didn't look fourteen years old at all;
or sixteen, or twenty. She looked like someone standing beside you in a
mirror, someone so familiar that her presence, her identity, wasn't even
something you thought about.

Come lie with me, Turner could absolutely have sworn she said. But
that was not the way any present-day teenager would have talked, was it? Especially with the little prick dancing beside her, as if he was itching to make
himself a pain in the ass. So Turner must have imagined this part, or Maridel must have tricked him somehow into thinking it. And it was also unlikely that he said himself, at the end, before he was gone down the road:

—I'm afraid of you. Afraid that you will betray me.

GETTING
TOGETHER

1

Like on the road

"Where has it gone," said Black Malachi, with a histrionic wave of the hand—"that famous Ashenden uncertainty? You have been sitting here for the better part of an hour now, telling me things that may, for all I know, be the truth. You have not posed a single vapid question. You have minimized your use of trite remarks. Even your grammar has been unexceptionable. Truly, old friend, I am at a loss. I do not know what to do for you. Why have you come back?"

"Come back?" said Turner. The words sounded funny, like a euphemism for something else. "Why do you say that—come back?"

"Well . . ."

But that was the end of it.

At the beginning, the new and unforeseeable beginning, the first day of Turner's life as an Invisible Man, there had been the discoveries. The recognitions.

Like on the road. The old highway straight as a ley-line rolling down from the mountain toward Candlemas where Turner's story once upon a time began. Where we saw transports runners hawkers pilgrims students off for the Duration and slogans painted on the chunks of age-old, New Age paving—Damn the Souls Fuck the System Join the Resistance New Reason God Save Us!—and somehow felt none of it, the passion hurry fear wan hope even the indifference of people moving past us in both directions driven by things that eluded them but that Turner lately down in the core of his brain seemed actually to understand. That dance of themes, of players, metaphors, *leitmotifs*, archetypes: the oldest war. Humming like molecules, buzzing, swirling, bumping to the next higher energy state as the government wagons groaned by with their holo systems playing the same old song, some speech from last week at the University, the well-remembered sward of open ground become a stage and staging-area now that classes were cut off. Blurring at the edges, Uncle Rodarch stood at the edge of something, we thought probably a flatbed. (Was this a new symbol, a link with the truckin' proletariat?) From his soporific box, the Chief Admonisher dished up a steady diet of the week's top twenty words or less—*Inevitable movement toward a state of greater coherence* . . . *Restraint of inappropriate social impulses* . . . *Committee to choose suitable topics of instruction* . . . *Screening of faculty credentials* . . . *My student associates* . . .

Or maybe like, on the beach. Like you were backed up, waiting, wondering when it would all roll over you. Turner figured that what the guy was talking about, as he floated above the road fuzzing in and out of resolution, was some kind of shake-up at the University. Suitable topics of research, ha. And student associates. Would that be idiots like Dinder? Turner thought about the way it had always been, the way he remembered, the two or three hundred years of nothing happening much but parties and hanging around, going to classes if you felt like it, buying books that you loaned to friends who swore to return them *tomorrow*, man, which you would obviously never see again, like for example what about that screenplay of *El Topo?* Turner was still a little burned over that one. But it had been a decent life, a strange and yes disorderly sometimes way to live but pretty much the way people had been living in lots of places, not just the valley, for quite a while now, until lately it had begun to seem like there was only the valley left, out of what there used to be everywhere, and now the valley itself was going the way of all distinctions.

No, it was like, on the bench. Turner was tired of sitting on the bench, watching all this shit come down on the field while he waited for the coach to give him the nod. The coach had taken him for a *ride*, man—to the top of the godless mountain, no less, and stuck him on the bench to wait for God knows what stirring in the crowd or injury to the first-string defenders—whatever it took to cause the Home Team to pull out its secret weapon, its ringer, the invisible player who could take his place in the huddle without anyone, even the other guys in the line-up, being the wiser. Blue forty-two left on three, hut, hut, fucking A, man, Turner was tired of Gloomy Gussing it. Whether or not Harvey Goldaster or anyone else particularly wanted him around he was rolling back into the valley, de-sparked, psychologically disturbed, harmless by any rational measure, but where had rationality gotten anybody around here until all this Festival of Renewal business got started? So get used to it, guys. The bad boy's back in town.

Black Malachi said, "Well . . ."

But Turner's question, see above, had been mostly rhetorical. Whatever the self-certified practitioner had meant by *come back*, it was probably apt. Anyway Turner had decided among other things not to stop unduly often to worry about this sort of stuff.

"Look," he said, "I might possibly have a problem. See, there's some reason to think that I'm going to die. I mean, if I stay like this."

"Like this?" Black Malachi smiled: curious, friendly, undisturbed. You got the feeling he had been waiting for someone to come along, someone to listen to. You got the feeling he had missed us.

"See—" Turner pointed down at himself. "I'm not all here, actually. I've sort of, lost my spark."

"Indeed." The round face, bearded a bit more thickly, but why not, with the goddamned heat pump turned down to lower October in here, broke into a familiar smile. "Lost your spark. Of course."

"A-And, there's some precedent. To suggest." Turner wished he had let Gwendola finish her story, back there. "To suggest, ah. That people this has happened to, like who've gotten separated from their Akashic Others or whatever happened—it's pretty weird, whatever it was—that anyway these people don't make it very long if they don't hang around the mountain. But I just . . . you know. With Maridel and all. Couldn't stand it anymore."

One might have expected an objection at this point: some little reminder that we weren't bothering to make a whole lot of sense. But Black Malachi was considering. His small ardent eyes stared down at the *Quik-Reference Materia Medica*. After a few moments he gave a little nod.

"I believe," he said, "there may be something about this in the literature. I'll have to look it up. In the meantime we might try a brief course of *Quercus robinia*. Many people swear by it. And we must try to keep your spirits high. How long were you planning to stick around? Perhaps we should have a little get-together."

"Now that," said the Invisible Man, "is really the *last* thing my spirits need."

Getting goats

At the outset of the pre-party supply run, Vinny Hawkmoth declared himself to be on the lookout for a couple of nice goats.

"Otherwise," he said, "we'll never get the strings right. Cagliostro's given it his best shot, but the chemistry just isn't there. The upper register keeps sounding like, you know . . ."

"Crumb," said Turner.

Vinny paused, his foot on the running board of the official party supply wagon—a large malodorous vehicle that had done some time in the cause of solid waste management. RECYCLE NOW, urged the signboard on its flank. "What?" he said.

Turner stood a foot or two below him, in the ruins of the vegetable patch. "George Crumb," he said. "*Black Angels.* The last movement, 'Return.' With a quotation from—"

"Gotcha." Vinny aimed a thumb at the lowering sky and climbed the rest of the way into the cab. Cervina glanced from one of them to the other, holding a spice-scented cigarette and looking confused. Which was not, Turner thought, without good and sufficient reason.

The tall girl said, "Does anybody want . . ."

Her voice did not exactly trail off; you got the feeling it was still going on quite loudly, inside her head. Turner wondered if a thunderstorm was really going to happen. If it was, he might stay outside a while, to watch the build-up. Then he wondered if anybody could really answer questions like that. Were there methods, for example, of divining the inner intentions of stormclouds?

"Don't forget the blankets."

—from a second-story window, Black Malachi's voice, disembodied, came down.

"He won't," called Turner, more sharply than the occasion might have required.

"My, my." The round head popped out a window. "Feeling skittish about the party, are we? A touch of pre-minstrel tension?"

"Blankets?" Vinny glanced up from the broken instruments on the dashboard. "What blankets?"

"Quite so." Black Malachi nodded earnestly. "Sixty or eighty should do. Or make it a hundred, and charge them to Goldaster. Really, we must take better care of our houseguests. Otherwise they shall all take cold, and I am completely out of *Natrum mur.*"

Vinny scowled, kicking over the engine. The old machine shuddered as its cylinders got a whiff of the stuff Malachi proposed they should run on. "Where in the *world*," Vinny shouted above the ruckus, "do you expect me to find a hundred blankets at the end of July?"

"Perhaps," Black Malachi said brightly, "the same place you find your goats. Take Ashenden along, if you're worried about it. He has a way of stumbling onto things."

Isn't that the truth, thought Turner. This was before he realized that Vinny was leaning out of the window of the truck, sizing him up like a piece of barterable merchandise.

"What about it, Turner?"—still shouting, as the engine sputtered and filled the air with yellowish smoke. "Want to come along for the ride?"

Turner wanted nothing less in all the world than to get into this grumbling contraption that looked as though it might explode at any moment; nor did it seem entirely prudent to go urging the inhabitants of Candlemas to RECYCLE NOW, even if he *was* invisible.

"Take him," said Cervina, phasing back into it. "He and Blackie have been snapping at each other all morning."

Turner looked around to find the cigarette being placed between his fingers. "I don't—"

"Well, hurry up then," cried Black Malachi from on high. "People will start rolling in any time now. Oh, I *do* hope we get a good turnout."

. . . So Turner found himself bouncing along in the cab next to Vinny, passing what seemed to be an immortal joint. No kidding, the thing lasted all the way to town and it was finally the sight of the great blue banner there that caused him to toss it out. By then, of course, he was feeling pretty jumpy.

"God," he said, as the brakes shrieked and the supply wagon turned onto the road leading past the University, "this smell is awful. Isn't there anything we can do about it?"

"Yeah," said Vinny, manhandling the wheel. "We can keep moving, and let other people smell it too. Now listen: where should we look for goats?"

As though Turner would know. As though Turner were even paying attention, instead of staring with a sort of characteristic dumb look on his face into the fuzzy screen of his memory. "Vinny," he wondered, "what did that sign back there say?"

"Harvest Festival," Vinny recited. "Aug 2. Assembly and March. *Discard the chaff of the old order!*"

"Yeah," said Turner. "That's kind of what I thought."

He slumped deeper in his seat. Beside them, a post-Dissolution film-scape reeled by, one grayed-out frame at a time. The old lanes of student housing, lately half-swallowed by berserker boxwood, were now shorn of their green buttresses and surrounded by a post-and-wire fence. A few student types were in evidence, but they seemed like maybe they were just passing through. Several of the windows were broken, and the whole place had an air of recent abandonment.

"What's going on?" said Turner.

Vinny didn't give it a glance. "You ought to know. You started it."

—No, wait, that's not f-fair, I . . . But what's the use? Turner kept his mouth shut, and the truck rumbled past the arched and guarded entrance to the grounds. He didn't really want to look, but you couldn't help noticing this sort of peripheral haze of Newport blue. It was like, there was nothing left.

"How about the shops?" he said. Expecting the worst.

"There's basically only one these days—one big shop. The Provisional Product Distribution Center. The good news is, it's really cheap. In fact, most of the stuff you can walk away with for nothing, only you have to fill out this Statement of Financial Irresponsibility or something. A pain in the shorts, but still. The bad news is, all your major items are off the market."

Turner imagined what *major items* might be. Probably everything you needed for one of Malachi's get-togethers.

"Well," said Vinny, "I guess we might as well check it out."

He yanked the hand-brake, bringing the truck to a peremptory halt in the shopping district.

"Aren't we going to park?" said Turner. He glanced around paranoiacally, eyes just clearing the bottom of the window.

Vinny snorted. "Where do you park a goddamned garbage truck?"

He hit the ground walking fast, and Turner had to hustle to overtake him. Until now—actually trying to coordinate his limbs and so forth—it hadn't occurred to Turner how blasted he was. But I mean, it was Toasted Dendron City. These people around us looked like they were being done in claymation, and we're not necessarily talking about friendly natives, either.

As Vinny had more or less described, the shopping district that once possessed, if nothing else, a little topological variation had been leveled and graded and cleared of the unexpected. The sign said Product, and Product was what you got. Art, craft, and off-the-garden-path provenance had vanished without a trace. Undaunted, Vinny advanced through the sparse and rangy-looking crowd to the nearest stall that looked like it was prepared to Distribute.

"Yes," said the young woman behind the table. A tag sewn crookedly onto her blouse said STUDENT ASSOCIATE.

"I need three thousand two hundred and fifty plastic cups."

The young woman gave Vinny a look that would probably have caused Turner irreparable neurologic harm. She said flatly, "You do."

"That's three thousand, two hundred . . ."

Those few extra years made all the difference. "Fill this out," the woman instructed him. "It's just a routine explanation of the use to which the items will be put."

"I need one of those other ones, too," said Vinny, licking his pencil-tip. (Why do people do that, Turner wondered.) "One of those Statements of Financial whatever it is."

"You're *poor*?" the young woman said. Clearly not buying it.

"As a titmouse," averred Vinny.

Turner thought that neither the species of rodent nor the emphasis with which his companion named it was entirely correct; nonetheless the woman handed over the necessary paperwork. Vinny smiled, even stooped his shoulders a notch: just a poor father out buying three thousand plastic cups for his thirsty family.

There were other transactions in this vein. The clouds seemed to grow thicker overhead, and a dusky sameness to blur the edges of the goods displayed on shelves and tables, though for all Turner could tell it might be his rods and cones finally giving out. Dragging several bags and feeling like some refugee weighted down with all his worldly belongings (which in truth had amounted to only a fraction of this) he followed Vinny back up the street toward the double-parked supply wagon. The whole thing had cost them less than one of Malachi's old vegetable runs, and they had been allowed to pay it off with worthless government currency. What a trip.

At the truck, they found a thin woman in blue overalls busily writing out a parking ticket. Turner bunched up his bags in such a way that they concealed most of his face, leaving only a little eye-hole. Vinny, however, elected to make a frontal assault.

"You've got to be kidding," he said. "A parking ticket? In Candlemas? Is this some form of street-theater?"

The young woman looked up from her pad. "Don't tell me you haven't heard about the travel restrictions." There was something about her voice. Turner sized up the distance to the passenger door. The woman said, "You're operating this bus without a current permit in the window. I'd confiscate it right here, but it's like, probably some health hazard or something."

She peeled the top sheet off her nifty little pad (if nothing else, the government produced first-class paper products) and with maddening officiousness slapped it in Vinny's palm.

"You look familiar," she told him. Turner would have looked familiar too, if you spent a lot of time staring at shopping bags. The woman stepped closer. You could sense this: a moving mass of bad vibes.

"You're some of those guys from Pantera's house," she said, "aren't you? That Temple place? Maybe you better show me some identification."

Turner had assumed he would probably die or dematerialize or something like that before he ever heard this sneering, nasally voice again. But alas. He was still alive, and so was Dinder.

"Identification?" said Vinny. It was a classic wartime encounter: your advance forces are out there thrashing around and making as much noise as possible while your main body of troops, your real strength, sneaks around under cover of potato chips. Turner glimpsed a piece of the truck, a dirty tire, which looked pretty good at the moment, and thought maybe he had caught the Fates napping here. Vinny said, "Maybe you should show *me* some identification. *Student asshole*, is that what that tag says?"

"Cut the shit," said Dinder. "Back away from the bus."

Turner thought, It's not a *bus*, you idiot.

"Well, this is it," murmured Vinny.

From the bed of the truck came the clatter of three thousand plastic cups.

"Hey," said Dinder. "Hey, stop!"

Turner—sensing an opportunity—prepared to ditch the bags and make a run for it. As usual, his body-language must have shrieked this plan at about a hundred decibels. Vinny glared down from the driver's seat.

"In the truck!" he shouted. "Throw it in the truck!"

This is how the concept of Inevitability came to be known and loved on several continents. Turner walked back to the truckbed in no big hurry, giving Dinder a chance to, as they say, share the experience.

"My God," she gasped—so astonished that her voice fell into a register that sounded almost normal. "It's Ashen."

"Get a mirror," suggested Vinny. "If it's truly Turner, all you'll be able to see is the reflection of Delmore Schwartz."

The engine kicked over with an offensive venting of gas.

"It's Ashen!"—screeching now. "The outlaw, the murderer! Somebody stop him!"

There was a little bit of an audience—attracted by the truck, probably, more than by this slight commotion—and Vinny gave everyone a politician's wave as he put it in gear and eased forward. Turner climbed into the cab, feeling strangely invulnerable, which was surely some kind of drug-induced delusion. Dinder, dead-center in the roadway, was trying desperately to stop her mouth from opening and closing like a fish's and to do something sensible with it. The truck rumbled down toward her.

At the last moment, she seemed to find the formula. She threw herself sideways, meanwhile shouting:

"Goldaster's lackey! It's the agent of the Old Souls, and we've got him trapped right here in the town square!"

The mention of Bad King Harvey had an instant effect on the crowd. Everybody who looked like, how shall we say, a "civilian"—students, shoppers, the usual hangers-around—found some revolving door in the wall of spacetime which allowed them to pop out of existence. Through the same door, spinning in, came about twenty-five guys with blue shirts and billy clubs.

"Got us trapped," said Vinny. The concept seemed to amuse him. Turner caught sight of Dinder's head—the thin yellow hair held together in little strands by grease—as the truck rumbled past her. Vinny flexed his muscles at the wheel. He quoted: *"They've got us surrounded, the poor bastards."*

Turner was amazed into immobility. Otherwise it's possible he would have laughed. The blue-clad security people did their damnedest with those little wooden sticks as the truck chugged by, but the worst they could manage was to dislodge the sign that said RECYCLE NOW. Vinny had it up to forty by the time the Grim Dyke came into view.

"Whoops," he said.

Beside the statue was an obstacle nobody had counted on. This was the frontier, remember: the Rift, beyond which Goldaster was holding his own. To mark it, one army or the other had gone to great lengths to tear up the roadway, piling up chunks of pavement to form a barricade. There were a couple of platoons' worth of soldiers and—on the patch of ground where the Dyke bared her chilly breast—a large black priapic device that looked disturbingly like a cannon. Fortunately this was pointed the other way, toward the hills from which the shit was expected to fly fanward.

Vinny said, "I don't think . . ." at pretty much the same time that the fellows with the big gun seemed to flash on to what was happening. They looked at the truck, then past it, toward where Dinder was still squawking. Sooner or later you figured they'd have to get the idea.

"Maybe we should turn around," said Vinny. His hands worried the gearshift.

"No."

Vinny looked surprised that his passenger knew how to operate a vocal chord.

"There's another way," said Turner. "A back way. Here—turn here. Through this old neighborhood."

The truck groaned around a corner, barely squeezing past the muscular flanks of lindens. Up ahead, there was some activity around the gun emplacement. Turner thought he heard a shot, but it could have been the truck backfiring. He looked out the back window, but there were only dust and oily truck-fumes.

Vinny mashed the accelerator, producing mainly noise. "Check the glove compartment," he said, "and see if you can find any more dope." As Turner blanched, Vinny waved enthusiastically out the window. He said, "This is *great*. This is how it used to be, before a party."

And Turner, not to be outdone in the folksy quotation department, said, "Yeah—it's like déjà vu all over again."

Crossing paths

Smoke made lace-patterns in the trapped air at the center of the cab. The wind sucking through both open windows nipped at the edges of this, causing the formation of tiny motes to revolve slowly, bleeding from the tentacles, like a spiral galaxy inhabited by googols of infinitesimal dope-smokers. Turner watched it all in a kind of stupefied delight. There were clouds overhead, but the sun had dropped below them. It was probably doing some kind of harm to Turner's right arm propped in the window, but by the time the disarranged DNA caught up with him, he'd be long dead from some less natural calamity, so why worry about it?

"Where are we?" said Vinny.

The truck was moving about ten miles an hour down a narrow road that felt like the bottom of a stream. On both sides, fat trees sat there holding up limbs that met fifty feet in the air; the light drifting down was green from the leaves and blue from the sky. Behind the trees were fields of something yellow. The land was flat, which you didn't see much in these parts.

"So where are we?" Vinny said again. "Turner? Are you with me?"

"I don't know," said the guy in the passenger seat. Everything, even Vinny's very sensible concern, seemed like a private joke. "I'm of *two minds*," he said, playing it for what it was worth.

"Yeah, well. We should've brought a map. I don't even know which side we're on."

"It's funny," said Turner, "that you should say that." He sat up, took a look around. His brain seemed to be getting a second wind here.

The truck was making a peculiar noise, something like a cow begging to be milked, and Vinny slowed it even further. "Say what? Look, Turner. You better get your head together and figure out where we are."

Turner felt a surge of confidence, of clarity. The whole thing—the drive, the road, the sunlight—seemed full of importance. He hadn't felt like this for quite a while. He wondered if he had *ever* felt like this.

"Do you know," he said, "how they used to pick the sites for cathedrals?"

It seemed like a useful line of discussion—you know, throw a little perspective on things.

Vinny tightened the muscles of his forehead until the phrase *Are you fucking crazy* oozed out into the numinous undercurrents of the cab.

Turner said, "Well, actually it varied. But see, quite a few of your oldest cathedrals are sited according to ancient principles of geomancy. For example, they might take some animal and turn it loose—"

"Some animal," Vinny repeated. The tightness in his forehead worked its way down to his lips.

"You know, like a chicken. Or a cow. Say a cow. And they'd kind of let it run loose."

The truck was barely moving. The countryside seemed to rotate around them, as though they were at its very hub. Vinny stared at the broken gauges on the dash. He said, "Do cows run loose?"

Imagining this, Turner was seized by the giggles. "I don't . . . oh! hee! I don't know *what* cows do. Ha! But see, the cow, it would like, *do whatever it did*, until after a while, it would, stop!"

Vinny shook his head. "It would stop," he repeated. He pulled out the hand-brake. The countryside quit spinning. "Turner," he said sternly. "Get your shit in one sack. We're lost, man. And I'm worried about this truck."

Turner looked out the window into a motionless yellow field. "We're not really lost," he said, after a moment's reflection. "We've just . . . stopped."

"Great." Vinny opened his door. "Well, while we're just *stopped*, I'm going to take a whiz."

Turner joined him at the roadside. The feeling of clarity was still upon him. "Speaking of water," he said, "do you know what they found at the place where the cow stopped?"

"A hamburger stand."

"I mean this was later, usually. When some dowser showed up. But they, usually they discovered two underground streams, at least two, coming together right underneath that very spot. Sometimes there would even be a spring or something."

Vinny gave him a sort of wistful smile—like, he had stopped wondering whether Turner was crazy or not, and had settled down to wishing he had a cold beer.

"What this *means*," said Turner, concerned that he might just conceivably not be making himself one hundred percent clear, "is that geologically speaking you have two separate things going on, two levels of history—at least two—right at the same place, where eventually maybe a cathedral or something would get built. Standing stones, maybe. Sort of an intersection, a crossroads . . ."

"Oh, sure." Vinny walked back toward the truck, making cross-signs. "Lines of power. Dragon paths. All that retro-pagan bullshit. Right?"

"I was just talking about water," said Turner, growing uncertain. "You know, like in the ground."

Vinny wiped something, probably hallucinatory, off his lips. "I know dope-talk when I hear it. You were about to tell me how you can create these mystical alignments where you stand right *here* and look in the rearview mirror, and every year on Guy Fawkes Day you're lined right up with . . . damn." Vinny blinked. "Got the sun in my eyes there for a minute." His gaze moved past Turner. "Hey, man—what's that over there?"

Over there was the yellow field, and it looked to Turner like that was the beginning and the end of it.

"No," said Vinny. "See? That shadow or something?"

Well, now that you mention it. Turner thought he saw something rise and fall, a darker region within the burnt gold of the field grasses. He felt himself at the threshold of some recognition when Vinny clambered into the cab and cranked earnestly at the starter.

"What are you doing?" Turner said.

The truck made a muttering sound, like someone unwilling to be roused from a deep sleep.

"Son of a bitch," said Vinny.

"But . . ." Turner glanced over his shoulder. The shadow in the field had grown a tiny bit more distinct. "I mean, it's probably just some farmer. Maybe we can find out where we are."

"That's no farmer." Vinny gave it one last shot with the broken starter, then began rummaging around under the seat. He came up with a shiny piece of metal, a keg-tapper, which he hefted like a club. "Come on," he said, "get something for yourself."

Turner was pretty sure that these actions were irrational. Nonetheless, like in a contact-high, he felt a tingle of excitement that was a kissing cousin of fear, and despite what was left of his better judgment he crouched behind the truck with Vinny, where they waited to see what was going to happen.

Across the field came sounds of slow, rhythmic thrashing, like a harvester advancing steadily with his scythe. The image was not exactly comforting, what with all the popular associations. The sound got closer, then stopped. Seventeen weeks or so seemed to pass in absolute silence. Turner knew that any second now he was going to cough or faint or start singing "Bali Hai." Vinny, detecting this, shook his head in consternation, but Turner ignored him and peered over the truckbed. He drew in his breath.

In the roadway stood a tall man wearing clothes made out of leather, with a beard down to his stomach and a walking stick as big around as a bat. He looked like Rip Van Winkle after an especially long afternoon at the bowling alley. His eyes were bright—as Turner's would be too if he could only get a few decades of good sound sleep—and his posture suggested considerable energy.

"Who are you?" the man said. There was a peculiar quietness in his voice which managed not to be reassuring.

Vinny brandished his keg-tapper. "That's not the question," he said. "The question is, who the hell are *you?* The Ghost of Lammas Past?"

The bearded man appeared to size up the situation. He stuck the end of his stick into the ground. He said glumly, "It appears so."

This had a disarming effect, even upon Vinny.

"We are homeless," the stranger went on, "and have been living in the woods for several weeks now. Unfortunately we have not been doing terribly well at it."

His beard was brown and gray, with tiny bits of leaves or grass-chaff caught in it. He was not quite so old, Turner supposed, as he had looked at first glance. Nonetheless his appearance was unsettling—like a figure out of history, a New Age homesteader, crossing paths with the present day.

The man gestured over his shoulder, across the field.

"My wife," he said, "is back in the wagon. She has fallen ill, and I am taking her to a doctor."

Turner stood there feeling dumb. One just doesn't know how to behave toward an articulate wild man. "So you're, um,"—saying something, anyway—"you're headed to Candlemas, then? To the government clinic?"

The man's face darkened. (Actually it might have been the sun passing behind a cloud. Things were still tangled up in Turner's mind.) He said, "We shall have no dealings with those people again."

"Those . . . ?" Turner had a sense—an outgrowth maybe of his unusual confidence—that he knew already what the guy was going to say.

"They drove us off our farm." The stranger thumped on his stick, driving it deeper into the ground. "We took pity on them, because they were poor, as we imagined, and new to the valley. We invited them to stay with us, and offered them food, and a share in our profits, in exchange for helping with the harvest. But they wanted everything—the land and the crops and the livestock—and they accused us of absurd crimes, anything that came into their heads. They called us *destroyers of the soil*, and *usurpers of the common heritage*, and *thieves of the bounty of Nature*."

"Exactly," said Turner.

The man gave him a wary look, which by now Turner was pretty well used to.

"We left one night," the man continued. "It had become unbearable. They took over our house, leaving us nowhere to sleep but the barn. And the young men among them . . . my wife was very much afraid. So we gathered up what we could, and we left one night with the wagon."

"Those assholes," Vinny said, shaking his head sympathetically, but with an appraising look in his eye. "So what'd you make off with? Some crops or something?"

"Oh, no." The man smiled. "We were actually not very adept at farming. Our real income derived from making quilts. We sold them to local merchants—mostly to Mr Goldaster. I always felt that we were being somewhat exploited. But in retrospect, it does not seem so bad. Perhaps we simply should have negotiated more firmly."

Vinny said, "Quilts?"—sounding inappropriately cheerful. "You mean, you've got a wagon full of *quilts?*"

The man nodded. "We were planning to go to Upper Moat Farm, and ask for Goldaster's protection, before my wife became ill."

"How many?" said Vinny. "I'm sorry to get off the subject, here—but, like, how many quilts?"

The man gave him a look of mingled sadness and pride. "Nearly a hundred," he said. "We were much better quilt-makers than farmers."

Vinny handed Turner the keg-tapper—an emblematic gesture that seemed to indicate he was clearing the decks for action. "I think," he told the stranger, "we can cut a deal here. We'll take the quilts—the lot of them—and we'll pay you in real money. Only, we'll need to get a ride back to our place on your wagon. Our truck seems to have . . . stopped. We live west of here, I think. But Turner can tell you about that. Anyway, *then* we'll get your wife to the doctor. We can scarf up somebody's car, with a travel permit and everything. What do you think?"

The man glanced back across the field, toward where one envisioned his wife languishing among the hundred quilts. After a period of unhurried thought he said, "You are certainly welcome to a ride, if you need one. If you live in the west, our paths may be much the same. On the way, you can tell us more about what you mean by *real money.*"

"Terrific," said Vinny. "Oh, and look—do you have room for a couple of bags of vital supplies?"

He was pulling things out of the truck before the man could answer. Turner, seizing the chance to feed his own curiosity, said, "Why were you going through the fields? Are the roads dangerous around here?"

The man pulled his stick out of the ground and gestured with it, tracing a line in the soil. "We have been following the old track."

He showed no inclination to elaborate. Turner said, "I, um . . . old track, you say?"

"Right here"—gesturing with his stick again. "It's difficult for some people to make out, but it's there, if you can follow it. It goes all the way to the mountains—and beyond that, I would guess. But we are not going so far. Just to the other side of Candlemas. There is a great healer there, and I am taking my wife to him."

"A healer?" said Turner. He spoke rapidly and quietly, as though time were running out.

"Black Malachi Pantera," the man said gravely. "Some people say he is the greatest physician in the world."

"Some people . . . ?"

But his time was up. Vinny said, "Let's shake it, Turner. Here, take this stuff, and we'll help our buddy here get it loaded onto the wagon."

The stranger had one final look for Turner—of interest and curiosity, as though he sensed that some critical point had just been touched upon—before leading them into the field. His voice, soft but carrying, mingled with the rustle of dry grasses.

"I hope," he said, "that neither of you is allergic to animals. We left most of our livestock behind, but we did bring a few of the goats."

And Vinny whooped; but for Turner it was all anticlimax.

2

Contemplation of one's Omphalos

"What day is it?"

—someone kept asking, in tones of voice that oscillated from nervous to wheedling in sawtooth-wave fashion, never lingering at the peak. Or if not that, the most memorable thing was the lady singing in the refrigerator. She had chosen her text from God knows where: a real period piece. Turner took to strolling in and out as though insatiably interested in ice. There she sat on a big chunk of steer, the white-boned carcass of an animal guaranteed never to have been fed a single kernel of anything grown west of the eighty-third meridian, and bearing an official-looking stamp in indigo vegetable dye attesting thereto. The steer, not the singer. The latter was dressed in a vintage thinsulate hunting vest and olive drab bush pants, cuffed up a couple of turns so you could see the flannel lining. She was barefoot, and crooning in a strange contralto:

> If you study the heuristics
> And logistics
> Of the mystics
> You will find
> That their minds
> Rarely move in a line.

On about the fifteenth trip, a certain rationale presented itself to him: the refrigerator was the only place in the Solar Temple where you couldn't detect at least the moody undertow of the house band. Partner Trefoil had dragged the pulsers from the dining room to the more centrally located banana court, where something akin to organ music boomed off the tile and was slightly damped by banana leaves before striking the glass of the second-story ceiling, where the notes got mashed together until you couldn't find the holes between them—an arrangement that pleased Vinny as being "like in a cathedral, or something." Cathedrals and such were on his mind, which also may have influenced his choice of programming for at least the early stages of the party, before things got really out of hand. There was some predictable stuff for a few hours until, in mid-*Kyrie*, Black Malachi emerged from his private suite and succinctly pronounced:

"Fuck Bach."

Malachi then disappeared for a day or two, and Vinny switched centuries. He flirted with Ives for a while, pleasing no one, before moving up to the Beginning of the End, musicologically speaking, and performing with faithful fancifulness a suite of Ned Rorem mood-pieces called *Views from the Oldest House*. You couldn't exactly dance to this, but it was too strenuously colored to talk above; if you wanted to pinpoint, for historical purposes, the turning-point of the party, it was now. The stockpile of psychotropic peptides stored in little canisters in the pantry had been drawn down considerably by the time the final movement rumbled out of the foyer and faded a few inches short of the refrigerator. Turner was just coming out, rubbing warmth back into his arms, as the music ebbed away.

"*What day is it?*"

"Tuesday," he said irritably. "Time to pay for your hamburgers."

Which was as near as anybody could have guessed.

Variations

In the Morning Room, some math-major types were arguing over the latest rage in Reality. It seemed that somebody somewhere had managed to replicate the first few hundred steps of a legendary proof attributed to one

Professor Tyrone Drode, deceased for a decade or so, wherein it is established that the world is not, in fact, infinitely complex; that indeed the entire concept of infinite complexity is a transcendental boner. This idea, known as the Horizon Principle (i.e., there *is* one), had been kicking around in certain academic and other, murkier circles since the word got out that Drode was on to something big. Sadly the proof itself, along with the rest of the good doctor's effects, had sunk behind some mysterious horizon of its own. Drode had gone *pffft* during one of the last continental gatherings of persons capable of understanding what he was talking about (these guys in the Morning Room, Turner judged, not being among them)—just vanished, like between one round of drinks and another. No one knew what had become of the famous Proof, either. As to its complexity et al, there was room for discussion.

"Take for example," urged a young man with black hair stacked high on top of his head, but nothing worth mentioning around his big red ears, "a computer program. We know all about bugs, of course. But even if you were to assemble the most talented programmers available and work for an arbitrary period of time, checking and rechecking every line of code, you would still come to a point where there would be foul-ups. A subroutine might be coded properly but get recorded wrong on the storage media. Which in turn might have been caused by a glitch in the power supply. Or some guy punching keys might have gotten distracted for a moment and let his fingers do the walking. Naturally you can design fixes for problems like this, but then you find that the error detection system is *itself* subject to error. You can have cyclic redundancy, you name it, but beyond a certain point the probabilistic nature of the thing is going to catch up with you, and it will become overwhelmingly likely that a flaw will occur—a *critical* flaw, if you expand the parameters sufficiently."

It sounded reasonable to Turner. The world was full of fuck-ups. For all he knew, the world was itself a rather embarrassingly colossal quantum mistake. He was about to set off in search of some more, you know, normal kind of conversation when Cervina popped her head into the room. The sonic sculpture, which had been buzzing like a high-voltage wire, gave a fluty little trill at the sight of her.

Hi—Turner raised his cup in ritual greeting. Cervina smiled uncertainly and settled into the doorjamb, looking oversized and awkward.

"Now," said the red-eared guy, "it's worth looking at *how* these flaws occur," causing the sculpture to buzz off again. "If a typist hits the wrong key, we tend to call it a 'mistake.' Likewise for a glitch in the power supply. 'Random fluctuation,' we say, and let it go at that. But if we think a little harder we realize that there's no such thing as a 'mistake.' What appears to be a random happenstance always turns out, if you really look at it, to be entirely deterministic. The guy might have hit the wrong key because he was thinking about his girlfriend. Or he was hurrying to get done by quitting time. Or maybe he hit the *right* key, but at the same moment there was some other highly improbable event—a little shot of background radiation, say, tripped up an electron racing toward a logic gate. The point is, there's always a real, physical cause of any of these problems, and if you have enough knowledge of the systems involved—the relationship with the girlfriend, the state of the guy's health, you name it—you will always find that the thing we are calling a 'mistake' is a perfectly rational and predictable event—*if* you've got the full perspective.

"It's like a territorial conflict. The computer program has intruded into the space of some other system. *That's* the heart of Drode's argument—that as any system grows in complexity, it starts interpenetrating the other systems in that particular stratum of reality, and eventually there's going to be conflict. Borders will be crossed, information stolen, processes disrupted. It doesn't matter—and this is crucial—it doesn't matter whether the system involved is an artificial one or not. The same thing applies, perhaps with greater force, to processes so vast that they seem to be part of the structure of the universe. Human history, for example."

"Very clever," said a member of the audience—a fat and sleepy-looking teaching assistant. "But it's a bunch of romantic sap. Drode said nothing of the kind. All he did was to observe that as things get more complex, they come increasingly to resemble the Ur-system, the fundamental reference point: specifically, that which you are naively calling 'the universe.' Thus, as they become larger, systems become subject to the same laws that we have deduced for physical reality as a whole. Any given system *may* be, in fact, entirely predictable, a piece of clockwork. Or it may be governed by processes that are truly random and hence unknowable—a possibility that your own simplistic analysis has not taken into account. What Drode said was, *all we can know is how little we know*. In other words, we can measure the limits of our own understanding, and that's it. To the extent that we are ignorant, our ability to manage complexity is constrained—not just in trivial undertakings like computer programs, but in such more, shall we say, interesting problems, such as governing a nation-state. Drode proposed a rigorous but essentially self-evident method of judging how far we can go before our efforts are doomed by their own ambition. It's fundamentally no more than a sort of base-versus-height calculation. If Drode had been at Babel, he could have told them when to quit with the tower-making.

"The *other side* of Drode's equations, the outcome, is simply a limit. It's stated in terms of density of information. Beyond this limit, unexpected and unexplained phenomena will *inevitably* occur. Maybe the program adds extra zeros to your pay check, maybe your girlfriend starts greasing up your buddy—whatever. Maybe you'll start seeing ghosts. And since the complexity of the world-at-large is *way* past Drode's limit, we can expect that from our point of view it will always be a pretty irrational place. That's something we all know anyway, but Drode managed to prove it."

Turner sighed. He was about to say something, interject some question (he was disturbed, for example, by the idea that even equations have an *other side*); but Cervina surprised him by getting into the act herself.

"Why don't you guys give it up?" she said.

Her eyes were like dark little slots, as though she had been sleeping too long, or smoking too much. But something in the way she moved her long limbs suggested an unusual restlessness, a need for a break—in the discussion, the party, the sameness of life. Everything.

"Why don't *you*," suggested Red-Ears, "take a swim in the punch-bowl?"

Ah, thought Turner. The spirit of pure science. But Cervina was really *there*, if you follow me.

"Here's how I look at it," she said. "First you guys fucked up the yardstick, and now we don't know how big anything is anymore. Not really *know*, I mean—like we know fingers and feet and paces. Then you fucked up the dirt, so nothing will grow in it. Then you fucked up medicine, so everybody has to take drugs to stay healthy. Then you fucked up the economy so that everybody's broke and can't afford the drugs, so they're dying. And now—after you guys have proven what great things you can accomplish when you just apply your wonderful can-do scientific method to things—*now* you want to know why things don't work the way they ought to. Well, I can tell you all about that. Nothing works because *scientists are so stupid.* The only things that still work at all are the little things here and there that you haven't turned your computer models loose on."

Turner was much more suprised by this than Red-Ears seemed to be.

"That," the guy said, shaking his black coxcomb in let's-pretend regret, "is classic Know Nothingism. The same unreasoning fear of scholarly inquiry that precipitated the Dissolution. I suppose you also believe in witchcraft and reincarnation and *everything is alive, we are one in spirit with the earth, the trees, the coffee table—*"

"Fuck you," said Cervina. "And for your information, tomorrow happens to be an ancient holy day and I hope some immortal earth-deva rises up and bites your dick off. If she can find it."

With which, she spun out of the room. Turner's thought (as he stumbled over people's legs and broken plastic cups, running after her) was that living with Black Malachi had really done something to her. Or for her. He overtook her in the Bug Walk, where she had slowed to snatch a blossom off a lipstick-red streptocarpus.

"Pretty amazing," he told her. From a jaded man, the highest form of congratulation.

She gave him a cagey smile; her perpetually half-closed eyes lent themselves to this expression. "I'm not really upset," she said. "Those guys do aggravate me, but . . . you know, it's mainly, just, with Blackie or something. Ever since you came back—it's like there's something on his mind."

"He seemed to be in good spirits, the last time I saw him." (Though when was that, exactly?)

"Oh, sure, he's . . . I mean, he's in an okay mood. But it's like, underneath that, he's been brooding about things. And he keeps having visions in the bathroom."

Visions in the bathroom?

"Yeah," Cervina nodded, "I know. But he just says, Well where do *you* have your best visions? Then he rattles on about the confluence of inversely empowered waters, or whatever. But you know Blackie."

They stepped aside to allow two underclassmen to pass, wearing detox suits. It was the third night of the party, and already the gathering had evolved its own folk-legends, its own epistemological creeds. The detox suits were the outward symbols of a belief—especially strong around the greenhouse, the kitchen, the Moon Deck—that certain psychoactive chemicals had been released into the ventilator shafts by agents of the Chief Administrator, or possibly of the Souls (the movement having spawned two major subjects); and once started, this style of dress had passed from clean-cut paranoia into the darkest reaches of *couture*. Turner could have showed them, if anybody cared, the vials of brown moldy goo Malachi had emptied into the muffin mix before popping the trays in the oven.

"Let the cake eat *them*," the smiling chef had declared.

"He can be so weird sometimes," said Cervina.

Turner shrugged. On the other hand, life itself was pretty implausible; so maybe Malachi was extraordinary only in being closer to the grain than the rest of us. At the end of the Bug Walk, the Quilt-Maker of the Woods appeared, his gaunt frame looming above a stagger of tequila drinkers.

"I've been meaning to ask you," said Turner quietly. "Has Malachi been, like, treating people? I mean, does he see patients or something?"

"Patients." Cervina's mouth tightened in an ironic smile. "He isn't even really a doctor. He could have been. But after he got the whole examining board over here—I could tell you the story about *that*, if you've got a couple of days—he sort of went crazy and paced up and down in front of everybody telling them that Hahnemann had his head up his ass, whatever that means.

"But yeah," she added, looking up. "People have been coming here. I don't know what he does with them—they go into one of his dressing rooms, and usually they come out again looking fine and dandy. Though I swear I think a couple just vanished into thin air. He seems to be building up some kind of reputation. The weird thing is . . ."

She looked at Turner as though to be certain she had really caught his eye; as though the next higher level of concentration were required for this.

"The weird thing is," she said more quietly, "he isn't even doing it for money. He may *take* money, now and then, but I know for a fact that some of the people he's seen have come up from the Settling Out Camps—you can tell by the way they stare at you, and their clothes never fit—and those people don't have any cash at all. I mean, imagine: Blackie doing something really good like that, just to be doing it."

The Quilt-Maker was ambling down the Walk and seemed to be

seeking out Turner personally. Still a couple of steps away, he began
speaking in that quiet but weighty voice of his.

"I am so happy"—no more greeting than that—"that you and your
friend crossed paths with us. My wife is completely cured, and Doctor
Pantera has invited us to stay with him for as long as we wish."

He was quite close: Turner could smell the warm and rather pleasant
earthy scent of his leather clothes.

"The old track," he continued, "passes right through here." He was
pointing down the hall, toward the stairway and the bedroom wing. "This
house appears to have been sited at a major crossing."

He walked on, barely having come to a full stop, and no matter what
he had said Turner wouldn't have thought of detaining him.

"You see?" said Cervina, pouncing on this latest bit of evidence.

Turner saw.

"And you know what he *says*?" she demanded. "Blackie, I mean—
if you ask him about it? He says that medical practice is just that. Just
practice. Every time you treat a patient you're just warming up for that
one really big cure that's going to make you or break you. He says that."

"I can hear him," said Turner.

And he could, actually. Somewhere amidst the drug-damaged tissues
of his mind a stocky little figure with tiny hands, from which light streamed
in many colors, seemed to be addressing him, and Turner could make
out every word.

What the hurricane told the palm tree

"Ashenden!" said a stoop-shouldered, goat-bearded boy. "How'd you get
here so fast? Weren't you just out in the greenhouse? I guess it's one of
those secret passages or something, huh. Jeez, this place is a real maze."

Seeing as how the boy was propping up both ends of the conversation,
Turner didn't do much more than nod and smile and refill his plastic cup
from the bottle of something purple, I hope it was wine, the guy was
carrying. "Have you seen Malachi?" he asked.

"Sure," said the goat boy. "Just a day or two ago. He was looking for you."

"Where?"

Backing away down the crowded upstairs hall the boy shouted: "In the Operating Theater!"

B-But, there *isn't* any Operating Theater.

Ah, well. At least he wasn't invisible anymore. Now he was being spotted in places he hadn't even been. Meanwhile the party precessed like an astronomic phenomenon, one phase twirling into another.

"What *day* is it?"

—the voice grown listless, little hoping for an answer after all this time, because of which as much as anything Turner opened his mouth to reply.

" . . . "

Which is to say, no sound came out. He tried again, for some reason very interested in making a statement, a definitive remark about anything at all, and it did happen that he knew without having to think about it what day it *was*, actually. Though he was fuzzy as to the hour.

" . . . "

There was only, from downstairs, Vinny's pretty decent cover of *Dead Can Dance*. Turner swallowed and checked out the inside of his mouth, running his tongue around. Everything seemed to be in order. So perhaps the words were coming out, after all, and he was just too blitzed to make out what he was saying—which after God knows how many days without sleep and several pounds of Malachi's muffins wasn't even tickling the limits of possibility.

"What *day* is it?"

—growing fainter. As Turner thought, August the second, damn it. And who wants to know, anyway?

He shambled down the hall toward his bedroom, unsure whether or not he was about to cash in his last couple of chips. He passed the usual sequence of open and closed doors, the laughing and moaning and throwing up, bodies in sundry degrees of indecency, furniture being sat on, leaned against, smashed up, thrown into the fire—nothing ever changes around here—and just as he was picturing the inside of his own room, the famous mountain-climber staring reproachfully, he bumped once more into the goat-boy, who gave him what Turner felt to be a downright *avid* smile.

"Did you hear," the boy said excitedly, "about Turner Ashenden?"

T-Turner who?

"You remember. The famous outlaw who used to live here. As a matter of fact, I'm a personal friend of his, myself. That's what Pantera's throwing this party for—to celebrate his return from hiding. Ashenden's supposed to make an appearance or something in the Operating Theater."

Now this, thought Turner, sounds like something worth staying awake for.

Where's—he started to say, but the boy was gone again, spreading the news, and Turner was left to put his question to the backs of some undergraduates leaning dangerously hard against the balustrade, cantilevering their torsos out over the banana court, which Turner felt was putting far too much faith in the science of structural engineering, not to mention their own senses of balance, no doubt presently impaired. — *this, um, Operating Theater?* his mind dribbled on. The boys seemed to have a bet going, and one of them was more or less successfully aiming a stream of, oh God, toward a banana-planter fifteen feet below. Well maybe the nitrogen, you know . . .

As his attention dipped parabolically, following the structural logic of gravity and paying homage to the enduring roguish appeal of schoolboy antics, a figure below cut across the very corner of his eye, and Turner— craning his head too late, the figure was lost in shadows bumping like zombies to the throb of Vinny's band—abandoned for the present the thought of going to bed, instead shoving off toward the staircase in hopes of catching up with his former employer and comrade-in-arms, Harvey Goldaster.

What Harvey would be doing at a party like this wasn't for Turner to worry about. He was having enough trouble talking. Even the likelihood of its having been Harvey in the first place, after that bare peripheral recognition, was pretty debatable, probably. But the off-chance was worth a shot. Turner had spent a night or two, up on the mountain, selecting the piece of his mind that he would give to that genial villain, in case they both lived long enough to come face-to-face again. He still believed that Goldaster was to blame for much of his recent misfortune—drawing him in, as he had, to a conflict that was nobody's business outside a few higher-ups on either side of the Dyke-line, the cool heads of government versus the Old Souls of, of . . . well, it's just a metaphor. No amount of lecturing by Madame Gwendola could persuade him otherwise; though it might appear, if you listened to what the whacked-out woman was saying, that it had been Turner's own appearance here, a fresh-faced matriculant whose gnarled and horrid Past was about to metastasize inside him, that had sealed *Harvey's* fate. Turner didn't believe it. He reeled down the stairs as the band undertook the eerie descent into its final movement.

"What *day* is it?"

—now coming distinctly from the bank of equipment on the bandstand, which made you wonder if the whole thing were not part of the performance, a sleeper-routine in Partner's software, maybe the band's way of laughing at itself as it mined the accreted brilliance of a thousand days past, scattered like jewels across the centuries. Where do you go after *Dead Can Dance*? Maybe into the very Underworld: a lighthearted medley from *Orpheus*.

—Harvey?

It was so noisy down here that Turner couldn't tell if his voice was audible or not. For sure, nobody seemed to be paying him any attention. He bobbed along on the currents of the crowd until he spotted, from a point or two abaft the beam, the well-appointed figure steering himself as one imagined a captain of commerce very well might, smoothly despite being rocked from either side while navigating a narrow channel between banana trees, already half lost in a yellow-gray smogbank. Turner paddled after him as fast as he could, but as he pulled alongside—an ancient battle-cry welling up from his gut—the cap'n turned to regard him and it wasn't Harvey at all. In fact the man resembled Harvey only in the matter of attire, and in degree of self-possession: he was heavier by a good three-and-a-half stone, with a dipsomaniacal redness about the cheeks and with eyes that were glazed to a stately luster, like old brass. His gaze fell upon Turner, and he smiled—swaying a little, but keeping it to a tight orbit, as though the two of them were being held gyroscopically steady while the party rocked, storm-tossed, around them.

"Ah, Mr Ashenden," the sleek stranger exclaimed. "Our most honored guest. Or is it our most esteemed host? The invitation was rather vague, I thought. Still: an honor to meet you. Am I in time for your, ah, appearance?"

Waves of something like dizziness lapped against Turner's mind. He got the feeling that he and this fat guy were moving slowly around some mutual point of reference, but in opposite directions. Correlated, but out-of-phase. Moreover he discovered that he didn't give a rat's ass one way or the other.

—Appearance? You mean in this what was it, Operating Theater?

(Words seemed to fall from him like something he was carrying too much of. Whether or not he was actually speaking them aloud was beside the point, then.)

The stranger's eyes withdrew a bit, back to a safer distance, their brightness now as chilly as diamonds.

"Well, I s'pose I shouldn't detain you"— he said, leaving no trace of an answer to any of Turner's uncertainties.

—Perhaps you shouldn't walk like you had a champagne bottle up your ass, so much.

The party was an engine turning on and off. Its noises doppler ed down; then they revved up again. The elegant stranger never ceased to smile, but their correlation had gotten attenuated; Turner wasn't sure they were still onboard the same gestalt.

"Such a fantastic assortment of people," the man remarked, though he did not deign to look at them. "I s'pose in your position one becomes rather amazingly eclectic. It must strain your open-mindedness."

—Oh, hey. A closed mind is the last thing I'm worried about. Hey—

[Was the guy really weaving, or was it me? Or is the imbalance an aspect of my memory? His face seemed to tilt and slide up close to me, like a drunk's-eye view of the guard-rail at Dead Man's Curve.]

—my mind is like, Big Sky Country. We're talking wide-open spaces here. I mean, you could hold an *opera* in it or something. Hey—

The big man changed faces like an actor getting off work. He laid a hand on Turner's shoulder, and whether Turner had really been going off the deep end or not the clutch of those manicured claws checked his fall for the next few seconds. With very resolute evenness of tone the man said:

"We are not stupid, you know. We are not effete or feeble-minded or whatever else you might think. Above all, we are not naive. I have come here from a considerable distance and at no small risk or expense to myself, because I am impressed by what you have accomplished, and because I am an old friend of Nicola Quoin. But do not doubt, young man, that I have brought all of my critical faculties along with me. And I have brought a few highly capable friends. I am prepared to be disappointed by whatever it is you're offering. But I am not prepared," a comma dropped here for emphasis, "to be made a fool of."

—Well I hope you're prepared (Turner declared or imagined or wished later he had said) to hold on to your nuts. Because like the hurricane told the palm tree, this ain't gonna be no ordinary blow-job.

Turner's imagination

may have been to blame or maybe not. But weren't there a lot of pretty strange people at this party? And I don't mean just, you know, *strange*, because God knows you had to expect that sort of thing. But for example, the Old Soul in the foyer. Who was not, by the way, the only horsey type snorting around here. And what exactly had induced the entire faculty of the Semiotics Department to show up, *en masse*, exactly? Not that their presence was any great shakes, life-of-the-party-wise, except by way of establishing a little beachhead of recondite jawboning on the far shore of the Game Room (whose name referred to the large stuffed rat a former housemate had killed and nearly eaten there, at an earlier party). But the question remained. And then there was the other question, the unspoken inverse or converse or conundrum, viz:

Where's Black Malachi, anyway?

"As far as I'm concerned," a lady professor remarked—or did she— in Turner's ever more enfeebled hearing, "the whole notion of *gay content* is an effort to block off the old Chip. You can be touchy-Feeley or creepy-Crowley, but just lie down on the Proustian bed and you'll wind up 86'd, if not TKO'd."

Well, all right, but. What about the goings-on downstairs, in the subbasement used now mainly for storing tubers and propagating fungi, which Black Malachi was pleased to call the Root Canal? Turner ambled down there on a slender lead: a dreamy-eyed coed had murmured that Blackie "went to get something for his nerves." Which sounded plausible enough at the time; but when Turner thought about it later, down among the spider webs and jars of homegrown tomatoes, innocent-looking enough, which happened to be the media of choice for a certain psychoactive mildew . . . she might equally well have said, "something for his *nurse.*"

Sounds of hot damp breath came from behind a mattress sagging on end like a lean-to, as per your Scout's Handbook, Post-Millennial Edition. Turner preferred to imagine a pair of lovers sucking at the unhealthy air, naked flesh pressed into the eerily warm concrete (the house was as thoroughly insulated as your costlier type of child-rearing), than to contemplate the trillions of discrete microinhabitants of the Canal having symbiotically unionized, Slime, Goo & Mysterious Fuzzy Growth Local #108. Strangely enough, the copulatory scene, which is what we're supposed to be focusing on here, did not have its usual effect. Turner did not, for instance, turn back with a sigh from the two-part harmony rising in pitch and volume behind the mattress, his vital organs swelling painfully from the build-up of hormones merging into the beltway of his bloodstream. What he felt, in fact, was a whole lot of nothing. At most, a kind of sexless *tristesse.* He tried to remember his last erection, his most recent purely prurient thought. But the only place his mind found to go was a crime scene it did not care to revisit—namely, his unrequited eyeful of Maridel, the night of the Chastity Ball. And if you don't find *that* disturbing, your name must not be Turner Ashenden.

The celibate houseguest gallumphed listlessly up the ladder to the basement proper, where a large-scale séance was in full shiver. Light twinkled from so many bayberry candles that the room (which was full of dark furnishings left over from the Hartfell Chalet era) had the look and smell of some decorator's private, Colonial-Revival circle of Hell. Twenty or thirty students were sitting around in bad simulations of the *padmasana,* which was supposed to divert the energy of the lower chakras toward more spiritual pursuits. In his current state of mind Turner found the idea depressing. Gather ye rosebuds, was how he looked at it. The ringleader was an unremarkable young man wearing a queerly painted robe. Magickal glyphs, Turner supposed; though to his eye it looked like a cheat-sheet for Art 203, "Graffiti and Other Emblems of Decay." The kid was mouthing some heavy-duty stuff about *old lost witnesses* which probably meant the Dead, you know, and waving an incense-stencher as though it might wake them. None of which was what really grabbed Turner. What did was this feeling he had, all of a sudden: a little tickle like the irritation you feel while listening to a braggart shooting off about a matter that wouldn't otherwise interest you. Turner frowned and tried to trace the thing, this feeling, back to its source—but as near as he got was the kid coughing a bit on his own hot air, going on about *ancient Defender stand before us*, blah blah blah.

Hold on a minute. That kid . . .

As Turner stood there annoyed by the whole creepshow, the notion stirred in him that this guy doing the incanting was a fraud in more ways than the obvious. Between painted bathrobe and dangling hair, Turner was pretty sure he could make out a layer of greasepaint—the opaque kind you wear for *dramatis personæ* purposes. It was a pretty thorough job, ears and neck and everything, which made it hard to see what was underneath, who the imposter-at-large really was. Turner, an accomplished fraud in his own right, sensed a territorial challenge here. He moved closer, up to the edge of the circle, from where he could see that he wasn't dealing with a single *persona* but a whole troupe of them: every face in the crowd wore a second skin of oil and pigment—the pallid, unlined complexion of undergraduates had been laid on top of something else, something older it looked like. Check out those wrinkles there, around the mouth, rippling like tiny serpents as the lips draw tight around their syllables.

Come with us, the chief caricature croaked. *Come lead us into battle once more.*

Turner was disgusted but nobody noticed that, nobody was looking at him. Whatever these old theosophic thespians were into, they were into it deeply. At least now he understood the problem with the lotus posture.

He figured on getting out of there, looking for some less depressing *divertissement*—like, you know, young lives being squandered in mindless depravity. Anything. But as he turned to go there was this generalized stirring around the room—the circle-jerks getting their act together, maybe to take it on the road. Their principal groaner fell silent, or maybe just forgot what he was doing there; the old are prone to such lapses. All of a sudden the bunch of them stood up (pretty spryly) and before Turner could do one thing or another a big fellow approached him carrying what's this, a sheet, or . . .

"It's time," was what the guy said. He was wearing a costume similar to the others'—a robe with little signs painted everywhere, only Turner could see things better now. Like the symbols for example were not magickal thingums at all but, check it out, *mathematic*. And the robe itself wasn't just any old thing out of the closet, no, but one of those gowns people unaccountably want to wear whenever they step into a laboratory, as though proclaiming their double-blind purity, their state of scientific grace. The whole thing brought new depth to the notion of "witch doctor." But that ain't all.

It's Turner's turn to speak, right? He's just been told *It's time*. But as he looks into the imposter's face, grease and powder failing to hide the wrinkles below, he sees for the first time that even the wrinkles aren't the end of the story; up close, the craggy skin looks to be just another layer, a kind of mask, stretched taut over the guy's cheek- and jawbones. God, it's like an onion. So let's see. These guys are laboratory assistants of indeterminate age, pretending to be aging actors, pretending to be young magicians. Or are there more layers below that?

"It's time," the guy tells Turner again; there is no easy way now to classify him, which practically eliminates the possibility of a response, even assuming Turner was still able to talk. "Do you need any help?"

—H-Help? Turner feels something turn over in his mind, tumblers falling in a creaky old lock. *EERRRRR*, door falling back, hall full of rusted armor, skeletons . . .

The guy looks up. Something's happening upstairs. Maybe Vinny and the boys are testing some new equipment, though it's hard for Turner to think so. The foundation of the house seems to shudder. It's not a noise so much as a fundamental sense of agitation. You can *sense* the shouting, the bodies hurling themselves one way and another, though none of the actual sounds penetrate the heat-slab.

Now there are feet on the basement stairs. People are clambering down—Turner can barely make them out in the odorous candlelight—detox suits, frayed denim, tailored oxford cloth, unseasonal tweed, God there's no end to it, and from overhead the sense of disruption grows stronger. The troupe of weirdos have packed up their medicine show and formed a knot around Turner, which under the circumstances is both alarming and comforting, as though one feeling were a mask over the other, but which is which?

—What's going on? it seems appropriate to wonder.

At the foot of the stair, the goat-boy appears, tossing his arms above his head as though giving some long-awaited signal. When this doesn't seem to get the point across, he breaks into a balls-to-the-wall holler:

"The Settlers! From the Camps! There must be *hundreds* of them! With *guns!* They're crashing the party!"

Well, why not, thinks Turner. Everybody else is here, why not them?

At the same time this news fills him with a more distilled sort of fear than he's known for some time now. You'd have to look really far back to find the likes of it. The only thing that comes to mind is that first visit to the Institute, the realization that he's lingered too long on the mountaintop, lights are coming on in the valley, he'll have to drive home in the dark . . .

A hand falls on his shoulder, rests easily there, a warming pressure.

"Come on, now. It's time."

The guy with the robe. Eyes peering out through the how many layers of makeup. Something, ah, *clinical*, Turner thinks, about his voice. And it's odd: at a moment like this, with people everywhere screaming and running around and the terror eating its way up his spine, the dispassionate air of this guy with his hand on Turner's shoulder is bizarrely reassuring. Like sure, they'll probably open your guts and rip your heart out, but we have some *very effective* anesthetics.

The guy motions Turner in some direction, toward a wall of swaying shadows. As more feet come booming down the treads. Unfriendly feet, we begin to feel. And are those popping sounds just synthesized percussion? Of all the things that have ever happened at Malachi's parties, Turner cannot remember there having been a gunfight before.

"This way," the masked man is telling him.

Th-this? But there's nothing here, it's a dead end or something, a cul-de-sac. Despairing of his ability to speak, Turner thinks impatiently —What? Where?

The guy presses his arm. The rest of the actors, or whatever they will turn out to be, form around him like an irresistible wave, a movement. Talk about your peer-group pressure. Turner is borne back, back,

back to the shadows again,

back where—

while pointing to a patch of darkness the size of a TV screen, the guy, the actor, the attendant—

the nurse, man—

presses Turner into the shape required to fit—and as though some explanation finally were required, mutters diffidently, "It's one of those secret passages"—

and sure enough, after a suitable amount of twisting crawling climbing and cursing in the dark, we emerge into the glaring light of—

The Operating Theater

You had your gleaming metal, hard as ice. You had your lamps burning hot on tripods artfully zeroed-in like spotlights tracking a performer. You had your yards of white fabric, laundered without mercy, and in the air all those things so sharp and clean they hurt your nose to smell them. And because this was a progressive sort of establishment, you had a bit of gentle music fluttering from somewhere offscreen—a tune Vinny had conjured up from his boyhood called "A Trip to Philadelphia."

Outside the ring of theater lights, it was dark. Or mostly. There was a faint aqueous glow from walls you could barely make out, and over your head the night sky (for it was night) was shot with incandescent motes that fell like bubbles, fiery, thousand-colored, drifting on the wind. These were fireworks. There was a celebration going on: a Harvest Festival. And though at first it seemed very quiet, shortly you realized that this was a strange misperception; there was a drumbeat of small concussions—the fireworks, exploding in the sky—and nearer than that, pitched more sharply, there were oddly timed outbursts that began with a fricative sound, like fingers on styrofoam, and ended in a hollow-throated syllable like *hump.* These were grenade-launchers. The Solar Temple was getting the shit blown out of it. There were also screams and shattering windows, but they were not quite so loud.

But all of that—lights, screams, explosions—seemed far away. The scene around you was astonishingly calm. There was a "hush," as people say, as though speaking of a silence that is palpably present—if not in the air then in the æther. The *akasha*. Just above eye-level, at the twilit fringe of the night, faces were looking down at you, like spirits drifting, and nobody was saying a word.

What was this place? You must have wondered, as everyone else did, drawing up to the edge and catching their breath. A wide hollow in the earth, a squared-off, symmetric crater, its walls were made of slick mostly-mineral composite, its floor crisscrossed with footprints, paint-marks, beads of silicon sealant, hoses, electrical wires, its deep center seeming to float in a pool of light.

Ah, of course. A pool . . . The neglected and empty and, as Turner had thought, forgotten swimming pool gouged out of a downslope behind the Solar Temple. Hidden from view by a fieldstone wall (which explained *some* of the silence), and surrounded by broken trellises, cast-concrete settees, rotten leaves of past seasons, and some more romantic debris that would turn up later, at random, as you took off your shoe to shake out what you would suppose to be a speck of grit, a piece of something ruined . . .

So *this*, we saw, must be our destination. The terminus of the "secret passage" (if, in truth, there was such a thing). Where a hundred terrified partygoers—surrounded, even interpenetrated by their enemies—had come to make a final stand. You could see their faces, if you tried, if you cared one way or the other: students, drop-outs, drop-ins, old friends and strangers, people from the University and people from places as distant and hopeless as Wine Barrens. They were dressed in the summer linens of the Old Souls, the soiled cotton of undergraduates, the leather of eccentrics like the Quilt-Maker. You could even make out, here and there, the blue-gray uniforms of the Settling Out Camps; but if any of the Settlers were armed, there was something here that made them keep their weapons out of sight, at least for a long uncertain moment.

It is hard to overstate our surprise. As we fled from the Solar Temple to find, arrayed before us, in a hollow in the ground, not the chaos or destruction we had left behind but the sterile white cloth hot lamps gleaming metal et al. of a just-add-water operating room. Or yes, Theater. That hush in the air. And of course the odd procession just starting—just this instant—down below.

Down in the pit, before the eyes of the hundreds of us huddled in the gallery, Turner Ashenden—famous outlaw, honored guest, hero of the Resistance, man of the hour—was carried in by a dozen oddly dressed attendants on an improvised stretcher, a pole-and-strapping thing made largely from his own clothes. He was laid out cold on a platform at center-stage like some doomed Cortázar protagonist: trapped in a dream, frozen in a photograph, strapped to the *piedra roja*, so irresistibly helpless he's been ripped off by everyone from A to D. Which must be pretty much how *you* felt at that moment, if you felt anything at all. It was not apparent whether you were conscious or not. But we'll see about that.

We've got some catching up to do, old buddy. 'Cause like one of your fellow archetypes sez—

Long time no see.

3

Dissimilar spirits

There was trouble on the road. We were expecting it, of course. The main routes north and south had been all but surrendered to highwaymen, and there seemed little that could be done to improve one's odds, beyond a few obvious precautions. Flaunting even these, Nicola Quoin dismissed her escort of farmers only a few miles north of Wine Barrens. They were needed more immediately at home, she said—with the government occupation scaling down, there was the prospect of total collapse; and I suppose what she meant was, What a wonderful opportunity! Anyway, we went on alone (or should I say together)—Nicola and myself and that chimerical spirit we will call, for a while longer, "Turner Ashenden." We carried guns, and Nicola, at least, must have known how to use them; but in a deeper sense we were armed with nothing more substantial than a destination. We had promised to be in Candlemas by the second of August, and none of us, probably, was thinking much about anything but that. We had begun to talk less among ourselves; but companions will do this, after days on the road.

By the second week out, Turner's attention started to wander. Often he seemed to have no clear idea of where he was, or whether anyone was with him. But none of this—and for that matter, none of the privations of a long journey on foot—bothered *him*, and I suppose if I were an astral entity I too would take a more equable view of worldly inconvenience. He strode ahead blithely, eyes on the horizon, as though something there was becoming plain to him that the rest of us could not yet see. Nicola, though, started to worry. She addressed me at night in hushed, furtive tones, and showed great impatience when, as I sometimes did, I failed to make any effort to reply.

But what an odd and vexatious position I was in. Turner, I was fairly certain, could overhear my thoughts, if he chose to attune himself, whereas Nicola understood me only imperfectly, in moments of strong intuition. But Turner during most of those days said virtually nothing, and Nicola —though she remained always civil and usually quite chummy with me —clearly would have preferred being alone with him. Who seldom paid her the slightest attention. So. That was the state of our little imbroglio, our skewed triangle, with its one vertex lapping into the void, on the morning when we met the Brown Witch.

In the old days, they say, the land that rolled westward from the great highway, in the highlands north of Wine Barrens, was a favorite haunt of people with peculiar spiritual proclivities. Having grown up in the sphere of Madame Gwendola, I do not use the word "peculiar" lightly. I mean, people still loyal to magic-men dead two thousand years; people given to rites of, at least, symbolic cannibalism; people who foretell for their theologic rivals the most sadistic, evil-minded forms of perdition. I suppose they have names for themselves, and for their sects, but this one I can only think of as the Brown Witch.

But clear your mind for a moment. Imagine yourself in the cool light of early morning, breathing air swept clean by a storm that blew through during the previous night. Imagine the sun just peering above the massed pines of the southern woods on both sides of the roadway. Imagine yourself walking lightly, your thoughts far away, beside two companions as silent and peaceful and distracted as yourself. You can press this as far as you like, pretend yourself to be in love with one of them—however far into the story you wish to go—but the point is, the last thing on your mind was any sort of danger.

And there, in that innocent moment (ah: innocence again!), the morning split open like an egg, and before you could understand that the sudden burst of noise had been automatic-weapon-fire, onto the road in front of you stepped a woman as bulky as any two of us taken together, and as terrifying as though she had been something other than a human being.

"Lay *everything* down," she told us. "I do not desire to slay anyone today."

She waved her gun and came close, I thought, to giving us a big smile—cocking her head to one side, as though wondering if *we* were human, if we were capable of following her line of thought.

Perhaps it was reasonable to wonder. Perhaps she was more completely developed than any of us. Certainly, to look at her, the woman was a perfect composite of the things that we three travelers, we dissimilar spirits, were not. Where Nicola seemed to lack an element of vitality, as befitted the last of a line, the Brown Witch overflowed with the vigor and plenitude of life. Where Turner was barely corporeal, she was fleshly to excess. And where my skin was almost colorlessly translucent, the Witch was as dark as healthy earth.

"*Now*," she said, sounding pleased with herself, and with us, when we had placed our weapons and our other small possessions in a line beside the road, "you come with me—*come* now—and we'll see what kind of clouds you are, blowing across my sky this fine morning."

She spoke with an accent, but not an expected one. Mixed like sharp seasoning into her tropic-coast patois were the clipped syllables of the city. The woman was, or had been, an Easterner. With a flourish of her weapon, she aimed us up the hillside like a pack of dumb animals. Our own guns, with all our other belongings, were left there by the road.

The Brown Witch seemed so jolly about this whole encounter that I half expected her to burst into song. I really believe there was music in her heart as she marched us though hills and hollows for perhaps three quarters of a mile, until we arrived at a place that had more the air of an encampment than of any fixed or well-thought-out abode. There were structures assembled from poles and fabric—the latter, I guessed, meant to be packed about and stretched on new timbers at each stopping-place. There was a fire-pit and, around it, all the fittings of a well-equipped hearth: jars of oils and spices, cooking gear, portable lamps and other small devices wired to a rack of sun-cells, staple foods neatly stockpiled in crates, and a fiberglass frame that looked suitable for gutting and dressing fair-sized animals. Beyond these things rose a kind of stone pillar, head-high, a couple of notches more upright than one would expect of a natural formation. Somehow it looked at home here. Though there were no other people in sight, it was hard to believe that the Witch lived in this place, in this manner, alone.

She confirmed that almost directly, when Nicola (tired of being ordered this way and that, as she grew tired in due course of anything) pointed a finger at the woman and demanded: "Who are you? What is all this? What are you going to do to us?"

The Brown Witch looked only a little surprised. She didn't dither about replying.

"We are governors, girl. Governors of the new day. *All this*, as you see, is our domain. For that matter, you have been living in our domain all your life, if only you knew."

She gave Nicola a . . . well, a rather sisterly smile. Still she held that nasty little weapon in one big hand. Only someone so capacious could have made the two things—the smile, and the threat of death—seem other than wickedly incongruous. She said, "What I will do with you," omitting the *we* here, "depends entirely on who you are. Who are you, girl?"

Nicola liked being called *girl*, I guess, less than she liked being held at gunpoint. Probably the experience was less familiar. She said, "We're just travelers, and we're running late to begin with, and if you wanted money or something why didn't you just take it back there at the road? Are you going to put a curse on us or something?"

The Brown Witch had a way of laughing inside—somehow you could tell she was doing it, though no sound or specific gesture gave it away. She chuckled in this way for a few moments, then she raised her gun. Bullets passed within an inch of Nicola's head; the whipping sound they made was audible as a kind of after-effect of the explosion.

Nicola's skin, beneath the suntan, went very pale.

"We may elect to kill you," the Brown Witch said, "but certainly we shall not involve your souls in it. Such things must be handled *very* carefully, if one is to maintain the balance."

"You're really incredibly stupid," Nicola declared. Though she was trembling, this did not detract from the *hauteur* with which she spun about, strode across the campsite, and seated herself by the smoky remains of the fire. As I have said, you had to hand it to her.

—Turner, I said.—Why don't you just . . . I mean, she can't hurt *you*, can she?

He shrugged, which caught the Witch's attention. He had not spoken at all during this ordeal, and even now, after the shooting, looked strangely apathetic.

"You," the Witch said, turning to him, "you are the leader? I believe you are. Come sit with me, and we shall see what we are seeing here."

She led him to a collection of logs and blankets arranged in the cross-cultural semblance of a sitting room. Turner followed indifferently. The Witch gave herself the best seat in the house, symbolically speaking— diametrically across from the upright stone, which in context acquired a certain active importance, like a work of sculpture that dominates a hall-way.

"So," she said, gesturing for him to sit beside her, which he ignored. "Tell me, then. Whose side are you on, in this big quarrel? The land-owners, or the refugees from the coast? The old law or the new?"

Clearly, things hung on this question. I drifted over, hovering near Turner as though there were some attachment between us—beyond, that is, my own hopeless sentiments. The Brown Witch (sensibly, I'm sure) did not even glance at me. Nicola sat apart, drawn into herself, but listening. I could tell.

Turner said, "Why do I have to be on anybody's side? I just want to . . . to *be* here. I don't want any part of all that."

Nicola made a little sound with her nose, as though this were too namby-pamby for her taste. Lay the cards out, was her philosophy.

The Brown Witch said, "You don't know your own mind, then. Or you are lying to me. But look—I have something here that will interest you. *You*, I believe, more than most people."

She motioned toward the pillar of stone. Turner looked intrigued by this. He walked closer, to study it with evident fascination. I was alarmed, for it seemed to me that a change in the psychological terrain had just taken place: Turner had formed some new connection with the Witch, and had grown thereby even more distant from Nicola and me. He lifted an arm—raised it very near but did not quite touch the standing rock.

"It's still working," he said, sounding surprised.

—What? I asked him, quickly, a panicky feeling rising inside me.

"I don't know," without thinking, he answered me. "It feels like . . ."

—Get away from it, I urged him.—Turner, it might be dangerous, some kind of trick—

The Brown Witch looked amused, glancing from me to Turner as though she had followed our exchange of thoughts. "Take your time," she told him. "There is no single path to the center. Just approach it in your own way."

"But the coils," said Turner. He moved his hand around: up and down, almost touching the stone, forming patterns in the air. "The spirals. They're so, like, *familiar*. It's like I've, you know . . . somewhere . . ."

"They are all connected," said the Witch.

I found her tone to be smug and offensively didactic—perhaps it reminded me of Gwendola. She stood up, moving gracefully for a woman of her size, with a quick look toward me and another toward Nicola, as though to assure us that no, she hadn't forgotten the gun. She was only a step or so away from Turner when his index finger fell (at last!) to the rough-textured face of the rock, and that was the end of anything any of us might have thought was going to happen.

It would be helpful, for artistic purposes, to place something here like *Poof!*

—but in life the truly epochal changes occur between one instant the next, in the indeterminate void between quanta. Offscreen, to put it another way. Beyond perception. Neither I nor Nicola nor the Brown Witch had time to press our mental RESET buttons before we found ourselves joined in the campsite by a short, frizzy-haired youth about midway in age between Turner and myself. The newcomer looked surprised, too . . . but not *that* surprised. He moved his eyes rapidly over each of us before allowing them to settle upon Turner.

"Malachi!" Turner cried.

"*Black* Malachi," the youth said, "please."

He paused, as though still getting the feel of things; raised his head theatrically; sniffed the air. His attitude was one of great satisfaction—though at what, precisely, I could not have guessed.

Turner seemed pleased, indeed delighted, to see him. "Malachi, what are you doing here?" he said. "What are you *doing?*"

The person or image of Black Malachi Pantera (I guessed, by now, the latter) made a beckoning gesture at Turner. His expression was thoughtful and a shade sardonic. He said, "Come here, Ashenden. I need you."

Turner's finger still rested lightly on the stone. He looked down at it, then up. "Should I just . . . let go?"

"Yes," said Black Malachi, firmly.

"No!" cried the Witch. She lunged forward, waving her gun.

Black Malachi regarded her scornfully—which took some doing, really, since she was three times his equal in sheer bulk, and her marksmanship was not to be disregarded. He chided her: "Now, now. One must strike while the irony's hot."

Then, all in the same moment, the Witch opened fire and I cried "Turner!" and Nicola shouted in excitement and Turner lifted his finger from the stone. But as I have argued, great changes don't happen in one moment or the next, they happen *between* them. Black Malachi was gone before this particular moment got started, and by the time it was over Turner was gone too. Not that he had ever exactly been . . . But you know.

That was not quite the end of our morning with the Brown Witch; there was still the little surprise to be sprung by Nicola. But I was too weary, just then, for more surprises. I sat down heavily near the stone— just distant enough to be safe from its swirl of energies—and by the time I heard the shriek of astonishment I was already lost in a secret, silent delirium. Nicola must have recognized this and even, in some measure, shared it. She let me rest for a little while, before concern about the Witch's comrades, whom we assumed must be about, made her rouse me, and we retraced the path to the road. Of all our belongings, we found only my record book. The rest must have been stolen. Anyway, they were gone.

Dirty Dick

Anything is possible. Maybe Black Malachi, having seen us in the clearing, did something, intervened in our destiny somehow. Maybe Madame Gwendola is wrong and there *is* such a thing as coincidence.

We had not been on the road for half an hour before we became alarmed by the sound of a vehicle on the parallel track, the more overgrown of the two "lanes" of the ancient highway, overtaking us. We tried to conceal ourselves in the underbrush, but although bushes and tall weeds and the like are supposed to be ready at hand in such moments, we happened to be walking through a dismal region where the prevailing vegetation—mostly ailanthus trees—had few leaves anywhere close to the ground, and even those were hardly enough to hide behind. So the best we could do was to crouch in a stand of narrow trunks and hope for the best. Nicola held the Brown Witch's repeating-gun with her usual air of competence.

It should not have worked. But as things came to pass, the people operating the rugged-looking transport that soon bumped into view were thoroughly intoxicated. Their laughter and off-key singing were almost as loud as the growl of the old-fashioned, petroleum-driven motor. They did not see us through the narrow windows, or did not care, and it was a wonder if they could see to drive.

I had just dared to stand up to watch the transport bounce on its merry way when Nicola stepped onto the roadway.

"Dick!" she shouted. "Dirty Dick!"

She stood in the dusty wake of the transport, waving her gun like a semaphore flag. The driver either ignored her or, as it looked to me, increased his speed.

Nicola said, less loudly, "Asshole." Then she shot out both rear tires. The vehicle groaned to a halt, and Nicola gave a nod of satisfaction. I believe if there had been smoke coming from the barrel of her gun, she would have puffed it away.

I had no idea what to expect. I was not even sure whether to leave my hiding place. Not, I guess, that it really mattered. The hatch of the transport—a heavy, armored thing—slid open. Out of it popped a fat man with thick gray hair, dressed the way one dresses, I think, for duck-hunting, and carrying a golf club. A putter. He looked at the tires and looked at Nicola, who pointed her gun at him.

"Damn you," he said. His voice was strong but mellow, like something that has been carefully aged. "Now, who do you s'pose is going to change this?"—with just a hint of a slur.

"I don't give a damn who changes it," said Nicola. She fired off a couple more rounds, into the air. The man did not seem to notice.

"Well, maybe we can drive on it," he said.

"Dick, you're really an idiot," said Nicola. "Don't you know I could be a robber? Aren't you worried about getting shot?"

"What's that?" The fat man squinted. "Nicola Quoin, is that you? My God, come closer, let me have a look."

She shook her head—privately, I think. She signaled me to come out, but by this time I had gotten the drift of things. The fat man approached with his arms wide, wagging his putter, and I marveled at what a gigantic fool he must be.

"You really should wear your glasses," said Nicola. "Here, say hello to my friend Tristin. He doesn't talk, so don't think he's being rude."

"Glasses don't help," said the fat man, peering about for me. "Ah, hello young man.—Something wrong in here, they say." Tapping his forehead.

"Tristin, this is Dirty Dick. He's a hundred years old. Can't they do something about that?"

The fat man gave a bitter little laugh. "For one of *us?* Come, now."

Nicola looked downward, thoughtfully. After a moment she said, "Well, there's not much to look at, these days, anyway. Have you got room for two more?"

In the transport, the singing had started up again. Dirty Dick woke at once into a smile—his habitual expression, you could tell—then seemed to remember the tires and looked worried again. But only for a moment.

"We'll drive on it," he decided, and ambled back toward the hatch.

"Dick," said Nicola. "You're being an idiot. Who have you got in there?"

Fallen angels

The seven passengers, plus Dick, who bad eyes and all was driving, were a new experience for me. A new reminder of how limited, despite everything, my life had been.

Of the passengers—youngish men, all—one would say looking back
that they had the air of fallen angels: festive, now that they were out of
the grim eye of the Almighty, but melancholy underneath, and faintly
bored. They were drinking heavily and holding it as well as might be
expected. The transport was reasonably well appointed, but not at all
luxurious; it had a nonspecific ambience of *sport*. The particular sport at
which these angels appeared to excel was that of staying alive—even, after
a fashion, prospering—in an inhospitable world. I don't know who they
were or what they did before or after I knew them, but for at least those
couple of days they seemed to exist for no other reason than to bring a
certain agreeable rhythm, like the jostling vigor of the transport, to our
journey. Or if that is saying too much, let's agree at least that they were
happier than me and Nicola, and they sang a lot.

[CHOIR OF ANGELS]

> Welcome, welcome, every guest,
> To our doomed heroic quest.
> Music fills the poisoned air,
> As we trudge from here to there.
>> [Enter baritones, repeating first verse, *rondo*-style.]
>
> Join us as we sing this round,
> Though our miseries abound.
> Rodarch brings us naught but woe,
> So to Candlemas we go.
>>> [Enter basses.]
>
> Turner Ashenden's our hope,
> Though it seems he's wont to mope.
> Let us toast him in good cheer—
> To his health we raise our beer.
>>> [& seq.]

Dirty Dick's role in all this was less well defined. I assumed he was
simply an elder version of the same character type, a sort of overweight
Lucifer, but other things are possible. He spoke rather little, chiefly about
obstacles in the road (some of which I believe were armed patrolmen,
whom he tried to run over), and seldom joined in the general revelry. He

never, that I remember, sang. He poured drinks, and decided when to stop for a meal, or a nap, or what he called a "pit stop," and every so often addressed a remark to Nicola, who for her own part remained distant and preoccupied.

"Your father," he said, "had some luck with that odd little plant, didn't he—that sage, what was it?"

"*Salvia divinorum*," said Nicola. "How do you remember that?"

"I remember."

This, you see, being typical. Since it was interesting and odd, like most of Dirty Dick's remarks, I have it jotted down in the record book, and can trace certain connections that were more elusive at the time. A couple of hours must have passed, and some miscellaneous adventures [It says here only, *3 killed with BW gun before got past roadblock—worse ahead?*] and then there was some follow-up:

D. Sage of seeing, was it?

N. Hm? No, sage of the seers. *Is* it.

D. Ah . . . ?

N. Ah.

And another break, which was probably nightfall. We stayed in the transport almost constantly, which was not such a hardship as you might think, since we had walked so far and been afraid so long, and somehow all jammed together inside that close-smelling enclosure, with the endless jabbering and carousing of the Angels, the horrors of the world seemed far away. I slept surprisingly well, pressed into leather upholstery. In the morning, when I awoke, the transport was moving again.

D. Well look, Nicola. Your father I remember said things . . .

N. No he didn't.

D. Oh, nothing direct. But there were certain . . . implications.

N. [starts to reply]

D. It's simply this, Nicola. I'm old and I'm frightened. I want to see the end of the journey. Spare me the indignity of . . . Just tell me what you know.

N. It's nothing, Dick. As far as I know it's mildly hallucinogenic, and that's that. It doesn't have anything to do with really seeing [emph]. Really, I tried it once and it was pretty boring. For years I've been shipping all we grow up to the valley. There's somebody there—

D. [exclaims]

. . . Then nothing. We had driven for two days, and I think at this point we must have come into view of the fortifications around Candlemas. Dirty Dick brought the transport to a halt. Peering out the narrow windows I saw that we were not the only vehicle on the road. The fields around us, stripped long ago of whatever had grown there, were full of all manner of wagons and motorcarts, with hundreds of people of various types milling between them. There was nothing as grand (or as dangerous-looking) as Dick's transport, unless you count the armored government vans that puttered up and down the edges of the road, like herd dogs keeping the rest of us in order. One of these was approaching us already, though I doubt that Dirty Dick had seen it yet. I nudged Nicola, who shrugged and began groping around in the mess of everyone's belongings for her gun.

Shortly there was thumping on the hatch. Dirty Dick drew the bolt and eased it back. A face appeared at the opening: youthful, with that gleam in the eyes I associate with zealotry.

"Here for the Harvest Festival?"—invoking a Courteous Greeting routine, his voice seemed more mechanical than alive.

Ah, I thought. The Harvest Festival. Here on the trampled, infertile dirt of the field, amid a flock of smoking vehicles, this concept acquired a certain ironic shadow. Though the voice of the young patrolman did not sound like one very much attuned to irony.

"You'll have to leave your car here and present your possessions for inspection. Do you have a place to stay in Candlemas? Are you carrying weapons or dangerous material of any kind? Are you affiliated with the University?"

Dirty Dick had not answered the first question yet—the Courteous Greeting—and already we had moved on to Routine Inquiries.

"Dangerous material, I should say!" Dick chuckled. He called back to the Angels: "Would you all mind stopping that noise for just a few moments?"

The Angels stopped singing. For just a few moments. Dirty Dick said:

"Look here, young man. We are on our way to a terribly important meeting upon which the fate of the known universe might very well depend.

Now get out of my hatch, please, so that I may proceed without shearing your head off."

The patrolman seemed to be scanning his mental directory, trying to decide whether this constituted Failure to Answer, or perhaps Threat of Violence. I was doing some rapid calculating myself. We were all, I expect, quite relieved when Dick gave a laugh and said:

"The Solar Temple—which way is that? That's where we'll be staying, you see. And no, to the best of my knowledge none of us has any business at a university."

The patrolman, unexpectedly, smiled. "You mean Pantera's place? I hear he's having a big party out there. Are you friends of his? Listen, is it true what they say? I mean, about those parties?"

Dirty Dick gave a wide and, I'm sure, sincere smile. He was on familiar ground now. He beckoned to the armed and indoctrinated adolescent, who ought to have been warned about such things.

"Come with us," he kindly suggested. "We'll introduce you."

Really, a moment's uncertainty was all that was required. As the young patrolman grappled with temptation at the mouth of the hatch, one of the Angels reached over and—with surprising strength, though I hear that's how Angels are—lifted the youth bodily into the transport. The hatch boomed shut. There was a brief thrashing of limbs, following which various badges and passes were found in a pocket and handed around, the poor boy's weapons were divvied up, and I was instructed to try on his uniform, as all of the Angels seemed saddled with overly broad shoulders. I rolled up the sleeves and legs like a child playing dress-up.

"All right, then," Dick proclaimed, sounding even more the Merry Old Soul than usual: "To the field! And remember—if we become separated, we shall meet again at the party! Or if not, then at some other party!"

We laughed, and disembarked. Naturally, the Angels knew a few good marching songs. Nicola and I started off trying to keep up with them, but we soon decided it was rather too exhausting—mostly in a philosophical sense. Angels and mortals do not mix. In which I could have found an important lesson, if I had looked. But there was enough else to look at, then, as we approached the strange calamity that had once been the town of Candlemas.

What they mean by madding

If you wanted proof that the world was *not* coming to an end, you would have had to go someplace else. Streets teemed, yards had been turned into campgrounds, tumbledown houses were converted to cheap hotels. The disparate clutches of people swarming everywhere, or huddled in shadows, had little enough apparently in common beyond that look of self-abandonment one saw so much of in those years, unless one were living on a mountaintop. It was most abjectly in evidence around the long tables, each with its attendant queue, at which bored- or worried-looking representatives of various sub-bureaus went about the business of Administration, whatever that entailed. There is probably a technique for keeping one's spirits up while standing in lines like that, but none of these people seemed to have mastered it. The end-result of the process was, I gathered, most often a stack of paper, whose colors ran toward a drab, yolky yellow. Scraps of this paper, soaked by rain and disintegrated by muddy feet, filled every cavity of the town, making for the most depressing kind of litter I have ever seen, like the nesting material of some demoralized rodent. Whatever information the papers had once conveyed was thoroughly lost, and nobody seemed to regret it. It is hard to remember why we once thought the choice would come down to fire or ice. Clearly, the world will end in gritty dampness.

What had brought all those people here? Most likely it was a pressure-release phenomenon, as Nicola had said on that first evening: *Just open up the highways and they will come.* Which makes one truly curious about what things are like in the East. Or perhaps it doesn't. I missed the Institute for the first time in my life, and I was growing very worried about Turner.

Nicola walked close to me, glancing frequently to make sure I was not lost, big-sister-style. We tried asking our way to the Solar Temple, and inquiring about one Black Malachi Pantera, but got only a series of looks which were hard to interpret. Had we committed some *faux pas*? Were we speaking words better left unuttered? Was everyone who knew Malachi already there?

Was there something we ought to know?

"It can't be this hard," Nicola said. "There's got to be something we're not thinking of."

We had passed from one end of town to the other. Yet we seemed to have gotten nowhere. There was a homogeneity about the place that made it difficult to get one's bearings. Gradients, as Malachi might say, had been smoothed over. The town had become a crowd scene, and we were only faces within it. I did not like the idea any better than Turner had.

"I've got it," said Nicola.

She took my arm. Beside us was one of those government vans, the only form of transport allowed within the bounds of Candlemas itself. Young patrolmen (they were always young, though, weren't they?) sat inside. They were watching things—for example, me and Nicola—without much evident enthusiasm. Probably someone had told them to "keep an eye out." From the roof of the van, a projection of the Chief Administrator, which I assumed to be lifelike though I had not seen the original, delivered a lecture on *Taking One's Place in the New Order*, which I believe had to do with making the most of this face-in-the-crowd business. It was hard to understand. Nicola strode purposefully to the door of the van, dragging me behind her.

She knocked. I tidied up my ill-fitting disguise. The Newport-blue cloth was made out of some stiff, nonporous fabric, inappropriate for summertime. From the van we heard a voice complaining, asking a question—something—in a loud voice.

"We have some *clues*," said Nicola. "About a fugitive. Open up. It's important."

Only one fugitive came to mind. Perhaps the people in the van were thinking likewise. A door slid back and a face—another of those bright-eyed empty-minded faces—looked down at us, stupidly.

Nicola was a fairly dynamic person. Such concepts as "inertia" and "momentum" (which, if you remember *very* well, you will recall that Turner had never quite grasped) were matters of native intelligence to her. She shoved a piece of paper into the patrolman's hand and glanced beyond him, in the manner of an investigator. There were three of them.

"Do you have a radio?" she said.

The patrolman nodded, distractedly. What she had given him was one of her own handwritten invitations: *To meet Turner Ashenden* . . .

He read it slowly, then over again, as though it contained concepts that stretched the limits of cognition. Finally he looked up at Nicola.

"Does this mean," he said, "that someone is actually giving a party for . . . here in *Candlemas?* Right *now?*"

"We mustn't waste time," said Nicola. She grabbed my arm, as though to thrust me into the van. "You'd better take us to this Temple place."

The patrolman continued to block the door. "So it's really true, then," he murmured.

"True . . . ?" (You could feel her falter.)

"Just like Mr Rodarch says. *We need not seek out our enemies, for they will come to us.*"

Nicola gave a devout little nod. "He's so smart," she averred. Then she struck the patrolman on the chin with her elbow. He lost his balance; Nicola shoved past him into the van, brandishing her stolen weapon.

"Are you coming?" she snapped at me.

By the time I clambered inside and closed the door, Nicola had the three patrolmen bunched together in the cab. For all their leader's prophesies, they did not really seem prepared for this kind of trouble. "I knew this would work," Nicola said.

Everything took forever. First the patrolmen attempted to have a whispered conference among themselves; they gave this up after a perfunctory single-fire discharge from Nicola's handgun. Then there were long exchanges of terrified looks while everybody wondered who was going to drive. This straightened itself out eventually, with one patrolman settling into the driver's seat and the other two scrunching against the opposite door, so Nicola could see that no one was attempting to work the radio. The van crept forward, parting the crowd before it, and eventually we were passing the last sentry-post at what was obviously the western edge of town. The sun drooped ahead of us, a weary-looking red.

"No signals," said Nicola—though it appeared the warning was superfluous. The sentries outside seemed chiefly interested in something over our heads. One of them nudged another, and soon a dozen pairs of eyes were focused a few feet above the van's roof.

Oh, yes. The projection of Rodarch. Nobody, evidently, had turned it off, and it must have been striking enough, in the fading light, to attract attention. You could hear the voice—I assumed it was a recording—but you couldn't quite make out any of the words. The van rolled onward and the Chief Administrator continued to talk. Somehow it all seemed entirely consistent.

I could see the mountains ahead of us. If we kept going this way, I would be home within a couple of hours. For a little while the thought preoccupied me; I imagined with startling poignancy the serenity, the safety, even a certain warmth that now mysteriously had become associated with Bad Winters in my mind. Well, they say memory plays tricks on you. Thinking of Maridel, of Gwendola, even of the barely human Nurse Tawdry, was like remembering one's own family. It was all poppycock, of course. Thank heavens we turned at last off the road into the modest grounds of the Solar Temple, or it might have gone on and on.

Turner had never bothered to describe the place—or at least he had not said much about how it looked from the outside. I was impressed, perhaps principally because it was so unlike the Institute. There was an aura of *concept* about it, of a unifying style or design. From the front it appeared to be an octagon, or some other figure that did not bother much with right angles. The sky was just beginning to darken, and around the glassy skin of the Temple arose a cool blue-violet radiance, like a fluorescent aura: the glow of Black Malachi's grow-bulbs. Walls and roof were of a piece, so that you didn't quite know what to call any given part. Tall trees and clambering vines made it hard to get an all-over look at the place. Moreover the parking lot was crowded with vehicles of every description —a different, rather more cheering display than the one at the other side of town—so that it was necessary to stop a good distance out, at the base of the low hillside.

"Well," said Nicola.

This was a moment of decision, and it lingered awkwardly. Nicola did not, in actuality, have much personal experience with violence; mostly things had been done in her behalf by her cadre of farmers.

"Okay, Tristin"—obviously temporizing—"you get out."

I scrambled to the parking lot. When the light begins to fail the darkness comes quickly, and I was no sooner on the ground than my attention was caught very dramatically by the projection above the van. It really shone in the twilight. The image of the Chief Administrator had such intensity, such *presence*, that I found myself thinking of it as a witness to our crime.

—Hurry, Nicola.

She was saying something, making some threat, inside the van, but things had reversed themselves: now it was Rodarch's voice I heard clearly, while hers was muffled and indistinct.

Let us join in celebration, the projection said solemnly. *Let us prepare to reap the fruit of our long season of struggle.*

By God, I thought. What charisma. You can see why the people are willing to obey him, why his followers are so starry-eyed.

—Nicola!

I tried to force my thoughts upon her. Standing here, at the foot of this strangely compelling image, was having an odd effect on me.

—Nicola, hurry, before it's . . .

Too late?

I looked up, and the Chief Administrator looked down at me.

It is too late already, the illusion said. *Your part in this is over—you have brought us to Mr Ashenden. I shall repay you for it, someday.*

I have no explanation for this, for any of it. I only stood there feeling more dumb than ever—truly believing in that instant that the illusion was addressing me, and that it could understand my thoughts.

Now, the fireworks. Rodarch lifted his head, as though speaking once more to the multitudes. *Let the light of reason overcome the darkness!*

Nicola had come to stand beside me. The patrolmen were leaning from the van, but nobody was doing much besides staring at the Chief Administrator. We watched for as long as he kept speaking—something in the illusion itself seemed to require this—and it was only when he paused for breath, just like a physical being, that Nicola found the presence of mind to yank her attention away. She yanked me as well—quite roughly.

"We've got to find Turner," she whispered. Growing beneath her voice was the first hint of hysteria. "I've got a feeling this place is about to have the shit blown out of it."

4

Vibes

Black Malachi Pantera, lately turned nineteen, felt himself to be at the peak of his inexplicable powers. Which is not, he thought, an entirely happy circumstance. For as the advice columnist told the bride: If *this* is the happiest day of your life, what does that say for the rest of the marriage?

Nonetheless his powers—whatever, exactly, they were—seemed to quiver just short of his fingertips. Somewhere around the cuticle, in fact. Black Malachi examined in turn each stubby hand. The fingers were short, the nails carefully trimmed, the backs preternaturally hairy. He wondered, as he did from time to time, where he fit in the scheme of things— whether, in an evolutionary sense, he was a prototype, or a throwback. *There were giants on the earth*, after all. Merlin got those bluestones to Sarras single-handedly, by levitation—and they came *not* from Prescelly but from Tipperary, just as old Geoff's informants claimed. Check it out yourself with a pendulum. And while you're at it, check out the Bright Lands, which figure prominently in a forthcoming . . . Oh, but whom am I talking to?

He was agitated. There were no two ways about it. The past day and night (or had it been longer?) holed up in his suite of rooms, however comfortable he normally found them, had done little for the state of his nerves. Vinny's godawful selection of music thumped at him round-the-clock through the floorboards, and Cervina was developing, God love her, a case of cabin fever far beyond the reach of *Pulsatilla*.

Still, one hesitated to pop the cork. We shall sell no djinn before its time. Black Malachi made a ritualistic gesture for the benefit of his mirror—can't be too careful of those things—and went back to pacing the room.

Cervina turned from the window.

"It's getting dark," she said, in a tone of voice that strongly suggested, *without me.* "Something weird's going on in the parking lot."

"Something weird?"—always a sucker for omens.

"Like, there's this guy standing on top of this truck."

The hirsute little wizard stroked his chin. No particular interpretation suggested itself. He shrugged.

"It's hard to believe," said Cervina, peering outward again, "people are still showing up. *This* one's got on a Settler's uniform about three sizes too big."

"I suppose they're down to drafting children now. Ashenden must really have got them rattled."

"He's got *you* rattled."

There was a good twelve inches difference in height between the two of them, but Malachi had a way of looking at you. He and Cervina exchanged stares for half a minute, until they had both forgotten who had started it. The stout youth gave vent to a sigh.

"I do hope," he said, "it does not go on much longer."

"What? What is going on, Blackie? Why have a party in the first place if you're just going to stay cooped up in your room? Don't you like *people* any more?"

"The vibes," said Black Malachi.

He moved back to the mirror, turned half aside, regarded his undistinguished form for several seconds.

"The vibes," he said again. He liked the sound of it. "It is important," he continued—noting with approval the way his expression remained fixed even while his lips moved—"to have people here, keep them dancing about, keep the music going. Thus we arouse and concentrate the vibes —all this chthonic energy swirling around us. Encircling the *Omphalos.*"

Cervina curled herself like a six-foot cat into a window seat. "Blackie, are you just talking? I mean are you just, like, going on, or are you really serious about this?"

"I try never," he said, "to be *really serious*. It damages, I believe, one's nerve endings. Nonetheless I am telling the truth. As always. As, in fact, I must, for that is my part in this. And I am not the only one who recognizes it. Look out there," pointing over her head, toward the blackening gap in the window-frame, "if you doubt me. Look at everything *he's* doing to bring the vibes up. I don't know who he's got whispering in his ear, but the Stainless Steel Savior really knows what he's doing."

Cervina regarded him, open-eyed. Black Malachi seldom addressed himself to questions of *realpolitik*—nor, for that matter, spoke so directly about anything. Hoping to hear more, she said, "What makes you think he's got anyone whispering in his ear? Maybe he's just, you know, smart. All by himself."

Malachi took a few steps toward the window and stopped. One might have thought something was making him hesitate, causing him to feel uncharacteristically uncertain. Cervina did and did not like to see this.

"Well, you know," he said, "I suppose it is possible. Anything is possible."

"And what do you mean"—determined not to let him escape into platitudes—"your *part* in this? And just what the hell is *this*? Are you trying to lay down some kind of all-the-world's-a-stage bullshit?"

Black Malachi stood with his back to her. Without turning he said, "When you arrived here, Cervina, from your daddy's big place back East, with that preposterous accent, you did not, whatever your other and more grievous rhetorical shortcomings, sink so low as to employ great numbers of hyphens in the manufacture of unnatural adjectives, simply to modify the word *bullshit*. Have I done this to you?"

Cervina stared at the middle of his back until the tension made him turn around—something else she couldn't have done a year ago. She said, "I love you, Blackie."

"Yes," nodding readily, "I believe you do. And I cannot think that is a very sound practice, either."

Still he gave her what, under the circumstances, must have been his very best smile. Like many another peculiar couple, they remained together because they were genuinely fond of each other.

Breaking the mood and their eye contact, he pointed over her head, out the window. "Oh, good," he said. "We're having fireworks."

Pop, pop, the explosions sang, filling the evening sky.

Parallel narrative (2)

If the synoptics are suspiciously tight-lipped about what an itinerant mir-
acle-worker had to say for himself during his trial for practicing medicine
without board certification, it's most likely because the author—the first
one, known to us as "Q"—being only a writer after all, had trouble
imagining what such a person would say at a time like that. And there
were, as far as we know, no official transcripts. We face a similar difficulty
vis-à-vis Pantera, regardless of whether strictly speaking we "believe" in
him or not. With Cervina, on the other hand, there is nothing especially
in which to believe; besides which we have a body of personal testimony.

"Well, there was this pounding," she informs us, "like on the door?
Which really you could hardly tell wasn't part of Vinny's music, maybe
the drum part getting out of sync or something. Only also there was this
sort of BOOM, BOOM, and the whole house would shudder, but even
then if you'd ever been to one of those parties you wouldn't necessarily
think it was anything that like you shouldn't have been expecting. I mean
there was this one time where somebody wanted to see what would happen
if you landed a sunglider in the middle of all those skylights. But I mean,
what did *you* think? You were there, weren't you?"

Well. But I had never been to the Solar Temple before. From the
moment Nicola and I stepped into the foyer, with those banana leaves
drooping everywhere and that music—the first music I had ever heard,
incidentally, that had not been chosen by Madame Gwendola for some
occasion, but rather was actually being performed—I was fairly certain
that I had stepped into a riot-in-progress. Or perhaps into a brothel (if
there are such things) in the middle of a raid. The first people we saw,
after all, were wearing detox suits. And the next people we saw were wearing
very nearly nothing. Fortunately the *next* people we saw were old friends
of Nicola. They were wearing exactly what you would expect old friends
of Nicola to wear. All I remember now is thinking, tweed in August?
Turner used to say (quoting Malachi, I suspect) it was a racial memory of
the Lost Isles.

"The what? But anyway, so you see my point. So when the BOOM
BOOM started, I didn't even pay it any attention at first. So then when

Blackie went and started getting all dressed up, in those whatever you want to call them, robes or something, I didn't have any idea what was going on. I still don't. All I know is, I said Blackie what are you doing, are you going out or something, and he just said, all ominous and everything, I *do* hope the vibes are high enough because there's no more time left, or words to that effect. He put on one layer on top of another. Silk, if you can imagine Blackie wearing silk. And all this time he was talking—Silk is the only natural fiber which is fila*mentous*, he said. Just like that. There is good *reason*, he said, to believe that if the Shroud had been made of silk, the pattern would never have been recorded. The vibes, you see, don't penetrate the serpentine interlacings. Which may underscore old Bill's point about the worm, mayn't it. I mean, come on—*mayn't?* Then he said, silk is the oldest method of containment. Spirals are quite good and crosses also, and in silk we find both structures in tandem. Just rattling on, while all this time the floor was shaking and it sounded like the house was having the shit blown out of it."

Ah, there. The first author. Upon whom all the synoptics have drawn.

"But Blackie you know wouldn't be rushed. He did act a little irritable—like there was this glass breaking, it sounded like in the greenhouse, and he said, naturally they are the sort of people who will *break in* when every conceivable portal is unlocked. But mostly he just kept putting these robes on and when he was finished he went really calmly over to this closet, and he turned around and said Cervina, are you coming? And I said to the *closet?* And he said, to the secret passage. Which I really figured was a joke, a pretty *weird* joke, at a time like that, but I went over anyway. It was a secret passage. We went down and twisted all around and came up again. You could hear the noises, but I never knew where we were or where we were going. It's the craziest thing that ever happened to me, until later on. Then like *that*, we came out of it. We were standing in this place where the light sort of hovered in the air above us, and all of a sudden even though things had been noisy as hell just back there in the passage, all of a sudden they got really quiet. Like . . ."

Making smooth-as-silk hand-signs.

Nicola and I had experienced things a little differently, but Cervina's memory rings true. There was a very peculiar feeling of orchestration. As though, even while yes, there was a riot going on, and yes the house evidently *was* getting the shit blown out of it—even so, there was for some reason a kind of natural gravitation drawing everyone down the hill, where of all things there were doors opening up, trap-doors, hidden in the bushes, and in just that handful of moments the party seemed to reassemble itself around the great glowing cavity in the ground, which we now are calling the Operating Theater, though at the time it might have been the inside of a flying saucer and made just as much sense, been no more astonishing at all lying there glowing wide open in the night with the fireworks still exploding in the east and two hundred of us or more huddled there in the shadows, looking down, completely paralyzed by the mystery of the thing, when they carried Turner in.

"I didn't see that. When Blackie and I stepped out, right into the pool down there, Turner was already laid out naked in the middle of all this, this *light*, and the lamps were so hot you sort of felt like maybe you were standing beside a fire or something. And there were smells—"

Hospital smells.

"But also *fresh* . . . you know how a thunderstorm sometimes . . . or like a waterfall, when the air makes your nose tickle?"

Those are ions, I believe. Something to do with volumes of water, or the movement—

"But see, that's just what Blackie used to say! Don't you remember? *The confluence of negatively empowered waters*, don't you remember I told you? And you said yourself, that stuff about the Solar Temple being situated at an especially active site, a natural crossing, the old tracks—*I* remember."

She had gotten off the subject.

"Bullshit. You're the one. I was just talking about how the smell . . . And then I saw all those people looking down at us. But the weird thing was, that wasn't what bothered me at all. I figured, well what the hell, I'm with Blackie and it's his party, or whatever it had gotten to be, but what *really* made me feel funny was this feeling that for some reason I wasn't part of the show. I mean, that doesn't make any sense, right? Because I didn't know what show I was even talking about. Or if there was going to be a show at all. But it did feel like a theater, down there, and Blackie was dressed up in all that silk like a magician or something, and there was Turner . . ."

At the time, I didn't even know which Turner we were dealing with. The flesh-and-blood Ashenden, or the other, the Akashic Other, the ghost, Nicola's bed-partner. God this is strange. I guessed it was the *doppelgänger* down there—hadn't Black Malachi snatched him from us, back at the Witch's camp? But there was something in the way the poor thing was strapped down. It was hard to imagine that an essentially nonphysical being—or if you like, a *meta*physical being—could be so constrained.

"I feel sorry for you, Tristin."

. . .

"Just let me finish, though. Blackie walked really slowly out into the light, where Turner was all tied down. And the way things were so quiet? It got even more . . . pronounced, I guess you could say, and it was like all those people, all *you all* up there, around the pool, were like holding their breaths, your breath, while Blackie raised his arms up into the air and began to do that sort of chant."

[A CHANT]

> There is an ancient General
> And he sleepeth a century.
> Then he open up one glassy eye,
> And he sleepeth another three.
>
> Pantera's doors are opened wide—
> Can you hear the merry din?
> The band's well met, and plays a set,
> And the Enemy waltzes in.
>   [Stirring among the audience]
> The General, yet, is loth to wake.
> "Who gives a shit," quoth he.
> But all the noise has stirred him up,
> And he riseth so to pee.
>
>   [Titters]
>
> Now the Enemy's a steely man,
> A governor of fame—
> But he takes one look at the General
> And he's blinded and he's lame.
>
> He raiseth up an army, then,
> And girdeth for a fight—

The General for to drive away,
Back to that great long night.

The General sayeth, "What the fuck."
—'Tis vulgar but 'tis true.
He layeth hands on a wizard stick
And cleaveth himself in two.

[Groans of displeasure]

The one half is a sullen lad,
Who's wont to sit and read;
The other half's a lusty brute
Who slippeth it in with speed.

Now the Enemy bethinks himself,
This is a jolly thing.
I'll poke my pecker hereabout
And see what luck it bring.

Fair maidens, prithee, go from hence,
For the Enemy's aim is true.
He'll gladly stick you with his shaft,
Now the General's split in two.

[Murmurs of consternation]

But wait! Is there an ancient sound,
A voice all pure and sweet?
Doth the General's famous Consort
Haply come to make ends meet?

Doth the æther sing at her approach?
Do angels hum along?
Or do my ears to fool me ring
From Vinny's deaf'ning song?

I reckon that I heard it right:
The Consort doth draw near.
The General soon shall stand erect;
We'll see the Enemy's rear.

Oh wond'rous night, that such a thing
Might happen in these dugs!

The General shall be two-in-one,
And he oweth it all to drugs!

[Mirth, applause]

"I don't know. Do you think we all imagined it? I remember reading
something about the madness of crowds. How hundreds of people could
think they saw the same thing, and you could like explain the loaves and
fishes and all that . . . and he *was* right about the drugs. I mean how
many days had we been living on those muffins, and that punch, my God,
I never did find out what was—"

Nicola and I had just arrived, though. And the Angels—would they
have taken anything?

"But that's not . . . but what I'm saying is, like maybe it was some
kind of big collective hallucination. I mean, don't you remember it *at
all*? The moment there when Maridel just—"

Some things I remember.

"That was the really strangest part. I mean, that's at least as weird as
anything that came after. Don't you remember? How the lights sort of
shattered, and the glass flew everywhere? But it was bright, too, like an
explosion or something, and all of a sudden people were shouting everywhere, there were people pushing in all around us, people being shoved
over the edge down into the pool, guns going off, and Blackie just—"

One thing I remember most of all. Nicola and I were right at the
edge, leaning over—it wasn't even a conscious thing, we were simply both
of us straining to be as near Turner as possible. So when the Settlers arrived
and did whatever they did—I suspect somebody must have damaged the
power system—the lamps exploded and suddenly the only light was coming
from flares or fireworks, I don't know which, up in the sky, and from . . .

"See, you *do* remember. From Blackie. Say it."

Perhaps. Who am I, at this point, to deny anything? But the thing *I*
remember was this. Nicola and I heard the commotion behind us, and
figured out pretty quickly what was going on, and Nicola just grabbed my
hand like it was no big deal and tossed me over the side. Confident, I
suppose, that as always I would contrive to land more or less on my feet.
I landed on my knees, actually, in the middle of something soft, and when
I looked down, by what light there was, a kind of strobing, I saw that I
had landed right on top of Dirty Dick.

He must have fallen, or been pushed. Nicola jumped down beside us and when she had caught her breath and crawled over she just stood there looking down with tears in her eyes. *Oh shit*, she said. *Oh Christ, Dick.*

—Nicola, I tried to tell her.—Nicola, I think *I* might have . . .

But then we looked up, something made us both look up at the same time, and there was Black Malachi standing there, not terribly big or impressive, which surprised me after that, how shall I say, performance —and he just stood there—

"*Glowing*, say it. I can't stand how you always leave the important stuff out."

Turner used to say that the important things are the most difficult to perceive. Black Malachi just stood there, is what I remember, and all I remember. Dirty Dick sat up. *Hello Nicola*, he said. You would think he had just taken a little cat-nap. *Do you know*, he said, *I can see quite well now.*

"What about you, Tristin? I wonder why Blackie didn't . . ."

Listen, Cervina. I do not believe this really happened. But somewhere in my mind . . . I don't know, the way you remember things that you used to wish for, impossible things, perhaps when you were a little girl? Things that you wished for so very fervently that it sometimes felt as though some magic were really starting to happen, the impossible wishes were starting to come true? Well somewhere in my mind, in a place like that, I seem to remember that Black Malachi took my hand and said, *I'm sorry, my boy. But not now.*

"Ha! I bet you've never told anyone that before, have you?"

Am I telling anyone now? Really?

"You're such a smartass. So what about Maridel?"

. . .

"Fuck off, then. I'll tell *you*. There were lights falling from the sky everywhere, and guns going off, and fire in the Temple. Some of the Souls had guns of their own and they were shooting back. People were falling into the pool, and you would have to think a lot of them must have been dead before they hit the bottom. Still, from what I remember every single one of them just sort of stood up and brushed himself, or herself, see how Blackie crammed that pronoun thing into me?—brushed herself off and got back into the swing of things. At the same time, though, in the middle of all that, there was this clear peaceful light that was everywhere around Blackie, like firefly-light, that kind of cool glow. Luminescence. Turner was in it, too, and it made him look sort of . . . reposeful. I'm really a lot more articulate than the way you've portrayed me in this goddamned thing. But anyway. All of a sudden Blackie spun around, so that his robes flew apart, and from inside all that silk he whips out this little wooden box. I guess I'd noticed it before, just sitting around with all that other crap on his desk. Weird stuff seemed to come and go in that place anyway. So Blackie holds this box up in one hand, and in another hand there's this little rod with trailing wires, I guess I don't have to go into much detail. Blackie waves this stuff around like it's some big mystical business, which of course it *is*, but Blackie just has to make a sort of big grandiose charade out of everything. And it just sort of *occurs* to everybody that there's this beautiful young girl standing around, like just lurking back halfway in the shadows. It wasn't as though she suddenly materialized or something, but more like she had been standing there all along and you sort of felt foolish about not noticing before. Because nobody reacted. There wasn't a single gasp or shout, you know *Look, there she is* or anything. None of that. So it was almost like, reality had changed right there in that instant to an almost identical reality except that it had Maridel in it, and we were all playing along like we hadn't noticed a thing. I'm having a little trouble expressing myself concisely.

"About Maridel, though. She was standing there and wouldn't come any closer, and Blackie was getting pretty impatient. Maybe I was the only one that noticed, but I knew him pretty well. God, didn't I. So after a minute he turned to look at me and he said, Cervina, I can't do a thing. See if *you* can make her listen. And he hands me the little metal rod, and holy Christ all of a sudden it's in my hand tingling and like, it felt like it was jumping around, twisting around, trying to jump away from me.

"I had a pretty good idea, already, what Blackie meant. It just seemed so *evident*, the way it had been about Maridel being there all along. I got this really strong sense of a stubborn little girl—only it was more complicated than that, as you can imagine. But at the heart of it, basically, even *with* the complications, it came down to that: a stubborn little girl. I'm not sure what I did. I just sort of thought . . . actually, it's kind of like talking to *you*. And poof."

. . . She changed in some way?

"The Consort. That's what I was thinking, after Blackie's chant. And I mean, the word's got certain connotations. So I was pretty weirded-out when all of a sudden I felt like I was really staring at this . . ."

Not a stubborn little girl any longer?

"Well not just. Although she does, she did—she *does*, I guess, right?—have that quality about her. But suddenly there she was. I mean, really *there*. Standing like that with her arms folded in front of her and her little hips sort of cocked up sideways, as though she was too young and innocent to know what that looked like. Whereas really you suddenly saw that she was this . . . like she was really a lot older, a *lot* older, and had seen so much, done so many awful—"

I know Maridel.

"Mm? Yeah, well. Maybe I'm being a little unfair. She was very beautiful. I mean, in a funny way she was so beautiful, so *perfect*, that it was almost hard to look at her. The way when you've got something really wonderful, you don't want to use it up all at once. I remember those hands."

I remember those hands.

"Poor Tristin. What a weird childhood you must have had. *She* had nothing to lose, did she? It was like, she feasted on you, on both of you."

. . .

"She walked so slowly. She came forward, into the light, until she was standing right at the center, next to Turner. Turner lying there helpless on the table. You couldn't tell if he was awake or not. It was like somehow the life had gone out of him, but he wasn't dead yet. Maybe he *couldn't* die. And Maridel . . ."

Yes?

"You're really enjoying this, aren't you. You want me to go over it slowly, I bet—how she reached down with one of those slender little hands and took Turner's dick and started playing with it—"

Come on, Cervina.

"—and *then* how she bent down like a fairy-tale princess—"

Do you have to do this?

"Only for another minute. You want to know, don't you? I saw you down there—looking the other way. You couldn't stand it, I guess. That's when I *knew*, you know. So don't you want to get all the facts, now? For your history? I mean, isn't that what history is all about?"

The answer to that

The thing with which History is concerned is that on August the second, just after nightfall, an attack on the Solar Temple by militant followers of the Chief Administrator, many of whom appeared to have been specially trained and equipped for the occasion, was repulsed. The incident is especially important to us, as historians, as students of the past, because it provided the first clear demonstration that the Old Souls were capable of putting aside their traditional rivalries—which had often verged upon internecine warfare—and uniting their collective resources, which were substantial, even then, in a coordinated resistance. It also marks the emergence of Turner Ashenden as the *de facto* leader, or at least the field commander, of the rebellious coalition.

Ashenden is nowadays almost universally given credit for winning that first skirmish at the Solar Temple, though on the night of the event, as those present will attest, the exact nature of the contest and the factors leading to its outcome were to say the least not fully clear. Speaking personally, it seemed to me that the center of the battle was an old, disused swimming pool on a terrace behind the house. In the intervening years, however, having spoken to a number of other witnesses—there were, after all, at least three hundred people at the party—I have come to realize that the fighting was intense throughout the house and, indeed, on all sides of it. It must seem strange to you, in what I imagine is a very different era, that so many people, in a single place, should have happened to be so heavily armed. But such was the nature of the times. We had been, in varying degrees, at war with ourselves and our neighbors, or in fear of being overrun by the faceless masses that were being "settled out" across the countryside, for so very long, that even on the mountaintop, at the Institute, we were seldom without the means of self-defense. It would be disingenuous to pretend now to have been above all that.

The interesting common thread in all accounts of the fighting is that Turner Ashenden appears to have been many places and done many things, commencing at a certain moment, before which the battle had seemed to be hopeless. From the time of Ashenden's appearance, however—and I think I use the word *appearance* appropriately—things turned about very nicely. He is reported to have rescued a band of partygoers trapped in the refrigerator, where a young woman evidently kept singing throughout the ordeal. At about the same time, he is said to have offered counsel to a group of socialites making a stand in a second-story powder room, following which the aroused matrons forced the Settlers back down the hall and established a tactically important stronghold along the balustrade, commanding a view of the open foyer. Perhaps the most colorful account is that of Ashenden appearing at the head of a small choral ensemble, half a dozen strong, whose members were uniformly broad-shouldered and toted a variety of captured government weapons. With this squad at his back, Ashenden seems to have fought his way up the back staircase, retaking one by one each of the bedrooms in the residential wing, stopping briefly at his own room to retrieve something described as a "roll of paper, like a poster" then proceeding down the Bug Walk, into the greenhouse, through a maze of pantries, and finally into the kitchen, where the choirboys prepared trays of sandwiches and beer for their comrades at the front.

The fighting went on until morning, at which time Black Malachi Pantera appeared on a second-story balcony to announce that a victory breakfast was being served. By this time, however, Turner Ashenden seems to have vanished. It is widely thought that he pursued the retreating Settlers down the hill to Candlemas, and perhaps directed some mopping-up operations in the town itself, heedless of the concentration of government strength. No reliable witnesses have come forward to confirm this, however. What *is* certain is that the breakfast at the Solar Temple was the largest single gathering of Old Souls ever recorded, before or since. Harvey Goldaster presided in Turner's absence. He claimed—and was believed, on the strength of long association—to have been requested by Ashenden himself to negotiate the terms of a unification pact, formalizing the structure of the Resistance. This was accomplished with remarkable dispatch, considering all the complications (though as one primary source claims, the negotiation was made more cordial by the presence of *Salvia divinorum*, sage-of-the-seers, homeopathically potentized, in the scrambled eggs). By eleven o'clock, Turner Ashenden had been awarded the provisional title of Field Commander, and accepted by all parties as the leader of all forces currently, and henceforth, arrayed against the Administration. The written pact itself was drafted by a tall young woman who seemed quite competent, thank you, for the task. Her words are now a well-known part of History.

The answer to your question, then, is No.

The other answer to that

As Maridel took him in her mouth Turner arched his back, involuntarily, and groaned. She wrapped herself around him, on the table, pressing their bodies into a tightly joined singularity.

Nicola could not, or would not, stand for any more of this. She stepped forward. She had nearly reached the operating table when someone grabbed her arm.

It was Turner Ashenden. It was more precisely the "other" Turner —the one whom she had known in Wine Barrens. He stood there, holding her arm, as though perplexed by the goings-on at the center of the Theater, where his physical counterpart was now locked (a fitting term) in Maridel's embrace. The look of perplexity evolved into one of faint disgust, then resignation. Turner released Nicola—who by this time, in yet another reversal, was clinging to *him*—and faced the operating table. His expression read something like, Very well then.

He slipped out of Nicola's arms like the insubstantial thing he was. He stepped forward, but at the same time in a more meaningful sense he seemed to be stepping *inward*—into some constricting dimension where he did not easily fit. The mortal coil, perhaps. He did not grow smaller, exactly, or fade out like a special cinematic effect; he simply allowed himself to be subsumed by the "real" Turner, the fleshly one. The only one. The once and future Ashenden.

"Very clever." (Cervina again). "But what happened, really? I mean, *specifically*. Did she make him some offer? Did she threaten him? Couldn't you read what he was thinking?"

Turner sat up, with Maridel in his arms. She moved with him, or against him—or both at once—in a kind of silent dance. Still silent, they embraced, and great things appeared to pass between them. Maridel's eyes were deep and black, like bodies of water whose infinite depths pose always the same question.

In the next moment—as I realized—Turner would give his answer: the other answer, the one which of course he must give, as he must have understood.

Ha! cried Black Malachi.

"You don't mean *Blackie* was doing all this."

He was still there, of course. Still somehow presiding. He looked . . . back to normal, I would say. If there had been a mysterious glow, it was gone now. He turned to smile at Nicola, at you . . . and at me, I'm sure he sought out my eyes also. He crowed: *What did I tell you? You just have to get all the pieces together!*

If I could have spoken then, I would have shouted a reply. My eternal refutation, my denial of everything. All that I had seen, or was seeing then, or would ever come to know.

But Turner, pressing himself against Maridel, murmured in true Turner-style:

Well, what the hell. Why not?

STAYING
UP

1

Tea at Bad Winters

" 'Winter kills'," said Turner, leaning back. "Where's that from?"

Nobody—Gwendola, Tristin, Maridel, Vinny Hawkmoth, Harvey Goldaster—answered him. A hero hath no honor, and all that. Might as well help yourself to more scones.

"It says here—" (Vinny: not looking up from a badly bound book) "that the satellite dish used to sit right out there in the middle of the lawn. Do you think that's why the place is so level?"

Maridel made that little sniffing noise. "There is no more satellite dish. There are no more satellites. What difference could it possibly make? I *much* prefer the lawn just as it is."

Which was empty, at the moment, and covered with snow. Their view of it was screwed up by the presence of old leggy boxwoods, whose hollow insides were most of what you could see from the windows. The low January sun had the same problem getting in; otherwise it might have been warmer. Nobody had thought of this, it seemed, at pre-Millennial planting time.

Vinny flipped pages. To Maridel he said, "What a cynic you've gotten to be." One lip twisted up: the notion seemed to please him. "And so young. It took me till I was twenty to get as bad as you. Where's your sense of wonder? Where's your *joie de vivre?*"

"Sense of won-der," Maridel played back, a syllable at a time. "Is that what you have to have before you can lose yourself in poorly written novels? No thank you. I'd just as soon remain cynical, if that's what you call it. The literature of cynicism is so much more . . . trenchant."

"Like a grave," said the music man. He was into the book again. "Listen here. It says that *at its highest point of development, the network designed by Doctor Drode was often employed to interconnect Psychic Explorers at otherwise isolated reaches of the globe, including the staffs of limited-access Reporting Stations such as those lately established under the Balance Act.* Pretty amazing, huh?"

"Amazing convoluted," said Maridel. "That must be the part my father didn't write."

Madame Gwendola threw a glance across the coffeepot at her precociously insolent daughter, and Turner followed her eyes. It made you think. As far as he remembered, Gwendola had never made a single mention of her late husband, nor for that matter shed the tiniest light on her own feelings about all this. This project, I mean: Vinny's farfetched and already over-budget scheme to tap into whatever was left of the old global culture net. He proposed to accomplish this by setting up a transceiver [a horrid word-splice, worse by a nose than *cultivar*] smack in the middle of the lawn. Clearly what he wanted was a wider audience for his music than the Solar Temple crowd; but all he'd admit to publicly was a spirit of scholarly investigation, a rather morbid desire to see *how dead* the past really was, and a neighborly concern for the Resistance. We would certainly (he murmured in the ear of Harvey Goldaster, whence all possibilities sprang) stand to gain from a faster means of talking to the boys at the battle front.

Where *was* the battle front, though? Was it a physical place, a divide as sharp as the broken pavement around the Grim Dyke? Or was it some murkier thing altogether, a philosophic DMZ, spawning-ground of future historians? I wasn't at all sure, and Turner—if he was even paying attention—gave no sign of agreement. On the other hand, he made no objection to Vinny's siphoning-off of funds: there was no end of them that year, and it is agreeable to have musicians about the house. Vinny and Partner and Twill Gavotte, the band's mostly silent third, had pretty much moved their whole operation up to the Institute, where the food was better and the beds softer and the company, in its way, even more entertainingly bizarre than down at Black Malachi's place. They had left behind, by now, little else but Cagliostro. The Stradivarius thing had sort of fizzled out there, what with parties and guerrilla attacks and political rallies and Souls showing up at all hours to consult with the *dux bellorum* (Gwendola's phrase, though Black Malachi made the same connection) on someone's latest conspiratorial brainstorm. Here at Bad Winters, the air was cleaner. Or maybe just thinner. Who cares. Vinny was busy assembling scavenged copper pipes into something that looked like the skeleton of a giant teepee, Erector-Set-style, and was the sort of person who could only really concentrate on one project at a time.

"You know," said Harvey Goldaster, preening crumbs from a bristly wool sleeve, "there's something I'd like you to attend to, if you could."

Though he wasn't especially *addressing* this, everybody looked across the drawing-room at Turner. Who sat in a cream-colored, fleeting pool of sunshine, oblivious.

"Winter kills," the object of our thoughts said, almost silently. To himself now—or maybe to me. His constant witness.

Jaunt

They were having trouble (Harvey told us) at the Peels, a weary strip of truck farms and small-scale factories a couple of days' drive—by the safe route, skirting lands under Administration control—north of Candlemas. Turner spent an hour either ignoring this or thinking it over, then surprised everyone by declaring that we ought to make a jaunt of it.

"A jaunt," said Harvey, diplomatic though rather plainly bemused.

"Yes," said Turner.

"Oh," said Harvey. "Well, then." (Seeking other eyes.) "Good."

"It ought to be fun," said Turner.

Perhaps he was remembering other days, other companions. Vinny and I were a cheerless pair, and of course on my part utterly silent. Maridel was not permitted to go, which proved I suppose that Gwendola, at least, remembered that her daughter was fourteen years old. Harvey demurred, sending in his place half a dozen members of his Faceless Brigade—or they may have been Fallen Angels, the types were much alike—who went everywhere with Turner in those days, I suppose as a form of symbolic ballast, giving weight to his entourage, as much as for their nifty touch with firearms. If there are still such people in the world, they must have moved on since then, westward, deeper into our collective sunset. One certainly doesn't see them anymore.

It was a dismal time of year, and the countryside through which we drove was bleaker than I would have imagined; though of course I had not yet inherited Black Malachi's copy of *Through the Heart*. Imagine a desert of corn-stubble, with the rusted hulks of old machines and black, frozen stumps where trees had died of a withering fungus or been taken for firewood. We traveled daringly (as it seemed) on the main roads, by winterlight, in the Institute's old blade motor carriage. Fortunately the most strenuous opposition we encountered was a small troop of absolutely fearless cows who refused to move off the highway, barely even deigning to acknowledge our shouts and gun-blasts. Disembarking, we watched them lick at the dirty water that had collected in tire ruts, sealed against evaporation by a skim-coat of ice. They broke the ice with their hooves in order to reach the water, which looked distinctly unappetizing. The cows didn't look too savory themselves. Their undersides were bloated, and they stared idiotically out of yellow, rheumy eyes.

"I wonder who they belong to," said Turner.

"Nobody." (Vinny, in his capacity as Older and Wiser.) "Probably some old farmer got killed off, or just turned them out—I mean, why would you want to keep things like this? You can't eat them, with what they've been living on, and who the hell would want to drink their milk? Not that it looks like they're giving any."

We lapsed into a disheartened silence. The cows didn't care much about being shoved out of our way, and that was the last problem we faced before arriving—at sunfall, naturally, on a windy but not very cold evening—at the headquarters of the Peels.

It was a kind of industrial compound. There was a wide buffer area surrounded by metal fencing and an inner wall of concrete block, broken down or blown apart in places and patched with rusty metal, of which there seemed a lot to go around. The buildings at the center of this were arranged in a huddle, like circled wagons, and made mostly of corrugated aluminum panels, which had warped and discolored over the decades much less gracefully than the humble, vernacular materials of the local barns, whose architecture in a general sense these structures emulated. Everything at the Peels, including the dirt, from what we could see of it, was gray.

To my surprise (even, I admit, my disappointment) no guards were posted at the outer fence; there was no challenge to our arrival. We simply drove our carriage into the center of the compound, where a single spotlight shone down on eighteen or twenty other vehicles and farm machines, and walked to the door under a sign that said OFFICE. Inside a large room there were ashen-faced men and women drinking from mugs around a trash stove, and one of them greeted us:

"So which of you is the hotshot from down the valley?"

One of the Angels (let us say) nodded toward Turner, and the man who had spoken turned away in evident disgust.

"God, I'd heard it was a young guy," he said. "But this is fucking ridiculous."

On previous trips I had made with Turner—his "organizational visits" to the strongholds and settlements and beleaguered outposts of the Resistance—he had been most often received with a certain skeptical deference, an acceptance however grudging of his importance to the cause of the Souls, and occasionally even a taste of honor. Here at the Peels the prevailing attitude seemed, from this first sampling, to be one of resignation or even annoyance—as though Turner Ashenden belonged to a class of inevitable phenomena alongside soil corruption, fungal blights and thunderstorms: things with which one simply learned to live.

I barely had time to wonder how Turner was going to handle it. He stepped in his characteristic manner (off-handedly, as though apologetic about something) across the room and stuck his hand out to the man who had spoken. It was a modest, disarming sort of gesture—old-fashioned even, as though it should have been accompanied by such folk pleasantries as *Put 'er there, pardner.* The man, who was on his feet but propped back against a desk, succumbed to the bodily logic of the situation and received Turner's handclasp. I think that the instant of their physical contact was the important one, really—the moment at which the primary interaction took place, stone striking surface of lake—and that the following conversation was a kind of ripple-effect.

"Are you in charge here?" Turner asked.

The man did not look surprised, exactly. But he stared at Turner, whose hand he was shaking, as though the room had just become brighter and he was able to get a better look at him. (In fact the room was strangely lit by a number of bare bulbs strung from wires, which caused a lot of glare but mainly served to accentuate the shadows everywhere, and the wrinkles on everyone's face.)

The man said, "We operate as a collective. We don't have that labor-management problem you've got down where you come from. Each of us rotates among the various positions of the organization."

"I'm speaking to a *position*, then?" said Turner. He said it innocently enough, releasing the man's hand and glancing around the room. A dozen people, plus myself and Vinny, were watching him. I daresay I was watching more attentively than anyone, for in a paradoxical way I felt I was in the presence of someone I knew quite deeply, and yet also someone I had never seen before. Turner In Action. How's that for a contradiction in terms?

"Don't give me any crap," said the man, moving his eyes edgewise, taking bearings. "We've got some serious problems here. The Administration's threatened to stop dealing with us completely if we don't accept another batch of their relocated workers. We can't do it—our yields aren't high enough to meet the payroll we've got now. But we can't risk losing our markets in the cities. So we've had to make some concessions on other issues. The thing they're *especially* sensitive about is any dealings with the Resistance. We shouldn't even be talking to you. But as a matter of courtesy, we wanted to give you at least an explanation. Let you have a look around, if you want to. Just so you know where we stand."

Turner continued to stare for a moment or two without reacting—making certain, maybe, that the man was done. Then he nodded. He turned to me and Vinny.

"This guy is the problem," he said. As though one of us should mark this down on a notepad. "Harvey was right. They've been selling us out."

"Now just a minute, asshole."

The gray-faced man pushed off the desk and moved his body-weight toward Turner, squared off for confrontation. Turner did not look back at him. He motioned over his shoulder: a teacher making a point before a roomful of unperceptive students.

"He's not a fighter," Turner said (maybe to reassure us). "And he's not a farmer, either. Look at his hands. Look at the way he moves, with his head bent forward. It's been a long time since this man has taken his turn in the fields. Hasn't it?"

He shot his head around, forcing the sudden question into the eyes of the other residents of the place. With theatrical flourish—learned from where, I couldn't imagine—he let his gaze rest on each of them singly, omitting only the man who still hovered ominously behind his shoulder.

"Now listen you little cocksucker."

True, the man's hands were free of calluses, but they were big, and formed mean-looking fists. He seemed to swell up behind Turner like a baleful cloudhead above the horizon.

Turner looked around. From where I stood, the larger man filled all the empty spaces around him. There was a thrilling sense of suspension —the pressure-drop before the winds begin to blow, when a stray dollop of rain blotches the ground in front of you, harbinger of finality. These digressive metaphors are not beside the point—they are *exactly* the point, no matter what it seems like. The point being, it was somehow impossible to experience those instants, in that place, as a distinct succession, or to respond sensibly to that pattern of events. For instance, Turner's teeth were almost certainly about to be smashed back into his throat. And yet we stood like the statues of idiots, immobile, Angels and everyone, staring vacantly, blind to this swelling danger. It was as though (this is not a metaphor but a guess) Turner's glance had left each of us mesmerized: capable of looking on but of nothing else, even comprehending. He alone was in motion, and the big-fisted man before him.

Their eyes aligned in the high-voltage silence.

"What is it?" Turner said so quietly, you couldn't be quite sure you had heard it right. "What's the matter? Are you ill?"

"I'm not," the man said, smartingly, like someone accused. "I'm perfectly well. You can see that, can't you? Just look at me. You can't see a thing."

It was a peculiar little speech. It had the effect of dissipating his store of hostile energy, so that his face was left sagging, like something deflated.

"No." Turner shrugged. "I can't see a thing. But I haven't got any training. Is it very far along?"

The man chewed his lip. He seemed to understand that this was not purely rational, that the laws of orderly behavior were breaking down; but absent any clues or reinforcement he could only stumble onward, like a guest at one of Malachi's parties, with the muffins kicking in.

"I . . . it isn't me, so much. It's . . . some of the others." He drew in some air, held it, puffed it out. He shook his head. "It's the children, mostly. And there isn't much . . . I mean, what choice do we have? Treatments are expensive, you know."

"Ah." Turner nodded: he understood, he sympathized. It was not an easy thing, he knew, to talk about. (Or thus bespoke his general demeanor. In his eyes I thought I saw something different—a confusion, a sense of doubt as great as anyone's. Perhaps he was not directing these events so much as riding them, going with the flow.)

In the next heartbeat whatever spell had been cast on us fell away. Throughout the room, arms and legs and eyes made tiny movements: the Peels crowd adjusting to this strange loss of place, of momentum, and the Angels puffing up their shoulders touching pockets where weapons may or may not have been, to solidify our newly taken position. Seeing all this, the big man who remained the other side's spokesman [ah—*the other side*] ended his hesitation by saying:

"Yes, of course. I'm sure it's been a long day for you." He attempted, and almost achieved, an earnest-looking smile. To someone back in the shadows he called out: "Noey—?"

A young woman stepped forward (thick black hair, athlete's limbs, a conspicious lack of humor in her eyes) and said to the group of us generally, without making eye contact:

"The guest rooms are this way. You'll have to carry your own bags. One of the things we do without here is servants"—and strode off without waiting.

Thus, our welcome to the Peels. Would you have followed her, do you think, if it had been you?

Through the Peels

I have never experienced worse cooking. Perhaps it was a means of purification, boiling the mutagens out. I arrived at the end of the mostly silent meal with the podge of bleached-looking and metallic-tasting vegetables still cooling in its gray broth on my plate. There was a lounge or recreation area off the dining room, and we shifted ourselves there afterward. The ceiling was high and black, with tiny lights like pinholes, tungsten stars. I carried my record book, supposing this was where the real negotiations would commence. Vinny found an old disk-playing machine, its plastic casing garish yet somehow forlorn, with yellowed embellishments and most of its buttons cracked off. Still it worked to an extent, serving up without complaint such iconographic ditties as "Willie the Pimp" and "You With the Stars in Your Eyes." I stationed myself across the room from it (choosing sides, we might say) while most of the others fell into formation near the bar, forming subgroups no larger than your basic primordial hunting party, or football huddle. There must be something quintessential in this—a function of the width of human shoulders combined with the maximum distance over which one's murmurs can be heard. Maybe the Dissolution began when the functional cells of society—government councils, corporate bodies and the like—exceeded this natural and fundamental order of size.

Forgive me, but I am drawing this from my notes.

The woman Noey, it says here, with nothing further to cue my recollection. Well, perhaps nothing further is needed.

Having conducted us, as I mentioned, through the Peels, this Noey (black-haired and fit-looking, as though she had been taking her turn in the fields) attached herself to Turner, though without making a point of it—keeping a slight distance away but always within eye- and earshot. Turner may have felt flattered by this, by her attendance; the residents of the Peels were an uncomely-looking bunch, and Noey did not have to be much more than decent-looking to stand in relief from that background. She was more than decent-looking, though. Her eyes were dark and animated beneath thick brows, for a woman, and her speech was articulate, though the local dialect was slurry. With her confident and slightly forward stance, she looked like a daughter of the mythical Land of Sunset. I did not much care for her.

"How did you do that?" she said.

Turner had eaten a lot and was drinking the local wine, which tasted awful, out of a jelly-jar mug. He looked around, seeming amused. There were a couple of Angels an arm's length away, and they sized her up suspiciously, which more or less spoke for all of us.

The woman pressed it. "How did you get him to talk to you like that? I mean we all of us know he's been kind of depressed lately, but he's never admitted anything before."

Turner raised his drink, acknowledging nothing, and it occurred to me as something that should have been obvious that, of course, he didn't know. He didn't know how he had done it or even what he had done; and he certainly didn't know what to say about it. He was just playing it out, revving up the dharmic engine called *The Defender* and hanging on for the ride.

"Well . . ." said the woman. She took a new stance—moving a step closer but facing a quarter-turn away, so that she stood like an adjutant at Turner's elbow. Her eyes were wary and they seemed to find me especially worthy of staring at. From there she said: "I thought it was impressive, anyway. What's this one, your kept boy?"

Turner smiled *[smiled!]* and said, "This is Tristin. He's sort of a record-keeper."

Sort of.

"So," she said, "look. What do you want from us, anyway? We've got nothing to give you, you know. Really we'd rather just stay out of it."

Turner must have learned by now that it was not an especially good idea to think before he spoke, as this would muddle things. He said immediately, "I want to look at the children."

The woman was a shrewd one, I decided. She knew that showing any surprise was *not* the thing to do at this instant. She did turn to look at him, though: slowly and with no attempt to hide her curiosity. "Do you really? Really want to meet the kids, I mean? Or do you just want us to put them on display for you, so you can have your picture taken doing the human compassion routine?"

Turner shrugged, which was honest enough. "Where are they?" he said.

Noey shook her head. "You'll have to get someone else to take you. I'm assigned here, to Product Development. The dormitories are—"

—*out there.* She said it with her eyes, staring past us into an unseen night the color of coal dust. Turner looked into those eyes for a while and then followed them through the Peels, into the darkness. A breath of winter moved like a feather across my skin.

Laughter, from the direction of the music machine. I saw Vinny inclining his head toward a group of gray-faced . . . farm administrators, I guess they were . . . among whom the big-fisted man who had nearly attacked Turner stood quietly, like a boy on his best behavior. The men smiled, eyes alight after an hour of drinking. Vinny dropped a punch line in their midst like a small explosive. It detonated; thighs were slapped, unaccustomed merriment found its way up the zinc-plated hallways of the Peels. There were more drinks. The music machine offered up "Romeo is Bleeding." Vinny had considerable talent for the Big Schmooze.

I looked around at Turner, at the woman Noey. But the winter had taken them. I stood in the open door for several minutes, becoming very cold.

Turner's night

We stayed up till dawn. We drove around. We talked. Somewhere there were clouds, the smell of decaying chemicals, a sound like doves in the gables; the warmth of tears that turns quickly to cold and brittle dryness. That's all I remember now.

Ask me later.

A trap

After I had turned away from the open door, but not long after, one of the Angels came and took me by the arm.

"It's a trap," he said.

We moved fast down a dark hallway while somewhere behind us things were happening that might be of great interest to a historian. There were spotlights, voices electronically amplified telling us to halt, warning shots over our shoulders. I had an urge to take notes, if only to give the experience a kind of structure, make it feel less like a nightmare.

"I figured something like this would happen," said Vinny; we overtook him and another couple of Angels and that was all of us, the others were lost in the Peels; and Vinny said, "Now we're all boxed in, I told Harvey this whole idea sucked, who gives a shit about this place anyway is how I look at it, it's a regular Tropic of Cancer without the sex scenes. Plus I think I'm drunk. What the hell time is it?"

It was the middle of Turner's night. The Angels were passing weapons around, putting drops in their eyes, smearing dark greasepaint over one another's cheekbones. There was a kind of foreordained efficiency in their movements. Voices came quite clearly through the metal walls: search parties being organized, I guess. It was strange how clear it all seemed, considering how little rational sense anything made in those dark moments.

"Well, okay," said Vinny. "Here's what we'll do, I guess."

He had actually, out of God knows where, produced a joint. An Angel, alarmed, but only by the match-light, blew out the flame. Everyone looked at Vinny, accepting him against all logic as the second-in-command, now thrust into leadership. He blew sweet smoke at us.

"We'll try to work our way to the parking lot and see how many there are of them. Probably it's about half the government army if they've got any idea Ashenden's in town. But that's okay because it'll mean plenty of confusion. Then we'll shoot the lights out and steal an armored truck or something and blow up a couple of buildings and hit the road." He paused for a toke, which he held contemplatively. "Or what do you think?" he croaked out, looking around. "Does that sound too crazy?"

The Angels laughed, at a safe volume.

"All right, then." Vinny crouched, hunching his shoulders, a bizarre night-creature readying itself to spring.

—Wait a minute. I clutched his arm, willing my thoughts into his bleary eyes.—What about Turner?

Vinny squinted in my direction, barely focusing. He said, "Now don't be worried about Ashenden. He's the asshole that got us into this."

I must have looked like the tragic fool that I was, or am, because Vinny took me by the shoulder as I tried to turn away.

"Look," he said, a shade more gently, with a drunkard's sincerity in his voice. "He'll turn up. He's the fucking hero, isn't he? Or haven't you noticed? I thought you were the one keeping track of all this shit."

So saying, he resumed his ridiculous predator-pose, and an Angel handed me a gun.

I shook my head. The golden-haired young man smiled down at me, as though wondering what sort of mythic creature I was. Then he pocketed the gun, and I will try to do some justice to the mêlée that immediately followed.

The compound at the Peels was laid out, as I may have mentioned, in a sort of irregular ring. Some of the buildings were connected by breezeways made of the cheap stuff of commercial greenhouses, through which klieg lights blazing in the courtyard shone in warped colors and patterns. We passed from one building to another unimpeded, as evidently someone who didn't know much about Angels must have decided (you can hear the voice now, can't you?) *They can't have gotten far.* Or maybe they were ignoring us, concentrating on Turner. Or maybe Turner was already in their clutches. The point is, we were safe enough for the moment, but without a clue as to what was happening in the overall scheme of things.

Somewhere along the line Vinny tossed the stub of his joint onto the floor, where it landed in a pool of some flammable liquid and promptly started a fire. The trail of flame ran back the way we had come, following the drainage contours of the concrete floor like the birds that gobbled up the trail of breadcrumbs leading out of the forest—or are we mixing myths now?

"God," said Vinny. "These assholes must bathe in industrial run-off."

We ran on, finding our way without trouble now. The glare from outside entered through rust-holes in the walls, and now and then we stepped across a narrow stream of fire; I think the rivulet of burning liquid must have taken a quicker route through the maze of offices and storerooms, but it's certainly possible that we were crossing and recrossing our own trail. In either case, anyone following us must have been badly confused.

We came to a huge loading bay, its cargo doors standing open, with stacks of crates bearing the names of Eastern cities that by now were almost legendary; it was hard to imagine that people still lived in places like that; it was like coming upon a letter plainly addressed to someone in Sarras, or Camelot. And who knows, maybe those crates had stood in that loading bay for generations, a final unclaimed shipment of the Dissolution. Or maybe everything we believed in those days was wrong, and the "New Age" had never ended at all; maybe our own era, our whole weary world, was no more than a fragile seedling, struggling to gain a foothold amongst well-established competitors. This is the business of History, though, isn't it—to sort out such things.

On certain nights, if one stays up long enough, one's understanding of the world is apt to melt and reconfigure.

Without waiting for Vinny's command—seemingly without giving it a thought—the Angels began setting fire to the piles of boxes. Flames licked up toward the drooping metal of the roof, and night air was sucked through the doors in a low-pitched, horrible inhalation. We ran outside heedlessly—not into the courtyard but the other way, *the other side*, the direction of destiny, the unsleeping night. Cries and whispers seemed to follow us, but I think that was a trick, an echo-effect. Something, of the many things now on fire, was giving off a nauseating stench. There were sparks in the sky, like fleeing meteors. We kept running, outward now, one million rats can't be wrong, toward the perimeter of the compound, where I distinctly remembered having seen a fence.

Remorseless, I scribbled in my record book. We must have stopped to take our bearings, to rest; but what was I thinking of? Turner's unglimpsed children? Turner himself? Our abandoned Angels, who may have been trapped inside? Or the whole mélange—explosions, leaping flames, the threat of asphyxiation?

My thoughts, whatever they were, kept me busy long enough for one of the Angels to hack through the decrepit chain-link. We stepped out of the compound to face the next problem, a more timeless and less tractable one—namely, what to do in our new state of (relatively speaking) freedom.

At least we could get a look at things. The compound, whose nearest building was now a hundred strides behind us, was not so thoroughly engulfed in flame as I had imagined. There were a couple of structures in bad shape, and the fire looked to be spreading, but on the whole the place was not a lot more hellish-looking than it had been a few hours ago, at sunset, which may not be saying much. At least, though, the fire was giving everyone something to think about. Vehicles were being moved a safer distance away. I could make out streams of water being played here and there, mainly on buildings not yet burning, but endangered. A growing body of people (in blue-gray uniforms? or was that my imagination?) was being mustered in a field, in the middleground; it was amazing how orderly this seemed. But that was their great rallying-point, wasn't it?—their unifying principle. At the Solar Temple, everyone had just grabbed his drink and gotten the hell out. (If even that. For all I knew, that woman might *still* be singing in the refrigerator.)

An Angel gave a soft moan beside me. It took a few seconds for me to understand that he had been shot. At once everything seemed to converge on me: the shock of it, the memory of a string of small explosions, someone's hands yanking me to the ground. I came down elbow-first and would have cried out if I could. (I managed a feeble sort of whimper, but that neither betrayed us nor did justice to my degree of pain.) There were more shots, some of which tore at the metal of the fence while others scored the ground. My comrades were deathly silent, except for some minor scurrying about, sliding into trenches. There actually were a lot of these; we were in an old field whose furrows had eroded into ripples like blown sand. Barely below the horizon of our unseen sniper, we wormed our way along in the direction we happened to be facing. In thirty minutes I suppose we covered a quarter mile, at much cost to our skin and clothing. Reckoning that a mopping-up team must now be headed our way, we risked (at Vinny's command) getting up as far as necessary to crawl, turning our backs now to the compound. We heard movement behind us but saw nothing—only the fire—until we found ourselves scrabbling in the gravel of the roadway.

We looked at one another, each of us I think performing the same quiet roll call. The Angel who had fallen must have died. There were five of us, a nice round number. I entered this in the record book. Vinny said, "Well, shit. At least we're out of the trap."

Against the felty backdrop of smoke and darkness, fifty yards or so down the road, rose the pale limbs of an old princess tree, silvery-pink by firelight. It was one of those inexplicable things that should not exist: a tree—in the middle of cracked and contaminated farmland—that owed its survival to having inexplicably been overlooked during the preceding century of unsparing monoculture. Vinny had his eyes fixed on this tree as he said:

"Tristin, you go on over there."

—Over . . . ?

He went on, "You're the only one light enough to climb it. Get on up there and keep a lookout. Drop a shoe, or something, if you see anybody coming."

I sighed. I wasn't sure I had the strength, at that point, if indeed I ever had, for tree-climbing. Besides, if our enemies were coming after us they would surely track us down, so what was the use? Vinny gave me a firm clap on the shoulder. There there old boy buck up, that type of thing. For all my dismay, I rather admired him for his relentlessness.

"Well look," he said, "I'll stay up too, maybe, and keep you company. Everybody else can get some sleep. We've got to be ready whenever Ashenden shows up."

I looked hard at him, trying to determine how seriously he believed this. In his eyes I could find nothing but the purest and simplest form of faith—the kind that is accessible only to those to whom the possibility of doubt has simply not occurred.

"You never know," Vinny went on, as we trudged side-by-side toward the old tree. "You just can't tell what he's up to. But sure as hell he didn't drag our asses all the way here for nothing. So just stay up there till he gets back. Then we'll see what the fuck's the story."

Turner's night (2)

All he could say was he wasn't sorry. All he could have explained right then about what was going on inside his head wouldn't have added up to much. Only, there was this thing or two, a memory, a bit of stage-makeup smeared on a napkin, the unexpected profile in a mirror, someone's words etched and weathered in his brain. A pattern, was all. Maybe what you could hope for, and it was only hope, nothing certain, was to discover a pattern in it somewhere.

Like a while ago, I had a certain notion about becoming enlightened —an impossible state, in which things always are perfectly clear. And now I see, though murkily, that actually it comes in dribs and drabs, not even flashes, little fuzzy pictures way back in your mind like the answers to an exam you stayed up all night cramming for which now are slipping away so fast that if you have to wait much longer for the little blue books to be handed out you're going to be S.O.L. But that's a student metaphor and one's present position in the supernal stacking of the deck derives pretty directly from having put all that unhappy student business forever behind one.

Turner had gotten the vague impression from somewhere that women are worried about driving at night—maybe insecure when the day's referents aren't there anymore to touch with the eyes like a visual rosary. And here, if you want one, is a perfect example of how one blurry little piece at a time the big picture becomes clear: it's men after all, isn't it, who do the rosary thing, wallet keys money fountain pen, always in the same order, pissing in the same place, drinking with the same bunch of losers night after night, stirring the same stuff into your coffee next day and listening to Vinny swear all over again how much better it tastes with goat's milk. Whereas it's women who handle the really horrible times without flinching, without deviating from the course, fuck the referents, God he was my husband for twenty-three years and only your father for twelve, and even at the blackest of times knowing where the horizon is, how much money's in the bank, whether we'll need more coffee cake with all those people coming over after the funeral, and at what point that unmarked side road that leads off to the most sacrosanct precinct of all is coming up in the godawful darkness while you're shivering with something more than cold and can't keep up a decent conversation without all these crazed digressions. So, if you've managed to remain attentive despite it all, another splinter of the divine is left sticking in some soft spot of your brain and you're one step closer to the big E.

Let's take a definitive stance, then. Are you sad that the other things, the experiences whence the splinters came, are gone from you, the other souls saved or lost, the other arms as distant as other lifetimes? Or is it better to be here where at least you have an itsy bitsy idea of what's going on, what the pattern is, what kind of shit is waiting around the next blind turn, including let's say a 50/50 shot at getting this swarthy little hotrodder here between the cool white ones?

Jeez, I don't know. I mean, I see what you're getting at but I really can't decide.

And that, Ashenden, quoth the wise native healer, *is why we love you.*

But wait, but look—I wanna ask, I wanna know—

"Here," said Noey, "do you like music? I've got some tapes on the floor someplace."

Yes. An assortment mad enough to donate to an asylum somewhere. If there still are such things, as distinct from say the hallowed halls of government. Let's get past this *Shaker Loops* crap and *Ionisation* (a worrisome bent toward the austere, maybe the odds just dropped to 40/60) brings us to speak of the devil, *Orfeo*, and here's something, the label worn away from repeated fingerings, surely not *Winter Into Spring?* Ah, no, of course, the famous suite, here in its original chamber scoring which debuted by happenchance in the museum right next door to the very fucking graveyard, a coincidence so tragically ludicrous that tears formed in our aging orphan's eyes and the odds just leapt up to 70/30, drawing a gasp from the bettors in the crowd. A manageable number of strings and woodwinds began playing softly under the seat of the pickup truck, and the headlights picked out twin rows of pleached limes you wouldn't have thought, would you, were still among the possible things in the world.

"Quite a place," said the jaded field commander.

"Thanks."

Turner looked at the woman in curiosity, thinking no big thing, nothing like the old Frenchman acknowledging a remark about the weather, but Noey's cheeks in the half-lit cab seemed to register his attention by flushing darkly, wow, you could feel the warmth of blood running into them, a certain musky presence in the cab, make that 80/ 20 and get the nags to the starting gate.

"I just meant," she said, composure snapping back, "it's my family's home. It used to be. It belongs to the cooperative now. We use it as a sort of dormitory. And hospital."

What she was talking about, not quite but sort of apologizing for, came into view slowly around nice terraformed hummocks of lately untended soil where in a couple of months you could bet ten thousand daffodils would be jostling with the crazed hybrid lawngrass for a bit of sun—people used to think dandelions were aggressive until they turned this monster loose. But anyway. Through the brown stalks you could see a house, and I mean the kind of place that gives ostentation a good name, first one wing and then another and then the main body of the thing, a Normanic torso in which Harvey's little hilltop demesne could have been digested with room for the Solar Temple between courses. What had become these days, Turner wondered, of this once apparently epidemic baronial compulsion? Were bigname bureaucrats even now hurling up rockpiles like this back East? Or were they content to go the bolshevik route, making fixer-uppers out of the captured lairs of Old Souls? In this context the humble chattels at hand presented a sort of intermediary case, a finlandization.

"I don't come here much anymore," said Noey. Still flirting with that apology. I wished Tristin were along to get the exact words, the nuance.

"Too bad," said Turner Ashenden.

The dance bit, which he liked, along with pretty much all the rest of it, was coming up. Abruptly the woman cut the engine. Here's a *koan* for you: where does music go when the electricity's turned off? The truck rolled fifty feet farther up the drive, then she parked it.

"The brakes don't work," Noey explained. "That's the only way to stop."

Turner contemplated this, reviewing some of the high-speed highlights of the drive from the compound as he followed her up what was left of the private lane. Her haunches were as perfectly muscled as a tiger's, and as much on display through those dungarees. He had to hustle to keep up, and worried about betraying one aspect or the other of his lamentable condition by breathing hard. God, how can she see in this darkness? But of course: she's a woman, and she grew up here.

They took what must have been a servant's entrance, cavelike amidst the yews that fendered the wall, and found themselves in a long corridor lit just brightly enough to make one's way, which gave Turner the unpleasant idea that other ways might be made by other way-makers when he would have preferred to play This Old House, or some other old-fashioned parlor game, with Miss Noey alone. But she, if not he any longer, as it developed, remained mindful of why they had come.

"There are offices in here," pointing right, she narrated. "And up there's the old butler's pantry that's now sort of a lab. You know, for blood tests? My sister and I used to live in *that* wing but we've kept that closed off for the past couple of years, to save energy. My sister died two years ago in the storms."

Or, the Storms? Something in her voice suggested capitals, a calamity so great that she assumed everyone in the world must have known of it. Whereas much to the contrary, two years ago did she say? That would be, let's see, Turner was probably in decent academic standing, more or less, and the thought that someone's sister might actually *die*, for God's sake, in the normal course of existence would simply not have shadowed the Ashenden brain. Though of course he must have known—surely he had—about the routine atrocities back east, the wasting plagues, the rest of it. The government had turned the whole horror show into a box office bonanza—cutting only a few frames of full-frontal contagia—in the cause of building sympathy for Settling Out.

In the end, Turner had the sense not to say *The Storms . . . ?* and trail off like an idiot, but simply to murmur, "I'm sorry," a completely banal remark which, however, has the advantage of being exactly correct.

"That's all right," said Noey, if he doubted it. "That's what you have to expect these days, isn't it?"

Turner said nothing this time. (Also quite correct.) They were still moving down the *very* long hallway, door after door opening up on either side of them, to blackened rooms. The way one was meant to make through here was obviously just the way they were making. At last they came to something you wanted to call the "back stairs," for they were inconspicuous yet functional, risers quite tall in relation to no-nonsense treads, with the telltale nightlight that marked this as the intended passage.

"Okay," said Noey, perched two landings up not huffing in the least, a reproach to all of us. "You'll have to be quiet now. Everyone's asleep."

And only I am left awake to tell thee. Turner sensed the turn onto the backstretch. Time to finger one's stub hopefully; a bit early to be whipping it out and welcoming one's chosen filly home.

"Well," he said, "and I guess this must be a, a *nursery*" (showing a tad too much excitement), "right?" He strolled into a long room with fanciful safari-scenes muraled across the walls. The pigments had dimmed unevenly, so that the once well-camouflaged smaller animals, your gazelles let's say, were left hanging out there with blotches of sunny ochre shining through a thinning umber coverlet. In short, tiger-bait. On the floor there were the usual sort of playthings. Turner gave it all a nice smile.

"Don't look so insufferably smug."

Noey's voice pounced at him. He turned in surprise to find the tigress backing him into an alcove.

"Now were you serious about what you said, or what?"

Turner nodded slowly, with no idea what she was talking about. He *meant* the things he said, sure; only he seldom understood, later, what had bestirred him to say them. But what was it this time, exactly?

"Then follow me," she said.

They were most ferocious (tigresses, as he should have remembered) when the well-being of their young was at issue. Every muscle of Noey's back seemed to scrutinize him as she crept through an inner doorway and into a place that was, for the first time, totally dark. Turner felt his way along using much the same guidance system as a heat-seeking missile, though in this case keeping his warhead half a step behind its target. He had the eerie sense of breath coming from all around him, but this was no doubt some cloaking mechanism designed to throw him off. Noey was still out there, in the night. He thought he could smell her. He smelled something fleshy, anyway. He felt a *presence*. It was agreeable.

The target halted, and the missile, colliding with her coccyx, crumpled back into its booster stage. There was a click, and suddenly the two of them were in the middle of this huge open space as large as . . . um, a dining hall maybe, suffused with this darkroom-style dull red light.

Turner held his breath, provisionally.

"This used to be the library," said Noey, which told you how much time Turner had ever spent in such things. "We use it because it's so quiet."

So *keep* it that way, is what she was implying.

He nodded dumbly. He turned this way; he turned that. He felt something like vertigo rising inside him: that fleshy smell, the breathing. Was the room here spinning, or was he just pivoting too fast? Or—

". . . it easy," the voice flooded back to him. Noey grabbed him by the arm, a steadying pressure. She hissed, "What the hell's the matter with you?"

How did Turner know? He just . . . all these beds, all these kids in them, the warmth, the *presence* . . .

The grip on his arm became tighter. "You can't even look at them," she accused him. And when he didn't even bother to deny that, she went on: "You can't stand to look real life in the face, can you?"

Um, I don't know. I mean, *life*, sure. No problem. But this was something a bit different. This was like, I don't know. Decay. Corruption. Turner opened his mouth and made an inarticulate noise.

"What?"

"I said," taking it from the top, *da capo al fine*, "what is the matter with them."

Noey gave him the angry eye. "Oh, nothing much. Some of them have got no arms, is all. Or no legs. Or half a cranium. Or blood vessels that leak. Or skin that you can see through. Other than that, no problem."

"I wasn't—" Turner tried to get a grip on this. "I didn't mean to sound . . . it's just something in my voice, I think. I really do feel, I mean, it's really horrible, it's—"

Noey turned away from him in disgust. On the nurse's console in the center of the room she touched a button and the world slid once again into merciful blackness.

[Only now the blackness will never be empty, will it? They'll always be there, in the dark, the bandages, the shrunken limbs, tiny sallow faces, everywhere around you. But you couldn't have told Noey that, no matter how you tried. As you said: it's something in your voice.]

"You're really pathetic," she informed him, no longer bothered about protocol, or even common politeness, back in the jungle-room—which, too, would be transmogrified in his memory. "You just can't *connect*, can you? You stand there like you're in some other dimension. But people really are *dying* here, Mr Ashenden. Our children, and the rest of us too if you just wait long enough. So if what you came up here for was to see for yourself why we're a little apathetic about your brave little Resistance, then now maybe you've seen with your own baby blue eyes. Or maybe you haven't. I actually don't give that much of a shit. But the thing is, we don't have much choice, and we don't have much time. Or I should say, considering how little time we've got, all the choices are pretty irrelevant."

No.

"What?"

"No," said Turner. Once more with feeling. "I don't think that's true. I think there's something . . . another . . ."

"I don't believe you," said the dark-haired daughter of sunset. "And I think it's time for you to go."

St. Elmo's fire

It sounded like singing, though who would have believed that? But the closer the battered motor-carriage came the more clearly I could make out, from my berth in the princess tree, the odd snatch of lyrics borne on the smoky predawn air.

> . . . We had walked and we had scrambled
> Through the moors and through the briars
> Through the endless oleanders . . .

The others, including Vinny, though he had given it a decent shot, were asleep in some leggy underbrush, bayberry or something, ten feet below me. The first few times that vehicles had rumbled by I had been terrified, but step-by-step I came around to believing that, as Vinny assured me, "The assholes've overlooked this tree for the last fifty years, I don't think they're going to notice it tonight." Indeed, the search teams had passed practically underneath me, all but clipping the wings of the sleeping Angels, but as yet none had so much as slowed down to investigate what should have been an obvious hiding place. There must be some theory to account for this, and I hereby offer these anecdotal data in confirmation. It was getting light enough see the latest transport pretty well as it shambled out of the south. The singing, also, was growing rather distinct.

> Through the nights and through the fires
> We went surging down the wires.
> Through the towns and on the highway,
> Through the storms and all their thundering . . .

It was discordant, I thought—not the singing, which was perfectly in tune, but the whole raucous advent of this beaten-up machine. I thought of dropping the other shoe on Vinny (the first, let fly hours before, had provoked him only to mumble in his sleep) when I noticed that the Angels were rousing themselves, perhaps exhibiting that intuition that Milton, for one, was so impressed by.

It would not be overstating the case at all to say that I was so astonished that I almost fell out of my tree when, like a bunch of sleepy choirboys straggling in late for Mass, our Angels joined in the final chorus now coming loudly from the approaching van.

> And we rested in a desert
> Where the bones were white as teeth
> And we saw St. Elmo's fire
> Splitting ions in the æther.

At this, even Vinny woke up. He slapped around ineffectually for his sidearm, but the incongruity of the moment got the best of him. We watched stupidly while the vehicle came to a halt, a hatch popped open, and Nicola Quoin (of all impossible people) stepped onto the road.

"Where is he?" she said.

She was looking up at me, but Vinny replied:

"Last seen riding into the sunset with a local heiress."

"Ah." Nicola nodded. "That would be Noey, I guess. It's really a shame about all that. But what can you do? Well, come on. We'll head on up to her place. Dick, have we got room for a few more? Where *is* all that smoke coming from?"

I transcribed this with no idea whether anyone, ever, would believe me. At times the role of witness seems a futile one. Suppose, for instance, there is no hearing at which to give one's testimony?

Anyway, we found Turner an hour later, standing in the middle of a private road, with the rust-colored sun at his back. He wore a very strange expression, about which I can find nothing written in my notebook, though it remains—the eyes, above all—quite vividly recorded in my mind.

Staying up

It used to be the thing we always wanted. And we were right, though as usual we didn't know what the hell we were talking about. Because see, the problem with staying up is, if you do it long enough, you never really come down.

2

Finger on the pulse

"It is counted, of course," Black Malachi held forth, "a great victory. After all, a number of armored vehicles were destroyed by fire, and as I hear it most of the attack force that was supposed to bring *your* ass back in a sling managed instead to get itself smoke-cured. On account of which, presumably, the Souls have acceded to an urgent request from the Peels for medical supplies, though not without the usual Tampon Clause."

Cervina not Turner raised an eyebrow at this, which was just what Black Malachi had hoped for and, indeed, depended on.

"A *string attached*," he proclaimed, on a note of triumph. "All hail, then, the Midnight Perambulator! Party Animal Emeritus, Knight of the Garter-Belt, and Role-Model to Disadvantaged Youth! Cervina dear, while you're up could you bring us another pot of tea?"

Cervina was not up, but no doubt correctly perceived this as a suggestion that the two old friends might like a little time alone. She bowed out, sliding past the Angels who hovered like a brood of broad-shouldered hens just outside the door, ever protective of their favorite gobbler.

Back in the Morning Room, Black Malachi nursed his customary twelve-o'clock eye-opener and after a moment's thought wondered aloud:

"Haven't we done something like this before?"

Turner stood by a window, perusing the months-old and still unrepaired damage to the courtyard below, where herbs had grown once in neat beds. "I wouldn't know," he said. "Are we doing anything? It looks to me like I'm just standing here and you're making vulgar remarks."

Which, come to think of it, did sound like that same old song.

Black Malachi sniffed and carefully laid his cup down, as though its contents were explosive. (Well, you never knew.) "Now listen, Turner. My well-known good cheer is genuine but not limitless. If my voice has grown tiresome to you, allow me to propose that you favor me with your own. I presume you had *some* reason for wanting to see old Blackie—after," he indulged himself so far as to add, "all these months."

The sonic sculpture, having behaved itself till now, underscored this tough talk with a low-pitched metallic clangor, which faded slowly like an underworldly carillon. Turner had felt himself once to be a sort of Invisible Man; now he felt more like a Transparent one. He turned from the window, another sad perspective, with a sigh.

"You're right, Malachi."

"Of course I am. I suppose I am right, also, in believing that you will never use my true and complete name."

"I suppose. But I mean, really. You're right that I was being arrogant—"

"I did not say that."

"Well, but. And you're right that I haven't been around for a few months."

"Not since the party," said the offended host; and despite there having been a million parties in this place, give or take, there was no doubt between them which party he was talking about.

"You're right," said Turner, "and I'm sorry. Really I'm sorry. That's why I've come back."

"No." Black Malachi brought a certain eloquence even to finger-twiddling. He paused with one of those stubby digits pointing upward, as though signaling for quiet. Obediently the sculpture shut its trap. "That is not," he proceeded, "why you have come back. Oh, I don't disbelieve you. You're a good-hearted lad, in the final analysis. Though the final analysis is not for me to make. I'm sure you *are* sorry enough, and I do appreciate your finding the wherewithal to say so. But you certainly didn't mount this little expedition just to stand in the middle of the rug and make contrite utterances. And by the way, Ashenden—"

He cocked his mop-head in Turner's direction, signaling a desire for secrecy, though there was little chance of being overheard. He said, "Do they go *everywhere* with you, those fellows in the hall? I mean, are they present during your nightly minings of Miss Maridel's tight little shaft?"

"God damn you." Turner's contrition, which like Malachi's good humor had its limits, was promptly forgotten. "That's not *true*. I'm not . . . and you've got no damned business . . ."

"Oh, my!" The furry head shook in consternation. "Have I erred, for once, on the side of lubriciousness? Can it be true that, after such an awesome display of oral dexterity, the Ersatz Virgin has denied you access to her slippery sanctum?"

Turner really could not contend with this. There were too many things to explain, too many involutions. He lowered himself into a barrel chair.

"Tell me," implored Black Malachi, "it isn't so. Tell me you're drilling it at *least* twice per evening, excluding holidays, in which case thrice, or I shall simply not be able to look you in the eye again. Or for that matter the crotch. Or for that matter—"

"It's n-not what you think. There's more to it. There's something . . . And anyway, has *everyone* lost sight of the fact that she's only what, fourteen years old?"

"Fifteen by now, I'll bet. Going on five thousand. And what's that to her, anyway?"

Turner shook his head. "I'm not here to talk about that."

"Oh, Ashenden. I despair. I truly despair."

"Well, despair, then."

They looked at each other. They sighed. The sonic sculpture chanted something contemplative, Bly-like.

"Can't you turn that thing off?" said Turner—wondering why this hadn't occurred to him a couple of years ago.

"As with your sadly underutilized organ of plenishment" (the round face merry again), "it has a mind of its own."

Yeah, well, that figured.

With some hint of gentleness at heart, Black Malachi said, "Why have you come, then, old boy? In words of a syllable."

"For your ad-. . . your help."

"Very good. Then, of course, you may have it." The stout youth rose, rubbed his hands together. "And which is the affected part? The head, I presume?"

"It's not me. It's—"

—but see above. His experience at the Peels, which had made little enough sense while it was happening, made precious little more now, though perhaps something was gained by distance. At least Turner could be certain now that, two months and several hundred miles away from that awful nursery, the horror and the helplessness were as great as ever. Black Malachi listened to his recounting with what Turner felt to be too much of a good thing: absolute, unflinching attentiveness. The small bright eyes (has the image of a gifted rodent occurred elsewhere?) remained fixed on Turner, absorbing every word and gesture and, one would not have doubted, every thought. Turner wondered if Malachi had been like this in medical school, during the semester or two when he showed up for classes. If so, the instructors must have been pretty relieved when he quit; the more so when he denounced the profession altogether.

"Blood vessels that leaked?" the heretical healer repeated, when Turner was done. "Skin you could *see through*?"

Turner tried to close his mind's eye.

"Fascinating," purred merciless Malachi. The rodentine eyes were wide and alert, like a child's at a circus. "Entirely remarkable."

You would have thought he wanted to hear more of it.

"Is there anything more?" on cue, he asked.

"You actually," said Turner, amazed himself by now, "you actually *enjoy* this, don't you?"

"As a great general once said, It's not what you think. But tell me, were any doctors around? Was anything being done for them at all?"

"I don't think so. I mean, some simple things—bandages and such. But only stuff ordinary people could do, like to make them more comfortable and so on. Apparently they've been depending on medicines being sent from the East. Nobody said so, exactly, but it sounded like there was kind of a trade involved. Drugs for food, more or less. And now it looks like I've fucked even that up."

"Well, they can only thank you for that."

Turner watched in puzzlement as his former housemate, gathering the now dilapidated Cherokee-red bathrobe, strolled in a stately fashion across the room. He seemed to be headed for the window, but stopped short, as though remembering what little was left to see through it.

Turner said, "I'd just like"—struggling with his own voice, trying to find the sincerity that had been lacking when it really counted—"I'd just like to help them, somehow. That's all. That's what I came back for."

"I see. Well, I am sorry. There is nothing you can do."

"Yeah, but see, I know that—I mean, I know there's nothing *I* can do, that's why—"

"No. You don't see. There is simply nothing to be done. Those people—most people, in fact, I would say—have been energetically destroying themselves for some time now. If they have not *quite* succeeded in doing so, it is simply a question of incompetence, not a lack of diligent application. There is really nothing we can do, or ought to do, to intervene."

Turner pressed his lips together. He didn't believe this, but he couldn't say why. Moreover, he didn't believe that Malachi believed it. This was just part of some overreaching moral or philosophical lesson. (It did not occur to him then, because it was beside the immediate point, that this was the first time he had glimpsed even the shadow of Malachi's inner intent. But what a realization, when it struck him later on!)

"You see, Turner," the lesson resumed, "there are those who argue, including myself—or rather who do *not* argue, since if anyone takes the other side I cease to listen—but as I was saying, there *are* those who argue that, and please remember this:

"Everything we need is already present.

"Now you must struggle to grasp this in the broadest sense. Everything—emotional, spiritual, and of course physiological—everything that we truly need must already exist in our immediate environment. That is to say, in the resources of the world around us, or the world within us. This is nothing more than a deeper reading of the old story of Evolution. For consider: if we required something—really required it, for our survival—that was *not* readily accessible, why, we should simply perish, shouldn't we? So it follows directly that we have evolved, and our environment with us, in such a way that the world is populated with beings who require nothing more than what the world has to offer.

"But now this place, the Peels, was it? From what you tell me, the people there have succeeded quite remarkably well in reducing their little world to a state of depletion. So that whereas once upon a time it may have been possible to trot on up there and dig something out of the woods and supply those poor children with whatever pieces of the puzzle their bodies and souls were missing, that is obviously the case no longer. Where once there existed a state of self-sufficiency, or I should say *mutual* sufficiency, there are now imbalance and paucity. Or fuck that—for our purposes, there is nothing. The world in which those children's bodies were designed to live has been obliterated. What is needed is a new type of being, a creature adapted to the Peels as it now exists. Probably such a creature will come along. Maybe Rodarch is the prototype—the first of a new breed, spawn of forward-thinking social engineers, crafted for Better Living Through Chemicals."

This was really, Turner felt, too much.

"Look, Malachi," he said. "Can't you just . . . I mean, I just have this feeling you're being *difficult* about this. I'm not trying to argue or say you're wrong or anything. It just seems like there's got to be something you could do. Aren't you supposed to be this great witch doctor or something?"

Black Malachi folded his arms and put on an affronted look. With his floppy bathrobe, long curly beard and well-rounded physiognomy, he looked like some kind of house-gnome, and a moody one at that. Despite himself—despite everything—Turner gave him a smile.

"What?" said Black Malachi, glancing about, as though he had missed one of his own *bon mots*.

Turner shook his head.

"No, tell me." The house-gnome came a step closer, peering into Turner's eyes.

Turner didn't get it. Why the big deal over one little smile? Later he would figure that this had marked a kind of break, a change in the equation. Malachi couldn't see through him, or at least not *all* the way through him, anymore. The stout youth shook his head in fond perplexity, as a parent might. Turner decided to gamble with this tiny advantage.

"Come with me," he said, "to the Peels. At least come. Just to look. You don't have to do anything—or at least you don't have to promise to. We'll just drive up and then head right back. Just the two of us."

Black Malachi said, "No."

"It'll just take a couple of days."

"No"—dismissively turning, trailing Cherokee-red strands.

"As a favor? For old times' sake?"

"No," came back over the shoulder. "No favors. No bargaining. No."

"But why?" Turner's voice had a bit of a whine to it, as though the parent/child metaphor had really taken hold of him.

"Ashenden, I cannot explain it. I can only say that it is simply not possible for me to leave this house."

"Oh, come *on*. I mean—"

Black Malachi looked back with a gaze that would have silenced a symphony. "Do you want me to tell you? Do you really? Because I warn you—it will *not* make any sense, and it will give you one thing more to fret about."

Turner stood waiting. His expectancy was so sharp that it set the sonic sculpture on edge.

"Fine," said Black Malachi. He raised his hands, palms upward. He stared at them for several moments, slowly flexing his fingers. Then he held them out to Turner. "Here," he instructed. "Take them, and hold tight."

Turner did so, slowly. "What's this about?" he began—then the room began to misbehave, tilting or rocking back and forth, the walls changing direction, the floor bucking up like something big and hungry was moving underneath. Malachi's eyes burned like pieces of metal in a forge. Turner felt an electrical current move through him, something like the tingle of the Identity machine but amplified exponentially, yet at the same time painless, even exhilarating. These things occurred in a small number of seconds, a time you could go comfortably without breath (as Turner was doing). Then Malachi pulled his hands away and everything was immediately normal, right down to Turner's state of mind, which was as close to rational as it ever got.

"What the fuck was that?"

Black Malachi licked his lips. He folded his arms again, smugly. He looked more like a house-gnome than ever. "I don't know," he said.

Turner refused to accept this.

"Well, I do have a theory. It is as follows. *That*, Turner, which you just felt, is the energy that sustains the illusion, that keeps the story going. Your story, Turner. No," he said quickly, seeing that our mouth was open again, "I shall *not* attempt to clarify what I am saying. You either get it, or you do not. Naturally enough you do not. But I will say this: having lived with it for quite some time now, I have come to suspect that many things depend on my remaining *exactly here*."

"You mean you're never going to leave the Morning Room?"—feigning humor, but honestly spooked by all this.

"Not precisely. The lines are actually somewhat stronger in the kitchen. But you have the idea."

"But what's the point? I mean, what are you trying to accomplish? Do you think the world will, like, suddenly vanish or something if you dash out for a loaf of bread?"

Black Malachi must have felt himself back in control here, for he gave us one of his characteristic smiles. All-knowing, like. He said, "I think that *you* might suddenly vanish, Ashenden."

Bullshit (thought Turner, secretly terrified).

"Ha! You disbelieve me. But of course you understand so little of the nature of things. Well, never mind, then."

"No, wait." We decided to allow ourselves one more question—just one—and were trying to figure out how to make the most of it. "So what happens if you *don't* go out? What happens if you stay right here till hell freezes over?"

Black Malachi nodded, as though to say, Fair enough. "In the act of healing, Ashenden, one attempts to bring the body's attention, so to speak, to bear on the source of the problem. The theory being, you see, that illnesses are brought about by a misdirection in the natural flow: a broken wire—again speaking figuratively—or a clogged pipe. When the flow of life-energy is normalized, the body commences at once to restore its equilibrium. If a microbial invader is in question, the body produces an appropriate defender, and soon enough—but again, for only as long as the energy, the *prana*, continues to move freely—one's health is restored."

Turner said, ". . . Yes?"

"Quite." Black Malachi stood patiently, as though he had said quite enough, and was now waiting for the light to come on. "It *should* ring a bell," he said—sounding happy, though, that it didn't. "The invader, the defender, the parlous equilibrium—"

(Ding.)

"—but only for as long as the flow of energy is sustained. Nature is highly evolved, Ashenden. So is one's body, so is the body politic. Still, a physician is occasionally required. The steadying influence. The healing hand. Ah, look: more tea."

Cervina had that timing down. She wheeled into the room, carrying a tray, as though she too were part of some ceaseless fluid pattern. She looked at the two of them, Black Malachi and his unwilling patient, with a gentle, undemanding curiosity. She told Turner:

"I hope you're going to come see us more often. Blackie really misses you."

Riding high in April

It was the season for turnabouts, it seemed. When Turner Ashenden returned to the Bad Winters Institute, his headquarters and current home, he found a party in progress. It was a garden party, in a way. At least, everyone had gathered out on the broad smooth lawn, where there were daffodils in bloom, and Vinny Hawkmoth was making some kind of speech. Or was he just talking loudly? The wind brought snippets of chamber music through the open doors of the manor. Turner climbed down from the armored transport in which he these days usually got around, meaning to get to the bottom of this.

The first person who approached him was Dirty Dick, carrying two drinks.

"How d'ya do, my boy?" he said genially, his tone such that one could not give any answer but "Fine," or its equivalent, without feeling that one was upsetting a delicate sociological balance, perhaps the entire shaky edifice of Manners upon which all of civilization is hung.

"Fine, thank you," said Turner.

"Ah, good." Civilization's survival assured, Dick held out a drink, which by analogous reasoning Turner could only, as a civilized person, accept. It appeared to contain gin in large quantity. Gin is flavored with juniper berries, which as far as Turner was aware are not grown in these parts; thus the handing over of this drink had certain economic implications, and may have been both a means and a cause of the present celebration. But one must be careful of reading too much into things. Cautionary examples abound. Consider, for example, this little pantomime on the other side of the lawn: young Maridel, whose yellow party dress doesn't have a whole lot to say for itself in the sleeve department, leans forward to speak very much into the ear of one of those horsey chaps one catches sight of now and then at Harvey Goldaster's place, who as far as Turner can tell makes rather a full-time job of shooting whatever animal is in season. A rich asshole, in short. This particular R.A. allows just a bit of the rakish smile, for which they're fitted at birth, to crease the tanned expanse of beef-fed cheek, letting shine those fluorescent gnashers. As he directs now toward Maridel an eye from whose gleam we infer the action of three-and-one-half standard cocktail units (the glass in Turner's hand being the metric here) plus a set of highly energetic lower chakras, stimulated no doubt by the daily impact of saddle-leather against one's prostate. Young girls are flirtatious, of course. But are we sure that Maridel is being flirtatious *enough*? Is there a shade too *little* titillation in her manner, a hint of that dropping-off of excitement that comes from knowing what the answer to one's question, one's ever-underlying question, will be? From having had that answer given more than once—given freely and repeatedly, in fact—until one has come to know it, as the saying goes, inside and out?

So you see, it's quite wrong and actually often dangerous to go reading too much into things.

"As always, lost in thought."

Turner was startled and then relieved to recognize the voice of Nicola Quoin, who had somewhere along the line become (along with pretty much everyone whose wardrobe was not heavy on Newport blue) a habitué of Bad Winters. She stood elbow-to-elbow with Partner Trefoil—an unlikely pair, though they did share a certain out-of-the-mainstream sensibility. Turner strolled over almost enthusiastically, sloshing an ounce or two of gin back toward his mouth as he went. He tried to remember when he had started to enjoy drinking so much—if enjoy it was what he did. As near as he could recall it had been the predictability of the stuff that appealed to him. There was no risk, for example, during this little lawn fête, of the inadvertent out-of-body experience, manifestation of serpents in the bathroom, or any other of the unplanned entertainments that might befall one at the Solar Temple.

"Here," Nicola said, producing a fresh glass as though by sleight of hand. "You look like you're looking for one. We were really afraid you weren't going to show up for your own party."

My own party? Turner scanned his mental calendar, but found no red-letter dates in the neighborhood. De Vere's birthday was past, Blooms-day a month off, and we felt still barely recovered from Gwendola's equin-octial *rite de passage*. He gave up. "What's the occasion?"

"Occasion?" said Partner. He raised his glass in a toast to nothing, or everything.

"So that's it"—speaking out loud without really meaning to, then getting to like the sound of it. His own party, after all. "We don't *need* an occasion to celebrate. Life itself is a sufficient reason. These are the days of wine and roses. Here at Ca-me-lot."

"Well, gin and daffodils, at least," allowed Partner, eyeing him oddly. Nicola seemed to see nothing the matter, or to see everything differently.

"Turner," she said, "what are you planning to do next? Now that you're getting things under control in the north and you've pretty much cleaned up in the south and you've definitely got the winning hand in the valley. Where are you planning to go from here? Harvey was just saying he thinks you might try to press east a little. I mean, he said 'we,' you know, but we assumed . . ."

Turner said, "Where *is* Harvey? Why is he speaking for me? For the coalition, I mean. That's *my* job—that's the whole point of everything."

The tone of petulance that had begun in the Morning Room was even more pronounced up here, at his own party. Partner shrugged and wandered off—he was the kind of person who could do so and seem neutral about it—while Nicola continued to notice nothing. God bless her.

"He wasn't really," she said. "I don't know, I guess he's still around. Have you seen Vinny's antenna?"

Maybe that's what the cluster of people in the middle of the lawn was all about. (They were bunched so tightly, Turner had figured somebody must be making an amusing fool of himself. But that's my job too, isn't it?)

He couldn't deny what a trip it was, the way an aisle formed right through the middle of the crowd as he approached. Most people weren't even looking at him; they just stepped aside without a break in their conversations, as though yielding to some natural but irresistible phenom-enon. Like Death, for example—another great reason to throw a party. Turner wondered how well attended his own wake would be; probably by then it would just be a couple of the old gang down in Malachi's kitchen, with Cervina (weeping quietly) pouring tea.

Check this out, though. These conversations that Turner's arrival failed to break up, even as he strolled between the participants—well, a lot of them proved to be about young Mr. Ashenden himself. Like, the Field Commander. That one. He overheard bits of gossip, details of recent engagements, speculation as to whom he was sleeping with; but the really unnerving thing was the way it rattled right on even with the subject himself close at hand. There are turnabouts within turnabouts in this story. Once upon a time I thought I was impersonating an ordinary student, or a poor horseman, or a well-mannered dinner guest, but now it's come down to where I'm impersonating somebody called Turner Ashenden, the guy all these people are talking about.

"See, Turner?" said Nicola; at least *she* recognized him. "See, Vinny's erecting the first strut on the platform today, in your honor."

My honor. My party. And I'll drink if I want to. Turner stepped into the open space at the center of the crowd, and a sound of something like . . . let's see, a dogfight between paper airplanes . . . heavy-stock paper being struck and crumpled, pattering sounds . . .

"Yeah, let's hear it," said Vinny Hawkmoth. He looked at ease, at home, on a platform like a small bandstand. From the center of it protruded a copper rod, sticking at a funny angle skyward. He said, "Let's have a nice hand for the guy who's made this all possible, the guy who's got the world in his oyster, or ah, you know, with that Midas touch and all."

It wasn't that Turner didn't know whom Vinny was talking about. It wasn't that. It was more like, I don't know, not feeling like *that person*, not sensing the slightest overlapping of one's own identity with that of the hero of the play. Here was this hero, see, stepping onto the little stage, graciously gazing down upon his followers, his advisers, lovers, bodyguards, hostess with the mostest, the whole pile of them, and it's like, I mean, This isn't me. This is that other guy, the *real* star of the show, he's the boss he's the king but above everything—

"And now," said Vinny, for the benefit of those who'd lost their place, "we come to the Official Dedication. And we are deeply honored of course to have with us today, to mark this important union of Science and Art, this recognition in fact of the original *raison d'etre* of the Bad Winters Institute, blah blah blah—"

[Coy again. But of course it wasn't Vinny that anybody came to hear. It was the T.C. himself, who just this minute didn't have the slightest notion of what he was supposed to Officially Dedicate, but whose name sure as hell was about to roll off Vinny's lips.]

And suddenly Turner was, you know, *there*. I mean, ZAP, his dislocated consciousness guesses correctly the password to log onto the charisma system, his arms calmly rise to still the applause, his lips move and just the right couple of hundred well-chosen words come sloshing out. While those admiring eyes, inquisitive eyes, probing sensual eyes, keep looking up at him, the special electric bond of audience and performer crackling in the air like the approach of a storm-front, charging the æther. The nearest thing Turner can recall is that day on the open lawn of the University, watching his own *doppelgänger* thrill the crowd, and while this is not at all dissimilar in essence it is obviously a debugged version of the earlier routine; the two Turners are intertwined now to the point that we can't be sure ourselves which of us is really running the show.

Cheers. Paper tossed in the air. Eyes locking with ours, hungry now, feed us Turner your life your energy your hope, and my God our own eyes calm but desperate, both at once, searching everywhere for Maridel, who we only hope at least may be able to understand. But Maridel is not on the lawn anymore, it seems; nor is Gwendola nor Nurse Tawdry. Even Tristin, steadfast Tristin, has turned traitor for the afternoon. We are, of that small circle, left alone at our own party.

[No. Not a traitor. I was *forbidden*—but now, as with everything else, of course, you understand that.]

"Thank you," says Turner Ashenden: for once, at long last, the life of a party.

A certain distance from dawn

Madame Gwendola stared out from the large armchair in the downstairs sitting room as a sea captain might from the depths of a night so black that the running lights blinking on the masthead pierce only inches through the air of it, the ship's horn grows fainter and fainter like a voice gone hoarse from crying, and the arms of the helmsman hang slack and irresolute at the wheel. While still on an unseen horizon, where in minutes or hours dawn will swell like a flesh-pink tumescence, the captain holds her eyes.

There was a chill in the spring-night air, which Vinny made worse by a composition in taut strings that drew itself on and on through the paint-stained speakers. The violins alone, straining for overtones hidden high above the chords, could make you shudder. As always, as Tristin has noted somewhere, the amazing thing was just that everyone kept sitting there so still for so long, putting up with it. It might have been, it must have been, something in the aging woman's eyes. You stretched, you glanced toward the open door, you thought of going to bed, but that sense of the ineffable, the notion that something was about to happen that *must be witnessed* kept you sitting there—even uncomfortably, on the threadbare Persian coverlet stretched over the floor—until that indeterminate hour arrived that might be today but might, more probably, be tomorrow. Thus the whole experience was thrown into a subjective nether-realm; you didn't even know if you were violating the classic Unities. For example, were all the usual suspects on the stage?

Well, let's see. There was Gwendola, of course, and close around the coffee table Nicola Quoin, Turner Ashenden, Maridel, the unnamed R.A., Partner Trefoil, Dirty Dick, a couple of kids whose parents were still shelling out for the Institute, a young woman we'd seen around the Solar Temple, who must be some sort of weirdness groupie, and way across the oaken slab, on the floor like the rest of them, Harvey Goldaster. At the fringes of the room you had something like a chorus—Vinny and the Angels and a bunch of players without speaking parts who could have been anything, costume designers, payroll clerks, mercenaries, lawyers, writers—by this time the whole operation had gotten pretty unwieldy; nobody really knew who was on board and who had tumbled into the snotgreen sea; years from now maybe an excavation of the cutting-room floor would uncover hands and eyes and shoulders of people no one had noticed before, ordinary folks just hanging out, complicating the life of our editor, who in the last stage of production must sit down to make sense of all this, slice away at the swollen body of footage until the fine skeleton of a pattern is revealed. Thousands of takes, millions of frames, scenes conceived at different times and shot at different places might be stripped and spliced into composite sequences that hadn't really happened, but *ought* to have—hybrids more vigorous than the ancestral filmstock. But that's the business of History, right? And of Art as well: a once-over-lightly from which the extraneous has been purged, major themes drummed hard on, conflict boiled down to a few pivotal scenes between the principals, who are given lots of screen-time to laugh and sweat and fuck their way to a predestined climax. Following which you roll your credits or hide behind your bibliography, depending on how you're hyping it.

Take this scene from the downstairs sitting room. It's last night or maybe this morning, depending, and all the big names of this side of the struggle, the oldest war—Malachi's "Home Team"—are conveniently grouped in one room, smiling for the camera. And only the editor himself (who right now is working part-time as an *auteur*, to make ends meet) is left out. But somebody's got to be, right? That's that Art biz, too. That's where your point of view comes in.

128   INTERIOR—SITTING ROOM—NIGHT

Setting and characters as before, though hours have passed. We hear WIND at the shutters, EERIE MUSIC. On the table: empty glasses, crumpled paper, matches, books. Pan the room. One by one we see faces weary but alert, on edge, expectant. Hold on Gwendola.

CLOSE SHOT—GWENDOLA

Obsessed-looking. Sees things others don't.

CLOSE SHOT—CANDLE FLAME

Flickers as though in a sudden breeze.

GROUP SHOT

They sense something. Twitch nervously, try to hide it.

> GWENDOLA
>
> The father must not be of this world. That
> is a requirement.

SERIES OF CLOSE SHOTS—THE HOME TEAM

Nervous glances: This woman is crazy, right? Right?

> MARIDEL
>
> Oh, mother. Have you kept us up this late
> to make us listen to that again?

> GWENDOLA
>
> (as though to an unseen listener)
> The father is often a figure from legend, a
> fact that is misinterpreted. Scholars know
> that legends are significant folk memories,
> but conclude that they must be rather
> naively overstated or colorized versions of
> mundane events. The Noble Savage's Civics
> text. They do not imagine that legends are,
> on the contrary ...
> (gesturing, warming to the topic)
> ... pale renditions, with colors faded by
> time, of the Other Realms that few have
> seen. Blinding glimpses, sketched with
> whatever instrument lay at hand, details,
> isolated aspects captured entire but out of
> context—

> MARIDEL
>
> Mother, you're babbling.

> TURNER
>
> No, wait, I think I ...

Others stare as though <u>he's</u> the crazy one.

> TURNER (cont.)
>> (weakly)
> I mean, I thought it was interesting....

Side glances. R.A. looks smug, slides closer to
Maridel. Nicola moves to Turner, protectively.

> GOLDASTER
> Now wait a minute. Weren't you talking
> there a minute ago about someone's
> father?

> GWENDOLA
>> (in a world of her own)
> The undying father! As real and present as
> the son, but unrevealed to us. We can only
> know him by uncoiling the secret of his
> seed, the cipher inscribed by his offspring
> through the millennia. So that when we
> meet the Master's odd companion in
> Bulgakov, we recognize immediately the
> Checkered Demon from the comic books of
> our youth, who later will appear in the
> guise of a tree pollard. But matters are less
> straightforward with beings of a higher
> order, the Masters themselves. Here the
> signifying traits are not likely to be of a
> superficial kind, peculiar taste in clothing
> and the like. We must overcome, often, our
> limited understanding of personality, the
> notion of an isolated identity or
> consciousness.

3-SHOT—MARIDEL, TURNER, NICOLA

Turner bracketed by the woman and the girl. Fidgets.

The two females look at him, catch one another's
eye. They hold it. Sizing up.

                         NICOLA
               (looking away, but not at Gwendola)
          You know, I know what she's doing. It's
          really just this bogus mystic mood she's
          trying to put on. All these pompous
          allusions to prove how smart she is. She
          probably doesn't even really remember the
          Bulgakov guy's name. I mean I don't either,
          but why should you? What the hell does it
          really mean, for God's sake? That Turner is
          some new improved version of a literary
          hero? That's more or less what's she's
          saying, right? Oh, and the identity stuff—
          this sort of Jungian gloss or I don't know,
          Maharishi-speak or whatever on top of it.
          That's probably just to explain why none
          of this really adds up, none of the
          archetypes that come to mind really fit
          Turner Ashenden without a lot of round-
          peg square-hole nonsense. And anyway,
          who needs this crap at whatever it is in
          the morning?

Turner squirms, looks away, tries to be invisible.

                        MARIDEL
          Very impressive. I suppose with your
          superior knowledge of the world you can
          explain everything that's happened.

                        NICOLA
          I'm not saying ... Look, you said yourself
          she was babbling.

NEW ANGLE—DOWN THE TABLE

In the b.g. Madame Gwendola, somewhat out-of-focus. In the f.g. Rich Asshole fondling Maridel's bare arm. Maridel turns away from Nicola, angry. Sees R.A.—smiles. <u>Focus</u> changes, bringing Gwendola sharply into view. Dreamy expression. MUSIC swells, strings seem to tug at each other. First LIGHT of dawn very faint in a clouded mirror.

> **VINNY**
> This is great. Listen to this. It's where all the themes come together.

> **HARVEY**
> Well I'd just like to know what she meant by—

> **MARIDEL**
> Don't ask her that, she'll never—

> **NICOLA**
> I can tell you. She doesn't mean any—

> **RICH ASSHOLE**
> (under his breath, to Maridel)
> You know, this guy is a real space cadet. I don't know what you see in him

Turner stands up. The others fall quiet.

> **TURNER**
> I'm tired of staying up all night. I'm tired of being talked about all the time—like I was somewhere else, or dead, or something. I'm going back to bed and sleep for—

GWENDOLA

No!

Everyone jerks as though suddenly awakened.

GWENDOLA (cont)
(calmer)
Not quite yet.

Spooks do furnish a room

Turner Ashenden, many things to many people, was not yet asleep and it was not yet daylight, completely, when the door of his modest room in the east wing of the Institute cracked open and someone peered in from the shadows of the hall. As any two-bit *feng shui* honcho could have told him, you weren't supposed to put your bed where someone could peek in at you like this. Now Turner reckoned it was too late to repair the damage to his privacy. He opened his eyes, squinting through the ambivalent half-light that was very fitting here, and said:

"Who is it? Maridel, is that you?"

The door opened wider. From the hallway, shadows flowed across the floor, across the braided rug, over the chair where Turner's clothes were flung and onto the high old bed where his head still nestled in its pillow. It didn't seem like things ought to happen this way: darkness moving in to push away the light. But Turner was sleepy, and he had stayed up on this mountaintop for a long time now. What would it take to surprise him?

"Who is it?" he said. His eyes were heavy, closing again. He felt the smooth wrist brush his forehead, the weight of a body settling on the edge of the bed. Soft lips touched his cheekbone.

"Maridel," said Turner, weakly, rapidly losing conviction. "I'm not really sure this is a good idea. Maybe you ought to—"

Get out

Turner Ashenden was not yet asleep and it was not yet daylight, completely, when the door of his modest room cracked open and someone peered in from the shadows of the hall. Turner reckoned it was too late to repair the damage to his privacy. He opened his eyes, squinting through the ambivalent half-light that was very fitting here, and said:

"Who is it? Maridel, is that you?"

From the hallway, shadows flowed across the floor, across the braided rug, over the chair where Turner's clothes were flung and onto the high old bed where his head still nestled in its pillow. It didn't seem like things ought to happen this way. But Turner was sleepy, and he had stayed up on this mountaintop for a long time now.

"Who is it?" he said. Something odd was going on; his breath came faster. He felt the smooth wrist brush his forehead, the weight of a body settling on the edge of the bed. Soft lips touched his cheekbone.

"Nicola?" said Turner. "Are you sure this is a good idea? I mean, right here at the Institute, and all? Maybe we ought to—"

Get out

Now Turner reckoned it was too late to repair the damage. He opened his eyes, squinting through the ambivalent half-light, and said:

"Who is it? Maridel, is that you?"

The door opened wider. From the hallway, shadows flowed across the floor, onto the high old bed where his head still nestled in its pillow. It didn't seem like things ought to happen this way. But Turner had stayed up on this mountaintop a long time now. What would it take to surprise him?

"Who is it?" he said. His heart constricted in his chest. He felt the smooth wrist brush his forehead, the weight of a body settling on the edge of the bed.

"T-Tristin?" said Turner, drawing away in the dark. "What are you doing? Don't . . . I mean, I'm not . . . maybe the best thing to do is just—"

Get out

It was too late to repair the damage. Turner said:

"Who is it? Maridel, is that you?"

He felt the weight of a body settling on the edge of the bed.

"N-Nurse Tawdry," said Turner, weakly, trying to force the vial away. "Are you sure I ought to be drinking that? I don't *want* to stay up any longer. Something's the matter here, I keep getting this, seeing this . . . Could you just, like—"

Get out

Turner had stayed up on this mountaintop for a long time now. What would it take to surprise him?

"Maridel?" he said weakly. "I'm not sure . ."

"No, goddamn it. Wake up."

Turner opened his eyes, squinting through the ambivalent half-light. "H-Harvey?"

"Your little incubus has run off," said Goldaster, "with my son."

"Your s-s—"

Turner's heart constricted in his chest. It didn't seem like things ought to happen this way. "The R.A.," he murmured.

"What?"

It was too late now. His gaze fell across the floor, across the braided rug, over the chair where his clothes were flung.

"Where'd they go?" he said. But Harvey was just staring out the window, east, where the sun had dragged its ass up for so long you wondered if it wasn't getting tired of the place. Turner climbed out of bed and stood naked in the dirty light.

Harvey said, "He always talked about going there. I suppose he knew it would hurt me. But he never . . ." Then, turning, as though remembering whose room he was in: "What are we going to do?"

Never sleep again, probably. "Well," said Turner, reaching for his pants, "I guess the first thing—I mean, like, unless we can find out something more, where they've gone or maybe if they left a note or something—the very first thing is, I guess we ought to—"

3

On the road (again)

You'll never walk alone, is how Turner looked at it. You'll be lucky to crawl. They rolled down the mountain with about a tabernacle choir's worth of Angels crooning barroom ballads in the back of farm wagons that obviously hadn't gone very far since there were actually farms around here. Tristin wanted to go along on the strength of his long knowledge of Maridel—his understanding of the limits (very distant) to which she might go. Gwendola forbade this, but Turner overruled her, much to everyone's startlement; he thought he remembered this dream, or something. Anyway, he needed somebody who would remain sober enough to read a road map. Vinny offered to accompany him, but Turner said, "Stay here and work on your antenna," which was exactly what Vinny had hoped to hear. He slipped the Angels some sheet music, a little good-luck present. Dirty Dick and Nicola headed off to Wine Barrens, and Harvey Goldaster to Upper Moat Farm, awaiting developments.

"He *is* a bit of an asshole," Harvey conceded. "But family ties are . . . well, you'll see. Don't do anything you'll regret."

"Mm."

"I'm counting on you, Turner."

"Yeah, well."

Nobody was very happy about it. Nicola was convinced that Maridel's disappearance had been faked, perhaps by Madame Gwendola. Tristin thought [and still thinks, for the record] that Goldaster himself was behind it: a neat way to get Turner moving east, at last, blazing a trail into what your more farsighted running dogs regard as the Ultimate Market—whole cities full of people with money and little time left to spend it. Gwendola must have thought she'd never see her daughter again, for she kept muttering (theatrically, wringing an indigo scarf) something to the effect that *It shouldn't have happened this way, this early in the cycle, so soon after the Recognitions.* Yeah, yeah, yeah. Turner wasn't sure at all what to think, personally. He brought his wagons to a halt outside the Solar Temple.

"Take five," he told the boys in the back. "Smoke 'em if you got 'em."

The Angels sang as though they didn't have a care. The Solar Temple was an awful mess, with weeds as high as your head poking up from the parking lot.

"Back so soon?" said Black Malachi. No great shakes himself, wearing the Cherokee-red bathrobe and a general air of desuetude; though as he pointed out, "It's scarcely eleven o'clock in the morning."

"Sorry," said Turner. He stood awkwardly in the banana court, Tristin nervous and attentive at his side. Malachi smiled kindly at the youth, extending a hand to lay upon his shoulder.

He still had that touch, though. Tristin's eyes came open as though he'd just slipped into a nice warm tub full of electric eels. He opened his mouth and for a very long moment everyone present must have expected him to speak, because we all fell very quiet.

No? Still smiling, Black Malachi took his hand away.

He said, "Well, I'll see you."

"Wait—"

Turner stepped up, thinking Don't just act imperious like this, turn away like you're some kind of monarch. Malachi had an enigmatic expression every bit as maddening as Gwendola's, and did not shrink from using it.

Turner said, "Wh-What," struggling to get it all in order, "what do you think I ought to do? Or no, look—just tell me how you *feel* about this. I mean, do you like, *see* anything? Or anything?"

"Your speech," Black Malachi mused, "has become so labored. But this is the natural result of being *out there*, I suppose. In the world, among the great unwashed. Well, what is wrong with that, though? Don't worry, old man. Trust in Lug and keep your back straight. You don't believe in that, do you?"

"Believe in which?" said Turner—then, bitterly, "What do *you* believe in, Malachi?"

"My dear boy," (grotesquely going through a series of strange genuflections, finger-signs, passes of the hand, How Many Gods Can You Find In This Picture?) he concluded with gravity: "I believe in everything."

Turner felt miserable. How come Tristin gets the healing touch and I get Sister Boom-Boom?

"I'm going," he said.

"Goodbye," called Cervina, from the balcony.

"So soon?" said Malachi, which sounded like where we came in. "Well, do come back."

"I always do."

Tristin looked at him as though he'd said something odd. At the wagon, the Angels were making up new verses for that old favorite, "I Love a Gang Bang."

"I feel very strange sometimes," Turner said.

—Me too, breathed Tristin.

The difference between fairy tales and sea stories

Past Candlemas, past the ill-fated development, past the rolling hills where the horsey set frolicked, they came to some actual mountains which, Turner supposed, in all likelihood actually had been here all along but which *he'd* sure as hell never noticed. Well, I guess it takes two to make a valley, doesn't it? He searched the mountaintops, the skies, the roadside for portents, found nothing but the usual ambiguity (partly cloudy—what does *that* mean?). In these uncertain times, the Angels turned to religion.

Ohhhh—
Pilate had a headache
That wouldn't go away.
An hour with a holy man
Can really wreck your day.

He took some Bromo-Seltzer;
He took some LSD.
He smoked the root of Burning Bush
And bark of Hickory.

The headache was still with him;
At least that much was clear.
So Pilate told the Roman guard:
"Bring wise Pantera here."

Pantera said, "Don't tell me.
You're aching for the truth.
You've caught our tragic Hero with
A scantily clad youth.

"The fellow says he's tight with God.
The rabbi says he's queer.
Your lawyer says, 'Just wash your hands
And stick him with a spear.' "

Well, Pilate rubbed his temples.
He asked Pantera's fee.
—"Just pay me twice what Judas got
And leave the rest to me."

Ohhhh,
What followed was peculiar,
But this is what we think:
The Hero tired of hanging out
And said, "I need a drink."

The weather got real gloomy,
For Daddy sent a cloud.
An Angel rolled the stone away
And Mommy kept the Shroud.

But what became of Pilate,
And does his head still beat?
And what about that naughty boy
In nothing but a sheet?

Pantera isn't talking.
He blew his sixty bills
On a Resurrection Weenie Roast,
Then vanished in the hills.

Ohhhh . . .

"Hold on a minute," said Turner. "Be quiet, back there."

Not that the song disturbed him. (Though it did.) But see, just a hoot 'n' holler up the road here was this sandbagged tollbooth with a big gun sticking out, aiming east, where most of your more desperate or illegal type of travelers would be coming from. There was movement inside the booth as our strange caravan (well-dressed, broad-shouldered fellows riding rusty farm wagons, plus Tristin, plus Turner) shambled into view.

"Be calm," said Turner—surely not to the Angels, who were temperamentally unable to give a damn; and what did he care whether Tristin was nervous? [That can be taken rhetorically, if you like.]

A patrolman appeared—professional soldier type, nonchalant but alert-looking, with eyes moving everywhere. He more or less defined the situation.

"Are you crazy or what? Don't you know this is where the uncontrolled zone ends? I don't suppose you've got a travel permit, either. What is this, some kind of fraternity prank?"

Turner glanced back at the Angels, trying not to imagine the weapons tucked like folded wings beneath their cloaks. Yeah, he thought—fraternity prank. You might think that.

"Ah, hi," was all he could say.

The soldier scowled. His hand came to rest on something that looked like a billy-club, but with switches along the handle. Clearly, the situation threatened to deteriorate.

Something happened to Tristin here: purely physical, a neurologic twinge as intense as the eel-bath he had taken at Malachi's place. All he could do about it right away was suppress the urge to writhe in discomfort, but then it was gone and Tristin was looking intently at the soldier, and something made him think

—*He's on our side.*

"What?" said Turner, before he got the drift. It was like Wine Barrens again—that intimacy of awareness.

"What?" the soldier said.

"Um . . ." Turner twisted in his seat. He murmured, "Look, are you sure about this?"

—*He's a traitor,* Tristin told him, more deliberately now. —Goldaster's got him on the payroll. He helps get things shipped in from the coast.

Turner was bemused, but willing to roll with it. He pulled out a folded piece of newsprint. "Here," he said. "Look at this."

From somewhere, he had gotten a copy of the famous photograph: *Student, believed psychologically disturbed, shown here after attempted assassination of visiting dignitary.* The soldier stared at it and then at Turner. He did something only a soldier would do, in a moment of befuddlement. He snapped to attention.

"Field Commander," he croaked.

Turner blinked.

—Tell him who you're looking for, Tristin suggested.

"Yeah, um," muttered the befuddled Defender. "Look, there's this girl, see. She's about fifteen—I mean, you wouldn't know it to look at her—or actually it depends on what sort of mood she's in. You know, some days—"

Only by a twitch of the soldier's eye muscles could one detect a hint of concern for the Field Commander's sanity.

—Mention the R.A., I said. (Someone had to take charge here.)

"And a rich asshole," Turner blurted. "She was with this guy, this like young, sort of, horsey type . . ."

Ahhh. The soldier nodded, relieved. "I knew there was something funny going on," he said. "It was just around daybreak, so I figured they must have been driving all night. They had a travel permit and all, but you could just tell there was *something.* You get an intuition, sometimes."

—Did they say where they were going?

The soldier, full of energy now, ducked into his tollbooth and came out with a map. "See, I confiscated this," he said proudly. "They're illegal now, you know. And this one is *especially* illegal, because it shows the locations of sensitive areas. You know, chemical dumps, libraries, gray market trading posts—"

—*Libraries?*

"Here," said Turner. You could sense the act of will involved in holding his hand steady. "Give that to me."

The soldier complied reflexively. He said, "Is there anything else you need? Weapons? Fuel?"

Turner was already poring over the map, and it looked like someone else's turn to drive.

—No thank you, Tristin prompted.

"Um, no . . ." Turner looked up, confused, but it was safe now. "Hey, thanks a lot," he said, allowing us all a glimpse of that winning smile.

The soldier knocked off a quick salute, but we were already beyond him.

"Look here," said Turner. It had taken him less than a minute to misfold and crumple the map. His thumb rested astride a black dot which someone had highlighted with a large blue X. It was labeled THEME PARK.

Tristin passed his hand over the map, saving the blue cross for last. There was no way to sort out the origins of the tingling in his fingertips: dread, excitement, paranormal certainty. Black Malachi's eye, as dark as the dot on the map, seemed to wink at him.

The Angels, having run through Vinny's sheet music, went back to vulgar sea chanteys, which must have been their default mode.

Open the door you dirty whore, they bellowed, in perfect consonance.

"Do you know," said Turner, in a different-drummer kind of voice; "do you know what the difference is between a fairy tale and a sea story?"

—Yes, replied Tristin, but the connection between them must have been broken. Turner went on:

"A fairy tale starts off, 'Once upon a time.' A sea story begins, 'Now this is no shit.' "

End of the World

How long had *this* little fascination endured? Above the charred planet-scape, contorted towers of concrete and flexed metal stood in frozen rigor. Around them rubble spread outward for several square miles, but it was varied in size and arranged in artful mounds so as to prevent the mind from registering it as a uniform surface, a giant's gravel-bed. Here and there, but not with implausible frequency, you would come upon a crater that might be as small as a basement or as large as a baseball field. The excavations were smooth, with edges scored a clean gray as though by terrific heat—the last word in distressed finishes.

Nor had details been omitted. Of every cataclysm there are the freak survivals, oddments of human debris which one cannot help reading as symbols, manifestations of the Dark God's hidden intent, whispers from *the other side*. Here the symbols were made as digestible as possible, philosophic fast food, for the convenience of harried moms and dads getting hot in the post-Holocaust sun: a little girl's doll pinned from torso downward beneath a slab of heaved-up sidewalk (but don't try to pull her out; the doll's made of the same stuff as the sidewalk itself, painted with eerie delicacy); a singed copy of *The Fate of the Earth* whose pages turn but do not tear—a miracle!—though the prose still clings together in ponderous lumps; a desk calendar, the year illegible (is the first digit 1 or 2?); and of course the obligatory Shadow of Death, silhouettes etched into walls as though by a hideous radiance, then protected with three coats of polyurethane. Somewhere, Turner thought, there's got to be a big clock with its hands frozen for all eternity; or maybe that falls into the category of Not Invented Here.

"What do you think," he asked Tristin, "is this tacky or what? A fun spot for the whole nuclear family."

—A passing fashion, Tristin thought, and nothing more.

"Hm?" Turner narrowed his eyes. There was still *something* there—enough to keep him talking. "But it's like, this obsession with the end of things, with destruction and all . . . it just doesn't seem very healthy, does it? From the standpoint of a whole society, I mean."

—They were people who thought in absolute terms. Pressing the

RESET button. Starting over. Back to Ground Zero. *We can cha-a-ange the world*. Naturally they would interpret failure in absolute terms. Thumbs up or thumbs down.

Turner watched Tristin carefully, impressed perhaps by the intelligent expression on the boyish face. Hidden depths, as they say.

"Well, it gives me the creeps," he said.

Tristin shrugged.—Maridel would love it.

"I bet Maridel would like it, though," said Turner at about the same time. Perking up at this idea, he craned his neck around, scanned the death park for any signs of life. There was only the snoring of the Angels, stretched out among the wreckage for a collective midday nap. Turner frowned. "Well, they've had a long morning," he decided.

As though we had not. We had stayed up all night, as I remember.

"Let's walk around a little," Turner said. "Just to get our bearings. There ought to be an information booth or something, don't you think? I mean, I *know* nobody's going to be . . . but like, maybe there'll be signposts or something. Just to get an idea."

—It doesn't sound very sensible to me, said Tristin, with the blitheness of one who knows his opinion will be utterly disregarded.

Turner was already skirting the ruins of a movie theater, a bit of the marquee still intact though partly entombed.

"What do you figure?" said Turner. "*Apocalypse Now?*"

He probably knew only the title. —More likely *The Last Picture Show*, it seemed to Tristin.

On top of the original, scientifically designed and artfully laid-on patina of the "theme park," a newer and more crotchety mantle of age had been deposited. Inasmuch as the world had not expired, on schedule, in the manner the prophets of the era had foreseen, these bone-white skeletons of buildings that had never been were now faded to what seemed to Turner a guano gray. Probably most of this was farmdust, brought east on the hot summer wind. Well, at least it cut the glare down. Through cracks in the cast fiberglass streets, weeds from other continents put on a spring show that was no big deal, but beat fake concrete: oxeye daisies, dandelions, crownvetch, and the eccentric flash of a self-sown, stunted magnolia, not a native kind, as grandly out of context as (for example) Nicola Quoin in the dessicated fields of Wine Barrens. Mostly, though,

Nature had given up on the place, which lay dead but had not the decency to decompose.

Beyond the magnolia the ground fell away into the largest crater yet, a real amphitheater, *The World We Have Lost* playing nightly, which rose again on the other side in a steady incline culminating in a low mound that evoked (in Turner's mind, already filled with the light of distant oceans) Glastonbury Tor, almost perfectly round and smooth, hard to believe it's really natural. And on top of this was the most remarkable and, in its way, distressing sight in all the End of the World: a very large tent.

At first we thought we recognized it. Both of us, Turner and Tristin, thought it was somewhere we had been taken, interviewed, et cetera, once before. After a few moments we realized that this, too, was part of the old illusion. The tent must have been made of something brittle, for it had cracked in ways that genuine canvas (which would simply have sagged and rotted) could not have done. It was an exhibit, then. An attraction. Perhaps you had once needed a ticket to get inside of it. Of course we had no desire to go inside just now. Still, it was perversely irresistible.

An old trail led across the rubble-pit. We scrambled down and up again. Soon we stood before a sign that explained it all, or at least a good part of it. More, anyway, than the sign-maker had known.

> As the weeks and months pass [said the sign] there will arise in the land a new order based on knowledge, reason, and rigorous investigation. The survivors will embrace this new way, though they have resisted it in the past, because their faith in the old doctrines, the old systems of belief, will have been shattered.
>
> Temporary headquarters like this tent will be set up across the countryside, as cadres of specially trained doctors, teachers, and technicians will assist the survivors in beginning their lives anew. In some places these tents will be preserved as shrines by a grateful populace; while in others permanent centers of study and fellowship will be erected where the tents once stood. We are privileged here to glimpse the first light of the coming day.

"Jeez," said Turner. "It's like they *wanted* it to happen. I mean, it's like a pep talk or something—go on out there and blow the place up so we can start over again."

Tristin's own line of thought was a bit more complicated, or perhaps there were just more shadows in it. *Onward Christian Soldiers* was just the beginning. He thought about how oddly and how neatly this place took up where Gwendola's lectures had left off—celtic twilight and all the rest of it, snakes chased off the island, new temples on ancient foundations, a blazing end of the old nameless faith, a whole racial history lost in translation, papish grafitti etched on dolmens, an immigrant savior enthroned, white vestments drawn over battle-scars—it was the Oldest War, all right, and the newest one too: a war that hadn't even happened yet, so great, so final, so purifying, they made a family pasttime out of waiting for it to come, programmed computers to spew forth Revelations at the click of a mouse, death tolls throw weights alert conditions scenarios symmetric and otherwise, fire and brimstone pacifists fairly *pleading* for it to happen, God grasp thy mighty rod and spew forth thy awful jizzum, and what a great disappointment it must have been when the world rolled over and the generals belched and the prophets died intestate, with nothing but this fiberglass Waste Land and a few tenured evangelists to carry the tidings of annihilation to a new generation of just plain folks, broken-down farmers and lonely heiresses and ordinary students out for a drive.

"Let's get out of here," said Turner. "This place makes me want to throw up."

Which was, Tristin figured, the difference between a hero and a historian.

They turned around. They looked out from the small hill across the crater and into the early afternoon sun. From the distance ahead came the sound of popping or thumping or . . .

"My God," said Turner. "It's guns. Somebody's *shooting guns.*"

Tristin drew closer in fear, but what scared him was not the now-familiar sound of small arms fire nor any concern for the Angels, who could jolly well take care of themselves. It was a peculiar sensation of some last thing falling into place, a fragment of a pattern, dire oracles coming in right on the money.

—Betrayed, he thought, or recognized.—We've been . . .

Turner said, "Well, we can't go back there. I mean, not right now. God, this is so stupid—we haven't even got a pistol or anything."

Tristin only waited. The sound of gunshots came from a diffuse area, a broadening arc, as though an ambush were expanding into an honest-to-God firefight. One could imagine the Angels, leaping gracefully from one pile of rubble to the next, or tumbling in showy, operatic death. Stray bullets chipped the surface of the hillside, bouncing like tiny rocks. Turner cast a troubled look toward Tristin: not really worried about those weary projectiles, which had lost most of their velocity, but disturbed as always by anything that might be taken as an omen. Still, through all these minutes, Tristin only waited.

Turner said, "M-Maybe," scuffling his feet, "we ought to go inside." Gesturing. Inside the tent, he meant. The fiberglass big-top on the hill behind them.

Tristin closed his eyes. This was the piece he had felt falling, like a latch, cold steel slamming into place on the prison door, and he just stood there motionless while it fell. Bullets tapped like sparse hail on the hill around them.

"Just for cover," Turner mumbled on. There was a sort of hitch in his neck, from glancing again and again back over his shoulder.

—All right. Tristin sighed. Only this combination of circumstances —gunfire, troubling intimations, the memory of Black Malachi's "healing touch"—only all this balled up in his mind could have made him turn around. Only this could have driven him a step closer to the tent, the *trompe l'oeil* precursor of the place where he had met his interrogator, where his view of himself and the direction of his life had forever changed. And you know, the fact that this *was* happening was probably itself a message of some kind, a little postcard from the Fates: *Don't tempt us, Jackson, we'll do whatever we have to.*

The battle at the End of the World seemed to grow distant as Tristin and Turner moved quickly the rest of the way to the tied-back double flaps (a fake, like the rest of it, but convincing enough, as though one's eye really wanted to be fooled) of the big tent. They stepped through, each in his own kind of hurry. Light came down from the open center and sideways through jagged holes, and of course the painted floorcloth here was pretty much the same as the others. Only they didn't notice it, this time around. Really, there was too much else to think about.

Just to give you an example. Near the entrance, leaning on a stainless steel counter at ribcage-height, was a Physician. (This is *not* narrative coyness; there was a placard on a post in front of him, the kind you see at zoos. The placard explained:)

> The Physician will be equipped with advanced diagnostic and therapeutic equipment, as the technology previously devoted to creating instruments of war is turned instead to the prolonging of life. With such equipment, a single doctor will be able to deliver health care to an entire community.

" 'Deliver health care,' " mused Turner. He seemed to be searching for a suitably wry follow-on. Failing, as he most often did, he said, "Pretty lifelike, though, isn't it?"

It was. It seemed more than an ordinary wax sculpture or mannikin. Actually the only thing wrong, as one drew closer and studied the thing, was the expression in the eyes: determined, weary, strong-willed but compassionate—all in all, if this makes sense, rather too literary. It was too obviously a collection of attributes, a character-type. Real people, as I'm sure you've noticed, are always a little jumbled up. The sculptor might have thrown in just one detail that was totally out-of-keeping—for instance, the Physician might have had an unattractive haircut. This would mean nothing; the vast plenitude of life means nothing, in scattered contexts; but it would be one of those artistic sparks that brings the monster to life. Well, so much for Art. We moved down the line.

Next came the Systems Designer; and I mean here you had visionary verité at its most extravagant. Her placard (for it was boy-girl-boy-girl here) read:

> Once it is appreciated that social systems are functional constructs like any other, coherent management of human resources can be instituted on a society-wide basis. While not supplanting democratic institutions, advisory personnel like the Systems Designer will be available at every level of public administration to optimize the efficiency of the government process. Her contributions to the new leadership may vary from rapid communications one day, to food distribution the next.

"This is the kind of thing," said Turner, "that gives stupidity a bad name."

Tristin was prepared to be open-minded, though maybe that was due to his lack of a University education. [—I don't know. It's touching, though, isn't it, in its way? As with all essentially religious movements, this one certainly had its tender spots, its endearing little pockets of blind faith to leaven all that pessimism. Have you ever read "science fiction"?]

But Turner was already walking away. He strolled twenty feet or so to the next stop on the tour. By the time Tristin overtook him, he was reading the job description of someone called the Administrator.

> Society will function more smoothly because the role of elected policy-makers will be supplemented by a corps of specially trained Administrators. These career managers will be assigned on a rotational basis to all jurisdictions in which the new government is operational. In addition, they may oversee specific programs or projects of civic importance. They will act fairly and impartially, for they will be serving the interests of society at large, and not a transitory political agenda.

The exhibit consisted of a sort of portable field-office: a folding table, a couple of chairs, some kind of electronic device (perhaps a means of keeping track of transitory political agendas) and, to lend gravity to this flimsy operation, a set of lawbooks. The only thing missing was the prodigal Administrator himself.

"Maybe they couldn't find anybody to take the job," said Turner. (He sounded bitter, though about what?) "Or maybe nobody was qualified. I mean, what did they think, the radiation was going to produce a new breed of tight-ass Supermen?"

Tristin felt very edgy. He looked at the empty chairs, the folding table, like a detective who expects to find tea standing warm in a cup, a cigar still smoking in the ash tray.

At the next station they met the Technical Adept. This appeared to be a sort of anachronistic Jill-of-all-trades; tools and wires and alligator clips sprouted like spines from her coveralls.

"Why is it," said Turner, "that it was considered egalitarian to stick women in ridiculous jobs which obviously some man thought up in the first place, which no woman really would want?"

—You're just being cranky, thought Tristin. Then the burst of a mortar shell, harder to ignore than simple gunfire, shuddered through the hollow flooring of the tent, and they never got around to reading the placard.

"Holy shit," said Turner. "I wonder what's going on out there."

He didn't wonder enough, though, to go have a look. Instead the two of them moved to the middle of the tent, where at least there was a sense of enclosure. At their feet spirals of paint played an over-and-under game, snakes and ladders, red-blooded serpents trying to get a piece of tail. Tristin opened his mouth, as though once more he were on the verge of speaking. Someone else spoke instead.

"Well, you're safe here, Mr Ashenden."

They looked around and of course they saw him standing there, a big man in silhouette, but really what was most remarkable was not the man but everything else, afternoon light streaming across his shoulders, the open plain behind him . . . no, look, it's all around, a projection or something: an old pasture, warm breeze waving new shoots of grass as luminously green as this lampshade, the night the story is recalled. There was a sound, vaguely musical, hard to recognize at first, that rose on the wind and fell; then all at once you saw bright hats bobbing over last year's almond-colored stalks, sprays of hair; finally a slip of pure translucent color, small as a child's T-shirt all pressed out, tore zanily skyward, its string invisible, hovered for one long hopeful moment, and dove for the field amidst a chorus of innocent, disappointed voices.

The big man said, "Too bad. But perhaps it will stay up, next time."

Turner faced him with an angry look, the look a little boy might wear who has been reproached, or embarrassed. "Where is she?" he demanded. "Did you trick her into coming here? Or has she been on your side all along?"

The big man only smiled indulgently. Then he shook his head. "I'm afraid I can't help you with that."

"Look," said Turner, "I don't know what the fuck this is you're doing. B-But, I've got a bunch of guys outside that'll be happy to make your face even flatter, if you don't tell me where Maridel is. That's all I came out here for. I'm not looking for a fight."

Tristin didn't think this a very promising line of inquiry. He drew up behind Turner like a trainer, ready to pull his contender away if the fight looked hopeless. Besides, there was something about the vastness of this . . . projection, illusion, whatever it was . . . that made you want to band together, pool your strength.

The big man, whom still Tristin failed to recognize, having known him only as a figure from legend, looked at the two of them with a kindly, tolerant sort of smile. *Avuncular*, Turner had said about this smile, and Tristin (who had never had an uncle) supposed that must be about right.

"When you speak," the big man said, "of coming *out here*, I assume you're referring to the old amusement park. Well, you aren't in the park any longer. As to what you did, in fact, come out here for, I'm afraid we must defer to you on that. There must be something here that you want. Perhaps some place you'd like to see?"

Turner shot his eyes around. "Ah, no, I don't . . ."

But Tristin thought, Of course. This was the missing figure from the sideshow—the Administrator, the tight-ass Superman—right? Because like the other mannikins he was a little too composed, too all-in-order, to be fully convincing. Maybe that's why Turner wasn't afraid of him, wasn't trying to get away or turn the projection off.

"Look at that tree," the mannikin suggested. "Maybe that's a kind of landmark."

He pointed at the tallest thing around us: a very old princess tree, spreading its limbs above the field. Its emergent leaves were the same glowing color as the grasses. The children, flying their kite, ran toward it then veered away, making a sport of near-entanglement.

"Yeah," Turner said. "Maybe . . ."

—*What?* Tristin wanted to shout.—What is it? Let's get out of here, Turner.

It was, instead, the Administrator who gave Tristin his attention. "And who is this?" he said. "Have you got a new bard? I'd have thought you would stick with Pantera."

"I'd have thought you'd stick it up your ass," Turner said viciously. "This isn't funny, you know. And it isn't going to work."

The big man winced as though Turner had struck him, and even Tristin felt that this was a little harsh. Could you really be angry at someone so . . . *composed*?

"He doesn't mean to be cruel." The big man was looking at Tristin, kindly. A terrible sensation crept up the boy's spine. "He's just surprised. And as you know, he doesn't like to admit his feelings, to acknowledge his true nature."

—No, Tristin fervently thought.

"Yes," said the big man.

—The Invader. (Naming the ghost at last.)—The Enemy.

"Well," said Rodarch, "that all depends, though, doesn't it? On which side you're on. And on who is writing the history books."

Turner was staring at the children in the field. Sensing our attention maybe, he said:

"So what is this, then? A trap? Like, was the whole Maridel thing a fake? Just tell me—"

"Oh, no." The big man shook his head. "This is simply the answer to a question. A question that was posed but not answered at our very first meeting. He couldn't tell me. Pantera is . . . unapproachable. And Gwendola—" (He glanced at me; his look of regret was very convincing.) "Gwendola has been hanging on for a very long time now. But maybe you have answered the question yourself. Maybe this," gesturing: the field, the children, the sunny sky, "is what you really want."

Turner sighed, as though he wished things weren't so easily summed up.

"Well," said Rodarch, "it's normal enough, isn't it?"

". . ."

"Sadly," Rodarch continued, "it is difficult to envision any future— for them, or for the rest of us—other than continuing misery. Continuing decline. As long as this struggle, this Resistance . . ."

"You're a fine one to talk." Turner wheeled toward him, shoving a fist very close. "You're a, you've got a lot of nerve, a-accusing *me*."

"Nonsense," said Rodarch. "I wasn't accusing anyone."

"Bullshit. I know where you're headed. Just lay down your arms Mr Ashenden and there will be peace and those children will be healthy and a New Day will dawn in the world. Which is all just so much garbage. You aren't offering peace or health or jack shit, really. Just a . . . a *program*, for God's sake, like we're all a bunch of fucking computers—this terrific program you've got with laws and camps a-and, all that paperwork—"

"And hope," said Rodarch. He was utterly placid. "Don't forget hope.

The hope of justice. The hope that a brighter day *will* come. That someday reason will prevail, that we will come to understand. Isn't that right, Mr Maleish? Isn't that what the, the *offer* has always been?"

Turner looked at Tristin, taken aback. I suppose he had never considered that, just like a real person, I might have a family name.

Rodarch pushed on, as any field commander would have, sensing an advantage: "That's where our real strength has always lain. We speak of the future. We do not deny the contradictions of the present. We face them squarely. But we look beyond. We offer—indeed we promise—that some day, it will all make sense. Isn't that right?"

He looked hard at Tristin, and Tristin could only nod.—But you've never delivered, I pointed out.—Justice, reason, understanding . . . it's always just a series of promises. It never—

"That wasn't the question. The question was, I believe, though Mr Ashenden wouldn't have phrased it quite this way: Which of us is the most convincing champion of *that?*" (Again, gesturing toward the children.) "Of hope. And health. Of—and this is important—of order. Calmness. And a future, any future at all, for the innocents of the world."

This was too much for Turner. "You self-righteous bastards are all alike. It was you guys that made them sick in the first place. All this *calmness* of yours, this *order*. Fucking *death* is about as calm and orderly as you can get, and that's all you guys have really got to show for this New Day of yours."

"And you guys," said the Chief Administrator, picking up Turner's phrase but enunciating it more precisely, as though such loose speech were really beneath him, "what exactly are you defending? What is it, really, you're hanging on to?"

Turner looked at Tristin—at me—as though it were my problem, as though I were the spokesman for our side. I might as well have been; silence was as good an answer as any other.

"Well, let me tell you," said Rodarch, "if I may. You offer, or I should say you represent, a memory of greatness. You offer ancient melodies, forgotten poems. You offer mornings of fragile winter sunlight."

(We passed a look of surprise back and forth, Turner and I, both of us more than ever taken off-guard.)

Rodarch rolled onward. "You offer, in fact you embody, that awful splendor, and that awesome beauty—everything in fact, the comic and the tragic—that is the summation of a certain strain of humanity, a certain path of evolution which has, if I may say so, worn itself very thin. That is what you offer. It is what you are. And it *is* great, in its way. But it's a blind alley. It can adapt no further. It is a relic, a hold-over, more and more estranged from the challenges of life, the selective pressures."

The Chief Administrator turned aside, gazed across the field. He looked like THE EMPEROR, on the fortune-telling card. Before us, joyful shrieks of children (an unfamilar sound to all three of us, I suppose) made an ironic counterpoint to his words.

Rodarch said, "Your greatest works of art cannot save them, Mr Ashenden. They couldn't begin to comprehend the stories that fill your mind. Your most beautiful music can only soothe them—if even that— while they weaken and die."

I looked to Turner, our champion, hoping for some rebuttal—some blunt dismissal that would slice to the gut of the argument, which was not (I believed) about art or music or anything of the kind. But Turner just stood there, looking shaken. He was in the midst of a different confrontation than I knew, and neither Rodarch nor I played a role in it.

"It is not," said the Chief Administrator, softening his tone, deigning to be generous now, "that your cause is unworthy. You will always, in every age, have your followers. But they will grow fewer, over time. The ideas with which you are associated—*tragedy*, for example, or *transcendence*, or *the other side*—these are preoccupations of the privileged. Ordinary people have more pressing things on their minds."

—Yes, I thought.—You've seen to that.

"But don't worry," Rodarch went on, ignoring me. "You will always be remembered. There will always be someone—hermits, historians, readers of books—who will understand what you were."

Turner, thus relegated to the past tense, faced his ageless Enemy with an expression the Enemy himself might have designed: an exact antithesis of hope.

"What," he said in a moment, timidly, "what about Maridel?"

The Chief Administrator only smiled.

At such a moment, I could not help wondering what Black Malachi would have done.

Well, since you ask

Black Malachi leaned out from his scaffolding, body-weight shifting ominously, to deposit a glop of raw umber on the not-quite-finished latest
version of his Ideal Mandala. The thick oils drooped a bit in painterly
fashion but did not run. Black Malachi let his breath out.

"That may have done it," he said—cautiously, as though his breath
might ripple the canvas.

"Done what?" called Cervina. She came out of the bedroom to stand
tentatively, afraid to take this as a positive sign, in the door of the studio.

"I was speaking," said Black Malachi (but not irritably, for a change),
"to myself. Or rather, to the greater being who drowses within me. Or
perhaps we are the same. Or perhaps I need a little something to smoke.
How are you this morning, my dear?"

Cervina felt as though a happy melody were trilling inside her. Blackie
hadn't been so jovial in weeks. Things were not the same here, anymore.

"It's two o'clock in the afternoon," she pointed out, thinking this was
something Turner might have said. Turner had been the great tonic, the
elixir, in Malachi's life.

"God—and my eyes are wide open. Clearly, the order of things is
disrupted. Come closer, then, why don't you, and tell me what you think."

Cervina felt herself on new, unsteady ground as she stepped up to
the scaffolding and peered through it at what was nothing more, apparently,
than a random series of swirls and knots. "Um," she said, "ah . . ."

"Precisely," declared the proud little prophet, from on high. "*Um,
ah.* Really, that is quite the effect I had hoped for."

He clambered down, showing a good bit of his hairy bottom as the
Cherokee-red bathrobe got hitched on the scaffold. Cervina resisted a
welcome and lately unaccustomed urge to laugh. It looked like a lovely
day, through the unwashed windows of Solar Temple. Did she dare suggest
a stroll out on the balcony? Black Malachi's skin had gone the color of
paper, from not getting any sun.

"Well," he said, heavily alighting on the paint-stained floor. "Shall
we see if it works?"

Understanding only that her Blackie had said "we"—and did not seem to intend it royally—Cervina nodded.

"Very well." He turned with stagey gravity to face the canvas, twice as tall as himself. He raised his hands on high. He chanted:

> "Give us your feet, if we be foes,
> And lick the crud between your toes."

Cervina grimaced, though fondly.

"Now," he said, motioning for her, "help me here. I can't quite reach."

She came to stand beside him, following as he pointed up to a streak of color no different than any other.

"Just place your hand there. And give me the other one. No, *there*, damn it."

She almost drew back, frightened again, but the earnest little fingers, squeezing hers, held her steady. He gets so caught up, she thought. She laid her index finger where he was pointing.

He said, "Now open your eyes."

"They're already . . ." she began.

Then she saw what he meant.

Before them, around them, swirling out of the center of the mandala, came a kind of synesthetic stew: warm wind the smell of flowers decaying leaves tender treble voices shouting in counterpoint sunshine everywhere and warmth, she could feel warmth like the pure blood moving inside her, dry grasses brushing her skin, a flash of color, dream-blue sky, billowing thought-clouds moving in no direction, from nowhere into *now*, caught in the act of becoming, and what Cervina realized (among other things, amidst everything at once) was that "open your eyes" had been a metaphor and that metaphors are the only way to wrap your mind around the Truth, the way characters are needed to fool you into believing a story, though the Story itself is nothing but artifice, empty conjuring—or no, it's full, exploding, the characters springing to life and Cervina becoming a character herself, a metaphor made flesh . . .

. . . and when she couldn't stand it anymore she "closed her eyes" and the mandala was there, empty, just hanging, a symbol of nothing anymore but itself, and her finger was oily with paint.

"Ahhh," said Black Malachi, a happy sigh. "I knew I'd get it right eventually."

"Blackie," said Cervina, seriously, facing him, "that was . . . I mean, really, that was amazing."

He wagged his head. "*I* am amazing," he corrected her. "That, the rest of it, simply *is*. It is devoid of qualities. Care for a puff?"

He had gotten a joint from somewhere and already smoked half of it. Time was knocked off-course: an effect Cervina had pretty much gotten used to. Sunshine fell at the wrong angle into the studio. In fact, she wasn't sure the sun ought to be shining in here at all. Weren't studios supposed to face north? So maybe the planet was knocked off-course, too. Big deal.

"All right," Black Malachi said, in a voice that had a hint of command in it. "Let's take another dip. Shall we?"

Cervina couldn't imagine what he was talking about, so he took her hand and turned her gently to face the canvas.

"Once more with feeling," he said.

. . . This time Cervina thought she detected, in the whirlpool of sensation, something that might have been a pattern—or maybe "a pattern" was only a metaphor for what she really perceived—something about the contours of the whirlpool itself, swirlings and windings like the trails of paint in the mandala; a secret language; or maybe it was all a contact-high. She tried to feel Blackie's hand. She even glanced sideways, looking for the round face in the maelstrom, but the face she saw wasn't Blackie's. Or actually it was, but it was something out of a memory, her own memory, some past moment, like a recording, only shot from a different place than she'd been standing at the time; remembered through someone else's eyes.

"It's scarcely eleven o'clock in the morning," Malachi was saying, the memory-Malachi, which ought to explain something, though Cervina wasn't sure what.

"Sorry," said Turner.

Ah, of course. Turner stood awkwardly in the banana court, with Tristin—remember Tristin?—nervous and attentive at his side. Malachi smiled kindly at the youth, extending a hand to lay upon his shoulder.

At the moment of contact, Cervina felt a spilling-over of energy that seemed to originate deep inside her—deeper inside than her physical body could go—and from there flowed outward, down her arms and through her fingertips, into the painting, down into the maze of spirals, back down into the earth. She saw Tristin's eyes open wide in astonishment and she thought, *I know what you mean, kid*, then Tristin opened his mouth and they all waited there, expecting him to speak.

But no. Still smiling, Black Malachi took his hand away.

He said, "Well, I'll see you."

"*Wait—*"

Cervina felt something hard before her, a barrier. She sensed warmth on the other side of it, laughing children, the odor of damp ground.

—*What are you going to do?* she asked Blackie in the secret language, which now she understood.

—*I've got the hook in him*, Black Malachi told her, a wry delight in his voice. *Now I'm going to reel the little sucker in.*

Overlay

Rodarch had that smile on his face. You remember that smile. If you're still in the mood for metaphors, try this one: spider, contemplating the harvest of his web.

Tristin was looking at that well-fed arachnid smile and at Turner's equal and opposite reaction (fly, concerned for future of vital juices) when from somewhere came the idea that they'd taken just about enough of this shit. What an odd thought: un-Tristinlike, if you see what I mean. But there you had it. He opened his mouth and, unable to speak, made a series of hand-signs—banks and dives of the palm, barrel rolls, round and back as though tracing out some mad hieroglyphic in the air.

It's hard to capture the spontaneous flavor of this. But in the following moment of mild surprise, a funny sort of wind came up in the field around the three of them, and the kite that the kids had been flying got stuck in the princess tree. There were cries of juvenile displeasure. Turner looked around, distractedly at first, then he focused on the kite—a pitiful, homemade thing, writhing before the wind—and an expression of relief came over his face. It was like watching the audience at, say, a performance of *Lear*, when the fool starts to speak; in this case the relief was tragic rather than comic, but it was scaled-down tragedy, a tragedy that could be contained. The one kite, the One Tree.

"Can you help us, mister?"

It was a voice as tiny and delicate as a crystal figurine—you know, you can just tell it's going to shatter and the play end miserably and the poor girl never ever get laid. (Tristin couldn't entirely believe he was having this chain of thought, but the next thought in line was *What the hell, my boy—let's roll with it.*)

The little girl came running up, and son-of-a-bitch, it was a perfect miniature facsimile of Maridel. Eight or nine maybe: Tristin remembered her from that age, and he could have warned Turner that the innocence, the vulnerability, the whole Little Girl Lost routine was nothing but a world-class sucker play. Yet at this particular moment he found that he enjoyed a good sucker play as well as anyone. Better, maybe, because he knew in advance how the scam was going to come down.

"Mister, can you," she said, her face all eyes and narrow cheekbones, "can you help us get our kite?"

She held out a hand. Perfect tiny fingers. There was no knowing if Turner recognized her. He looked down and maybe just the slightest tremor of uncertainty—not even close to suspicion, yet—twitched at the corner of his mouth. But the body, the unrefined reflexes, ruled; Turner lifted his arm so the little girl could take his hand, and allowed her to tug him into the pasture.

"Wait a minute," said Rodarch.

Tristin thought the big man looked worried—though how could you be sure? These Administrator types seemed to be programmed for only a limited range of feelings.

Rodarch said, "Do you know what you're getting into?"

Turner looked back with one hand holding the little girl's and stared as though having a hard time divining what these words might mean.

"It's out of your control already," the Chief Administrator noted. (Smugly, Tristin thought; but this might have been an overlay, like a scribe heaping attaboys on the currently fashionable god in the middle of a manuscript. It happens.) Rodarch said, "Be reasonable. If you go any farther you may find yourself on *the other side*. We wouldn't want that to happen."

What mean "we," white man? Turner gave the mannikin a shot of his prize-winning smile. He took another few steps toward the princess tree.

Finest kind, my boy, said the overlay in Tristin's head. *Now you've got to get the Stainless Steel Savior to trot after him.*

Blackie, said another voice, this one a little less distinct, *why don't you leave it alone? Let them work it out for themselves.*

If we do that, Tristin warns her, *our friend Ashenden's going to wind up pinned to the mat like a butterfly*. Thecla halesus W. *The common purple prosewing.*"

What?

Never mind. Turner and the little girl were almost lost from view in the tall grasses. Owing to some point-of-view irregularity, Turner actually seemed to grow smaller as he walked away. The wind whipped old leaves around, bringing ripe smells, fertile smells, across the plain.

Next to Tristin, the tall man or mannikin moved his substantial weight from one foot to another, back and forth, cycling, like a cybernetic dream machine caught in a wait-state. It does not compute, it does not compute, my god cap'n it looks like she's overloadin', better jump ship before she blows. You could almost enjoy this.

—Well, said Tristin, I guess we ought to go after them.

Rodarch looked down at the boy, somewhat wearily. "But who are *you?*" he said. "And what's become of Pantera? I don't recognize half the characters, this time around."

—We're at the End of the World, Tristin pointed out.—Things have been forgotten, threads intertwined. It stands to reason.

The appeal to Reason, a ploy, seemed to work. Rodarch gathered himself up and looked out into the field. Turner and the girl were gone. You could barely see the kite, the princess tree, anything at all. Flecks of hay, grass seeds, dirt blew in their faces like spittle.

"It doesn't make sense," said Rodarch. Not complaining, really.

—It does or it doesn't, said Tristin.

This is the nuts, said the wily little wizard in an ancient, secret tongue. They walked out there, into the field, under a sun that cast no shadows.

The old sucker play

We are all children in this place. By the time we get here, to the flowering meadow, we've been expecting it, or at least everybody is too cool to act surprised. Turner Ashenden, a fair-haired twelve-year-old, stands awkwardly under the princess tree glaring at lanky Trev Goldaster, maybe thirteen, whose limbs and neck have entered the stretch of adolescence. Between them is little Maridel. The other children hang back a bit, fidgeting, like a school choir in the minutes before a show.

Maridel points up into the tree. From a child's perspective, the kite is twice as high as before. It's red, with a white tail flapping like a pennant. Maridel looks at Trev; she looks at Turner.

Trev says, No way we can get that, it's a mile high.

Turner hesitates. The tree scares him a lot less than Maridel does. She stares hard at him and he looks away, kicks the ground with his toe.

Now up comes young Rodarch—a big, jocky-looking boy at least fourteen—who would never have fooled with them if they'd asked him to, but now he gets to play savior. He says, You want me to get that? looking real serious, to Maridel.

She smiles.

Rodarch spits in his wide palms and wipes them on his jeans. He sizes up the tree like he's a scientist or something, like maybe pretending to gauge the height, the strength of the limbs, it's obviously a bunch of crap. Then he jumps. He snags the lowest branch and pulls his weight up onto it.

Suddenly Turner is there too. Before anyone sees him coming, he makes this stupid leap at nothing, misses the limb, winds up with his arms and legs hugging the tree like some animal. You know, a tree-sloth. The kids laugh. Turner seems to give up; he starts sliding down the smooth bark. Then he recovers. He squirms upward, pushing against the trunk with his thighs, and soon he's latched onto the limb across from Rodarch. The big boy gives him a smirk, for his trouble.

Turner and Rodarch head on up the tree, taking turns, so as

not to overload the branches, an instinctive form of cooperation that emerges in the midst of rivalry. They depend on each other, in a way. After a couple of minutes they have climbed amazingly high. The branches they're standing on are sagging, creaking, like they're about to snap off.

The kite hangs before them, about eye-level, but it's too far out. First you have limbs and then branches and then twigs that bend way down if you even lean on them. Turner stretches forward, trying to reach the kite, but everything sways so much that the kids on the ground step back a few more steps: not a good sign. Rodarch, a couple years older, is more calculating. He rummages in his pocket and pulls out a rock, a black rock. It must be a private treasure: it shimmers eerily in the sun. Rodarch takes aim with it but doesn't throw. He stares at the kite while hefting the rock in his hand, as though weighing what he stands to gain against what he will sure as hell lose.

Looking down, Turner sees that Maridel has led Trev away from the other kids, out to the field, among the tall grass. Now they are facing each other. She comes up to stand very close. She puts her hands on his skinny shoulders, runs them down his arms, his waist, his bony hips. She moves against him like a dancer. Trev does not do anything, especially: he doesn't go along with it, but he doesn't push her away. He is unnerved. Any boy would be.

Turner watches, in horror now, as Maridel drops down on her knees. She's almost hidden behind the grass-swells. Only her head, her wheat-yellow hair, is visible. Trev looks surprised—astonished—as the understanding spreads among them, the two children in the field and Turner in the tree, of what Maridel is doing. Her busy hands loosen the boy's belt, force the pants down his gangly legs, into the matted grass. Then she seizes his hips and pulls them forward, thrusting herself onto him. The golden hair falls in a tangle as the perfectly sculpted little head moves up and down, slowly, assuredly, shamelessly, and the tall boy arches his spine, letting his head fall back. His mouth opens in the beginning of a long slow moan.

Turner thinks he may be insane. Either that, or the whole world is. Heedless of his shaky perch in the tree, he lunges forward, grabs the rock in Rodarch's hand. He wrests it away. It tingles in his grasp, hot, electric, filling his arm with energy, glowing like dark glass with sunlight trapped inside it. Turner feels, he knows, that the rock is very important, maybe more important than anything—that if he stares into the rock even for an instant, eternal things will be revealed. At the same time he cannot know this; eternity means nothing to a twelve-year-old; the rock is simply a rock and nothing more. He draws his arm back.

Rodarch gasps. His face is filled with panic, desperation, as though some part of himself has been torn away. He holds his arms out, he opens his mouth—but the feeling is too great, too awful, for words.

Then it is done. Turner lets the rock fly.

Rodarch cries out, loses his balance, tumbles from the tree.

The rock whizzes an inch above Maridel's head, strikes Trev hard in the belly. The boy yells in pain, then jerks away from Maridel, leaving his penis exposed for a moment, pale and wet. In mortification, he bends to cover himself.

Maridel stands. She looks around with absolutely no expression at all. Her eyes meet Turner's, hold them for an instant, and drop them as Turner should have dropped the stone. It is too late now.

At the base of the princess tree, Rodarch lies on his back, rolling slowly from side to side. He is groaning, but his agony seems different, deeper somehow, than the fall can account for—as though Turner has merely reopened a very old wound. His eyes are wide and empty. After a moment, they close.

With their closing, a change comes over the meadow. The wind grows harsher, colder; the debris blowing up is dry and gray and infertile. Turner looks around, where the grass stood tall and green a moment past, but now there are only dead stalks rising from a cracked, eroded landscape. The sun is low, casting a dry wintry light on the children, on everything.

Maridel turns away. She is looking at nothing, she is tossing her beautiful hair; her chin is high, her eyes are calm and narrow; she faces north, her back to the enfeebled sun.

Unnoticed by everyone, through all of this, Tristin has stood alone, at the edge of the meadow, taking it in. His lips are pressed together. Finally, catching Turner's eye, he shakes his head as if to say *I know how you're feeling, my boy. I've seen it all before.*

And then, as all children know will happen, in the end, before life becomes unbearable, the Angels swoop down (amidst dust and cracking fiberglass and a hundred small explosions) and bear us safely away.

Commentary regarding the mandala, and the coming of May

"Lug help us," said Black Malachi, stepping back from the scaffolding in a state of quite visible surprise. "I should say that this thing actually does work."

Cervina said more tersely, "I should say."

Black Malachi shook his head. Preternaturally unflappable since birth, he gave every sign of having been flapped. "Perhaps," he said, "I should go back to homeopathy."

"And leave things like this?"

"Ah. Well. What month do you suppose it is?"

Cervina pursed her lips. The sun seemed to be shining backward now: outward through the windows, from the inside of the house. There was no telling what fundamental laws of reality had been disarranged. She boiled this down to a simple "I couldn't tell you."

Black Malachi nodded. He stared at his two small, meddlesome hands.

"Blackie?" Cervina came closer, moving unsteadily. "What's going to happen next? Do you know? Can you remember? Or is it different each time?"

He frowned; though it appeared that reverting to an accustomed role—dispenser of wisdom, knower of the Four Dark Things—had a steadying effect on him. After a few moments' thought, he was able to summon up an offhand shrug, an air of being above it all.

"Oh, a little different," he said, and raised a cautionary finger: "Maybe. A little. But basically the same, unless we've *really* jerked it around."

"We?" said Cervina.

Increasingly himself, Black Malachi snapped his fingers, and the sonic sculpture came on. It was doing its aged-jukebox imitation, complete with scratches and amplifier-hiss. There were even lyrics, of a sort. Ironic ones. Finding pleasure in this, Black Malachi smiled and raised his eyes up toward the ceiling, from where the music came.

"That's life," he said happily.

LETTING GO

1

"Golden hours"

Summer brought nothing new to the mountaintop: rain, the same flowers, familiar tales of battle, rumors of starvation, smells of decay. We sat apart in the upstairs sitting room with books, with newspapers, waiting for sunset, watching the breeze from the west billow the muslin at the French doors. There was music, but it wasn't Vinny's anymore. He had ceased to perform, or very nearly, since the antenna had gone up. Now he sat for hours listening to the eerie silences through which now and then, like a shooting star, some tune or political broadcast or plea for emergency aid would run its thrilling course, then fade, and the silence would rule again.

Once, on a very clear evening, a signal arose and held steady. It was a double-flute, an instrument out of fairy tales, warbling through the darkness. Vinny nearly tumbled from his chair. His musician's fingers played softly at the directional controls, turning the antenna one degree at a time, seeking the source of that astonishing music. The other performer, hundreds or thousands of miles away, played with a kind of languid certainty—tranquil, unhurried, an unconscious accompanist to Vinny's trembling hands. The antenna swung from east to northeast and still the signal grew stronger. At due north, Vinny halted.

"This is impossible," he said. What he meant was, he didn't want to go past the zero.

The flute changed melodies; now there was some hollow-sounding percussion, like wooden blocks.

"Impossible?" said Turner. The word had a funny sound—less substantial than the music that floated over the room.

"I mean," said Vinny, staring out the window, "there's nothing *there*. Just some outposts, you know, internment camps, research stations . . ."

Suddenly, there was singing. It was one of those crazy voices, a late-night tavern voice, weaving ballads out of the warm air.

> The passage of time
> Is flicking dimly upon the screen.
> I can't see the lines
> I used to think I could read between.
> Perhaps my brains have turned to sand . . .

> Oh me, oh my—
> I think it's been an eternity.
> You'd be surprised
> At my degree of uncertainty;
> Putting grapes back on the vine . . .

> Several times,
> I've seen the evening slide away,
> Watching the signs
> Taking over from the fading day;
> Changing water into wine . . .

Then Vinny touched the directional control, the antenna clicked past the zero, and the music stopped. The whole thing might have been a mistake, an electronic aberration; some piece of dying equipment might have chosen that evening to cry out its last melody; but we were feeling edgy, always alert for portents.

"That was weird," said Partner Trefoil after a while.

Turner nodded. He had recognized the old song. His fingers tapped absently at a book he hadn't been reading. *Prisons et Paradis*. Only a faint hiss, the usual night-noise, came out of the speakers. We stayed there listening many nights.

Without warning, years were gone.

La recherche

In those days Turner traveled freely, in and out of the government's zone of control. A certain aura surrounded him. Conversations tapered off at his approach, and strangers treated him with instinctual deference. Feeling no concern for his own safety—and wishing, perhaps, to distance himself from the violence being perpetrated daily in his name—he led the Angels on tedious and mostly senseless errands, out to the fringes of the populated world, places even bleaker and wilder than the Peels. These errands tended to involve something Turner described as "a black rock, like maybe some kind of jewel," which he seemed to believe had been lost in the north, and might be worth finding. Returning empty-handed, he let the Angels go: back to Dirty Dick, to Harvey Goldaster, to whatever Old Soul once had employed them. They were needed more urgently, he said, in the contested provinces. More urgently, he meant, than in our enchanted inner circle, which no ill-meaning spirit dared to broach.

What was in his mind in those days? Or more to the point, what was he looking for, really? All we saw, those of us immediately around him, was a sober-minded and punctilious young man with an increasingly preoccupied expression, who in his off-hours was growing more than ever bookish. He read novels, collections of folktales, travelogues; an occasional popular history, of the *Forbidden Rites of the Druids* sort; and gardening books, which he pulled out of dusty piles in the library and carried around with him for days, staring at the photographs and committing their captions to memory. I wonder if he was pining in some obsessive way for those dead flowers, or for the sea-fresh air of the lands that once had grown them. The Lost Isles.

On Maridel's sixteenth birthday, he ambled along the upstairs hallway and, with his usual lack of ceremony, took up residence in her rooms. They were sunnier than his own, with well-stuffed furniture, and walls that had been painted a warm pink not so many years before; and in any case, "home" was not a simple concept for Turner Ashenden anymore. He was as much "at home" in Maridel's bedchamber, I suppose, as anywhere else.

Gwendola grew peculiarly quiet. Her lectures in the sitting room ended. She ceased even to play her austere, chilly music, contenting herself with whatever Vinny put on. It was a relief; yet one could only wonder what was the matter with her.

There was, of course, a world outside the old house. Things were going on *out there*, to which none of us but Turner paid much attention. Our only tidings—and our only way of guessing at the trend of events, whether good or ill—came in the form of well-armed messengers who shuttled up and down the mountain, to and from the various estates and field-offices and mercantile encampments that made up the Resistance (a term which I began to think was something of a polite euphemism, less denotative than the Home Team). Sometimes Harvey Goldaster showed up in person, stayed for dinner or longer, late into the evening, and usually afterward Turner would slip into a motorized cart of some kind—whatever we had, at that moment, the proper fuel for—and be gone a couple of days. Maridel sulked in his absence. Yet she sulked a great deal in his presence, as well. I thought she must be waiting for something. At least she no longer tormented me.

I was, in fact, left very much alone by everyone.

Goldaster was clearly excited when he appeared one morning in what I believe was early May. It might equally well have been March or July; what I recall was the way the sun lay in yellow pools outside the windows of the downstairs parlor. The air was moist. The schoolchildren—those who weren't yet orphans, or permanent boarders—were away on some vacation or other. Beltaine, perhaps. No one was about, that early in the morning, which is how I happened to be the one to open the door.

"Where's Ashenden?"—getting right to the point, as his eyes swept across the hall, past the sculpted dragons, up the spiral stairs, around the balcony. Still detecting no one but myself (whom, I think, he had little use for), Harvey put his question again, slowly and loudly, as though speaking to an idiot.

—I have no idea, I was pleased to inform him.—And if you can't be any more polite than that, you can go look for him yourself.

People were always surprised, somehow, when they actually *saw* me. Harvey Goldaster, narrowing his handsomely wrinkled eyes, seemed to detect a degree of cunning or calculation on my face; he nodded curtly, as though recognizing a kindred spirit.

"All right, look," he said. "I don't have time to hang around. Just tell Ashenden . . . or, what I mean is, can you give him a message? Good, well. Then tell him, let him know that his friend Rodarch is on the move again. All right? Tell him he's rolling up the road with a whole goddamned army of Settlers behind him. And listen: make sure he understands this isn't a joke. Mention the *cable-laying machine*, all right?"

—Gotcha.

Harvey stared at me for another few moments, oddly. Perhaps I was smiling, which would have struck him as eccentric. The fact was, I had actually gotten to like this cocksure little autocrat.

"And tell him," he said finally, turning to go, "that I said he'd better get on the stick. Tell him to get his ass in gear."

—I'll tell him you dropped by with the usual load of clichés.

Harvey was gone, though.

To my surprise, at such an early hour, I found Turner sitting cross-legged on the back terrace, that week's gardening book unfolded in his lap, staring out at the plain where tufts of bleached-green broomsedge made what they could of the shale and red clay. He didn't seem much interested in Goldaster's appearance or hurried departure, until I jotted in the margin of his book, in a final effort to get his attention:

the Cable-Laying Machine (?)

Then he looked around at me.

"Did Harvey say that? What does it mean?"

He was half smiling, as though he suspected some form of inside joke. His eyes looked more violet than blue in the warm western light. There were creases around them. I wondered how Turner thought of himself now: years removed from being an unhappy student, yet still terribly young for whatever role had been thrust upon him—Lord of the Horseflies, Black Malachi once said. It was as though some hereditary position had descended to him before he'd had a chance to prepare for it. One meeting with the Chief Administrator, two hands on the hilt of the Identity machine, and Destiny had clamped its jaws shut.

Turner gave me a companionable thump on the upper arm. He must have sensed that I was going morose on him.

"Come on," he said, with something like inspiration in his voice. "Let's go, before anyone else is awake."

He must have meant Maridel.

—To Upper Moat Farm? I wondered, surprised that Turner would want to take me there.

He was *so close*, sometimes. "To the Solar Temple," he said, looking out again, toward the plain. "I'd like to see how Malachi's getting along."

Ducky, thanks

We had to wait several minutes while Cervina went to wake him. Taking advantage of the delay, Turner conducted me through the maze of the banana court, which I swear was more confusingly arranged than ever. Many of the dark glazed tiles were broken (I would have bet deliberately) and roots protruding from drainage holes in the great terra cotta planters had made their way back to the primal soil below, *tapping the source* all right as Turner may well have murmured. I had never seen a place look any more wild. We passed through the dining room (its constellation of tiny lights almost all extinguished, only a couple of bulbs still alive: the whole place was a kind of glyph, as perhaps it always had been) and thence to the kitchen. The Omphalos.

Here at least was a modicum of cleanliness, of organization—though creepers had followed us even here, curling their tendrils around drawer pulls and wine racks. The door to the refrigerator room stood ajar. Clouds of moisture—like the sublimating dry-ice-in-water concealed in the caldron, Scene 1, Community Theater matinee of *MacBeth*, edited down so that even sci-fi buffs could follow it—drifted across the room; it was marvelously atmospheric. Think of the wasted energy, though. The alarm must have been deactivated. Or maybe it was broken. Maybe the Solar Temple wasn't a self-maintaining system, a Turing cottage, after all.

"Well suck me blue."

One was never quite prepared for Black Malachi. We turned to find him no longer wearing that Cherokee-red bathrobe, which must, thank

God, have long disintegrated; but now his attire was even worse: a pair of boxer shorts all over which large blood-red valentines had been stenciled in glossy paint. On closer examination, which I was hesitant to make, but which the stridency of the pattern seemed to compel, I saw that the hearts all had been pierced with shafts of various kinds—swords, rocket ships, golf clubs, uncircumcised penises, severed arms dripping blood of their own . . . It was the most grotesque thing I had ever seen.

"Malachi," said Turner, "you look awful."

The *enfant terrible* did not deny it. He came a few steps closer, scratching his exposed furry stomach just below the years-long fall of his beard.

"I have a new name," he said; he sounded very pleased about it. "A nickname! You may now call me *Black Mal*."

"As in sickness?" said Turner.

The old roommates stared cannily at each other.

Malachi said, "Black Mal, the unwell healer. The physician who cures by sympathetically acquiring his patient's malady."

"You must be doing a lot of doctoring these days." (Turner glanced around, perhaps expecting rows of army-style cots, evidence of large-scale convalescence.)

Malachi came closer. "I have one patient only." His expression made Turner draw back, as though from something feral. "Tell me, Ashenden—have you ever read *Dorian Gray*? Yes, of course you have; I ask only rhetorically. For the benefit of your, ah, special friend here."

I did not like the tone of this, and I suspect neither did Turner. We all adjusted our postures a bit. Some subtle theme was being danced out; an unsuspected subtext lately discovered in the ancient tragedy. The refrigerator gave a long groan: the compressor complaining, I shouldn't have wondered. Around our feet, the fog of condensate thickened.

"Black Mal," said Turner, somewhat sarcastically. Also, I suppose, trying it on for size.

"Well, kiss a fish," exclaimed our slippery host. "What have I been thinking of? I have neglected to offer you anything to drink. Let me see, we have a few things here . . ."

He bustled over to the open door of a pantry. Things looked all atumble inside. Malachi plunged in heedlessly, throwing tins and boxes back over his shoulder.

"Forget about it," Turner told him. "We don't need anything."

—*I* wouldn't mind, though, I thought, to my own surprise.

Black Malachi, *Black Mal*, turned with a different kind of smile—his bedside-manner expression.

"Of course not," he said kindly.

Four or five identical bottles were balanced expertly between his stubby hands.

"A very fine Barollo," he explained, rejoining us. "Among the most kick-ass of all wines, which is seldom, however, given the chance to live out its right and proper lifespan, toward the end of which it becomes as tame as a . . . as Cervina, for example. This particular one came from a place called Wine Barrens, which I don't expect you've heard of. The vines down there are all dead now, I hear. You know, this is just about the last of the stuff which, how do they say . . . which *conveyed*, yes, thank you . . . with the house here. Surely we could all do with a glass or two. That is permissible, isn't it?"

"Are you, um, talking to someone?" asked Turner.

"Am I?" Malachi looked at us, innocent-eyed, as though caught at something by surprise. "Why, yes. Aren't I? Of course."

He had become very strange.

. . . A glass or two, indeed.

Cervina came to sit with us upstairs in the Morning Room. If she was, indeed, only as tame as this wine, then I had to hand it to her, for they both had a good bit of kick left in them despite years of being cellared. By the time, a couple of hours later, just past noon, that the sun actually did make it around here, we were all feeling a good deal more chummy.

"Lovely, lovely," said Malachi. He had been discoursing on one arcane topic after another—theoretic astrology, computer-generated folklore, the cultivation of houseleeks—and now stopped to regard the sunlight as it poured over a crop of some kind of cactus growing in small pots on the sill. The sonic sculpture, which still I hadn't quite grown used to, chimed an imaginary hour. Quite fanciful, we all had become.

"Turner," said Cervina, "are you still, um, with that girl, that . . ."

He looked away.

"Ah," chirped up Malachi, "the Immaculate Harlot. The Betraying Mate who becomes the Inconsolable Widow, after you've been sucked dry. A very symbol of womankind, you've got there."

"Misogynist," muttered Cervina; though it seemed she was quite accustomed to this kind of thing.

Turner said, "What do you mean—"

"Only when the occasion arises," said Malachi. "Without innoculum, there could be no antibodies."

Cervina shook her head. "I should have kept my mouth shut. Turner, I'm sorry I asked. I hope things are going well for you, anyway."

"What do you mean," keeping at it, "after you've been sucked dry? Is that just, like, some figure of speech?"

"Ha!" Black Malachi twisted in his chair. "Just a figure. I should say it is. A fine figure. A real *plié*, one might say. Or indeed, a split! Ha!"

"Be quiet, Blackie," commanded Cervina.

Remarkably, the little pontificator clammed up. Cervina smiled at us—a bit too tactfully, I thought. I wondered if another odd role-reversal might have occurred here.

"You know," she said, "it's sort of a coincidence, you all showing up right now. Because the last couple of days, you know, there've been like these little hints, like—I don't know, these rumors or something. Only not the kind you hear. Just like, something in the air."

Turner and I exchanged a glance at "rumors," and to my surprise, Cervina and Malachi exchanged a very similar glance at "in the air." Whatever is in the air, I thought, it ain't the smell of flowers.

"Nor," said Black Malachi—as unnerving as ever, again—"is it the stench of decay. Though perhaps it has a bit of both in it, as do most things in this benighted era."

Turner rose from his seat and, weaving only for a moment, went to look out the window. A small circle, big enough to gaze through if you stood close enough—and just the right height for Cervina's eye—had been cleaned out of the otherwise all-covering smudge.

Without looking around, Turner said, "I sort of figured we'd get to this."

"This?" (Malachi, like a prompter behind the curtain-wings.)

"This . . . this, Ah my son I see a dark and terrible cloud hanging over you, kind of crap. These obscure little private allusions that don't make any sense but are basically supposed to worry the shit out of me. I knew you'd start in on it sooner or later. After all, it's your specialty."

"Yes," Black Malachi surprised us by acknowledging. "It is. And I am so dreadfully good at it."

"Yeah, well." (Turner, off-guard, not altogether steady on his feet.) "All right, fine. Let's hear it."

"Hear what?" said Malachi. His tone was quite neutral. He seemed to have completely metabolized the same quantity of alcohol, or more of it, that had wrought havoc with the rest of us.

"Hear *what?*" repeated Turner.

Cervina stepped in, speaking low and fast: "Just tell him. Or ask him. Really—ask him whatever you want. He's in the mood, I think. He may actually be able to tell you. Or be willing to. Whichever it is that he's usually not."

"Um, okay." Turner bucked himself up, took a couple of breaths, stood with his back to the window. "Okay, um. What do you mean with all this stuff about Maridel? And this 'after you've been sucked dry'?"

Black Mal sat implacably. His mouth, nearly invisible under all the facial hair, was set in a twisty little knot. We waited for several moments, for nothing.

"Well," said Cervina, "I guess that isn't it. Try something else. Really," she insisted, seeing Turner's expression, "I really think he's got something he wants to talk about."

"Big deal," said Turner. But he looked both nervous and intrigued. He glanced down, for once, in my direction, as though willing to take counsel from any quarter. On an impulse (which I suppose means the same thing as "intuitively") I thought:

—The cable-laying machine. Ask him about that.

Turner frowned, maybe trying to remember. "Ah . . ."

Before he could utter another syllable, Black Mal began to speak.

"Life is complicated," he said. "Though perhaps not quite complicated enough. Sometimes we are undone by circumstances that seem to be oversights of the divine consciousness. Little chinks in the mortar of reality, through which inimical dimensions gain entry to our world. Take for example the condom. Truly, this is a product of some diabolic, alien sensibility. Though one must admit, it does allow one to spoil the rod and spare the child.

"—But anon," he went on quickly, as Turner tightened his lips. "That was just an example that came to mind. There are analogous instances, everywhere you look. The fact of the matter is, God hasn't been doing so well, these last billion years or so. Batting around 270, I'd say. Look at the fucking dinosaurs. Didn't see that comet coming, did he? His own boomerang flying back to thump him on the noggin. It's a bunged-up world we've got here, Ashenden. And there's only One Person to blame for it."

"He's babbling," Turner complained, looking at Cervina.

"He's just warming up," she replied.

Black Mal waved his arms for silence. He got it. He flashed Turner a weird, beatific sort of grin. "So," he said, "the Braille King has got a new toy, eh?"

Turner shrugged.

"St. George," Malachi pronounced, "making amends to the serpent, restoring it to its proper place in the earth. A real *feng-shui* Antichrist. The coil is unwinding, isn't it?"

Turner did not even stir himself to shrug this time; he stared impassively and Black Malachi stared back. Perhaps, like me and Maridel, they had known each other too long.

Malachi said, "It's as well. Your little holding action has held on past its time. Look at the Souls, back to their tricks again. Look at Harvey Goldaster."

"What about him?"

"I'm surprised," said Malachi, "he hasn't dropped by to demand the last year's rent on this . . . this hovel. Haven't you heard what's going on in the East? The riots? Starvation? The dead lying in bombed-out tenements, in culverts, rusted cars, decomposing so long you can't even carry them away when you find them—nothing but porous bones and slime, have to goddamned well use a firehose to flush them into the street, more or less an open sewer anyway from the sound of things. And meanwhile Goldaster letting his harvest rot in warehouses, grain silos, leaving it on the ground, feeding his horses with it, his insufferable kids. I'll wager you, even his rats are happy."

"B-But, how do you *know?*" demanded Turner. "I mean, about how things are back East, and all. How do you know what's going on there? Not to mention Harvey's place. Or anywhere else. You never get out of this filthy house."

"So you agree. And this is a palace, virtually, compared with—"

"Oh, what a bunch of crap." Turner took a step toward the window. "This house is exactly the way you want it. It *all* is. You had a hand in everything. Don't try to dissemble your way out of it now."

"Interesting choice of words. I, Black Mal, the Great Disassembler. Here to reduce the whole to a confusion of parts. Enemy of the system. Indeed, of systems generally. *Let aberration rule*: my credo."

"At least," said Turner, "you practice what you preach."

"As does Rodarch. Think like a machine, speak like a machine, no doubt fuck like a machine—you know, with all the creaking and meshing and pumping—making the grease with two jacks—"

"*Blackie*." Cervina shot a frown at him. Once more it worked. Malachi seemed to shrink a bit, back to his normal modest proportions.

"Oh, sorry. I am off the subject, aren't I?" He poured a new glass for himself, but seemed uninclined to drink it. For a few moments he swirled the wine, tinged orange at its edges, in the sunlight. Then, in an almost frenzied impulse of motion, he threw back his head and downed it at a gulp. When he lowered the glass his face revealed a quality of openness, a dropping of barriers, discomfiting to witness. I decided that whatever else he may have been, he was truly schizoid, if not worse; more souls than one seemed to contest for that uncouth, barely full-grown body.

"Turner," Malachi said, the syllables coming from somewhere far back in his throat. "My God, old man. I am powerless to stop this thing. You must know—"

He turned away. An inexplicable grief had come over him. His squat little figure trembled from bottom to top. He went on with obvious difficulty: "You must know . . . if I could . . ."

Turner was unimpressed. "Look, Malachi," he said, "or Mal, or Mulligan's Ghost, Cad Allagash, whoever you are today. I'm tired of riddles. I'm tired of obscurantism. I didn't come to interview the fucking Delphic oracle. I just wanted to see how you are. A-And to ask you about this, this cable-laying machine. Like, to see if you've heard of it. Or anything."

"You did?" (With glistening eyes.) "Truly, old man? Well, in that case . . ." Malachi poured another glassful, this time taking a modest, though noisy, slurp. "It's nothing. The cable-laying machine. Only a symbol. International Harbinger. *Dildo ex machina*. A clockwork porridge.

Food for thought for the working class, starves the soul but sticks to the ribs. Do you see now? It's just the usual sort of thing."

"No," said Turner. "I don't see."

"Then go to the Peels," Black Malachi snapped, deflecting a gust of anger. "Go see your lost children. See the fucking thing for yourself."

We all rather froze at this; we remained there a few moments very quietly. But the only thing Black Malachi did, in the end, was take another gulp of his wine. It ran out of the sides of his mouth, into his beard, rained in large driblets from his chin. Whatever violent mood had seized him a few moments ago, he seemed determined to drown it.

"But how kind," he said suddenly; apropos of what? "—how kind of you to ask. Why, I am quite ducky, thanks. How are you?"

Scenes of Innocence and Betrayal (1)

What if they gave a party and everybody came?

Vinny cranked up the band. (He had tired of the antenna; he had even allowed Nurse Tawdry to place a small rooted strand of ivy at the base of one of its stanchions. The vine raced up the metal struts with a vengeance. It was striking: an entwinement of unlike things. By midsummer the tower was covered along its northern and western legs by tough green leaves and hairy stems and looked off-balance, as though it were about to topple.) The band played waltzes, scherzos, serenades. Missas, sarabands, villanelles. Ballads in archaic languages. A dirge or two. None of it was especially partylike, but the problem went deeper than that.

"Ah, Turner," people gushed, "congratulations!"

Thanks, um . . . on what?

"Turner!" (Picture this from a hand-held camera, Allenesque, faces pressing around you.) "Hey, how've you been, man? Great job there at Deeping Lube."

Where?

"Wow, Turner. Don't you look nice today!"

Yeah, um, what's your name again? (The daughters of the Old Souls look awfully much alike, you think. They all have that sort of . . . soapy look.)

"Turner! Up here!"

Up here, right. On top of the godless mountain. Haven't thought of that for a while, have you? Here with the Home Team. Harvey Goldaster, coach. Madame Gwendola, trainer. Maridel, official team sweetheart. Keep them happy behind the bleachers, give her half a chance. Black Malachi Pantera, team doctor—unable to make the party, though, sorry, little touch of the *mal de guerre*. Silent Tristin, water boy. And what a line-up: Dirty Dick, Nicola Quoin, the Faceless Brigade, a choir of Angels, mercenaries, bodyguards, I bet there're two hundred people here packing guns. Makes for a very festive atmosphere.

And these soap operas, playing around you. Or detergent operas: family size, industrial strength, major league mendacity, deals affecting thousands, costing millions, being made and unmade in the afternoon sunlight, hearth light, cigar light, brighter-than-white light, years worth of dirt coming out in the wash. These sleek fat cats and slinky kittens purring together over champagne, smoked fresh fish from the last uncontaminated northern stream, heart-of-palm salad, one tree killed per plateful—might as well just do it right and dine on the flesh of one's slain foes. Flip a coin for the testicles. Loser keeps the coin. Plenty where that came from. Need a light there, young man, take this twenty. Made it fair and square off a boy who needed some medicine. Offered me his sister but I couldn't risk that. Have to be prudent, this day and time. Looked like plague-sores around his mouth if you ask me. If you ask me, it's better to get the cash and get going. Here, young man, let me fire you up. That and worse, everywhere Turner turned.

Sometime nearing nightfall, as the self-satisfied rejoicing waxed around him without him and perhaps in spite of him, never the life of a party anyhow, Turner went for a stroll through the very heart and endangered soul of his domicile. He left a group of quite happy heirs and heiresses asking Vinny who Stradivarius had been, name sounds Latin doesn't it, some revolutionary guitarist? and stepped out into the main downstairs hall, which he no longer managed to think of as a foyer; it seemed these days the most characteristic space in all the house, what with bad lighting awkward architecture this endless Hofstadter staircase foolish carved dragons and not a single window looking out at what a mess the world had become.

Maridel stood, one could not but think *waiting*, at the foot of the stair. One of her palms rested lightly on the laminated sundial. Her back was toward him; but she knew. You could tell that. She knew.

Turner thought it out. Were it not for Maridel he probably would have walked through the back doors onto the terrace and watched the sun plummet one more time beyond the weeds and shale and poison of the western plain. Now, he didn't know. He might invite her out to join him. She would go, but would not cooperate; one cannot get properly lachrymose with a little tart rubbing one's crotch. He might ignore her. That would assuredly make things worse. He might stand here until hell froze over and the damned Souls made a killing selling iceskates. Well, he might. Or he might do as he usually did, as his body would have done in a moment automatically: amble over like some grazing foolish foal and wait for the dainty rider to take her crop to him.

"Hey." He inevitably said.

Maridel's hair, by the faint high light of the cupola, was one of the colors grasses turn in autumn. You couldn't quite tell which. She moved her head slowly, letting a little bit of the warmth and fragrance trapped within it, next to her neck, drift up to Turner's nostrils. (God, why was it always so chilly in here?) Then she raised her mouth. She kissed him, or rather more exactly obliged him to kiss her. Her lips were as soft as the skin of babies, of tiny precious baby girls, though it must be said in all honesty that they were rather too thin. They pressed but did not enfold one. Her tongue, on the other hand, one could not complain about. It held back shyly between her perfect rows of teeth, darting out to tangle with Turner's with a fetching fond freshness. Her breath smelled of candles in dark rooms, of girl-flesh, of fading perfume.

Did I love her?

You'd think I would have decided, years ago, or at least certainly before now. Or else you'd think I wouldn't still be wondering about it. Ah, but what would you know.

She stood quiet when the kiss was over with. Typically. Waiting for Turner to make the next move, let slip the next clue.

Turner was of course empty-headed, or really as always his head was full of extraneous things, nothing but a clutter of memory, like a house teeming with guests and no host, nothing but a certain drift to the conversation. Should I say something? His hand lay on Maridel's on the base of the ridiculous sculpture, which he figured would do as well as anything. He could not endure those silences.

"What," he began, touching upon another topic he might well have gotten settled, in his mind at least, years before. "Um, Maridel? What's this thing all about, anyway? Are these supposed to be dragons? I mean, I've always figured it was supposed to *mean* something."

She smiled that ageless, maddening smile. No, I couldn't have loved her. Could I? She said only, "I think you're right."

I am? "Th-that it's a symbol?"

"That it's silly. That's what you really think, isn't it." Not a question, this. "It's just something my father did, in one of his Renaissance Man moods."

Turner's finger nudged one of the dragons—the red one, holding back, clutching the fin of the sundial. "Your father . . ." For a moment he thought he might have dislodged it; it seemed to give a little, half a millimeter, at his touch. But when he pressed it harder the little beast hung on as though cast in stone. He said, "Does this have anything to do with all that, you know . . . your mother's ideas about reincarnation, and all?"

Maridel stared down at the sculpture, regarding it with studious intensity like an art student calling to mind the current aesthetic dogma, the window of words through which one was expected to view a work of art.

She said suddenly, sternly, "Don't you *read?*" Knowing full well, of course, that no one alive read any more than Turner Ashenden; nor indeed ought they to.

Turner drew a bit back; Maridel's hand fell upon his and held him.

"Don't you remember it?" she said—less loudly but somehow more directedly, the words cutting right through him. "Don't you remember: the vision, the prophecy? How your father asked, and the bard answered . . ."

"What? No. I mean, *my* father? No. What do you—"

But *yes*, was the weird part. In some inexplicable manner, yes, he did remember this, something about this, a pattern, a configuration, less an independent memory than an aspect of some very deep sensation, like a tiny throb of the worst headache in the world.

"No," he said.

"Yes," he said.

Maridel watched him.

"Okay," he said finally, "look. Why don't you say what you're trying to say? Why do you have to jerk me around like this? You're as bad as Malachi, all this talking in circles and allusions a-and, weird images and all."

I am telling you, her most earnest self replied, *as well as I can.*

Turner stared at her, at the silent face of a sixteen-year-old girl. Who was she, really? It's amazing, all these questions I never straight-out asked.

I am trying to help you see, the other told him. *It's you who are pulling away.*

No. Well, maybe. I don't think so, though.

"Want to go?" she said. Only a girl in the hall before him. Her eyes green and passionless. In case he hadn't gotten the point—the invitation to another session of their consumptive and somehow unearthly lovemaking—she clarified: "Want to come outside with me?"

He stared at her for a second, as though adjusting to a new language, a new mode of thought. "I think," he said, slowly, "I was about to . . ."

He tried to remember. At the penumbra of his vision he thought he saw someone he knew—or half-knew, or wanted to know—step across the balcony at the top of the stairs. A dark-haired young woman, moving from shadow to shadow without a pause. He pulled another couple of inches away, straining to find his twilight-eyes. "I don't think so," he said. "I, um, think maybe I ought to just be alone."

Maridel watched him for another moment; and you got a funny feeling, like that was all it took. She nodded slightly, then shrugged. "You're going, then, aren't you," she told him. "You just can't stand it any longer."

"Hm? No, I'm just . . . stand what?"

Damn. The figure at the top of the stairs had vanished. Turner was, as they say, torn. He felt the certain unspoken pressure of Maridel's presence, but also the kind of tug a vacuum makes, emptying you, trying ever to fill the starless Void. Of these the vacuum was stronger. Turner extended the man-in-space image so far as to rather float up the staircase, leaving Maridel, with nothing more than a parting stare in her direction. There were shadows all around him now. There are shadows even in summertime.

Maridel disdained to wave goodbye. She turned and walked straight to the front door, and for a moment Turner wanted to follow her. He wasn't going to find anything upstairs; just empty bedrooms, or worse; and the party was getting a little old.

He let her go anyway. He moved through the darkness of the second floor until he came to a zig-zagging hallway known as the Research Wing. It was a dead zone: Gwendola's late husband had spent his time here, a lifetime ago, but not much use had since been made of the place. Sounds of laughter, damped by floorboards, then re-amplified by Turner's melancholic temperament, gave the only hint of connection with a world-in-progress. Sheets draped the corpses of sideboys, bookshelves, reading lamps. Turner walked slowly up this hall and another, peering into rooms, yearning for company, smells of ordinary food, wholesome pastimes he had never had. *I was the shadow of the waxwing slain.* Somewhere, it must be dawn. Somebody is just starting out. Most people's lives are unedited experiences, the raw stuff of stories, not mythic constructs. Most people have families, not archetypal progenitors. On the other hand, most people's stories make no sense. At least for Turner, darkly, there was a pattern.

At the end of the hall, a lithe form moved from one doorway to the next. The black-haired woman returned to Turner's mind. He began walking more quickly, feeling as though a cool breeze were slipping past him. Out of the silence he heard nightsounds—birds, a flummer of voices, the sighs of clouds blowing over the mountaintop—and reckoned there must be a window open somewhere. An animal called softly in the black woods; there was no reply.

Standing by the doorway where the shadow had gone Turner watched strange lights move across that curious inner eyescape where one's dreams are played out, feeling excited and somewhat intoxicated, a little sleepy, but hyperalert also, all at once. I am not alone here, he thought. Everything inside him changed alignment, the pieces of him reconfiguring for some long-postponed and possibly dreaded encounter. He wondered what he would say to her. Then his vision cleared, and a long room with many chairs and tall windows, or mirrors, filled with moonlight, took shape. Nearly terrified, he went in.

The room was empty. The chairs were old and weakened, victims of

unnoticed decay. In the mirrors you saw only more mirrors, shadows of
the chairs, brief glimpses of yourself and yourself again, regressing, but
always from a skewed perspective. Here's how you can tell you're getting
older: you no longer give a shit how they did it in *Citizen Kane*. Turner's
steps echoed in a muffled way, like dancers' feet on a stage heavily cur-
tained. Even the sound of his breathing was nearly lost. The double doors
standing open at the far end of the room were the only place light and air
were coming from, and Turner hurried there like a claustrophobe, gasping
as he stepped out to the small west-facing balcony.

What was it about Destiny he had read somewhere? A writer who
shared his birthday; something ominous in that. . . . *no qualities at all.*
It was light enough now still to see quite well once your mind was pre-
loaded with the right expectations, but until then things were very murky.
The red afterburn of daylight had left its scorch on the horizon, and its
heat clung to the bricks and iron rails of the balcony. From one side came
a sound like a night creature stirring. Turner spun to it.

Dark hair, skin almost luminescent.

Turner said, "Noey?"

. . . too soon, and maybe by that he betrayed himself, collapsed the
broad field of chance into a bitter particularity.

The pale face turned away, darkening.

N-No, gosh, I see now. It's just Tristin.

[Yes: the fatal *just.*]

"Oh, hey," recovering artlessly, straining his eyes in the half-light,
"how're you doing? I was just . . . I mean, I guess I thought you were
somebody else."

He stepped closer. Tristin, at the edge of the balcony, near a broken
place in the railing, drew up more tightly around himself something a
sculpted figure might wear, a sort of classical sash—or no, look, actually
it's a towel. Had he just taken a shower? This was starting to feel strange.
Tristin was staring through the balusters at the drop-off of the mountainside
below, a hopscotch board of light through the French doors downstairs
falling on the terrace, the sweet clematis clinging to the edge of the world.
He made no effort to respond; which after a while itself came to seem like
an answer of some kind. A fundamental instinct in Turner—the questing
for equilibrium—made him take a further step into this, throw his own
mass in a compensatory direction.

"Hey, some party, what do you think?" He strained to see Tristin's eyes. The poor kid after all hadn't really any friends except me and Maridel, a pitiful pair to say the least. And even then it wasn't like he had anybody to *talk* to. "Well, to tell you the truth"—close enough now to reach out and touch the young man's shoulder, but not—"I was getting pretty tired of the whole thing, really. Jeez, I wonder how long those people can keep it up."

—*Not much longer.*

Tristin looked around. His eyes were too big for his head, it seemed like. They welled out of their sockets black and glossy.

—*Only a little more* (the thought seemed to press itself into Turner's mind, as on that far-off afternoon on the rose-colored carpet). *They won't last long after you're gone.*

Turner's internal gyroscope started to wobble. He realized he should get the hell off this balcony and back to the party and have a couple of nice drinks, until the equilibrium returned. The interests of sanity, at least, required this. But maintaining one's balance isn't everything. That belief was part of Turner, too. Now and then you have to choose sides.

"Tristin?" he said. "W-Were you, um . . . I mean, I feel sort of funny asking this, but . . . were you about to, like, *let go?*"

He glanced down at the twin sets of fingers clutching the broken rail; his mind ran through various equations—the angle of the slender body, the heaviness with which summer lay on everyone this year, the coefficient of loneliness, distribution of body weight . . .

Tristin's mind seemed to brush against his; or maybe "mind" wasn't the half of it, something more essential yet more inchoate, a night-thing, child of desire, fluttering bravely out onto the currents that moved between them, then falling away, falling—

"No," said the hero, sharply. As Tristin hesitated, Turner extended his hand. "You're all worked up over nothing," he said, making it up as he went along; "it's not . . . what do you mean, 'after you're gone'?"

The two of them looked at each other, Tristin perhaps remembering that Turner had asked a question like this once before.

—*Didn't you hear,* the boy wondered, *what Malachi said? The Inconsolable Widow? The Betraying Mate?*

Turner's brain made up sentences that his mouth wouldn't articulate.

(Yeah, well, what about it? Everybody knows Malachi is full of shit. What's it to you, anyway?) Meanwhile his eyes were locked on Tristin's fingers, clutching the rail, the boy's body trembling at the edge of nothing but black air. It had seemed so early; and already, almost dark.

Turner needed, personally and quite badly, to get out of this. He had no business coming here, or staying, or getting involved. He had taken stupid turns before, but always he had kept on trucking, improvising, keeping the show on the road. But the road ended here. In some way, this was the end. Before him was nothing but . . . b-but *nothing*. The frontier of the night. Tristin had known it, and now Turner knew it also. Another word, the wrong kind of motion, and the weight of dread and guilt and longing would send him down the cliff too, side-by-side plummeting with the doomed, desperate boy.

—*Turner*, said Tristin, as clearly as though the name had been spoken aloud; and just as clearly Turner knew that it was about to be too late. The balance, the illusory normalcy of life, was about to be broken through. One more word would do it.

In Tristin's mind, the word took shape.

Turner moved, as always in crisis, by ignorant instinct. His hand fell with something like anger on the boy's thin wrist. He felt the androgynous body shudder, begin to twist away. The cliff seemed to rise up; *Der Tod* in the darkness beckoned.

But our hero—for the first time in how long?—did something inarguably heroic. As Tristin stood poised between this world and the next, Turner held tightly to his forearm, drawing him slowly back to life. The evening closed its eyes on their embrace.

Scenes of Innocence and Betrayal (2)

About the other part—*the other side*—we know very little. But an outline, at least.

1. Maridel, her eyes not quite dry after a bout of objectless tears, appears at the door of the Solar Temple.

2. Cervina admits her, escorts her to Black Malachi's tumultuous bedchamber, leaves the two of them alone.

3. Malachi sits at the edge of a dirty bed wearing nothing but his pierced-heart boxer shorts. The painted blood nearly covers them. He and Maridel watch each other a while, their wills wordlessly contesting. At the end of this, some silent treaty achieved, Maridel crosses the room and removes her only garment. Black Malachi rises to embrace her.

4. "No," she tells him. "Make it as sordid as possible. It's not enough of a betrayal otherwise."

5. Black Malachi, accepting this, proceeds quite deliberately not to make love with but simply to fuck her, repeatedly, at leisure, in the most demeaning of postures.

6. Sated, after a fashion, she leaves him well past the unforgiving dawn.

2

Upon there being days without wind

There were about a month of these. Maybe more. The air seemed to have come down from the sky. Now it filled all the spaces between every thing and every other thing.

The nature of breathing changed. Effort was required to empty the lungs. Perhaps if we had just stopped, we would have kept filling up until nothing remained outside us. Over the weeks, our relationship with summer grew strained.

Evenings, Turner got up and started toward the French doors in the west as though meaning to step out onto the terrace. He never did, though.

Upon the tendency to dissociate and regroup

Tristin and Turner and Vinny Hawkmoth and Nurse Tawdry and the students of the Bad Winters Institute, except one, slept in separate bedrooms. The other student, an athletic 15-year-old boy, slept in a room in the Research Wing with Maridel. Madame Gwendola, who lately had become quite remarkably silent, suffered the insomnia of the very aged and spent most of her nights in the downstairs sitting room taking some comfort in the music of other cultures than her own, virile drummings and chants and polyphonies, which she adopted and tried to love as a spinster or a lonely elderly historian may come to love a nephew or some other small child, for a time, or even a pet, though the intellect still reminds one of that awful gut-emptying truth, that one stands at the end of a line.

In Wine Barrens, Nicola Quoin and the regional administrator placed their initials carefully in the lower corners of each page of a memorandum of agreement, thus marking a new phase of their decade-old Accommodation. Henceforth, the supply wagons that returned to the coastal cities empty of wine would be loaded instead with modest but profitable quantities of another family crop, *Salvia divinorum*, sage-of-the-seers.

In Candlemas, the students and some professors at the University circulated leaflets critical of the Board of Regents, whose members the leaflets accused of being "in bed with the Old Souls." There were arrests, but no trials.

Upon the sterility of beauty, the vigor of repetition

According to the newspapers used as packing material in the crates of food delivered erratically to the Settling Out Camps, the most popular book that summer in the eastern cities was a novel called *Fallen Silver*. This book evidently was a further installment in a series of other books featuring common characters and suspenseful plots which arrived at satisfying conclusions. The author of them, on at least one occasion, had declined an invitation to speak at the University, citing the dangers of travel.

Vinny Hawkmoth surprised everyone by announcing that he had been quietly working for months on the Stradivarius emulator and was ready to give a demonstration performance. The program—attended by the shrinking inner circle of the Institute, plus Harvey Goldaster, who had come to dine—consisted mostly of traditional works, but included also Suleiman's *Warped Canon* and Rochberg's *Third String Quartet*. During much of the slow middle movement of the latter, Harvey sat with his head lowered and appeared to doze.

"You will never hear," Partner Trefoil said afterward, "that sound, exactly, again"—the property of slow inevitable aging having been made, as it developed, part of the software, since "otherwise we wouldn't have gotten the Strad idea exactly right."

Of course. As was once said of static, the decay is part of the performance.

Chief Administrator Rodarch, having picked his way through the lesser territories to the north, rounded the tip of a mountain chain and turned to face the valley. An enormous army of pilgrims and would-be squatters marched behind the coal-black telephone-cable-laying machine that had become his latest portable and practical symbol. The Chief Administrator was hopeful but grim. As much as anyone else, now, he believed that Turner Ashenden was the creature of some greater Destiny than his (rectangular, red-tape-tied) own. But this did not excuse the Chief Administrator from running again and again down life's checklist, until that last ineluctable item should be scratched through. He paused just north of the Peels for a brief, and characteristically colorless, address. The text of his remarks is lost, as far as I know. In a way, it doesn't matter.

Upon waking at night

having dreamt of forgotten things
of dry flowers
you lay there breathing shallow

lightly sweating, and
for one silvered moment
the astral edges of your fingers
strayed a last a lone a long
time

—and evermore you will remember up to that
and yet not touch it again,
pausing by that bed
as at some river's edge no longer fordable: wondering if
in the soft foldments of time
we spent
that final night
together.

Upon the habits of Nature

Except that they exist, we can only guess at the reason or need for them. They are like stories that She tells and tells again, comforting tales and terrifying, memory-prompting, admonitory, reeled off in her ancient awesome stuttering voice never quite the same, the themes getting often crossed and character traits transposed, symbols changing from one false skin to another, dragons and fair maids, knights and thieves and scryers, the Trickster, the Hanged Man, the Wandering Sailor. One suspects that Nature herself must change, along with the stories; as all tale-spinners do, lugging their harps and ballads up that road across the mountains, through the dark and the silence, into the north. Certain new connections are made and others severed. Perhaps the contingencies of Time are always surprises. Still the patterns are repeated, the customs observed, as the ancient threads are rewoven. Thanks to History, we know that. We take our comfort in habit, in repetition, even as we plunge as from the waterfall so very quickly and only once into that dark pool below.

Upon Turner's letting go

It was like sometimes, some days, you could hardly stand it. Waiting for the air to move, the weather to break. Sitting around the house while messengers came and went, making smaller and smaller decisions. Reading books—exhausting books, exhilarating books, not the crap they write anymore. Listening to Vinny's music.

Plus, it had gotten so goddamned awkward, anyway, what with Maridel.

A-and Tristin.

What about Enlightenment, though? What is that? That's still a little bit of a problem, there—the unchanging incommensurable et cetera. Seeing as how it looks quite clearly like the change or evolution of things is pretty thoroughgoing. It's like, you grow, you recapitulate every trip that's ever come down, and then you sort of bleed and die like old Van did, merging into his Ada, disintegrating into his constituent metaphors, though at least right up till the end he kept his shit together. You could maybe at any rate strive for that.

I think that is what I will strive for. It is after all a very imperfect world; see, there's one thing I haven't changed my mind about. There's *some* conceptual continuity. Maybe there's more I'm not thinking of right now. I'm tired, anyway.

Upon letting go of Turner

It was summer, yet. The sunrise spread in a disheartened bright haze like yellow gorse at the horizon, where the fields of dry hard dirt and toughened forbs—beardtongue, blazing star, rattlesnake master—reach even now beyond this house and beyond this view out to another one, the next one, where the road runs like a blunt weapon, through the heart.

3

Out here

There was a certain magnificence about the rutted fields and the fruitless hardpan underneath their wagons. Clouds were caught high in the gray sky like kites escaping; Turner alone seemed to notice them, frequently glancing up although it could have gone ahead and rained for all he cared. The rest of the crowd had its baby blues on the number one attraction.

Due to the likelihood of untoward weather, you had to suppose, they had gone ahead and set the Savior's pulpit up in the only sheltered spot anywhere near the scorched-out remnants of the compound. It was an aged princess tree that lately had shot out an amazing bunch of new branches. The heart-shaped olive-drab leaves flapped like fans in church. And lordy was it hot enough. Turner wore a T-shirt artfully faded, everything about him being artful in some measure these days; our boy was your basic full-length mirror held up to Nature, complete with toothless hag's head grinning back. Sheeit. If he'd ever been much into spitting, he would have done so now in the dirt.

He felt like a spy. Whereas in point of fact he was something more like an expatriate on the lam, an abdicating monarch. Even now, even now, wheels were ripping up the twin ribbons of the highway, cartridges clacking into guns, battle orders being rehearsed, the air beating at windguards like a wrath of avenging angels. There could only be a couple hours more.

At the podium, an overblown analog of Chief Administrator Rodarch outlined certain abstruse provisions of the law. Everything will be taken into account. Every ledger will be balanced. Certain small but necessary adjustments will be made in the coming fiscal quarter. Individual needs and rights will be respected of course but must be measured against the greater good et nauseum. . . . Or I don't know, maybe he was singing "The Green Fields of France." To tell you the truth, I wasn't paying much attention.

Turner's mind was focused for the most part on the setting or mood or how shall we say, the *mise-en-scene* of this morning's performance. Like a rival magician, he was looking for trap-doors, secret strings, the clockwork of the illusion. It was a pretty slick operation. As near as he could tell, the Man of the People was nowhere near the stage there, nor in the cab of the big machine behind it, nor hiding like your more brazen type of elephant in the middle of the herd. Turner didn't know what made him think this, but he got the distinct idea that this Rodarch persona wowing the crowd was being *piped in*, you know? Which was quite a trick, given what little anybody knew about those Identity boxes. It kind of made you wonder. But the first problem, really, was to trace the thing back to its root, tap the bloody source. But time was disappearing and Turner worried that he might be wasting it, out here.

Out here. At the thought, conjured out of the corner of his eye, a dark-haired figure flitted in and out of the crowd. For real, this time? Well, what difference did it make, though, figured Turner. The gradients had blurred to the point that you could keep philosophers employed beating the bounds between them, between *the other side* and this one . . . or had we already crossed? Never mind. Turner shoved off in hot pursuit of his vision. Anyway, there was nothing here worth hanging on for.

A few security types, card-carrying assholes in Turner's book, gave him the cursory law-and-order eyeball, the same look you've seen on the faces of prudes and petty scientists the world over. If anything, Turner was *too* off-the-charts to hold their attention. Had he represented some trifling deviation from the norm—a Resister, say, driven to violence by his beliefs—they would have sniffed him out in a heartbeat. But Turner was not a believer. He may have been an object of belief—or of disbelief, or of hatred. At this stage of his evolution, he was barely a discrete personality at all. The former Unhappy Student, Headless Housemate, Fugitive, Doppelgänger, Defender and *Dux Bellorum* had curled back upon himself, assumed a kind of closed-spatiality: keep walking around him, looking from all the angles, and you might discern the edges of the thing-in-itself—like the naked limbs of a sweaty young Scorpion, remember that? half seen through a shell of laserlight. But look at him straight-on and all you saw was a cutout, a gallery-piece. If there had ever been a "real" Turner Ashenden, an organismic entity with fixed, identifying traits, that character now seemed as improbable and as arbitrary as the idea of a "real world." You might still hope, as Madame Gwendola did, to discover that what there is, out here, is this One Thing—that *this* is what it comes to, *this* is what it meant all along; but meanwhile the rest of us cynics will content ourselves with shrugging it off as being just the way things turned out. That's all, folks. Shit happens. Turner is who he has become. He is an end-product of his experience, a collection of things of which he himself has been the collector. Stick *that* in your copy of the Holy G.E.B.

[Sure. And Albertine's nice round cheeks never grazed the upholstery of Marcel's motorcar.]

Behind the stage stood an oil-black monstrosity that Turner figured must be the famous cable-laying machine. It smelled of violated earth. There was hardly any earth left to violate, sure, but that was what Turner registered. Synesthesia, maybe. Heat from the engine block held you at bay. The limbs of the princess tree drooped low near your shoulders, and once again you had the odd notion that the many people present had their attention directed somehow around you, failing to sense your presence though you stood like an idiot in plain sight.

Then from nowhere **pop!** like an editorial afterthought, or one of those deeply embedded things you only notice the second time through, a dark-haired young woman laid her hand on Turner's arm. The house of cards collapsed, THE HIGH PRIESTESS landed on top, a nice Jewish girl if you want to know, and Turner jumped *into* his skin from wherever he had drifted off to.

"Noey," he said.

Thematically, theatrically, the dark-haired woman let go.

"I th-*thought* I saw you," he said. "I mean, just now, a-and a couple of months ago. Down at the Institute. At a party."

Such explanations were pointless. Noey shook her head. For just an instant, in midshake, she seemed to flicker at the edge of existence.

Whoa, thought Turner. Hang on, now.

The field stabilized. Noey looked hard at him. She said, "Have you come to help us?"

He didn't know. It sounded iffy; it sounded like some kind of trick question. Can a man marry his assassin's sister? Before his awareness got dissociated any worse, he nodded his head.

"Got a car?" he managed to ask.

Noey shrugged. Eternal female ambivalence. She said quietly, "I can take you there."

Turner looked around them. The intentions of the scriptwriter were no clearer than usual; there was no clue as to how to play this. Sunlight glanced for a moment off the lictor's blade. The "real world" had fallen pretty far behind Turner now.

"Sure," he said. Quoting Ashenden. "Why not?"

The crowd let its breath out.

"There is hope, then," said the ghost of the Chief Administrator. "There is hope of a new beginning, even now, even this late in the game."

The speech must be wrapping up, thought Turner. Noey motioned with her head—*out here*—and took the first step toward the field herself, to show him. Turner looked beyond her. He saw the princess tree holding its arms out. The crooks in its limbs looked like elbows. Its posture needed some work. Was this anthropomorphizing? Or was the tree doing a pretty good Turner-impression?

"Come on," said Noey.

Oh, right. Drifting again. We took a step after her, another, through the tall meadow grasses, funny the crowd hadn't flattened them. Noey seemed to grow happier; her step lightened. Turner had to hurry to keep up. He only overtook her once, when she paused to pry something from the dirt, something pinched between stubborn roots where it had sunk over the years, over the decades. She had to work at it. Turner, compelled, stared across her shoulder at the object reluctantly coming unburied: a rock, a black rock or a piece of broken glass of some sort, a crystal. It drank the sunlight, insatiable, more give me more. Turner blinked at it; he wondered if it was drinking him too, recording all emanations.

I'm melting, he thought. Dissolving into sentences.

Noey looked sympathetic. "You need help," she said, "as much as we do."

—H-Help?

She held the black rock out to him. Turner raised a hand, instinctively. A receptor. Before he could stop himself, before he had time to think, he was touching it: the *lapis exilit*, the stone from on high. For seconds afterward, the crowd blinked its baby blues at the light that came like a fireball consuming the princess tree.

Übermensch, flicking dimly upon the screen

The helpless gazelles in the mural were pale umber *pentimenti*, exposed by the continued fading of the savannah grass. Each blade of grass was a single vermilion brush-stroke, aged and translucent now as church windows. Turner admired the collaboration of technique and time. He glanced around the nursery with a sigh. Should Art make us remember, or make us forget? There were toys made out of plastic (look—they still have plastic here!) lying on the floor of the nursery, and music playing somewhere in the background. Turner grew cautious. In life there is nearness and distance, but only Art has a "background."

The young woman Noey made a kind of noise beside him. It was an almost silent stirring, a movement of waves. Turner closed his eyes and thought about her, about what he was doing here. It seemed to him that someone must have appointed him to make this journey into the dark north, that of the many possible candidates the others had been one by one disqualified until he alone was left in the running. Should this have struck him as unfair?

"We have always believed in you," said Noey.

There, now. That was pretty odd, wasn't it? When Turner no longer knew what to believe about himself.

"Um, the kids," he ventured. "They're, ah . . . are they any better?"

Noey gave him an interested look, the look a bright student gives an instructor who has just posed one of those thought-provoking questions. What is the origin of archetypes? Where does the idea of the Hero come from? Were our ancestors inspired by prototypic patterns of heroism, or did we create the Hero ourselves, in a sort of Platonic vacuum-mold?

"The kids?" said Noey. She seemed to strain, endeavoring to be correct. "The children are . . ."

Turner waited. The children are . . . ? He studied Noey's face, an amberish or maybe khaki-colored face, a face that would never be lost in a crowd. As he watched her he had a niggle of intuition. It dissipated fast; by the time the thought-bubble had made its way upward through the viscous goo of Turner's mind, it was gone.

"The kids are d-dead?" he said. Popping the bubble.

Noey made a motion with her head, a compromise between shaking and nodding it. "They couldn't come this far"—playing up the ambivalence for all it was worth. Her expression changed, her stance, vibes, something. She glanced over her shoulder. "It puts a strain on people," she said, "keeping up with you. There's this way you have. You press things to their limit. You bring out the worst in everybody. And the best. The final things. Whatever they are."

Turner tried to take a step back—away from the canvas, dramatically speaking. Is this a real conversation? It sounds more like, you know, dialog. I mean, does anyone really talk like this? Or only characters, *dramatis personae?*

"What it is, Turner," Noey was saying, "is that you had a certain dharmic duty to perform, and you've done that. You crystallized the Resistance; you posed an argument to which the government, the New Reason, Rodarch, all of that, is the antithesis. A dialectic was necessary. But in the nature of such things, it has to end somewhere." She gestured around the nursery: pint-sized furniture, a swing-set, a small video box across which old Superman cartoons swirled. Noey's manner became gentle, big-sisterly. "We're glad you came back, though," she said. "Really. But maybe it's just too late. Too late in the story."

"Hm?" Turner had gotten distracted. "You know, that guy looks awfully familiar. Or I mean, that . . . um, look, Noey? I know you're trying to say something important here. But to tell you the truth, I didn't really come to *learn* anything, so much. It's more like, you know, I just needed to *be* here. Again. To be sure."

Noey motioned around the nursery. "Here?"

"Well, you know. To flip ahead to the end," said Turner. "Which this is, right? I mean I figure this is where we're all heading, eventually. Only you guys got here first. So I wanted to see, like, how it's all going to come out."

"Well," said Noey. Her tigress eyes grew narrow.

From the dusty surface of a bureau she lifted a small porcelain cup, finely made and decorated, in which glowed something faintly odorous, maybe wine. She held it out to Turner. *Want some?* the gesture said.

"Ah, no, I—" But Turner thought the young woman's hand looked unsteady, there, as though she might drop the delicate cup. Without thinking much, he stuck a hand out—reflexive prophylaxis—and met the cup, the trembling fingers. A rusty smell grew unmistakable in his nostrils.

What the fuck, he had time to think.

Son of the End of the World

The "theme park" spread out gloomily, as usual, for miles. Beside Turner and Noey stood a totem pole covered with words and symbols, red-on-white. One of the signs said FIRST AID. Another said PARKING. These were accompanied by a Swedish cross and a graphic silhouette that reminded Turner, painfully, of his old spirit-burner. Arrows pointed the way.

But was this the same End of the World he had visited before? Or had this particular "theme" been so popular that innumerable fiberglass monuments, alike except in small geographic or cultural particulars, had been erected in its honor? A sequel, quoth the prophet, is worth sixty percent of the original. Turner gave a little sniff, as though an answer (not necessarily The Answer) might be drifting on the scant wind. He smelled only sun-baked pavement and dust; nothing poetic; no nerve-gas residues or stench of corpses—though he would have bet those had been supplied, via olfactive analog, in the heyday of this place.

No clues, then. No rotten smells, no poetry. How ironic, Turner reflected, I have become.

"Okay." He turned to Noey. "So. What now?"

She made again that movement of her head. Perspiration becomingly dampened her brow, her cheeks, her shoulders. Turner didn't have time for that. At the End of the World, you're down to the final things. Whatever they are. He thought about Maridel. There was something of her—the self-possession, the utter neutrality—in this young woman's eyes.

Noey touched his hand. Primed by his line of thought, his memories, he let their fingers entwine.

A rumble, like distant thunder, came from a direction that was not clear: one horizon or another, or perhaps the fiberglass plain beneath their feet. The sound grew louder. Their two hands were damp with sweat. Turner looked around for . . . what? Confirmation? Shelter? A swoop of Angels? A porcelain cup? He found only the *faux* holocaust, cheap family-oriented entertainment with an overtold story-line.

He listened carefully to the rumbling, the faint susurration of Noey's breath, his own stressed heartbeat. These noises ran like words through his brain—streaming, forming patterns, assembling themselves into stanzas and paragraphs and chapters. They offered explanations; they connected things. But they went murmuring by too quickly. Turner caught only isolated phrases. *To have come so far. We have done. With only a sword. Here at last. Ten thousand gray wings. Of the plain. For a long time. Make my stand here.*

He didn't like the sound of things. It occurred to him that he had not eaten since beginning this particular leg of the long, long journey—which would have been sometime yesterday, he thought. On top of the godless mountain. While everyone slept but Tristin: Tristin the watchful, the tormented, the insomniac. Cold beer and crackers; cakes and ale. It was only a thought, an allusion, like all the others, part of the web of connections upon which Turner Ashenden was inescapably strung.

Noey let go of his hand, and amazingly now she was holding a tray out before him. It was silver, shiny, heavy-looking. It bore a scatter of little sandwichy things, teatime shots of carbohydrates barely sufficient to get one the rest of the way to dinner. Noey waited placidly staring downward at the food, though clearly it was a job to hold the tray up, one-handed like that. It shook. But maybe that was the rumble, which continued to grow louder from everywhere.

Turner decided to try it. Saying "Thanks," at least, as though all this were no big deal. He lifted a single tiny sandwich—something thin and pink laminated with white bread—and raised it cautiously to his mouth. *The body of our Lord,* he imagined Malachi intoning; followed by a belch, if one could be mustered. He gave it a nibble. Then, seeing that the whole thing was really no more than a bite's worth, he mangled it up in his mouth. It tasted like, um, salt water taffy. Something bland like that. The plain vanilla flesh of the Savior.

The tray was gone from Noey's hands. Turner didn't give it a second thought; he didn't even glance around her, looking for trap-doors or hatches tucked into the fiberglass. Nah. Just another independent miracle. We got a million of 'em. If Turner had any balls, he'd ask for a gin-and-tonic. Just to see.

Don't press it, Noey's expression warned him.

Now about that rumbling . . .

Somewhere, across the flat artificial landscape, a shadow peeked Kilroy-style over the horizon. This could all be part of the packaged and demographically fine-tuned "theme"—that rumble, the vibration underfoot, and now the pop-up silhouette of doom. The noise grew louder: rhythmic, an arterial throb, as though thousands of feet were marching this way. Piece of cake, if your speakers are large enough. Anything is possible at the end of the line. All Turner could think about, really, was that the little sandwich had made him godawfully thirsty.

"Aren't you going to hide?" said Noey. "Or anything?"

Hide? Turner looked around, and there (of course) was the big tent. The cast panels of its surface seemed to ripple in an imaginary wind—a big blow at least twenty knots more serious than this faint summery exhalation. No way, he thought. What do you think, I was born yesterday?

But then, that was the point of this, probably, right? I mean, being born and all. Because from the viewpoint of the End of the World here, maybe I *was* born yesterday. Or maybe I'm pushing up plastic daisies.

Preserve thy body and soul, Malachi's memory advised him.

In the tent, everything was hushed and dim, with a chill that made you shiver.

This is the saddest story, thought Turner, recalling something—*The Good Soldier*—I have ever heard.

The tent had been transformed into a field hospital. Rows of cots were arranged by the hundreds in concentric rings; but that was the only discernible ordering. There had been no time for *triage*, grouping by severity; the dying commingled with the mildly feverish, shock-stricken amputees with wasted visitants of the Plague. The place stank of another era's palliatives, antiseptics, excrement. Here and there the requirements of body or soul were being expeditiously ministered to by wrung-out nurses, a surgeon or two, a bloody-handed priest. There was remarkably little human sound from anywhere, as though victims and survivors alike were governed by a supernal sense of decorum. Only Noey, clutching Turner's hand again, could be heard very privately, for just a few moments, to sob.

The oldest war, thought Turner. Malachi, this is beyond even you.

From within, the youthful and ever-sardonic voice came back: *For everlasting life.*

Yeah, right. Turner tugged on Noey's hand, pulling the young woman around to face him. He said, "Do we have to keep on with this? Is this like the Ghost of Battles Yet to Come or something? I mean, all right—I get the picture. It's horrible. I'll stop it if I can. Just tell me what you want me to do."

Noey was very pale. She twisted slightly in Turner's grasp, making a very poor effort to pull away. Turner saw that she was carrying a bottle filled with blood—a real bottle, open at the top, not one of those hermetic plastic bladders. He felt a squeamish urge to draw away. As he fought this down, he realized that the bottle was being fed by a catheter twisting up to Noey's elbow and worming into the major artery in her arm. Her blood ran down in systaltic gushes, a remorseless cataract that overfilled the bottle and spattered audibly on the dirty floor. Turner stood before her, stupid and stunned.

With a final access of vitality, Noey stepped back from him. She yanked the tube from her arm, splashing bright red liquid around her. Drops fell on Turner's leg, his outstretched arm, his reaching fingers. He stepped forward, grabbed Noey by the shoulders and tried to steady her, to keep her upright, even as the strength of life seemed to pass away from her. Her skin had blanched to a greenish white. One hand still held the bottle, the receptacle of her own lost essence. With a feeble and barely controlled gesture, like a child dying, she held the bottle up, offered it to Turner. He shook his head. Her grip slackened; the bottle tipped. In an unthinking motion—the same reflex that had made him catch the porcelain cup—Turner extended a hand, felt the warm slippery vessel lodge in his grasp, and heard Noey murmur:

"There, Turner. It's yours now."

Black Malachi's eerie, almost corporeal voice intoned, *And be thankful.*

Then Noey, with no other sound, not even a last breath, lay still and empty at the bottom of the tent.

Turner ran. He hurled himself through the double flaps with the bottle in his hand. He could not put it down; he could not continue to hold it. It was at once holy and untouchable. In some grotesque way he felt he had been tricked, the whole thing had been a set-up, the young woman had conspired with persons or forces or elements unknown; she had done this horrible thing *to him*. Such thinking must be the climactic form of megalomania. A breath of cool air, heavy with dampness, entered his lungs, and Turner came to a halt.

A change had come over the landscape outside the tent, the wasted field, the entire End of the World. Gray mist filled the hollows of the plain as though it had been stuffed everywhere like cotton. The tent was nowhere to be seen, lost in the fog. The rumbling had stopped and the dark shadow was gone from the horizon. Turner figured the rumble must have been the sound of this great change approaching, this metamorphosis, and the concentrated blackness at the edge of the world must have spread outward while he was in the tent to darken everything it touched, by only an increment or two. He took another step, and the ground underfoot responded to the movement, resisted it. There was a soughing noise. The fiberglass was transformed into dirt, into mud, its bleached surface as brown as a sewer-rat.

For an uncertain time Turner stared through the gauze of fog. The sun that had been in the sky, where now only low clouds bunched together, had come down to shine from the petals of cowslips, the bracts of dogwood, the watershot leaves of silver nettle. The world was alive again. All the dark gods had reawakened. The blood-red serpent reared up from the ground for a final stand-off against his eternal enemy, the white dragon of the sky. Long after you thought you had him pinned, the old bastard was still hanging on.

Yeah, well. Turner wasn't placing any bets on that one.

Still, he thought, as the living air moved deep in his lungs, it's nice to see dogwoods again. It's nice to smell rain, to get your feet wet. *It's, almost like being, a-*

He stopped, or stopped himself. He was holding the bottle of Noey's blood. It was strange how, even for moments at a time, you could forget something like that. It was as though that constant tension of consciousness—the struggle to remember, to keep things in mind, to retain your perspective on things—was a struggle you *needed* to lose, if you were to muddle from one instant to the next. Because to win it, to ever once really understand what the Christ was going on, would surely fry your brain in a heartbeat.

Meanwhile there was this blood. He could yet not bring himself to get rid of it; he formed a vague alternative idea, the notion of holding some kind of ceremony, laying this last part of Noey to rest. God, he hadn't really even known her. But that wasn't right, either. What he hadn't ever known was not so much who but *what* she was, this dead girl who had led him through the northern darkness. *Y Gododdin.* Was that answer enough? He felt tears gathering behind his eyes, and wondered how quickly blood coagulated. Scarcely believing that he was doing so, he peered down into the blackening depths of the bottle and gave its contents a little swirl.

Malachi could have warned him about this.

A moan rose up, as though conjured out of that awful vessel. It was a deep voice, agonized, that seemed to gain strength from its own mournful sound and grow louder and louder. All Turner could think of, being who he was, was the song of the dead father in *Ugetsu.* We mix myths with abandon at the End of the World. Turner was terrified. He drew the bottle inward, held it protectively.

I am utterly lost now.

Things became clearer, bit by bit. A breeze was tugging at the fog, and through the changing views of the landscape, like someone staring out the windows of a moving train, Turner deduced that he was standing at the foot of a little hummock, and that the moaning voice, which seemed to come from everywhere at once, was really just being deflected by that mound of earth, and was being made by someone—probably someone lying ill, or wounded—on the other side of it. This did not solve the problem but at least more sharply defined it. He took a step up the sloping ground, resisting for all he was worth the notion that the hummock had shifted slightly beneath his weight. *The world was alive* was only a metaphor, you know. Who's afraid of the big bad earth?

His perspective improved as he got higher—something else Malachi could have told him. The plain stretched out on all sides. The hummock rose from a patch of fallow land, an overgrown meadow, but everywhere around it lay fields of a different, more disciplined sort. Grain plants stood by the million in rows and columns like a great fatalistic army, indifferent to the absence of the sun, resigned to the inevitable harvest. Only where Turner stood did there survive the pleasant chaos of cowslips and silver nettle, oxeye daisies in bud, seedling oaks, poison ivy, native plants and exotics, defenders and invaders and the bastard hybrids of both, and on the opposite slope of the hummock, rising above all, its fan-shaped leaves as yet no larger than a child's open hands, a lusty spreading princess tree. Turner paused to admire the thing; no better than a weed as far as serious-minded arborists were concerned, but what a welcome sight to a fellow hybrid like Turner Ashenden!

He proceeded quickly down the hill, for the situation now was pretty clear. A figure sat half upright at the base of the tree, supported by the corky trunk. Straightaway the moaning stopped, as the figure caught sight of him. It was a man, we could tell, as we drew nearer, and a big one at that. He looked familiar. But Turner was a forgetter of things now, and happily so. His mind was emptying. The vast jumbled container of faces and names and unoriginal thoughts was bleeding itself dry, its once sterile contents bursting into fervid bloom where they touched again their source, the primal sod. Innocence regained; effects dissolving into their causes. God, this is great.

The big hunched-over man watched him from the bottom of the princess tree. His eyes were gray and burnished-looking, though the flesh around them was almost colorless, the features flat and static. Some vital essence or attribute seemed to be missing from him. I mean, this guy just wasn't *real*.

Turner, still a couple of paces off, called down to him, "Is anything the matter? Have you been hurt somehow? Can I help?"

The man looked at Turner with a momentary intensity, as though some hint of feeling or irony was about to present itself behind the aluminum-alloy eyes. This lasted only an instant, and then the flat, cartoonish quality of the man reasserted itself.

Turner thought, It's like déjà vu all over again. Or no, it's even better than that. It's like *you don't have to remember unless you really want to*. And one way or the other, this is the last time around; the final ride at the theme park. The End of the World. So like, meanings and implications and consequences and all are just so much crap you don't have to worry about. When it gets dark *this* time, we'll just hop in the car and get a jump on the weekend traffic. Heading home.

On the ground underneath the princess tree, the flat-faced man said, "So, Mr Ashenden. Once again you have an interesting choice to make."

Turner frowned. His own last name sounded funny, as though it meant something he hadn't thought about before, offered some clue; but that was exactly the sort of stuff he wasn't going to think about anymore.

He said, "I've already been through that. I didn't help you the first time around—or the last time, or whatever time it was. I mean, as if I could have." He looked around a bit, appraising the situation. "This is probably all a fake, anyway, right? I mean, I'm pretty sure this is some kind of hallucination I'm having."

A look of grievous pain came over the big man's face. His cheeks flushed with a hint of lifelike coloring, as though the unseen artist were determined to make a stab at verissimilitude. The hard lips and graven nose, the whole Roman-coin look, grew slightly more animated; but they remained stuck on that singular expression like a jammed play-back mechanism: *pain pain endless agony and pain*. Turner couldn't take it.

"Oh, what the fuck," he said, dragging a foot around, reluctant-schoolboy style. "What do you want, really? I hate to see you just . . . you know, *lying* here like this."

Never mind that the bastard was propped against the tree, actually, and probably just playing out his role. When you're a foreordained decent and self-effacing sort of fellow, certain things are simply expected of you. *Noblesse oblige*.

The man made a Saturday morning TV display of mustering his

strength. He sat more upright. "What do I . . ." oh it was such a struggle, "What do I want? What do I *really want?*"

Naturally this took a lot out of him, this little performance, and left Turner standing there feeling ever more awkward and shuffling a god-damned *trench* in the soft ground. And naturally Turner spoke again, just to fill the awful silence.

"I mean, look," figuring it out on the fly, "you could have just stayed put, right? You could have stayed back in the East where people *want* you, where they believe in all this Order and Reason bullshit. There was no sense trudging out here holding the lantern of truth and bringing light unto, like, the least of His fucking creatures. See, the thing about us least creatures is that we don't *need* it, we don't like to hear sermons, we were having a pretty good time with the light turned off. Why fix it if it ain't broke? Why pick a fight just for the sake of . . . of being *correct* or something? I mean it's not like there's going to be a fucking test. It's not like there's going to be this big Room Inspection someday and you're going to get gigged if there are any little corners where you haven't tidied things up. Why couldn't you just *leave* it?"

The big man, now sitting up and looking quite well adjusted to the idea of ultimate martyrdom, gave an appropriate lengthy and infinitely saddened sigh. Turner was disgusted. He turned sideways, keeping an eye on the guy but basically looking out across the field, westward, hoping to catch a last glimpse of the great hot ass-kicker before it set on all this. The rows of grain swayed dutifully. We all have our position in the scheme of things. Even though it is a highly imperfect world.

"I am afraid, Mr Ashenden, that you will have to answer all those questions for yourself."

Turner looked down in mild surprise. The big man, his impressive though presently rather dumped-on-looking adversary, stared up at him through those dull chromium eyes.

"It was you who chose the fight," the man went on. "I would not have attacked you with force. I have never depended on numbers alone. I have never overwhelmed you."

"That's true." Turner shrugged. "You've just always been more . . . organized. You're always wrapped up in like, this one big Idea. But it's all so bogus. You can't eat an Idea. You can't smoke it. All you can do is turn it into slogans and march around—"

"My Ideas have always triumphed."

"Shit. They've always been so stupid, that's why. They've been simple-minded enough that people can understand them, they can talk about them in *words*. You're like, Lord of the Left Brain. King of the Calculators. If it doesn't compute, you start smoking."

"I am able to govern, Mr Ashenden. What are *you* able to do? Paint pictures? Write poems?"

Ha, thought Turner sadly. Hardly even that. Unless you get points for listening to music. Or how about daydreaming? How about *feeling* things? How about making love?

The Stainless Steel Savior lowered his head. Argument seemed to have further weakened him. So much for the dialectic, Turner thought. Overhead, a late afternoon breeze played in the upper limbs of the princess tree. The world around was darkening like the oxydizing oils in a Rembrandt, turning a wonderfully moody, end-of-century gray.

Der Tod, Turner thought. Remembrance moved like electricity up his spine. *Der Tod und das Mädchen.*

This must have been the place where everything happened from, the formative world, *Yetsira*—because as soon as Turner's emptying mind turned up that particular title, the air all around them was filled with music of the most delicate, plangent, heartbreaking sweetness. The innermost resonances of the strings, the old wood, the intricate sounding-cavities all were present and all clearly audible in a perfect, inimitable synthesis. Vinny would *never* get this right, Turner once and for all decided. For in the end—and this was the End, if ever there was one—this experience and all experiences are not reducible to "information," however broadly or portentously that is defined.

He stood listening to Schubert's perfect melody, the magnificent rolling-out of chords, for most of the slow second movement. Beyond a certain point the music itself, for all its sublimity, could not quite compete with the clamoring certainty that this was the *last time* he would ever hear it; that indeed every moment of life was a final thing, an induplicable experience; that *der Tod* lurked within each note of every melody, for not one would ever be heard in just the same way, ever again. There was no return, only imperfect repetition. Eventually even that would cease, the playback mechanism fail, the music never be heard again except in the most abstract imaginable way, as an Idea in some hypothetic consciousness, and if you choose you need not believe even in that. Only in *der Tod* himself. Who always, every moment, is merrily defiling *das Mädchen*.

Turner looked down at his ancient adversary. The big man with the soul of a machine looked up at him. Well, what did it matter? Turner bent down a little, spoke more familiarly.

"Want me to help get you something? I mean, if there's like anything I can do . . ."

"Old friend," Rodarch told him, "it is in your hands."

Distaff

Did I mention that Turner Ashenden's mother was an obsessive reader, a woman who spent so much of her time with large old volumes open on her lap that the boy, a delicate child, not very good at games, spent a major part of his early lifetime sitting in half-darkened rooms in something very close to silence?

Did I tell you about an afternoon in early spring, a cold day but quite sunny, when down by a stream running past a cemetery the eleven-year-old stood with his pants down splashing water over his very first erection, growing frightened and hypnotized by the sunlight trapped in the tiny drops that clung to the stretched, vein-rivered skin?

Did I tell you about that first trip east, the interview with the schoolmaster?

Did I tell you about the poems he wrote, little songs without music, in the back of a classroom, and how the teacher destroyed them?

Did I tell you about the moon that cast webbed shadows through the skylights of the boys' dormitory on winter nights—how it slid with almost perceptible speed over beds and footlockers and cotton rugs, lighting the way to the bathroom, the tiled hall, the cold forbidden storage room to which the biggest boys always had a key?

And would these things have helped, do you think?

The body, the blood, and all that jazz

In Turner's hand was a cup of some polished metal so bright that you couldn't quite tell the color: it may have been a gold so reflective as to look like silver, or silver so pure that in this gray world it was colorless. The cup was rimmed with crystals that resembled tiny holograms, jewel-like things that sparkled with a light of their own and transfixed the eye, drew you into them as you raised the cup to your lips, made you laugh, helped you overcome your terror.

You were terrified anyway. You knew that inside this gleaming cup and behind that jeweled rim lay a dark bottomless pool of something that you must never, ever drink. You must never even stick your nose over the rim in case the smell alone, warm and briny and more mysterious than the odor of lovemaking, would be enough to send you over. Probably it would; probably it would be too much. Quite possibly even the thought of what was in this cup was too much. As was the very thought of the cup itself, the weight of it in your hand, the warmth that grew from the warmth of your hand where you touched it. Quite possibly even the knowledge that you were holding it, that the cup had been bequeathed or had seen fit to bequeath itself *to you* was enough, more than enough, to send you over. Over to the *other side*, beyond the jeweled rim, falling like a cataract

so quickly

and only once . . .

You were on the other side already. You were mad or worse than mad; your consciousness had no connection now with anything solid, anything normal, anything at all apprehensible to anyone else except this cup that you couldn't put down, you couldn't hold another instant, but the instant was past, you were still trapped in this, Achilles was a basket case and *still* hadn't caught the fucking tortoise, Jesus Christ in another

minute I'm going to take a drink of this stuff
    a big gulp
    just to see

Scenes of Innocence and Betrayal (3)

In the field where the Chief Administrator had set up his bully pulpit, the glow of light around the princess tree faded and—what do you know—there really is an explanation for everything. The lightburst had been produced by a very expensive weapon of which there were only a handful in the entire arsenal of the Resistance, though you'd better believe they were all here on the field today. The Angels, mounted on a variety of what military strategists like to call "platforms," were deployed in a parabolic cordon that tightened with dramatic speed and regularity. Sure, they were getting knocked down like bowling pins; the corps of professional soldiers assigned to the Chief Administrator had been caught by surprise but it wasn't like they were made out of wood. Whenever a hole appeared in the Angels' ranks, though, they just closed their formation to compensate, so that the cordon was tightening like a noose without interruption, and casualties among the government troops were mounting fast.

At the focus of the parabola was the very old princess tree, beside which hulked the cable-laying machine. This seemed like the most logical place for the Chief Administrator to hide. And barring further intelligence, the Angels were assuming, in their collective and purely intuitive way (but see the extensive literature on this), that the sheltered spot beneath the tree was where their leader, Turner Ashenden, was being held prisoner, or was perhaps himself holding the Chief Administrator prisoner, making a lone last stand. There was no sense in this: no reason why Turner Ashenden should choose to make a lone last stand, and no reason to think this is where he would do it; but an absence of logic is no problem at all for Angels. Nor for Turner Ashenden himself, wherever he might be.

The Angels felt pretty certain that he was alive, at least. They felt pretty certain that they had gotten here in time, as they always had before.

They may have been troubled by doubts or confusion of some angelic
kind—here even an omniscient narrator must bow out of it—but not to
such an extent as to undermine their efficiency in battle. They were in
fact pretty thoroughly kicking ass.

Behind them, outside the range of accuracy of bullets and mortar
shells, came the larger vehicles that transported the various lieutenants
and land barons and gentrified smugglers and moneylenders and horsey
types and their assorted spouses and sweethearts and kept persons of both
genders who more or less constituted the Resistance for which Turner
Ashenden was *dux bellorum*. They had turned out in unusual numbers
for this journey to a northern battle-plain—some of them no doubt genuinely panicked by the chance that the *dux* was in danger, and others
probably under the impression that this was some *de rigueur* albeit un-
conventional social outing which would culminate in God's own tailgate
party. The expedition had been mounted in haste and without much
consultation. Nobody had ever seen Harvey Goldaster so worked up, was
what had started it. And there had been rumors—the artful, titillating sort
that are most often planted, but irresistible anyway—that the notorious
reputed faith-healer Black Malachi Pantera, in whose very existence many
people did not believe, had emerged from a reclusion of years for the
occasion. Anyway, lots of people had come along, for their own reasons,
for the ride.

They were astonished, most of them, by what a messy and basically
incomprehensible affair a battle really is. When you do this sort of thing
from above, so to speak, by moving the pieces across a gameboard, or
manipulating symbols on a screen, you perceive it as an interplay of forces
as unambiguously defined as mathematic constructs—movement points
and strength and range and likelihood of a given action being successful,
time and motion displayed as a series of vectors, those classic fat arrow-
heads, like the color commentary on an instant replay. Forget that. What
you had here was fire and deafening noise and dirt being blown in your
face, all sense of direction obliterated by the first gust of stinking sulphurous
smoke that choked and blinded your driver and sent your vehicle slamming
into the one beside it. From there it was all on foot, not knowing which
way was inward and which was out. You ran until you heard a noise you
thought might have been your name, but the friend who had been running
beside you was lying in pieces on the ground and what you did then was

not make a reasoned evaluation of why this had happened and what it meant. What you did was crawl. What you did was inhale dirt and sob and rub black phlegm across your cheekbone. You heard machine-noises, shouts, explosions. You smelled roasted human meat. You cowered. You prayed. That was how you spent your afternoon in a northern cornfield.

Afterward, you appreciated how good the Angels really were. Because through all that death and stench and blindness they drew instinctually nearer to something that was not a target but rather a sanctum, a single vortex in the *primum mobile* of battle that must be left untouched until the very end. What a fine faculty of directness was required for that! For here there was no question of control, of understanding the causes of events and rationally shaping outcomes. The beast was running free here. The only thing you could hope to do was influence the Fates directly, slip a mickey into their drinks, pull their own wool over their eyes, whip your big angelic dick out—like, whatever it took, man.

But Angels are cool. Angels have a knack. The fighters of the Resistance moved in on the cable-laying machine and the princess tree like that stolid fellow, Tietchens of Groby, ambling between the trenches, somehow knowing that in the face of such audacity the Kaiser's boys would blow their wads. The government troops were driven back into the crowd that was fleeing toward the compound of the Peels. The whole mass of them became a broad, writhing target. A steady wind came up to hold the smoke down, so that once again you could see the general outlines of the plain. In and out of the smoke figures moved with the lurching motion of zombies. The Angels swept the field, identifying them, lifting some onto their "platforms," leaving others to continue staggering about, shooting the rest. There was not much methodical about this; it was not Order but Climax.

At last they reached the princess tree and surrounded it. Blueish smoke from the cable-laying machine drifted over the ground and hid everything lower than shoulder-height. Angels' shoulders are very high. They held back, unwilling to make that final plunge. They set about fighting the fire in the big machine, meanwhile securing a defensive perimeter. A small crowd—Old Souls and other survivors—gathered around what was clearly the center of attention, though nobody knew what it was.

Lingering battle sounds, somewhere in the west, provided a drumroll.

The wind swung around. The smoke faded to wispy gray, the color of fog. For a few moments you felt as though you were watching a routine cinematic dissolve, the old scene fading out as the new fades in, with a brief transitional phase in which both views are present together.

In the old scene, the world was black and white, peopled with tall beings who strode about with heavy weapons in their hands, divinely ruthless.

In the new scene, the world was an ever-attenuating gray, with two human forms at its center. One of these was a slender young man, lying spread-eagle on the ground a few feet away from the princess tree. The other, leaning over him, was a short, husky youth with wild hair and a beard of alarming length. He raised a hand—a gesture that seemed to demand silence, forbearance, a little more time.

The new wind held steady. Both worlds, both these incongruous scenes, remained in view. The Angels held their places, toes seeming to butt against an unseen circle inscribed in the earth. Behind them, one ring out, there was a murmuring and a hesitant pressing inward; the Old Souls wanted the best seats. The stout youth glared at them, and the demented ardor in his eye kept them still for a few more moments.

Black Malachi looked down at his old friend Turner Ashenden. Turner's skin, pale at the best of times, was the color of the flesh of some pale fruit. Say a banana. His breathing was shallow; the narrow chest was almost still; only the stomach, alarmingly sunken, and the eyes, twitching as though in some animated dream, could be seen to move. Black Malachi held one hand, palm-downward, over Turner's solar plexus, and an abstracted expression spread over his face.

There were footsteps in the tall grass. The Angels locked arms. Black Malachi, without looking up, gave the barest of nods. The Angels parted, admitting three newcomers, then the circle closed again.

"What's wrong? What the hell's the matter with him?"

Harvey Goldaster. He came on like the father-figure he was, complete with two children straddling behind him. He stopped when Black Malachi held up, once more, a small chubby hand.

More quietly: "What are you going to do?"—choosing perhaps unknowingly a deferential, doctor's-office tone.

Black Malachi flicked one finger, not so much pointing as redirecting Goldaster's eye to the central problem here, the heart of the labyrinth.

Turner's arms were spread widely and asymmetrically, as though he had been seized, while he dreamed, by Dionysian fervor. In one hand he clutched a shiny, cylindrical object—a shaft or handle of some kind. The end of the shaft was hollow; it might have been a curious sort of drinking vessel, except that from the base of it trailed two narrow wires. The wires led down to the ground and were lost there among trampled field-flowers.

Harvey looked thoughtful. The two children came up on either side of him. Girl and boy; boy and girl. It was hard to know what order to put them in. The first lover or the last? The devoted friend or the immemorial consort? They drew nearer from opposite sides and stared with very different expressions downward. For half a minute, longer perhaps, no one moved.

"Well, damn it all," said Black Malachi. He brought his hand up, stared into the palm of it like a sharpshooter inspecting a trusty revolver that has unaccountably failed him.

The gesture, just this side of comical, unfroze us. We four witnesses looked at one another, seeking common ground or choosing our stances or scoping out the competition—none of us appeared to know what to expect from the situation, nor from ourselves. Black Malachi's eyes settled finally on Tristin, whose own eyes were averted, tending rather to slink down to the form of the fallen hero.

What do you make of this, my boy?

Tristin nearly jumped. He looked into Black Malachi's dark penetrating eyes.

Seen anything like it before?

Tristin shrugged, accepting this; he shook his head.—I've heard it can drain you, is all. If you don't hang on. If you lose control of it. The Other gains strength and the material self grows weaker.

"Well I hope to heaven, then," (startling everyone, Black Malachi spoke aloud) "he can hang on a while more."

"What?" said Harvey Goldaster. The merchant prince glanced about as though to say that he didn't put much stock in the intangible, the numinous.

I suppose each of us felt the need to stake out some kind of position. Maridel, who had been uncharacteristically subdued throughout our journey, took two steps in a direction that brought her closer to Turner while keeping her distance from everyone else. She seemed particularly to avoid looking at Black Malachi—who on this very account, I guess, showed a growing interest in her. His sharp eyes pricked patterns out of her comely back.

"Look," said Harvey Goldaster.

Growing restless, he had begun to pace, and stood now about midway toward the hulking form of the cable-laying machine. He gestured to the ground. We discovered there a freshly dug trench, stretching from the back of the machine out toward the relative infinity of the eastern horizon. It was neatly carved about three feet deep. In the bottom of it lay a black rubbery tube as fat as Malachi's forearm.

"Ah," the little healer declared, at the sight of this. He raised a finger. "The Hitchcock principle: If you have a crop-duster, it must dust crops."

Tristin shuddered. He had the sense that other, nonartistic principles were involved. He walked slowly along the trench from the digging apparatus toward the place where it made its closest approach to the outstretched arm of Turner Ashenden, the hand holding the metal rod. He knelt.

—Oh my god, he thought. —Malachi, look at this.

Very carefully he lifted two small wires, which emerged from the grass at the edge of the trench and twined downward into the hole, terminating in a crude splice-job where they fused with the main cable. Like a lost child following the piece of string he has laid through the forest, Tristin worked his way back down the wires to Turner.

"Well, I'll be a son of a bitch," said Harvey Goldaster. "They've got the poor bastard *plugged in*."

"They do at that," marveled Black Malachi. "But to what, I wonder."

In Tristin's fingers the wires seemed to dilate and contract, as though they carried something more substantial than electricity. The boy looked hard at them: one a bright, plasticky red, the other dirty white. He found them unaccountably hideous—as though they were the capillaries of a disemboweled giant.

Black Malachi came to stand beside him. Gently the stout youth placed his hand on Tristin's shoulder: a healer's hand, preternaturally warm, its pressure enlivening.

"My boy," Black Malachi said, barely breathing it, "I believe you are onto something here."

He bent low, peering at the rod in Turner's hand. He started to touch it, then looked up at Tristin, one hierophant to another.

—I don't think I would, Tristin advised him.—You don't want to risk breaking the connection and leaving him . . . you know . . . *out there*.

Black Malachi nodded. He straightened up.

Harvey said, "So what now?"

And Maridel—out of mind, these last several moments—one always overlooks something, it seems—Maridel stepped without a sound from whatever stage-wing she had been waiting in. She gave us one quick look, not time enough even for Black Malachi to react, but sufficient to burn itself into all our memories, and to permit at least three distinct views of her intentions. Then she fell to her knees by Turner's side and picked up the hand with the rod in it. Their ten fingers entwined. Her head fell back—an involuntary movement, it seemed—and slowly she arched her spine. The slow-motion spasm in which Turner had been seized seemed to spread outward to absorb her. Now they were both lost to us.

Black Malachi's sturdy little form began to tremble. He looked, I thought, for the very first time, at the edge of losing control of himself. Harvey Goldaster and I exchanged glances.

"I don't know, Tristin," Harvey said. (It was the only time he ever used my name.)

Then beside us, speaking with a kind of subterranean intensity, the thwarted little healer said, "Hang on, old man. Blackie will get you out of there."

At the rim

The cup

—in your hands. Your hands on the smooth cool handle of the cup. Your lips at the rim of it. Beyond, a vastness. Limitless waters. A whirlpool, deadly and roiling. No bottom. A hole, a blackness, an end of time.

You lean forward. The sweet warm stench of those waters rises to your nose. You hear the music there, the *Four Last Songs*, the soothing pink-noise ostinato.

You loosen your grip on the handle. Your breathing deepens.

It is cool here. It is dark before you. The very shape of events, your life's curvature, moves you forward, past the rim, into the gravity-well of the cup you have sought and hold at last and long to drink from.

Hang on, old man.

You tighten your grip again. Something has happened. Something has changed. The crystals gleam around the rim, each one a story, a lifetime's worth of plot and theme and invention. Which was yours? This one, with the boy? Or this one, with the girl? Or were they different views of the same tale? You stare with growing curiosity, your eye moving into a crystal and out of it. The scene grows and somehow you are part of it. Or rather, a missing part. An actor offstage. You smile, shyly, uncertainly: have you missed your cue? It is all very interesting, and very odd.

On the ground, in the scene, a figure lies beneath a tree. This figure looks familiar to you. It is a weakened man, a man who has been wounded, who is missing some vital essence. The essence that would restore him is in a bottle in your hand.

You remember now. Or you *can* remember, if you care to. It is hard to decide. The figure turns weakly, looks up at you, little vitality remaining in those pale eyes.

"Give it to him."

This is another person. The voice surprises you. You turn, and it is a beautiful young girl. The sight of her thrills and frightens you. You draw the bottle inward, protectively.

"He needs it," the girl tells you. She points to the wasted figure on the ground. "You did this to him, and only you can make him better."

You are unsure. There is something circular or inverted about the girl's argument, but you can't decide what. The man on the ground has his eyes closed. His limbs move sluggishly, as in a dream.

"Now," says the girl. "If you wait it will be too late."

You mop your brow. You always meant to be a decent guy. Maybe there's been some confusion, misplaced identities, an improper diagnosis.

The girl speaks your name. Or is it your name? It sounds like a different name, a secret name, spoken in a secret or forgotten language. Without thinking, without really meaning to, you respond to this. You step forward, holding the bottle. Its contents seem to glow, red and bright and hypnotic, a combination of attributes not seen except at certain places, at certain sunsets. *Fin de siècle*, you think. See, you've got a few secret words left of your own. You feel as though you are standing on a cliff, balanced at the rim of the world, watching the sun crash into the poisoned plain.

The girl reaches out for you. Her eyes are green, full of meaning, damp with tears of no certain origin. Her hand touches your brow, your shoulders, your wrist. Slowly her fingers interlace with the fingers of your hand that holds the bottle. They slide up to the neck of it, the long smooth shaft, and in that instant you remember something else—

something very old, a-and
long forgotten, that had lain
deep
unmoving
as in sleep
at the bottom of—

Hic jacet

—*Malachi!* shrieked Tristin's mind.

The bearded little prophet lunged too late.

Maridel stood calmly with tears bleeding from both closed eyes. In her hand was the metal rod. With a deliberate motion she seized the wires and jerked them free. She hurled the shaft away from her. In the gray world where we stood, the metal seemed to lose its sheen as it flew through the air. By the time it fell to earth, a dozen yards from the princess tree, it was a lumpish thing as dull as charred carbon, as black rock.

Black Malachi bent down and lifted Turner like an insubstantial thing, a vacant shell. He did not bother to examine him. He began walking slowly toward the west, the barren cropland. The Angels parted to let them go.

Tristin, struggling to recover himself, ran after them, Malachi and Turner. Harvey Goldaster held back. Maridel stood alone, inaudibly sobbing.

—*Wait!* Tristin tried to cry.

Black Malachi gave no sign of understanding. His small limbs carried him and his pale burden with impressive speed. Everywhere he stepped, an early shadow, a patch of twilight, seemed to fall.

—Wait, Tristin called again. He drew alongside, reached out tremblingly to touch Turner's hair, his cheek, his lips. The skin was cool, not cold. Every single thing had become indeterminate.

Black Malachi halted. He stared at Tristin with an expression of such complexity that it—like Maridel's momentary glance—would admit of any number of later views. There was sympathy in it, surely. There was anger. There was despair. There may have been a touch of love. And there were other things, for which there may be words in some secret tongue, but not in the language of History.

"Tristin," said Black Malachi, after a time had passed and the shadows had deepened. He said it as gently as could be hoped for, under the circumstances. Then he abandoned language altogether and addressed me only with his eyes.

Tristin, they told me, *you wretched boy. It is time to let him go.*

COMING
BACK

1

Why

When I was very young my parents were killed during one of the earliest housing riots. A well-meaning aunt—who could not, as later I told myself, in a kind of private litany, *who could not have known*—heard about Madame Gwendola's husband, who was then still alive, and perhaps read some of those pamphlets that seem to have lain forever on the table in the hall. My aunt decided that Bad Winters Institute would be just the place to nurture what she called my "artistic temperament." That sounds like a euphemism, doesn't it? I was an undersized, nervous, dreamy child, and I don't recall having shown any particular talent for the arts, or indeed for anything. My aunt died soon afterward, and I became to all intents a permanent possession of the Institute.

That's one reason.

Maridel was the central, insurmountable fact of my growing-up. She was always present and always in control, one way or another. She experimented with various methods of emotional domination, as another child might have sought out new places to hide, new games to play indoors in rainy weather. She was very methodical. And I, of course—notwithstanding that I was two years her senior, which was of absolutely no importance to anyone—I was the perfect subject for her investigations. I cried easily, succumbed to puerile and ill-considered forms of blackmail, and fully believed the most transparent of threats. I don't know, even now, how much aware Gwendola may have been of her daughter's and my relationship. She was a distracted guardian, to say the least. Her interest in people lay mostly in deducing what *roles* they were intended to fill, not in what they themselves might think or want or feel about it. I believe in her way she cared for me.

That is reason number two.

We are all, of course, by fiat, great believers in Reason nowadays.

Maridel's *métier*, toward which she seemed to find her way by pure —one might even say "innocent"—intuition, was the invention of new and highly personalized forms of sexual torment. It was remarkable, considering her age and the sheltered circumstances of her life. She couldn't have been older than nine—for I was certainly no older than ten or eleven—when this particular New World was revealed to her. She crossed the frontier, dragging me miserably but complaisantly behind her, and we would never find our way back.

This is of course one of the larger, more prominent reasons, or I would not mention it at all.

Perhaps you have heard about the boy who was kept by his insane mother in a wooden box. When he was seven or eight, the mother was placed in an institution, and the boy was discovered by the authorities. Upon being told that not all boys are kept in boxes, his reaction was one of simple amazement—no bitterness, no rage, no regret for the lost precious years. Those things, one assumes, came later.

I have not read Freud. But I understand that much ado is made over the issue of sexuality in extremely young children. In the specific case of me and Maridel—or should we confine ourselves to the specific case of me?—I can say that indeed, some dark inchoate process that would later manifest itself as "sex" was certainly active, in what now seems to have been a morbid and terrible way, long before the machinery of reproduction began to operate. When Maridel placed her hand on my tiny rubbery penis, something happened to me, wicked and consuming and stupendous. Afterward I felt such shame as might have been expected of someone older, pubescent at least, who had been capable of a physically thorough response. Which was precisely what Maridel counted on. It was the decisive source of her power.

I have not read the Crowleys, either. Turner was the one who read things. Then he would forget most of what he had read, retaining only a certain quality of feeling, the gist of a scene or two, the names of the characters: just enough to allude to. *I* am the one who remembers. (That is a third or fourth reason, if you're counting.) I remember, for example, hearing that one of the Crowleys pronounced the syllable "crow" like the bird-name; and that both of them knew quite a lot about the mysteries of sexual magic. They are both here in the library. Perhaps I will read one of them, some day.

By the time Maridel was eleven and I was thirteen, she must have decided that the purpose of her investigations had been served. She had perfected a skill that would serve her well for the rest of her life—until it killed her, to be exact—and she had no further need of me.

But that wasn't all. It wasn't enough for her simply to abandon me —to open up my box and let me wander away. She wanted instead to nail the box closed forever. She wanted to prevent the possibility that, once free of her constant domination, I would warn others about her, tell them of what she had done. I'm sure she must have considered murdering me, which would have been easily accomplished. But for reasons known only to Maridel—and which only to Maridel, I suppose, would have seemed like "reasons" at all—she chose a more difficult and less definitive solution.

She forbade me to talk. Not just to talk about *it*, you understand. But to *talk*.

How she did it, really, fundamentally, I do not understand. Discussions of cause-and-effect have never sounded persuasive to me. The procedure itself was brief and deceptively facile. She sat me down before an Identity terminal, placed both of my hands on the rod, and ran her fingers over the coils engraved in the holly-wood. After a minute or two, having prepared her spell or written her program, she told me:

"You shall not speak again, ever."

And that, of course, is the strangest reason of all.

There are two more. In the interest of completeness I will mention them, though they are perfectly self-evident and in fact you know them already.

I loved Turner.

And only I am left.

What happened next

With Turner Ashenden presumably dead and inarguably vanished, the Resistance reverted in short order to its former condition of mutual rancor, suspicion, under-the-counter deal-making, and coming to terms with the government on an issue-by-issue basis, one Soul at a time. Soon there was no Resistance at all. A new order had insidiously asserted itself. Candlemas and the surrounding valley were reclassified as "population 75–90 percent below carrying capacity," which resulted in a stepped-up Settling Out program and an accompanying, out-and-out occupation by government troops. As the blue-jacketed soldiers began to outnumber the local independent militias, some of the more prominent landholders were arrested. They were placed on trial for assorted petty offenses. A few of them were sent to jail. Harvey Goldaster, against whom the charges were somewhat stiffer, owing I suspect to his former special closeness to Turner, was sentenced to be executed. The sentence was immediately commuted by Chief Administrator Rodarch. I'm sure the whole thing was done by prearrangement—a symbolic slaying of the King of the Valley by a triumphant invader.

At the University—always quick to respond to such things, which is how it had gotten to be so venerably old—a new round of faculty dismissals began. Committees were established to recommend changes in the curricula, and many of the former "student associates" were elevated to instructor status. I remember in particular one spokeswoman for the revisionist side: not so much the face or the name as the voice. Those awful whiny vowel-sounds, which seemed to originate chiefly in the sinus passages, remain fixed in my mind as the very voice of the New Reason. By that voice we were told of departmental reorganization, work-study centers established in the Settling Out Camps, the sale of certain architectural embellishments that had no place or purpose in the current era, and the numerous other good works undertaken by the University, or in its behalf. There were those who found this spokeswoman to be objectionably smug; but I think it was just the voice.

So time passed, and the sights and sounds and even smells of life—for the new cuisine ran to salt and hydrolized soy proteins and away from, say, ground-nuts and garlic—slowly changed, but not in a night-and-day fashion. It was as though one's favorite watering hole had kept its façade and most of its furnishings, but quietly hired new staff and changed the program of nightly entertainment, all beneath the self-effacing aegis of a small sign announcing, New Management. Under protest by longtime patrons, some of the changes might be reversed, popular menu items restored. On other issues, the Management stands firm. Over time the faces change but the establishment endures. One is left with something to complain about, and good old days to remember.

In History, I believe, this is the way things happen. There are glorious victories and crushing defeats, but they are, in themselves, of limited consequence—except of course to storytellers. The real business of History occurs in the tidal changes, the ceaseless give-and-take between sea and sky, the adjustment of boundaries that occurs like an anticlimax after the thunder and lightning have ceased and the rainbows have faded, out along the gray, indeterminate frontier of the horizon.

It is in that ambivalent world, the chilly no-man's-land of History, that I make my home nowadays. *Out here*, I am an ideal citizen.

The circle

On top of the godless mountain, wild grasses and weedy princess trees sprang up where the driveway had once run smoothly through rhododendrons. Where the purple-on-swami-yellow sign had hung, bare poles now supported a season's crop of honeysuckle. One might easily have driven past the Institute and not known it. I'm sure many people—government troops among them—did so. As Madame Gwendola intended.

So we lived for a time in ironic tranquility, quite safe and even permitted to enjoy what may have been a special, brittle kind of happiness: we, the inner circle of a famous dead outlaw.

There is little distinct in my mind about that period, even its duration. It could not have been more than three or four months. The weather stayed warm into autumn. We took our tea in late afternoon on the back terrace, overlooking the drop-off where once I had nearly thrown myself. I don't know why the thought of dying no longer attracted me. Perhaps Turner's death was so enormous as to leave room for no other. We kept our tea warm with little votive candles which it was Maridel's job to light. She did this mechanically, as she lived now. She had become as mute as myself, it often seemed. While the hot water lasted, we would stay there watching the sun go down and the sky change colors. Some evenings Gwendola rose early to go inside and play music that those of us still outside couldn't hear.

Vinny Hawkmoth stayed on with us. He kept us cheerful most of the time with stories of life at the Solar Temple and improvised games and, sometimes, a new ballad or sonata. Tentative and self-referential though he had become, he had begun to compose again.

Partner Trefoil and Twill Gavotte were gone, off to hunt for Black Malachi. I supposed they were safe enough. There were "stories," Partner had informed us before setting off (though where they came from, and how they penetrated our little circle, he did not mention) that Malachi had been sighted at some distant compound or trading post or research station—places where the New Reason did not yet prevail.

There were other stories, wilder rumors, of which Partner whispered only once or twice, after the sun was safely down, that the burly little wizard had gone into hiding deep in the wilderness (whatever *that* meant, in this age), where he was by forbidden means keeping Turner Ashenden half alive, a vessel without a soul or a soul without a vessel. To me this sounded like the kind of tale that the popular mind will invent for itself, if no professional storyteller is astute enough to do so first.

Nicola Quoin had left for good, even before the news about Turner. I imagined her alone in that grand and desolate manor, the seat of her family, at the end of her line.

Harvey Goldaster was abroad in the world, living the odd life of a deposed monarch. Such people always seem to survive. They always have a bit of money, though their circumstances are reduced; they have aides-de-camp and bodyguards; they appear before their remaining faithful on ceremonial occasions. Their old enemies first condemn then tolerate and finally ignore them; and slowly the world turns its head away.

The Angels, of course, were no longer among us. They may have been and may still be somewhere in our world, striding boldly and singing and striking down their foes with divine impudence. But they weren't part of our circle anymore, now that the center of it, the source of its magic charge, was gone.

So there were only the few of us, of all there had been. And even among ourselves, within the small world that remained to us, we were diminished. We cast shorter shadows. Our actions were of no consequence. The choices left to us were restricted to such matters as the selection of music, the duration of tea.

I could live like that. To me it felt quite fitting that life had become a series of slow and nearly silent rituals; for in ritual we find solace, a transcendence of time and its effects on us, a connection with the greater cycles and circles of the world.

Maridel could not. She could not live that way. She could not tolerate sitting around week after week with no direction, no object, no secret agenda. And as we soon discovered, she could not wait, also, on more practical grounds. She was living under a sentence of sorts. Facing a deadline.

Maridel was pregnant. And she knew the child would be Black Malachi's.

But we didn't know that, as yet; and even had we known, we never would have found the subterranean connection between that alarming fact and the other, seemingly independent fact that brought an end to our quiet rituals, our tranquil and almost happy existence on the mountaintop.

One day we awoke to discover a fire just subsiding across the perfect lawn. The grass and honeysuckle and weedy trees that had kept us hidden from the road were blackened and smoldering. Only the residue of the last night's thunderstorm, and a heavy morning dew, kept the flames from spreading through the surrounding woods and burning us out altogether.

Maridel stood at the head of the drive, holding an empty spirit-bottle and surveying her handiwork. Vinny was shouting at her, or perhaps just shouting. In response, Maridel turned slowly with a faint smile—the first smile she had worn for weeks or months, since Turner . . .

"I have sent for him," she said, with narrow self-satisfied eyes. "I have sent him an invitation."

Übermensch, in the drawing room

He—if whom Maridel meant by "him," to whom her invitation had been sent, was Chief Administrator Rodarch—accepted.

He arrived with a small entourage no more than three or four days after the fire had died and the earth had become lukewarm and the Institute was laid bare to government scouts. I was surprised that he came so lightly protected: only half a dozen soldiers, and these not even of the brutal-looking type. Had there been even a couple of Angels left, we could have made short work of them and rid the valley of the Chief Administrator and perhaps bumped History into a new "dharmic creode," as Gwendola would have said. But dharma is not easily amended, nor History bumped off-course. The Chief Administrator brought his vehicles to a halt at the edge of the lawn, a respectable distance from the old house itself, and came slowly and confidently toward us across the smooth green expanse. So relaxed was his manner, it would not have seemed out-of-character for him to greet us with "Croquet, anyone?"

To the victor go the smiles. All of us held back except for Maridel, who stepped out brazenly and took Rodarch by the arm.

"You must be tired," she told him, "from driving so far. Come inside and wash your hands and we'll give you a drink. Do you take wine?"

Rodarch allowed himself to be conducted through the downstairs hall (where he ignored that sculpture, the contesting serpents, that had so puzzled and fascinated Turner) and up the spiral staircase. He made the obligatory stop in the nobly appointed bathroom, then proceeded to the upstairs parlor, whose Colefax & Fowler furnishings were more frowsily genteel and comfortable than ever, having acquired a few more years' worth of the all-important patina of age.

The Chief Administrator sat down and waited easefully on a sagging Regency sofa while Nurse Tawdry made a nervous business of fetching glasses of wine. These arrived eventually on a tarnished tray. Tarnish, of course, went with the territory. Nothing was so carefully avoided here as the shock of the *nouveau*.

Rodarch eyed the tray for a moment with apparent curiosity. Then he plucked a goblet of zinfandel from among the unmatched glasses and smiled around the room at the rest of us.

I was gripped with disgust. It occurred to me that we were repeating, almost exactly, the ceremony with which we had received Turner Ashenden on an earlier, happier afternoon. The next step, I supposed, would be for Maridel to pull out an Identity terminal and offer it to him. Would he take it? What sort of web would Maridel weave *then*?

After a few moments of the blandest kind of chitchat, Rodarch·made an expansive movement of his broad shoulders—a sort of shrug that spread outward along his muscular arms—and said, "So, this is where he lived."

The remark, innocent enough in its way, silenced us. Or all of us but Maridel. She nodded; then after a moment she pointed down to a spot on the floor, beside the rose-colored rug.

She said, "And *that* is where he sat."

—And this is what he drank, I thought bitterly, staring into my glass of wine. Had I truly been able to communicate, I might well have gestured toward Maridel and added, *And that is who he slept with*.

But all of these remarks, made and unmade, were equally pathetic and equally futile attempts to capture the essence of a thing that was gone from us; that even while it was among us had remained elusive. It was as though we were a bunch of old pagans who might point to a rock and say, "There is where the great warrior-god stood in battle," or "There is where his bard once recited a prophecy"—as though the legends of these events, the places where they were supposed to have occurred, and the very act —itself a ritual—of referring to them, all were united in a kind of chain or family of phenomena through which those on *the other side* were connected with us on this one. But even falling short of that, our pointing to the rock was an affirmation of whatever linkage existed among ourselves.

This was an odd line of thought, where we old enemies in the drawing room were concerned. And Rodarch seemed to realize this—even to be interested in making the situation feel less awkward. He drew his shoulders in and hunched forward a bit, made an undemanding remark about something. The weather, I suppose. How unseasonably warm it had been. This was what Turner had referred to as his Ordinary Person routine.

But awkwardness was Maridel's native element, and this meeting—

or reception, or whatever it was—was being held because Maridel had wanted it, for unspoken reasons of her own. She cut through the soft padding of social nicety, speaking not loudly but sharply, her tone a complement to her words.

"They *say*, you know . . ." (She waited for us to fall silent before going on:) "They say that he may still be alive, somewhere. They say that Black Malachi may be hiding him."

She looked directly at Rodarch. "You haven't found Pantera yet, have you?"

The Ordinary Person reacted as any of his fellow citizens might. He looked back at Maridel quite surprised and, for several moments, speechless.

Maridel, evidently set on more of a response than that, kept pressing in with the same blunt weapon. "So you don't really know," she said. "You don't know whether Turner is *actually* dead or not."

The Ordinary Person vanished. His place on the Regency sofa was taken by another persona—the Stainless Steel Superman, a colorless, middle-aged authority figure who had outlived many a younger and more charismatic rival. He stared at Maridel through eyes as impervious as tiny shields.

"I did not come for that," he said quietly.

His words had a startling impact that belied the expressionless tone in which he spoke them. One really must, I thought, after all, give the devil his due. Rodarch went on:

"I just wanted to . . . to look. To see this place. To see *you*."

Now it was Maridel's turn at speechlessness. (Unless even this, as seems highly possible, was part of her act, like a dancer's circling of the stage, a quintessentially female process of enfoldment.)

In any event, she recovered. She performed her own little metamorphosis, from Sassy Schoolgirl to Smart Hostess. "Oh," she said, "but you must do more than just *see* this place. You must come again, as often as you like. You must *stay*."

The Savior softened a little. He looked at Maridel with an air of friendly interest, even amusement: one shape-shifter to another. He smiled a comradely sort of smile.

"Do you think so?" he said. "Really? Well, then, perhaps I will."

News and weather

Partner and Twill came back on the first cool day of fall with news of a murder. The sky hung low above the mountaintop as though if you wanted you could walk right up the sides of those clouds and visit the gods in their great gray offices. A young woman (Partner and Twill related, by turns) had been found slain in the most baroque manner. The tale was hard to follow; there was no clear chronology, and the double narrative diverged on key matters. "She was a collaborator," they said. The sky boiled above us. Clouds changed rapidly from dark to light, then dark again. "She was leading a search party to find Black Malachi." But was this before? Long before? Did it have anything to do with her death? "They had sliced up her face," said Partner. Twill said, "They mutilated her limbs." Who was *they*? Had our two informants actually seen these things? Was that a raindrop? "Well, this should teach them." We headed for the door, before the rain began in earnest. Partner murmured, "It might have been some kind of, you know . . . ceremony." Twill nodded. "A human sacrifice." The gods poured icy water down our backs. The old house drifted among the clouds like a ship, a limestone freighter. "We ought to tell Maridel," Partner thought; he grew inspired by this. "We'll see what *she* thinks." But Maridel was sleeping inside and Gwendola wasn't interested. The rain lasted for a couple of days, marking a definite seasonal passage. We were all restless by the time it ended. "Her name was Dinder," Twill remembered. Partner said, "I knew her."

Legends

The popular mind now had another thing to stew over, another key ingredient. Soon it was quite widely rumored—by which I mean, we heard it even on the mountaintop—that Black Malachi had returned from the barren West after a time spent fasting, gathering his powers, and that he was somewhere in the valley, plotting a horrid act of vengeance. The popular mind hadn't quite worked out what. The Chief Administrator was a cooked goose, by most accounts. I doubted it. On his visits to the Institute, which had become quite regular by now, Rodarch looked fit and shrewd and confident. He looked, as Turner would have said, like a man who's got the world by the short hairs. I, for one, didn't think Black Malachi was a threat to anyone. I believed Turner's demise had undone the poor little fellow—that like others who as teenagers showed such brilliance and such brazen verve, he made a disappointed and disappointing adult.

Thus spoke Tristin, from the world-wise and -weary perspective of his twenty or so years.

People say that the age of legends is over. The truth, I think, is very much the contrary. The age of legends has only begun.

Take a single example. When after several weeks, at Maridel's third or fourth invitation, Chief Administrator Rodarch did not drive down from the mountaintop as night approached, but sat through the long evening of wistful music and drinks in the downstairs sitting room, finally climbing the stairs like the rest of us and making his way down the hall to Maridel's large, east-facing bedchamber—just what exactly was he doing, then? Had he really allowed Maridel to seduce him? Or was he (as I would argue) still waging the oldest war along a new and more dangerous front? Having wrestled to the ground the fleshly person of Turner Ashenden, was he not now locked in combat with Turner's just-born and rapidly growing legend? If not, then why was he so assiduously gathering unto himself all those things that had been Turner's: the Institute, the entourage, the consort? Rodarch knew full well that his legendary foe was larger and more troublesome than a life-sized Turner could ever have been.

Why Maridel was prodding this rather macabre process along was another question. But I had learned not to wonder too much about Maridel's motives. She was a force of nature, as far as I was concerned: implacable, irrational and unrelenting.

Rodarch stayed for several days, that first time. As the weeks went by, his visits to the Institute drew themselves out and the periods he was away grew fewer and shorter. At some point, he must have learned of Maridel's condition, for it was becoming unmistakable. He reacted in no visible way. His manner toward her may have grown a little solicitous, even protective; but even this didn't happen all at once.

I wonder what Maridel told him, though. My guess is that she led him to believe that the unborn child would carry on Turner's bloodline. That would have fit the pattern; it would have made Rodarch's attitude consistent with my own view. The ultimate military occupation: taking the fallen enemy's child to be one's own.

It was a strange time for us. It was like one of those late-summer days, hot and enervating, when great tensions build up behind the heavy fabric of the atmosphere, waiting for some shard of lighting to release them.

In Maridel's seventh month, Chief Administrator Rodarch declared that he was dispatching search teams to find Pantera. (He never used the name "Malachi." Perhaps it was too biblical, or something.) I was taken by surprise. Was he planning further vengeance? Rodarch announced his plans at the breakfast table, in the midst of his usual bland meal of grains and juice, no meat, no coffee. He smiled, as though he were anxious to dispel the air of tension that ensued.

"Oh, I'll keep him quite safe," he said.

Maridel, beside him, looked suspiciously placid.—This is *your* idea, I thought, isn't it?

She let her narrow eyes pass over me.

"I just think," said Rodarch, having paused politely to swallow, "that it would be useful, now and then, to have the advice of a physician of such . . . repute."

—Ah. (*Repute* seemed to be the key word here. Another legend to attend to, this time by dragging into public view the modest and ultimately unimpressive little figure at the source of it—and, if possible, putting this figure on the payroll. Death by employment: Black Malachi would have been the first to savor the ironic tang of that.)

"I don't know that I want him here," said Gwendola—a remarkable little *obiter dictum* in itself, since she had raised no such objection to any of the other characters who had trooped through the Institute. "Isn't he said to be living like some sort of animal? Dressing in skins and whatnot? He must be a filthy thing. And what a *smell* he must have."

I think she was losing her grip; she no longer seemed able to concentrate on the really important things. That Black Malachi might possibly smell bad—as I imagined he certainly would—was almost comically irrelevant, when one was sitting contentedly enough at the breakfast table with one's great lifelong enemy, lingering over tea.

A gust of wind caused a momentary backpuff in the chimney, forcing smoke through the leaky doors of the Aga.

—We'll see, I thought.—Probably old Blackie has hidden so well that you'll never find him, anyway.

A common denominator

I believed Rodarch. I didn't think he wanted to harm or imprison or even humiliate Black Malachi—merely to *annex* him, as he had done with the rest of us, the remnants of Turner's circle. In this case the prize would be an especially juicy one: the court bard.

But my belief was not widely shared. All those people who claimed to have seen Black Malachi or to have heard news of his whereabouts suffered lapses of memory when questioned by government scouts. The search seemed to progress backwards: after several weeks, the area under consideration had not narrowed but widened. Patrols were said to be sweeping as far south as the pinelands above Wine Barrens, where Nicola and I had met the Brown Witch.

Early one morning, in the final month of her pregnancy, Maridel appeared at my bedroom door. It was not yet light. Her pale hair hung loosely, wisps of it floating before her face like a silvery veil. Because I knew her so very well, I guessed that this disheveled, insomniacal appearance was premeditated, aimed at achieving a certain effect—but that her tears were not.

"Tristin . . ." voice trailing pitiably.

—What is it? (I remained safely beneath the covers of my narrow bed.)

She crossed the room and sat next to me. Her stomach was immense. It was like a separate entity altogether, as though the child already existed at some remove from its mother. She had a way of placing her hand over it, not as though she were probing for it or feeling for movement within her, but as though she were trying to *hold it down*. When I showed no sign of sympathetic stirring (for those hours just on either side of dawn were the times I was most likely to pass into sleep, after lying awake all night; and besides, I had lost my taste for twilight melodrama), Maridel reached under the covers and seized one of my hands. This she pulled out and laid flat over that place where her distended belly met her ribcage, just below the heart. I could feel her heartbeat and the rhythm of her breathing, and the surprising body heat engendered by the baby.

"Tristin," she said, struggling with what really did seem to be an honest round of crying. "I'm so frightened. Mother told me—"

I was not unmoved by all this. Merely unconvinced. I think I had earned the right to be suspicious, where Maridel was concerned.

—Yes, I mentally prodded her, what did she say?

"Mother told me . . ." She lifted my hand from her stomach, held it close to her face, where she seemed to strain through the half-light to study my thin fingers. She whispered, "You're so gentle, Tristin. You're so kind. I know I can trust you."

—Sure, I thought bitterly.—What could I possibly do to *you*? Anything I could think of, you've already done to yourself.

She lowered her head, as though my thoughts were perfectly clear to her. I felt ashamed, despite all reasons not to. It was then, having gotten me in just the proper mood for it, that she told me the truth of her baby's parentage.

Another intimation of innocence: I was shocked.

"So you *see*," she said. Her head was upright now, and the first augury of sunrise highlighted the porcelain slope of her cheekbone. "You see why I must find Malachi right away."

I noted the pronoun here. Why *she* must find Malachi. It had not been Rodarch's idea then, I supposed, all along.

Seeing as how I was well awake and there was no escape from it, I climbed out of bed. I was naked, but of course there was no question of modesty where Maridel was concerned. Standing before the window, I thought how very large and secretive a place the world is, even this late in its history, even after so many people—Gwendola's husband, for example—had worked so hard to plunder its mysteries, and others—like Rodarch—to deny that any mysteries existed at all.

I wondered what in the world Maridel wanted from *me*.

"You are attractive, you know," she told me, "in a certain way. Do you think Turner could have loved you?"

I turned toward her, angrily. This was entirely out-of-bounds, as she well knew. She acknowledged my stare but only, maddeningly, continued her appraisal of my underdeveloped form.

"*I* think so," she said. "I thought he did, in fact. I was jealous of you. I wanted that . . . that closeness, that you had with him."

—You're the one who betrayed him, I thought coldly.

She shook her head. There was something like sadness in her eyes. She said, "You know I can't hear you anymore," with an overdramatic sigh.

For just an instant I felt the presence of a peculiar bond, tying me to Maridel. It was not love, nor friendship, nor even the camaraderie that exists between old enemies. I believe it may have been a simpler or more universal denominator that unites us, all of us: an intuition that we are *not* entirely separate, after all; that if nothing else, we are *personae* in the same long and inconclusive drama. I felt for that instant like crossing the room and touching Maridel, affirming this link. I felt like embracing her. Whether she wanted or needed it or not, I felt like offering her my warmth, my companionship, my solace.

Then I felt chilly, so I began to put my clothes on.

Anyway, I thought I had figured out what Maridel had come for.

Between the shadows

We drove, the two of us, down from the mountaintop in late morning, while the sun shone and shadows fell with such clarity that one could sympathize with the misguided scientists and politicians who believe that these things are all there is: light and shadow; places where photons fall and places where they do not; coins that when tossed must land on one side or the other; events that occur or do not occur, but not neither, and not both. For surely (they imagine) there is only one History. Surely any given story is a true accounting of the facts, or it is not.

One fact of which we were well aware, Maridel and I, was that the place where Chief Administrator Rodarch's emissaries had begun their search for Black Malachi was his old home, the Solar Temple. Not that they expected to find him there. Quite the opposite. But it must have felt somehow obligatory. A pilgrimage. One came down the mountain, turned off the government-maintained road, left one's vehicle on the weed-grown, rain-gorged, pale red clay of the parking lot, and walked edgily up the hill to poke through the broken glass, the dead banana plants, the cracked glazed tile and ruptured pipes of that old New Age habitation.

I was as much a sucker for the place as anyone. I loved ruins and relics as much as any classical scholar. (I was, after all, on the way to becoming a relic myself.) And certainly I am not deaf to the poetry of desolation. Winter kept us warm, et cetera. Still, it felt ghastly somehow, nosing about like that. It was as though we were joining in the desecration of a tomb. God knows the signs of death were everywhere.

The place retained its strangeness. We were barely through the banana court before we had gotten lost. I thought I was leading us back toward the bedroom wing, but we found ourselves moving instead across a wide gallery, through whose fractured glazing one looked down on the remnants of an herb garden. The garden was in an early stage of succession to a natural or "climactic" state: its more aggressive residents, mints and comfrey and horseradish, had crossed their original bounds into the territory once assigned to the likes of lavender, southernwood, dittany-of-Crete. And weedy interlopers, as though amazed to have sprouted in fertile soil, flourished everywhere. Among these was a tall aster, still in bloom, an exile from the arid western flats that had once been farmland, and before that prairie. Its violet-blue petals radiated from a hub of tawny orange. The trouble with this world is, you can never be sure where your sympathies ought to lie. I thought Black Malachi would approve at least of the aster, if not of all the other invaders of his garden. He had never minded gate-crashers, as long as they contributed something to the overall *milieu*.

At the other end of the gallery was a series of doors, some of which had been broken in and others yanked off their hinges. I permitted myself to choose one of these either by instinct or purely at random, depending on how such things really work. I was certain I had never seen this part of the Temple before. Yet when I stepped through the door, with Maridel trailing listlessly behind me, I found myself in the old Music Room, which

I remembered, though not in its present condition. Chairs lay on their sides amid strewn paper, electric cables, broken cups. I fancied that I could hear the traces of a last elegiacal melody. *The End of All Songs.* Perhaps between "instinct" and "randomness" there lies a middle ground, a kind of latent or intrinsic memory that resides in objects, locations, past events. Perhaps such a memory—of music I had never heard—had drawn me here.

Perhaps not.

Maridel touched my sleeve. I looked at her. In such a setting, the ruined pleasure-palace, the sight of that beautiful, eight-months-pregnant nineteen-year-old girl was poignantly appropriate. I smiled at her—at *this*, the whole situation. But Maridel had more down-to-earth things on her mind.

"I need something to drink," she said. "Where's the kitchen?"

That, as I recalled, was the great secret. The center of the labyrinth. I looked around, from one way out to another. The faculty of intuition or hidden memory or blind guessing—whatever had brought us here— was stubbornly silent. But I did not want to admit this to Maridel. Also I had the idea that perhaps we should be getting on. So I took her by the hand and led her to the doorway nearest where we were standing. Either it would take us deeper inside, toward the kitchen, or it would take us out. One or the other. Yes or no.

Remember?

There was water standing on the floor. It seeped from between the tiles and trickled with a slight gurgling noise down the length of the chamber we had stepped into. If water pipes ran under here, perhaps the kitchen was nearby. The place smelled of rot. It grew darker, as we progressed, but somehow there was more allure about this than danger, so we plodded on toward a faint warm-colored glow that seemed to come from around a corner.

There was no corner, though, that we could find. The room may have had a slight curve, as many parts of the house appeared to. I put my hand up to touch the wall. It wasn't there. The darkness had taken on a persuasive solidity. I gave Maridel a shrug, meaning to suggest that we might have taken a wrong turn, would she like to stop and rest? She surprised me by smiling.

"Isn't it *precious*," she said.

A light must have clicked on, toggled by a motion-sensor or a pressure-plate under our feet. We were standing just outside an alcove furnished as a child's bedroom. The chairs and bed and bookshelves were so diminutively scaled, the colors of the paint so jewel-like, the whole room so tidy and bright that I felt like a visitor to a museum, standing before a spotlighted diorama. One stood at some remove from this magical little room; one could not enter it; it was reserved for the curators, or for some future race of beautiful, perfect children.

Maridel squeezed my hand. I felt her draw close to me, shivering with delight.

"Tristin," she whispered. "What is it? Where are we?"

I felt that I should caution her. There was a certain problem here, a riddle to be worked out. I tugged her hand, leading her on. She resisted, but for once in our mutual lives my will prevailed over hers.

As we stepped away, the light clicked off, and that bedroom vanished into the darkness of my memory, from which it has never emerged.

At the end of the imperceptible curve, the faint warm glow took on the outline of a door. I reached for the handle and was filled again with that thing—instinct or memory—that seemed to flow in and out of me like some autonomous etheric presence. I took a breath, then pushed through it.

We blinked at sunshine streaming down from skylights.

We stared across the rose-colored tile toward the gleaming stove, the altar, the *omphalos* of the house.

Black Malachi stared back at us. He wore an apron, and nothing else. His beard fell to his groin. He held a large cooking fork, with which he seemed to have been badgering some bacon in a pan. Flames danced underneath it.

"All the elements," Black Malachi said merrily. "This place has them all. A few more weeks, young lady. Have you got a name picked out? Tristin, you're all grown up. And just in time."

"*Blackie*." Like an airy spirit, Cervina materialized in a far corner of the room. "Stop playing prophet and offer them something to drink. Here," she said, beckoning Maridel, "come sit with me."

Black Malachi continued to stare at me. "You've really got," he said more quietly, man-to-man, wagging the cooking fork, "your work cut out for you."

Where is he? (1)

Maridel's birth agony began on one of the long gray afternoons that seem to drag on for most of the day in certain seasons, certain types of weather, certain phases of History. We must have been sitting for hours in the upstairs parlor, watching the flames play like whips against the square tiles of firebrick, studying the clouds through the curtainless French doors for patterns or portents, while some sort of briefing was conducted for the Chief Administrator in a room across the hall. We couldn't make out the words—Gwendola had the music turned too loud, *Black Angels*, one of Turner's favorites—but there was no need to. The sense was clear enough. The Administration's political wing, increasingly sensitive of late to the rumors of Turner Ashenden's survival, improving health and imminent return, was up in arms about the implications of this other, related event: this childbirth. How would the populace react? Would it embrace the child as a sort of hereditary hero? Would irrational rumors once more begin to fly? Perhaps (the suggestion was always present, in those advisors' eyes) the Chief Administrator should leave the Institute and return to the East, leaving the valley to the military wing. There were problems everywhere; one must choose which of them one was best able to address. One could always—after things had calmed down—come back.

Maridel drew in her breath. The pain that no man can know had made its first intrusion into her gut.

Violins shrieked like a creepshow theme song.

Rodarch appeared in the doorway, trailing uncertain aides. He stood there looking the very model of the archetypal male: large and fumbling, strong and inarticulate. Maridel, her brow lightly touched with dampness, looked up at him. She said, "It's nothing yet. There's a long way to go."

Gwendola sat alone across the room quite concerned with a small ceramic trinket, a dragon, a huckster-room toss-off, on which she had discovered a hairline crack. I don't know if she had any notion of what was happening to her daughter. I really don't.

Vinny was practical, as ever. "Should you, um, lie down or something?"—moving toward Maridel cautiously, like someone in a waiting room checking out the pile of magazines beside you.

Maridel remained still for a minute after that first, rapid contraction. "Where is he?" she said at last.

Vinny looked at me, and we both glanced furtively at the Chief Administrator, still hovering in the doorway. Perhaps (we thought) he had misheard her; perhaps he assumed that by *he* she meant *him*. He came further into the room—a bulky, uncomfortable presence.

"He'll, um . . ." Even Vinny found it hard to be offhand about this.

—He'll be here, I thought almost angrily.—He promised he'd get here in time.

Maridel closed her eyes.

"Mother told me—" she began; but another contraction started, too soon, and after that we became all rather swept up in it.

Where is he? (2)

Black Malachi did not come as he had promised. Maridel's labor progressed quickly to the stage of frequent, prolonged, and immensely painful contractions, with no one to tend her but Nurse Tawdry, who seemed very little accustomed to this kind of thing. Maridel refused to be taken to her own bedroom, preferring evidently the center-stage position provided by the upstairs parlor which was, one must acknowledge, warm and reasonably cheery with the fire going. She sat curled into herself on the loveseat, on piles of towels, with a sheet drawn around her shoulders. Something about the ancient ritual of birth makes all women look like ageless Woman— contorted with pain, staring out through feral eyes, trapped in an eddy of time beyond reach of help or hope or solace. Soon, very soon, it was night, and we brought in candles.

"Where is he?" Maridel hissed.

There was no hiding it now. Rodarch sat looking baffled on the far side of the room. He winced at the shrinking of Maridel's womb, and kept silent while she rested between spasms. The ordeal was not progressing well.

Vinny said, sometime past midnight, "Maybe I should go and get him."

Helplessly, I shook my head.

"You'll never find him by yourself," said Maridel, which was exactly what I had been thinking. Perhaps our minds were joined again, by her misery. Maridel pointed at me. "Take *him*."

—But . . . there's nothing . . .

Maridel shut her eyes, straining into another contraction.

Vinny caught my eye. Despite myself, despite everything, I nodded. Increasingly I had come to believe that one's desires are as irrelevant to Destiny as one's rational expectations, which go right out the window *very* early in the game.

"Okay," said Vinny. He patted Maridel on the arm, though I doubt that she felt it. She only would have gotten the general sense of things, at that point. Nonetheless Vinny told her quietly: "We'll find him. We'll be back."

From Maridel there was only a rapid dry movement of air, in and out, an act unrelated to ordinary breathing. She may have tried to nod.

It was two o'clock in the morning when we arrived at the Solar Temple. Everything looked quite dead and long-deserted from where we stood in the parking lot.

"Yeah, well, you know"—Vinny, gathering up his resolve to enter the ruins of the house—"he's probably sitting around in the dark smoking dope and tickling Cervina on the boobs. He's probably lost track of time. We'll just trot on up to his bedroom and get him."

This was more or less an invocation—one of those speeches that are important to make at the beginning of some doomed undertaking, on the low probability that they *might* pull some weight. (Think of ship launches or weddings, by way of comparison.) We crossed the banana court with our mutual breath held, and it was only when our eyes had gotten accustomed to the faint misting of moonlight and it became obvious that no ghosts were about to jump us that we began to settle down.

"What a fucking mess," said Vinny.

I pointed in a direction that I thought would take us inward, toward the bedroom wing.

"What, the greenhouse? Okay, if you want. I thought I'd get going upstairs, though." Vinny turned away.

I lunged after him, terrified at the thought of becoming separated. We collided; he hadn't even taken a step, just stood there getting his bearings. I tried to signal an apology.

Vinny gave me a cockeyed smile. "You know, Tristin," he said. "You're just about the only one I like, anymore. Your heart's really in the right place."

This might have been comforting, but we had a difficult role to play out. Vinny signaled an angle of departure, and the two of us set off between dead plants into the echoing depths of the Temple.

If such a thing were possible, I would have sworn that the whole place had changed shape or dimension since my last visit, a few weeks ago. I mention this only to convey the extent to which my perceptions had become twisted. I had no idea whatsoever of where we were in the house, or how any particular room related to the overall scheme of things. Vinny may have been as disoriented as I, but he had the sense to conceal this behind a matter-of-fact façade. Such things are important, I think, to our unseen audience. You know: never let 'em see you sweat.

Taking my arm, Vinny pointed. "In here, I think."

It was a dark portico, whose pneumatic door was stuck perpetually open. I entered, trying to feel that tug of memory or intuition, feeling only tired. Further doors gave off this way and that. A suite, I thought. Or a rat's nest. Vinny prodded me from behind, forcing me deeper into it. Rats in a trap. Before us the chamber swelled into a tall-ceilinged space with huge windows and some kind of slender wooden framework, trellis, scaffolding . . .

I turned around, thinking Vinny might have spoken. He was staring at something over my shoulder. I tried to follow his gaze.

The wooden frame unfolded in its rickety manner upward, almost to the ceiling. It was silhouetted at low contrast by the expanse of windows beyond, whose thin mullions made a sort of counterpoint to the cat's-cradle of posts and struts. Vinny seemed to be looking at something near the very top, among the cobwebbed shadows. I steadied my gaze.

Like an owl on the uppermost planking, Black Malachi perched. At first I thought he was radiating a very pale aura; slowly I figured out that the light was coming from something on his lap or in his hand. An unusually bright wristwatch might have done it. It was hard to tell; he was a good twelve or fifteen feet above us. You could just make out his features, his closed eyes, and the way his bare stomach rose and fell with his breathing. His hands were clasped over his navel. He looked like a dissolute little Buddha, sleeping one off.

"Hey," said Vinny. His voice was diminished by the grandeur of the room, vanishing like a whisper. He raised it: "Hey, Malachi. Wake up, man."

Up above, the little wizard breathed more deeply.

Vinny tried it again. Black Malachi started to snore.

"The fat bastard." Vinny shook his head. "He's defying us. We'll have to go up and get him."

I would, he meant. Frail as the scaffolding looked, I was the logical candidate for this mission. I looked up doubtfully.

"I'll tell you what," said Vinny. "I'll go look for Cervina. She's probably used to this kind of thing. Maybe she'll know how to wake him up."

—No, I thought, shaking my head.—Stay. I'll do it.

The scaffolding shuddered and swayed, even with my slight body-weight, but I guessed it would hold. As I climbed from one level to the next I noticed that, besides myself and Black Malachi, the framework supported an enormous canvas which seemed to consist of a myriad tiny black-on-white swirls. It was as though Black Malachi were designing some wall-covering of mathematic intricacy, whose pattern could not be said, at a glance, either to repeat or not to repeat, but simply to continue as far as one could see in all directions. Near the center of the design was a bit of comic relief: a red arrow, labeled in a bright, cartoonish hand, YOU ARE HERE. Several inches away was a similar sign and another arrow. This one said REST ROOMS. The signature of Black Malachi.

At the top, I hoisted myself onto a platform of loose planking. The little prophet sat cross-legged and unconscious a couple of feet away. The glow that had guided me here came from something he held between both curled hands, still unidentifiable. With its center of gravity so high, the shaky edifice reacted to any twitch in a distinctly ominous manner. There was no time to worry about this. I tried to concentrate on Maridel. Her pain. My promise to her.

I touched Black Malachi's arm.

To my astonishment, he opened his eyes immediately, very wide, and stared straight into mine.

"I am prepared," he said, "to grant your every wish. You have only—"

He raised one hand in one of his patented, carnival side-show gestures, waved it mysteriously in the air, and extended it to me. Had he been a professional magician, it would have held a spray of paper flowers. As it was, it held nothing. Specifically, it held *no thing*: only that faint, immaterial glow.

"You have only," he told me, "to ask. Tell me what you want, and you shall receive it. But for God's sake do so *politely*, dear boy. You know I am a stickler for good manners. That's why we miss Ashenden so."

Vinny called up from below. "Damn it, Malachi. Cut the crap and come down the ladder. Maridel's in pretty bad shape. You said you'd come in time."

"In time," repeated Black Malachi. His voice seemed to warp the words into new shapes, new connotations. "*In time*, I shall be there. Just as I promised. But first, we have a minor miracle to undertake. Tristin shall find his tongue again, before we leave this place."

My trembling grew worse. Black Malachi held his hand out. The glow seemed to dim, to diffuse into the air between us. Then, in that astonishing way he had, the burly little man smiled at me—a pure, soothing masterpiece of a smile. He lowered his voice, so that only I could hear him, and just barely.

"A *minor* miracle, mind you," he said. "I don't expect you to talk. At least, not yet. But why don't you *sing* for old Blackie?"

At the word "sing," his hovering hand fell lightly to my shoulder. The light went out for good. At the same time, energy seemed to pass by direct conduction from those gentle fingertips. I found myself sitting mouth-open and trying very hard to make some sound. Hot damp air passed through my larynx, but no distinct noise. Maridel's spell was holding.

The scaffolding shook. Vinny called: "Malachi! What are you doing up there?"

He held me fixed in his smile. Slowly his hand moved along my shoulder, pressing softly into the sinewy tissues of my neck, easing its way toward my esophagus.

A vast weight of accumulated stress and fear and sorrow seemed to pass through my muscles, through my limbs, as though my body were flinging it away. My stomach quaked. Black Malachi's hand reached my adam's apple. Tears formed at my eyes.

"Now," he said. "Try now."

I tried. I made a tiny, croaking noise.

"Ah," said Black Malachi.

Vinny said, "You *know* the kid's going to be gigantic. You *saw* how large she was."

At my throat, those warm fingers faltered. I clutched for them, but Black Malachi pulled his hand away.

"You're right," he said. He gathered himself up, prepared to climb down from the platform. "I suppose I must—"

And to everyone's amazement, all quiet rage, I chanted hoarsely: "*Wait—no—come back.*"

Blood

It ran out of Maridel's open womb and down the sides of her stomach and soaked the towels and spilled onto the floor, more of it than I had ever seen. It dripped from the knife that lay on the coffee table. It covered Black Malachi's hands and wrists, as he yanked the tiny monster head that protruded from the incision. It drenched the rubbery body that came out in sections, like the jointed carapace of an insect, one brutal jerk at a time, into the wan daybreak. It mixed in lumpy clots with the mucus that covered the shrunken face. I thought the child must be stillborn, drowned in all that blood, as its mother was dying from having shed it. But Black Malachi wiped the face with his sleeve and performed the famous inversion: upside-down his newborn son was slapped until the first wail blew his lungs clean.

The next day, Maridel was dead. After the delivery she had not spoken. She slipped from this side to the other without so much as a sigh.

Chief Administrator Rodarch, who had remained at her side during all those final hours, rose at last and stepped drunkenly out onto the terrace, where he stared westward at the horrible thing the last century had done to the plain. Then he sent for his car and went down from the mountain. I thought, gone for good.

Madame Gwendola took to her bed and lay in what appeared to be stupefaction. I, for one, was relieved to have her out of the way.

˙Black Malachi—the only one in a position to do so—christened the infant "Destry." He handed him (a fat little boy, already sucking hungrily at whatever was placed in his mouth) over to the care of Nurse Tawdry. She whisked him off to some distant corner of the manor, perhaps to spare Gwendola from the sound of his crying.

In the kitchen, those of us still left—Vinny, Partner, myself and Cervina, who had come up with Malachi—were having an impromptu wake. Cervina was making breakfast, and Partner was mixing drinks. Vinny and I were just sitting at the table. I don't remember for sure, but I think none of us had slept yet. It might very well have been that none of us had even spoken.

At Black Malachi's entrance, a little shiver passed between us. I felt it; I'm sure we all did. It was as though Death had come into the room. This seems unfair, I suppose—but it was an instantaneous feeling, not a rational thought. And though no one had been talking to begin with, the room seemed to grow very still and quiet.

Black Malachi crossed the kitchen and stood beside Cervina at the stove. She looked at him with tragic fondness. He said nothing for a while. Eventually Partner got back to mixing drinks—five now instead of four— and Cervina poked a bit at some overdone sausage.

The whole world had changed, as it is wont to do, in a moment, or less than that: the moment in which Destry's spirit came in, or that in which Maridel's departed. As a token of how far things had come, it was silent Tristin, of all people, who broke the long silence.

"You tried to save her," I said.

My voice, from lack of practice, was weak, with no control over such finer points as inflection or intonation. Thus my epoch-marking sentence, innocent enough when written down, was a naive masterwork of ambiguity. It could have served as an uncolored remark, a vote of confidence, an inquiry, an accusation. Black Malachi studiously regarded me, and very slowly gave a nod that seemed to acknowledge my accomplishment. Beginner's luck, I suppose.

He said, "I did not try particularly to do one thing or another." He was quiet another moment, thoughtful, then went on. "I had no desire to see Maridel live, nor any wish to kill her." He looked at all of us, in turn, around the room. "Do you find that shocking?"

We had been shocked too much by now; we had reached our limit. Cervina rubbed his shoulder, as though the problem might simply be that he was tired.

"The truth," said Black Malachi, "the *truth* of the matter is, I don't think Maridel had any intention of living with that child. I do not think she cared so much which of them survived, as long as it was not both."

In this insane new world—a world in which Tristin Maleish could talk—such a remark seemed eminently reasonable. Vinny handed around a tray of full-pint bloody Mary's, and Cervina served scrambled eggs. We must have been not only crazy but famished, for these little emblems of death and fertility did not give us the least pause.

As we sat around afterward with empty plates and glasses in our hands, too weary even to carry them to the sink, Cervina said, "Well, I guess it's awful, but . . . I mean, she *was* a cruel person, you know. Look at Turner."

We looked—not at Turner but at Cervina. We held our silence. She may have discovered the one taboo that remained to us.

How, anyway, could one explain that Maridel had been no more cruel than any elemental force—than, say, a thunderstorm is cruel, or *der Tod* himself?

Black Malachi rose. To Cervina alone, though loudly enough that we all could hear, he said, "That reminds me. See you soon, dear." He made a motion of his hand, a half-distracted gesture.

. . . Then he was gone.

I don't know how to say it, other than that. He was simply not in the room any longer. It was a crazy world, with the craziness that follows great trauma and lack of sleep. Perhaps in such a world, anything really *is* possible.

However that may be, Black Malachi was gone. He did not "suddenly vanish" or any such thing; that would not be accurate. We just found ourselves sitting around a room that did not have Black Malachi in it. You will have to take my word for this, of course, but it did not feel so very odd, at the time.

No more odd, certainly, than it felt to hear myself say, to Cervina, "Will he be back?"

Or to hear her say, as she might have said on any number of occasions before this, "Oh, he'll come back. You know Blackie."

Destry

As you must have gathered, our story—"our" story—is virtually over. By now, there was almost nothing left of "us" to tell a story about. This is one of the really unsettling lessons of History: its impersonality. It goes on, though we as individual participants do not.

What will happen next, as the spiral of time bends past my life and past the lives of all those people I knew and have written about, is that the story—the same Story, though it would take a god's-eye-view to recognize it—will continue, perhaps even in certain ways repeat itself, but with a new cast of characters upon its stage. One of those characters will surely be the one who is now only a boy, the one Black Malachi named Destry. I will take a moment now to talk about him. Just a moment. For it seems to me there is a certain balance in this, a coming back to where we began. We know so little of Turner Ashenden's childhood, after all. Perhaps there is something to learn from examining Destry's.

He was a remarkable child. He was large for his age; he was quick to learn things; he was lovely. His hair was pale, nearly white, with a touch of Maridel's gold in it, and his face was round with brilliant eyes like Black Malachi's. His limbs were very well proportioned for his age—the legs long as though he was eager to be up and running, the fingers remarkably agile. He was good at drawing, for instance. He listened attentively. He did not babble on about nothing, as other children do. One got the eerie feeling that he was *waiting*. I imagine that a little prince might act this way, guarding his tongue, keeping himself alert and watchful until his own day should arrive. But there were no princes anymore. Even Harvey Goldaster's little grandchildren attended the government school. There was no child like this, as far as I knew, but Destry.

Naturally enough, he became the object of considerable public fascination. He was a legendary child, and he seemed to know it. People assumed, as there was no reason not to, that his father had been Turner Ashenden, the Defender, the last hero. And his mother, a beautiful girl barely grown, who had died in childbirth, made (if possible) an even more romantic figure. The boy was thus, in a sense, close enough to having been royally born for all practical purposes. He *was* a little prince, whose domain was that of legend, of poetry, of late-night storytelling.

It was not a trivial heritage. Such things wield great power in human minds and human hearts. And even in this new day, this new Age of Reason, we are still human. All question of governmental provenance aside, Destry was, or would someday be, a power to be reckoned with.

And that, I'm sure, must be just what the Chief Administrator came to realize. That must be why—one morning, one distant spring—Rodarch came back to the Institute.

We had long expected him. Or I should say, *I* had. Gwendola was enfeebled and to all appearances thoroughly senile, by this time. She spent much of her time in the sitting room, playing older and older music, and the rest of it in bed. Nurse Tawdry, who was frail enough herself, was needed less and less as Destry's nanny and more and more as Gwendola's cupbearer. Vinny and the band were gone, most of the time, traveling and performing in the East again; though the Institute remained a kind of home base for them. They came back for several weeks each year, especially on the holidays that Gwendola still devoutly kept. The burden, and the joy, of child-rearing thus fell increasingly to me, who was arguably the least qualified of anybody to have assumed it.

The reason I had expected a visit, if not from the Chief Administrator himself then from his local agents, was all this little-prince business: in an age and a society where egalitarianism ruled, by due force if necessary, raising a child such as Destry, alone on a godless mountaintop, must have seemed an act of subtle defiance. The boy was six or seven at the time. I had already turned down a dozen invitations to have him boarded-out at one of the schools in the Settling Out Camps. They would probably have taken him from me, anyway, except for a technicality that had to do with counseling the child's parents and obtaining documentary evidence of having done so. As mathematicians have discovered, there are unforeseeable quirks in any system, any set of rules. I informed the government functionaries that the child's father was Black Malachi Pantera, who was alive but not in residence here. (Gwendola had the wit, thank heavens, to corroborate this.) I gave Black Malachi's address as "Hartfell Chalet," as the Solar Temple was listed in government tax records, confident that —whether this were still true or not—no one would be able to find him. And this had, so far, presented the Administration with a procedural obstruction it had not managed to clear.

When I saw the Chief Administrator extract his stately bulk from an armored transport and begin walking (rather stiffly, I thought) across the flat but these days weed-grown lawn, I wondered whether the game was up. Rodarch had always struck me as an honorable man, but inevitably there are other considerations. In his mind, I'm sure, a child would truly be better off in more normal, more *ordinary* surroundings than those of this eccentric Institute.

The Chief Administrator waved at me. He smiled his well-known flat and insipid smile. I waved back. There must have been guards with him, but they remained in the vehicle. In my mind I was formulating and rejecting various plans. The truth was, I was rather stuck. Behind me, out the open front door, Destry appeared at a full run. He hesitated, catching sight of Rodarch, and ended by wrapping himself around one of my legs. I loved him terribly, you must realize. I was very afraid.

Rodarch came to a halt, a couple of paces away, and stared down at the boy even as the boy was staring shyly up at him. An odd look was in the big man's eye. I hadn't seen him, face-to-face, as I now realized, since the day Maridel died. That fact—that this was a reunion, of an odd kind—made the moment feel even more awkward. Rodarch had never seemed to mind awkwardness, though. Perhaps he just didn't notice it. He cleared his throat.

"They tell me—" (his voice husky, as though he seldom used it anymore) "—they tell me that he isn't Ashenden's, after all."

I shook my head.

"They tell me you are talking now."

I nodded. Then, thinking this was silly, I added, "That's right."

Rodarch nodded back. "They also say," and here I think he was speaking of a different *they*, no longer of government informants, "that he is Turner Ashenden, come back again."

I said, "That's just superstition."

"Of course." Rodarch was still staring at Destry, who peeked out from behind me, and at this point he gave the little boy a slightly forced—though still apparently heartfelt—smile. Destry beamed back. Rodarch's smile grew a bit brighter and more relaxed. "He *is* a bit like him," the big man said very quietly.

Like Turner, he must have meant. That smile. I said, "Would you like to come in?"

He shook his head. Then, in what seemed a very rare, spontaneous change of heart, he nodded. "Well, maybe so," he said, looking oddly at me. "I didn't come to take him away from you. I just wanted to . . . you know. To come back. Just to see."

The last party

Destry did not, however, spend the rest of his boyhood in my care. I kept him for years, and taught him many things—solid, objective skills like reading and mathematics, as well as other, more abstract things, like attitudes, ideals, daily habits. I think I did reasonably well, during my time as his guardian. I hope, and believe, I was a positive influence. To this day, I think, Destry retains something of my quietness, my penchant for keeping still and observing. I even hope that some of his gentleness and his generosity, more evident now than ever, might be attributable to me.

But by the day of the Chief Administrator's visit, though I could certainly not have known, my life with Destry—that fleeting and final period of relative happiness—was all but over.

Vinny and Partner and Twill came back to the mountaintop, bringing some new friends, a concord of young musicians, many of them women. I have always been slow to get to know people, but they were all very nice, and in truth it *was* good to have company. Good for Destry, of course, and good for me too. It was around the winter solstice. Christmas, if you go in for that. Or Hanukkah, the Darkmass, the night of lights . . . the worst time of the year to be alone, as I can now confidently tell you.

Vinny had brought an awful lot of whiskey. I guess it must have been

a good year for him. He and the others were all wearing new clothes, and
from the snippets of news they brought back from their travels I gathered
that things in general were not so bad that year. It was only a respite, of
course. They have since become much worse.

So there we were, on the third or fourth night of their visit, which
might have been the solstice itself or the day after. Since it was dark and
cold we tended to spend our time in the kitchen or in the upstairs sitting
room, which had the big fireplace. Mostly it was the kitchen. Even Gwendola emerged from her isolation and joined us—drawn by the spirit of the
occasion, even if, as I suspected, she wasn't quite sure what the occasion
was. She seated herself at the head of the kitchen table and played hostess
(though as usual, it was poor Nurse Tawdry who ended up doing the
hostessing). Night had fallen, but the only way you could tell that was by
looking out the very small window. The electricity still worked, in those
days, so there was plenty of light, and anyway in consideration of the
season Vinny had brought, and was burning, hundreds of candles. There
was a bowl of some kind of hot punch—the kind of thing that really, as
the saying goes, sneaks up on you. While the rest of us were getting drunk
and singing songs and acting foolish, Destry was running about allowing
himself to be made the darling of everyone.

At some well-advanced stage of all this, it began to seem to me that
there were more people in the room than there ought to have been. This
was an odd feeling; and what made it odder was the way in which it had
come to me. If this makes sense, it was less a matter of perception than
of reflection, of analysis. It was as though I had *concluded* (as opposed to
seen) that there were twenty or thirty people wandering about, where there
ought to have been ten or twelve.

Well, it's true that we were drinking, and my senses were dulled. But
that accounts more for what happened next than for my having gotten the
notion in the first place. What happened next was, I launched myself on
the misbegotten project of moving from one person to the next, looking
each in the eye, making sure that it was someone I had met and whom I
had expected to see at the party. Naturally, everyone met these qualifi-
cations. (Everyone also looked at me as though I were quite batty.) Still,
there were twenty or thirty people milling around—if not more, by this
time—and I was unshakably sure of it.

At last, in one of those moments of drunken inspiration, I decided to bring Destry in on this. He was, after all, my greatest intimate. I found him underneath the kitchen table, no doubt busy at some important project of make-believe; I knelt down to signal my intention to talk.

"How are you doing, Tristin?" he asked me gravely. His little face was worried up into a smaller version of Black Malachi's bedside-manner expression.

"Destry," I said, "how many people do you think are here?"

He frowned. Without looking at the crowd around us he said, "Twenty-seven."

Foolishly, I grabbed him by the arm. I whispered, "Are you sure?"

"No," he said. "But there could be. I *like* twenty-seven."

I let him go. Even precocious children think like children, it seems. I said, "I just felt like there might be people here we hadn't met."

"Ask Madame Gwendola," he said.

I am a historian; memory is my laboratory. For several seconds after this offhand remark, I tried to remember exactly how the boy had said it and why it had sounded funny. At last I asked Destry, "What do you mean?"

He shrugged. He seemed anxious to get back to his playing, as though he found these questions puzzling and boring. "*Someone* must have known them," he said, "or they couldn't be here. Could they?"

I did not understand this—I didn't know why, for example, he had said "must have known them," in the past tense—but I experienced one of those flashes of alarm that had always been a feature of my life with this boy. I imagine this must be how a parent feels when his child displays an impressive but dangerous talent—say, an ability to walk along the top of an extremely high fence—which one had not hitherto suspected.

Straightening, I looked down the table at Gwendola. She was still sitting in her chair at the head of the table. She looked half asleep. Her eyes were narrow, and her head nodded in a slow rhythm, as though in accompaniment to music no one else could hear. I turned to ask Destry something further, but the boy was gone. He was quick as well as clever: his father's legacy, I guess.

At the thought of Black Malachi, I felt a warm hand lie softly on my back. The touch alone gave me a jolt of recognition; by the time I turned around and stared into those sharp bright eyes, my feelings had progressed all the way to astonishment.

"It's getting late for her," said the vexatious little man. He was in his late twenties now and managed to look twice that. "You ought to let her go."

"Gwendola?" I said. "But . . . I'm not . . ."

Black Malachi patted me again. "Thank you," he said, "for keeping the boy. You've been good to him, he says. You've been a good friend."

I was more surprised by this, in a way, than by Black Malachi's unscheduled appearance (which, if you see what I mean, one *expects* not to expect). "You've talked to him?" I said. The words came out sounding hurt and faintly accusatory.

He gave me a sympathetic smile.

"Well, that is—" I felt very drunk all of a sudden; disconnected thoughts were swirling around in me. "I mean, of course he *is* your son. You have every right. I only—"

That smile, those eyes, touched me with an almost palpable pressure, like an extension of the healer's hands. Very solemnly Black Malachi said, "Tristin, I've come to take him."

Something escaped me like a sob—something utterly incoherent, a failure of my hard-won ability to talk. I staggered as though from a physical blow. "Are you . . . do you mean, *tonight?*"

He waved a hand around the room. "Look at this," he said. "The poor woman's drowning in holiday sentiment. Things are unstable here. She's hung on as long as she can, I'm afraid. I don't want Destry here when the thing collapses."

I thought, Like father like son. I said, "Blackie"—finding some comfort in the familiar form of address—"do you mean that . . . that this, that Gwendola is . . . what *do* you mean?"

He shook his head. "Never slow down," he said. "Never explain. Just keep talking. Keep the story moving. Eventually the truth will emerge, or you'll run out of story. Either way, the curtain will come down."

I think he might have been speaking of something very specific here: my effort, so far unsuccessful, to write down the history of the brief career of Turner Ashenden. Though of course with Black Malachi, there were always other levels of reference, possible connections to a less comprehensible realm. *The other side.* It was this—the implication of the numinous—that disturbed me most.

"Will he be all right?" I said, allowing myself an oblique connection of my own. "You'll take good care of him? I have a right to *ask*, at least. Don't I?"

Black Malachi took a long breath. For the first time in my knowledge of him, a degree of weariness was visible in those dark eyes. "Perhaps, Tristin," he said thoughtfully, "we could arrange a trade."

Only I

The longest evenings passed in silence.

Destry was gone. Vinny and the other musicians left a couple of days after the party. Madame Gwendola suffered a kind of collapse; the word is not really descriptive, however, because she did not fall down or sink into her bed or anything like that at all. Perhaps I should say, she *froze up*. She became very still. Nurse Tawdry helped her into the large chair in the downstairs sitting room, her favorite place in the house, and she sat there like a dying queen upon her throne—not speaking, not glancing about, not reacting to my presence or my absence at all.

I was frightened. I felt that something very odd was about to happen. My appointed meeting with Black Malachi loomed up like a mountain, the only relief at all in a very gray landscape. But even this was not necessarily a good thing. It was not a mountain I was sure I wanted to climb.

I spent those nights working on my narrative, trying to make a start or at least to establish a tone or find a voice or whatever one does, to begin with. I wrote out many pages longhand. Some of them contained whole paragraphs, the beginning of some scene or a little authorial essay. Others went wrong after only a sentence, even a phrase. After a while I grew tired of throwing perfectly good paper into the fire, so I worked on acquiring the discipline of composing in my head. *Decline and Fall* was written that way, you know: each of those well-formed paragraphs was inscribed entire after having been processed and perfected in Gibbon's mind. I grew gradually adept at this, but it only revealed my greater failing or unsuitability.

I had much to say and the basic means of saying it, but I lacked what Turner would have called "that spark."

Regardless of any of this—of me or my problems or indeed any human concerns at all—winter grew old and the days grew by tiny degrees longer, here on the mountaintop.

My meeting with Black Malachi took place, as scheduled, on the second of February. It was one of those evenings. Cold mist clung to the stones of the old manor. The moon was discernible only as a pale discoloration of the sky. There was not much wind: only enough to keep the clouds moving around us, forming ghostly patterns and dissolving them in the black void beyond the terrace rail.

At about midnight, wrapping a heavy cloak around my bathrobe, I ambled out onto the lawn. I was not cold; merely trembling. In one hand I held a glass of wine, still warm from being twirled over my candle. A few patches of snow, still hanging on from a January blizzard, lay between the rugged-looking clumps of switchgrass. I had come to prefer the lawn's new, wild look to its earlier, croquet-field incarnation. Snow got into my slippers and quickly melted. I felt silly, out-of-place here. But of course this *was* my place. It was, and remains, my home.

I took a sip of wine, set the glass down in the snow, and waited.

Ahead of me, one of the sheets of mist resolved itself into the plump, stately form of Black Malachi. He came forward like someone in a great hurry. I supposed he was eager to get our business done and return home to Destry and Cervina. I approved of this.

We stood for a moment with those shadows all around us, silently weaving and unweaving.

"Well, all right," said the bearded little man at last. He held out a hand to me. His expression was genial.

I raised my arm toward his. Then I paused. It was not doubt and not even hesitation and certainly—at this late stage of the game—it was not fear. It was more like excitement, a desire to prolong for a few more moments the anticipation, the wonder, the *innocence* that I was surprised to discover I still could feel. Imagine.

But Black Malachi looked a tiny bit impatient, and it *was* cold outside, so I stuck my arm out the rest of the way, so that our transaction could occur.

And then—

[Ah, dear reader. Have we met before, at a place like this?]

"Take him, by God," said the feisty little prophet. "Take him, and let me get out of here. And take his girlfriend too, while you're at it. Poor Gwendola! It's all a body can do to *die* these days."

"Yes," I whispered, feeling the certainty of the thing flow like warm blood through me. "Yes, I will . . ."

Black Malachi released my hand. He glanced at the ground. "Is that wine?" he asked me.

I did not respond. My mind was filled with other things—like the shadows that seemed to stir like a small army around us, a cast of thousands, in that midwinter night.

"You're right," I stammered. "You're . . . he's *out here*. He's alive!"

"No, damn it," Black Malachi growled. "*You're* alive. Don't you understand anything? You're goddamned well *alive*. You can sèe it now, can't you? See it all—the whole goddamned thing—the beginning and the end of it. *All* the beginnings and ends. All the bloody middles."

The two of us stood there, lost briefly together in the timeless story that it has been my subsequent task to relate. After a minute or so Black Malachi gave a wry nod, offered me a farewell hand. There was nothing in his clasp but an ordinary sort of warmth.

"Enough to drive you to drugs, isn't it?" he companionably said.

"No," I whispered. "It's . . . beautiful . . . it's . . ." I pointed across the snow that lightly, imperfectly, covered the ruined lawn.

"—I can see them now."

ABOUT THE AUTHOR

Richard Grant is the author of two previous novels, *Saraband of Lost Time* (runner-up for the Philip K. Dick Award) and *Rumors of Spring*. He currently lives in Maine, where he is at work on his next novel, *Through the Heart*.

Read a preview from Richard Grant's new novel: *Through the Heart* coming in January of 1992

A monstrous vehicle called the *Oasis* moves inexorably across the wasteland. A hulking form that symbolizes sanctuary, it dispenses a treatment for "The Crying," a plague of madness that has decimated the land.

When his wagon breaks down in the desert, Kem's father trades his son to the *Oasis* for a new engine. Thus begins Kem's new life as a galley slave aboard the *Oasis* where he is befriended, in turns, by the strangely androgynous Sanders, the enigmatic Captain Hand, and beautiful Davina. Slowly Kem is drawn further into the labyrinthian structure of the *Oasis*, for he cannot resist questioning the convoluted systems that govern life and death in this desolate world. . . .

The truth proves to be more shocking than he ever suspected.

The following is an excerpt from *Through the Heart*, Richard Grant's haunting new novel.

One day before the afternoon break a messenger came down to the galley bearing a piece of paper with Kem's name on it.

The galley boss (who neither read nor remembered names well) looked up from the paper with eyes still squinty from the effort and peered around the room. Kem watched the man out of simple curiosity—any break in the monotony of galley work was a relief—and he thought he saw a flicker of something, maybe disdain, as the boss's eyes brushed over him. Kem tightened his lips and returned to the hobart, where hundreds of dishes remained to be washed and the heat of the water had already turned his arms red up to the elbows. The sound of his name spoken aloud above the background din of machinery was so unexpected that in a way he did not quite hear it. In another way he did; he had expected such a downward turn of events. He looked up just as the galley boss was puffing out his chest to expel that single syllable again.

Kem.

But by the time he heard it a second time his heart was already going fast and his hands were dripping hot dirty water onto the deck.

"Come on, then," the galley boss said crossly. "This fellow's got a job for you."

The fellow in question stood just outside the galley door, sensibly declining to enter that steamy fiefdom. He was a youth just a few years older than Kem himself and not quite as tall. His expression was sympathetic; he may well have served his time in the galley, too, not so long ago.

"I don't know if this is good news or not," the young man said, already heading up the passageway. "One of the Residents asked for you by name." He glanced at Kem across his shoulder, making a genial sort of appraisal. "What'd you do, steal something?"

"I did *not*—" The moment of panic was long enough for Kem to construct the bare outlines of a terrible and pointless plot against him, a frame-up.

The young man laughed. He went on cheerfully, "Or is it some old lady who thinks you're cute? Well take it from me—get them to give you money. That'll last longer than *they* will."

Kem smiled; he tried to make himself companionable. The young man seemed quite at home in this part of the *Oasis*—indeed, in this part of life itself—and perfectly happy to be joking with a galley boy. He turned from one corridor to another with the ease of long familiarity, and the couple of guards they encountered seemed to know him, for they nodded as he passed. Kem wondered if his own life here would ever be so easy or so lighthearted. He wondered what the young man had done to arrange things this way.

They stopped at a hand-lettered sign, RESIDENTS AND GUESTS ONLY, identical to the one Kem had seen on the deck above, but this time screwed onto a doorway far from sunlight.

"You're on your own," the young man told him. He smiled, still with a faintly curious expression, and went back the way they had come.

Kem pressed lightly at the door, which swung on rusty hinges inward.

He was again, disconcertingly, alone. Before him was a dim chamber whose dimensions Kem could not judge (though they seemed immense) crammed as tightly as could be with rows of books. Some of the books were arranged on shelves and some in stacks and some more carelessly in piles. Whatever the original plan of storage had been, it was long lost in the flood of later acquisitions. Many of the aisles were blocked with cartons that had simply been left in the middle of them, not even unpacked. The only illumination in the place came from prisms set in the high ceiling. It was absorbed quickly by the shelves and their dark-spined contents; very little light made it so far as the bare, rusty metal of the deck. The air smelled strongly of mold, which must find a luxurious nest in these millions of rotting pages.

It was by far the most appealing place that Kem had ever been. There was a sense of quiet, despite the everpresent throb of machinery, and a feeling that however long you lingered here, you would be safe from interruption.

Even when interruption—inevitably—arrived, it did not startle him. A soft and oddly damp sound, like someone tidying up after a meal, came from one side, muffled by books. Kem turned without alarm to see the tall man, the Resident, settled on a low stool with only his head and shoulders visible. He was wearing (rather absurdly, it seemed to Kem) his palm hat. He looked around, not quite in Kem's direction, as though he were having trouble seeing in this light.

"Hello?" he said. "Is that Kem? Did I get the name right?"

Kem nodded, but the man still did not seem quite to be looking in his direction. He said, "Yes, sir. It's Kem."

"Ah, good."

Kem waited for the Resident to give him some explanation, some instruction at least. Instead the man sat absolutely still for several moments, more than long enough to make Kem fidget. Then he raised a hand to his face, dabbing it with a napkin or rag. Kem supposed he had caught a cold, up there in the chill air of the Residents' quarters. At last he motioned for Kem to come nearer. He lifted a book from the table beside him and held it out, wordlessly. Kem did took it, remaining an arm's length away.

Sun Tales and Moon Songs, the cover said in stark old-world graphics.

"They say I can have you for an hour," the Resident told him. "I have been having trouble with my eyes."

A partial explanation; though for a few moments longer the man offered nothing beyond it. Then he looked up, blinked once or twice, and seemed at last to focus on Kem without difficulty.

"I neglected to tell you last time," he said in a tone of courteous, even quaint, formality. "My name is Tallheron."

It sounded that way, one word and not two. Kem thought about this, the name itself, and the fact that the man had seen fit to reveal it to a galley boy. He supposed some sort of response was called for, but his background among the wagons had been short on social nicety. Inspired somewhat by the books all around them, he ventured:

"How do you do?"—which seemed like the sort of thing a character in a story might have said. Tallheron nodded slowly, which Kem took as a sign that the old-fashioned words were acceptable.

"Well, Kem," Tallheron said, "I sent for you because I believe you can read. I believe I saw you reading the signs in the hallway, and the cover of that book. Is that right?"

With some reluctance Kem nodded, then—in case the man could not see him clearly—he said, "A little. I can only read a little." This sounded funny to him, less than a full answer, so he added, "You know, from the winter camps."

Tallheron frowned. "The winter camps," he repeated, as though the term were not familiar to him. Then he went on, "I had been hoping, since you *can* read, that you would read aloud to me from there," motioning toward the book in Kem's hand.

Kem looked at it again, doubtfully. He opened it at random, to a page filled with small print and wide margins. It did not seem too complicated, though he had to strain somewhat to make out the print in the dim light.

"Sure," he said. "If you want me to."

Tallheron said, "Good." He settled back into his chair a bit. "Good. I would appreciate that very much. I would do it myself, you know, except for my eyes. I had quite a time even finding it."

Kem could imagine so. He hefted the volume in his hand, flipped a few more pages. All looked much the same, though some had longer sentences and paragraphs than others.

"The story I'd like to hear," said Tallheron, "is called 'Death in the Back Yard.' Oh, but . . . ." He gestured as though in impatience. "But sit down," he told Kem. "Don't stand there and tire yourself."

There was not much choice of sitting arrangements; over any of the nearby stacks of books Kem chose the deck. The metal was warm beneath him, and alive with the jolting and shuddering of the great landcraft. Kem negotiated the table of contents with some difficulty (Tallheron had gotten the title wrong) and, though very self-conscious, began to read in a loud voice:

DEATH IN THE ROSE GARDEN
A native folk tale, as narrated by Rowan Free

In the land that was once know as Fields of Wheat there lived a girl named Julia. She was an ordinary girl except for her eyes, which were very bright, and her hands, which were always warm even on cold nights. This was when winters were cold and the snow began to fall during Fly South Moon and kept falling for a long time thereafter.

Julia lived in a village where there were very few other children because the water was supposed to be bad. There were large houses on the hillsides around the village but not many of them had people living in them. Their big windows looked down through the tall grass and the trees and the bushes that the people had once planted, and Julia liked to imagine what the people who had left would think now if they came home after all these years and saw their houses this way. Sometimes the people who had stayed behind went into the big houses and took things away to the smaller houses where they lived. Sometimes they cut the trees down to make their cooking fires, but not very often, because the people in Fields of Wheat believed that trees were very holy and that it was bad luck to cut them. So mostly they burned other old things that had no spirit in them. There were many such things and there were not many people to burn them.

Julia liked to play among the houses that people had gone away from. She did not go into the houses themselves, for she was afraid they might be haunted, or unsafe for children. But she liked to go into the yards where sometimes she found wild beds of flowers blooming and rose bushes as large as trees. In a book she had there were pictures of roses, and Julia knew all their names. She knew the stories, too, that the roses had—where they had come from, what kind of plants their ancestors had been. In a way Julia felt that through the names and the stories of these flowers she knew something about the people who once lived in the large houses, the women and men who had planted them here. Sometimes she pretended to be pruning and spraying the flowers as her book told her she must do, or the roses would die. At such times, she imagined in her childish way that she was tending not the roses but the old gardeners, who must be dead now.

One day she was playing like this, pretending to spray a strong poison onto a fine, ivory-blossomed plant named Bishop Darlington, when a very old man approached her.

"You know—" (Kem started as Tallheron spoke from the shadows) "—you really don't have to read so quickly." His voice was kind, as Kem imagined a grandfather's might be. "The story will wait for you to finish it, you know. It has waited a very long time."

Kem nodded. He went on, making an effort to go more slowly.

"Good morning," said the old man to Julia.

"Good morning," she said, smiling at him with her very bright eyes. She did not run away from the old man because she was not afraid of him, even though she knew he was not one of the people from the village. His skin was pale and a little bit yellow, like the sheets of metal on the side of the old house. He stood only a few steps away and watched her with a funny expression on his face. Julia thought that he was probably a ghost, though he might be an old doctor from some other village gathering herbs, or he might be a crazy man dying of the plague who would try to kill her. She held up her hand to shield her eyes from the sun, so she could see him better.

"You ought not to come any closer," she said. "I am spraying this flower with a horrible fungicide which can make you vomit and give cancer to your children."

She reflected as soon as she said this that the old man's grandchildren and maybe his great-grandchildren, if he had any, were probably older than herself. But she felt it was important to let him know.

She was very pleased when the old man nodded gravely.

"I see," he said. He stayed where he was and did not come any closer.

Julia smiled again at the old man and put down her imaginary spraying can. "I think that's enough," she said. "Now Bishop Darlington will live through the summer."

She was glad that the old man did not point out to her that Bishop Darlington had lived through very many summers without need of the poisons in her spraying can. He just looked at the rose bush for a long time as if he were admiring what a good job she had done and what a very good gardener she was. Indeed, when he did speak again he said, "Well, thank you for taking care of my roses."

Julia looked at him to see what he meant. Her bright eyes shone in curiosity.

"You see," said the old man, "this was my house when I was a little boy—when I was a boy younger than you and not nearly so wise about flowers."

"Ah," said Julia. "So you *are* a ghost."

She was awfully excited. She turned all the way around to face the old man and she held her hands out with the palms facing him. She did this in order to protect herself, though in truth she was not really very much afraid.

The man surprised her by getting a big smile across his face. "I suppose I *am* a ghost," he said to her. "At any rate, I feel that way."

He looked away from Julia and he stood there for a long time just staring across the grasses that had grown up as high as his waist in the old back yard. As Julia watched him she thought that this was not the way a ghost was supposed to behave. Then she thought that since he was a very *old* ghost, he might have forgotten some of the important points of his profession. She cleared her throat, to get his attention.

"Aren't you," she said very carefully, when the man had turned to look at her, "aren't you supposed to tell me about how you became a ghost? You know, the awful way you died, and all? So that I'll feel sorry for you and not be afraid?"

The old man's smile had left his face and now he looked very unhappy, which Julia felt was much more appropriate. Like all little girls, she had a great respect for the manner in which things ought to be done. She waited patiently while the man recollected the sad and fateful details of his past life in order to begin his story.

"Well," he said at last, "I guess the truth of the matter is that I died many, many years ago, of a broken heart. Or at any rate the best part of me did. It was back in the early days of the age we're now living in, when this place still had another name besides Fields of Wheat. There were more folks like me living around here, in those days."

By *folks like me* Julia understood the old man to mean the people who had lived in these very large houses. In her mind she had certain vague notions about those people, but few definite or historical facts. It did not appear, however, that the ghost was going to educate her just then.

"I was in love," he said. "The girl I loved lived right up the street there, in the Tudor house. We had known each other since I was a little boy and she was a little girl. We were engaged to be married. Of course we had heard about the troubles everywhere. But somehow I guess we believed our little village here was immune, that nothing terrible would ever happen here."

He gave a sigh and looked away, into the rosebush that Julia had been spraying, as though something might be hidden there.

"Well, they came and they killed her. They were rather polite about it, in their way. They explained that they needed a girl about her age for their sacrifice, in order to make their medicines. I don't suppose you know anything about that, do you? I'm sure nobody believes in such things anymore. But those were awful times then, and people were desperate and they were willing to believe anything. So . . ."

The old man looked more than ever like a ghost now. He was staring blankly out of his dim cloudy eyes, and his voice sounded like something coming out of a machine. In this way he went on:

"So they took her away and they split her skull open and took something out, a little gland, which they needed to make their famous Remedy. They stayed out there all night, with electrical fires burning in their lamps, and tapes of some kind of ritual music, and their protectors standing there pointing guns at the people standing around. No one was going to stop them, of course. The town folk were afraid, and I think many of them were secretly glad, relieved that it had not been their own daughters who had been taken."

The old man paused to look at Julia, and Julia looked back with approval. This was a *wonderful* ghost story, she thought. It was certainly the most horrible thing she had ever heard from a grown-up. She held her very bright eyes on the old man, unblinking, in order to encourage him to go on.

"So," he said, "they stayed there all night, and they made their Remedy. Then they sold it, in the morning, for a very high price to anyone who could pay. And there were people willing to pay, believe me. In a way you couldn't blame them. As I said, they were desperate. The sick and the dying were everywhere. Doctors could offer nothing but consolation, if that, and pills to relieve the pain, in the final stages. The pain was quite horrible, we were told.

"It was then, I suppose," the old man said, "that the best part of me died. It was then that my first life, my innocent life, ended—and my new, longer, and unhappier life began."

Julia frowned. She had not counted on a new, unhappier life. She was expecting Death, for Death is the proper end of a ghost story. She held up to the man one of her small, very warm hands, signalling him to stop.

"Because," the man said, ignoring her hand, "do you know what they did? Do you know what they did, after they held her down and broke her head apart without even knocking her out first and left her body there still warm and oozing blood out?"

Julia felt odd and a little dizzy listening to the man talk this way, even though she thought he had gotten the story back on its proper track. Her very bright eyes may have blinked a time or two. Still she shook her head at the man's question, so that he would answer it himself.

In a much quieter voice he said, "They gave me a vial of their Remedy—the thing they made out of her. They did this, you know, as a gesture to us, the town folk. Someone must have told them the girl they murdered had a sweetheart, a fiance. So they gave me a vial of it. They called it the *Caput Mortuum*. Death's Head. They gave me that so I might live to remember her, who had died."

Julia thought that the very old man had finished talking, that his story was over, until he added in a matter-of-fact voice, a voice without any feeling left in it, "That is why I became a doctor. Because I believed there had to be another way. I believed there must be other medicines, *true* medicines, that are not based upon superstition or hysteria. And I resolved that day that I would find them."

So, thought Julia, the very old man was simply a man and not a ghost after all. Well even so, she told herself, she had been right about him all along. For she had thought as soon as she saw him that he might be a doctor from another village, gathering herbs. This was something of a disappointment, but Julia thought she must make the best of things. She asked him, "Are you here to gather wild berries and flowers to use in your medicines?"

"Not exactly," the man said to her, smiling kindly. "I am here to experiment with a different kind of treatment—something that I have seen used now and then with great success, though I have never tried it myself."

Julia nodded, thinking this might be informative to watch. She put away her imaginary spraying can and stood up, smoothing her skirt. "Do you need any help?" she asked the man. "I know all about the things that grow in this village. I am very observant, and I have lived here all my life."

The old man only smiled at her, and in his smile Julia thought she could see something else, something that very old people often feel that makes them stare at things absent-mindedly and sometimes sigh, which Julia thought must come from knowing how close to dying they are. After a while of looking at her this way, the man said, "Yes, Julia. I think I can use your help."

Kem paused in his reading. The story had made him uncomfortable. Tallheron was leaning forward on his stool and blinking his eyes again. He did not seem to be paying attention. Kem felt a bit annoyed, for he had been reading for a long time quite carefully and now his throat was dry. He said in a louder voice, "Sir, do you want me to keep going?"

Tallheron looked up. He did not seem sleepy or distracted, as Kem had supposed. Quite the contrary, his expression was alert and even agitated somewhat. Kem supposed that it might be that his cold was bothering him.

"You may rest if you like," Tallheron said. "In fact, perhaps we should leave off there and pick it up next time. That has given me enough to think about for the time being."

Kem nodded. He wondered when "next time" would be. Was this going to be a regular occurrence? He memorized the page number (one thirty-three), closed the book, and held it out for Tallheron to take back.

"No, no," said Tallheron, waving the book away, "you keep it"—exactly as he had done with the smoked glass bottle. "It will be simpler that way."

Since he said nothing else, and in fact did not seem quite to be meeting Kem's eye, Kem supposed that today's session was over and that he must go back to the galley. The volume of *Sun Tales and Moon Songs* felt suddenly heavy in his hands, an encumbrance, a thing that needed attention. Among other things, he was not sure how well it would fit into the tiny drawer under his bunk, or whether one of the other boys might steal it. Still he accepted the fact of the book being his to care for without complaint, because it meant a change, a subtle alteration in the terms of his life. He left without saying goodbye to Tallheron, who did not seem to notice or to care. Tallheron was an odd man, Kem decided, though perhaps that was the way with Residents.

As he stepped from the library, a guard eyed him suspiciously, glancing down at the book in his hand. Kem felt the accustomed twinge of paranoia, expecting the guard to demand proof of something—ownership of the book, the right to be walking down this hall. The guard just looked away, giving Kem as wide a berth as the passageway permitted. His contempt was reassuring. Kem was not a criminal, after all; only an untouchable.

In the galley, alone once more in the privacy of his own unhappiness, Kem thought about the peculiar little story for a while. He wondered why Tallheron had wanted to hear it—to hear that story in particular, out of a book that contained dozens of others, in a room that must have held millions. Something to think about, he had said. Or no, *enough* to think about. There might be a difference. Kem thought there was. He had trouble concentrating on the hobart, and scalded his hands. The galley boss inspected the blisters with obvious satisfaction.

"Have to put you on the cutting line tomorrow," he said. The cutting line was where vegetables were chopped, and there was a substantial risk of losing a finger. The galley boss smiled.

That night Kem stole some candles. It was a minor theft, at worst. The candles were tiny things that had been set out in glass holders on dinner trays that were carried to the upper decks, the wardrooms where senior members of the crew dined (as Kem imagined) in ease and splendor. They were half burned and would have to be melted and recast before they could be used again. Kem figured that two or three of them would burn long enough to get him through the story. He figured that if he read to the end of it he would be able to concentrate better and to understand what it really meant. Then tomorrow if he was summoned to read out loud he would be able to do so with the proper feeling.

It was a good secret, having the book. Kem lay in the dark bunk for a long while as the other boys grew tired of their nightly rude games and bantering and fell asleep. The Oasis was never really quiet, but with your eyes closed and only the growl of the engines below the deckplates you got a certain feeling of calmness, of things settling down. Kem spent some time savoring this and the knowledge of his plan before he allowed himself to take the trivial but thrilling risk of lighting a candle. The flame seemed to float in the glass of the holder. Kem watched it, thinking that in the dark room, the little fire in the glass seemed almost to have its own soft noise, a breathy sound like the wind, maybe the sound of the chemical transmutation inside the flame.

For a time the candle held his attention. Kem stared at it and though he did not forget about the book, the comforting weight of it on his stomach, he did not feel just now the desire to read. It was peaceful, lying there. The Oasis lurched and rumbled yet Kem felt very still.

After a couple of minutes he decided that what had seemed to be a faint sound made by the candle flame was really no sound at all: it was silence, or the closest thing to silence that he had known since coming to live here. What made it seem like noise was the ceaseless movement in Kem's mind, the current of his thoughts, which at other times he was too distracted to hear. They surged into the little circle of candlelight, roaring through his ears; and then, as the candle burned down and the silence deepened around him, they faded away.

The book of *Sun Tales and Moon Songs* lay open on Kem's stomach the next morning when the galley boss came through, shoving his way past the tangle of wayward limbs and the piles of discarded clothing that cluttered the narrow aisles of the berthing area. The man banged his wooden spoon on his soup pot desultorily, as though he held out little hope for the coming day. When he approached Kem's bunk, though, his mood seemed to change. He stopped his spoon-banging. When Kem raised his head, the galley boss stood abreast of him, his small oily eyes alight with a kind of menacing curiosity.

"So," the man said. "Taken to reading ourself to sleep, have we?"

Kem had the feeling of struggling upward through layers of semi-consciousness. Despite the unseemly fact of the galley boss glowering inches away, part of his mind was still caught on the shards of the night's last dream, and part of it on the dream before that, which may not have been a dream after all. A secret: a candle: and then, this mind-gate having opened, he felt the weight of the book still there where he had lain it. He had not meant to fall asleep. He had meant to finish the story and then put the book back in his drawer, hidden and safe.

It was too late now. The galley boss lowered his head into the confined space of Kem's bunk, investigating. You could smell last night's mescal on his breath.

"Ah," he said, lifting a glass candle holder. "Just borrowing this, I imagine?"

Kem struggled up, onto his elbows. He bumped his head; the book slid sideways off his stomach. Kem made a grab for it, reflexively, but the galley boss caught it first.

"*Sun Tales*," the man read slowly, squinting at the spine. "*Moon Songs*. What the hell is this? Who'd you steal it from?"

"No," Kem said, feeling confused and somewhat panicky. He always had a feeling, when talking to the galley boss, that he was guilty of something, that he had committed some serious mistake. But this time he hadn't. "No," he said, "I . . ."

He stopped in confusion. Behind the galley boss, a few paces up the aisle, Sander had materialized, drawn as always to the momentary source of entertainment. He seemed to be signaling to Kem, shaking his head, forming words with his small mouth. Kem got the general sense of a warning, but he could make nothing more of it than that. The galley boss was riffling the pages of the book with his greasy thumb.

"Stop that," said Kem.

The galley boss did stop, but only to look at Kem in amazement. This changed to a look of something like evil glee.

"No," struggling to explain himself, Kem stammered, "It's not . . . look, it's not even mine, it's—"

The galley boss snapped the book shut, making a pop. Sander, behind him, looked up at the ceiling.

"But I didn't steal it," Kem blurted. "It was—"

"A *present?*" the galley boss said sneeringly. "From one of your many *admirers?*"

Kem felt himself growing warm in anger, in embarrassment. Everything seemed to be out of balance. More quietly, struggling for control, he said, "It was just given to me. To keep. Until later."

The galley boss glared up and down the aisle as though warning the other boys to be about their business. (Sander, presciently, had already vanished.) Then he looked back at Kem. "Lying is a serious thing, boy. Who'd you take this from? What do you want with a book, anyway?"

Kem wasn't so afraid of the galley boss as not to feel affronted. He straightened up as best he could in the cramped space of his bunk.

"You can ask him yourself," he said. "His name is Tallheron." And he added, having saved the clinching point for last: "He's a Resident."

The galley boss stood still and without expression for a second or so, absorbing this. Then he dropped the book. It landed in Kem's lap, heavily. The man took a step back.

"A Resident," he repeated, each syllable falling cleanly from his mouth, as though the word had shaken his dull mind to alertness. "You got that from a Resident," he said slowly, "and you brought it here?"

"He gave it to me," Kem said—feeling now that he, not the galley boss, was having trouble grasping the point.

"I'm sure he did," the man said. "I'm sure he did give it to you."

He hardly seemed angry at all now. He acted as though the conversation were over, or all but. He turned up the aisle, addressing Kem as a judge might address a criminal already convicted, the question of his guilt settled beyond doubt.

"Pack your things," he said. "You're moving to the engine

flats." He turned away, symbolically and physically putting Kem behind him. To the other boys, the room at large, he muttered, "They don't pay me to train idiots here."

The last thing Kem saw as he was led by a pair of guards down a badly lit passageway was Sander standing behind him, watching, shaking his head with an expression that might possibly have contained a hint of sadness, though it also implied another thing, maybe that he had tried to tell Kem something, to make life easier for him, but now Kem was going to have to learn the hard way, he was going to have to discover things for himself.

Then Sander was lost from sight, and
   Kem followed the guards around a corner and
      toward a dark stairway,
         leading down.